THE PRODIGAL DAUGHTER

Jeffrey Archer is a master storyteller, the author of ten novels which have all been worldwide bestsellers. *Not a Penny More, Not a Penny Less* was his first book, and it achieved instant success. Next came the tense and terrifying thriller *Shall We Tell the President?*, followed by his triumphant bestseller *Kane and Abel*. His first collection of short stories, *A Quiver Full of Arrows*, came next, and then *The Prodigal Daughter*, the superb sequel to *Kane and Abel*. This was followed by *First Among Equals*, considered by the *Scotsman* to be the finest novel about parliament since Trollope, the thrilling chase story *A Matter of Honour*, his second collection of stories, *A Twist in the Tale*, and the novels *As the Crow Flies* and *Honour Among Thieves*. *Twelve Red Herrings*, his third collection of stories, was followed by the novels *The Fourth Estate* and *The Eleventh Commandment*. A collected edition of his short stories was published in 1997.

Jeffrey Archer was born in 1940 and educated at Wellington School, Somerset and Brasenose College, Oxford. He represented Great Britain in the 100 metres in the early sixties, and entered the House of Commons when he won the by-election at Louth in 1969. He wrote his first novel, *Not a Penny More, Not a Penny Less*, in 1974. From September 1985 to October 1986 he was Deputy Chairman of the Conservative Party, and he was created a Life Peer in the Queen's Birthday Honours of 1992. He lives in Cambridge with his wife and two sons.

By the same author

Novels

NOT A PENNY MORE, NOT A PENNY LESS
SHALL WE TELL THE PRESIDENT?
KANE AND ABEL
FIRST AMONG EQUALS
A MATTER OF HONOUR
AS THE CROW FLIES
HONOUR AMONG THIEVES
THE FOURTH ESTATE
THE ELEVENTH COMMANDMENT

Short Stories

A QUIVER FULL OF ARROWS
A TWIST IN THE TALE
TWELVE RED HERRINGS
THE COLLECTED SHORT STORIES

Plays

BEYOND REASONABLE DOUBT
EXCLUSIVE

JEFFREY ARCHER

THE PRODIGAL DAUGHTER

HarperCollins*Publishers*

HarperCollins*Publishers*
77–85 Fulham Palace Road,
Hammersmith, London W6 8JB

This paperback edition 1997
7 9 8

First published in Great Britain by
Hodder and Stoughton Ltd 1982

ISBN 0 00 647869 7

Set in Baskerville

Printed and bound in Great Britain by
Omnia Books Ltd. Glasgow

To Peter, Joy, Alison,
Clare and Simon

THE PRODIGAL DAUGHTER

Prologue

'PRESIDENT OF THE UNITED STATES,' she replied.

'I can think of more rewarding ways of bankrupting myself,' said her father, as he removed the half-moon spectacles from the end of his nose and peered at his daughter over the top of his newspaper.

'Don't be frivolous, Papa. President Roosevelt proved to us that there can be no greater calling than public service.'

'The only thing Roosevelt proved . . .' began her father. Then he stopped and returned to his paper, realising that his daughter would consider the remark flippant.

The girl continued as if she were only too aware of what was going through her father's mind. 'I realise it would be pointless for me to pursue such an ambition without your support. My sex will be enough of a liability without adding the disadvantage of a Polish background.'

The newspaper barrier between father and daughter was abruptly removed. 'Don't ever speak disloyally of the Poles,' he said. 'History has proved us to be an honourable race who never go back on our word. My father was a baron . . .'

'Yes, I know, so was my grandfather, but he's not around now to help me become President.'

'More's the pity,' he said, sighing, 'as he would undoubtedly have made a great leader of our people.'

'Then why shouldn't his granddaughter?'

'No reason at all,' he said, as he stared into the steel grey eyes of his only child.

'Well then, Papa, will you help me? I can't hope to succeed without your financial backing.'

Her father hesitated before replying, placing the glasses back on the end of his nose and slowly folding his copy of the Chicago *Tribune*.

'I'll make a deal with you, my dear; after all that's what politics is about. If the result of the New Hampshire Primary turns out to be satisfactory, I'll back you to the hilt. If not, you must drop the whole idea.'

'What's your definition of satisfactory?' came back the immediate reply.

Again the man hesitated, weighing his words. 'If you win the Primary or capture over thirty per cent of the vote, I'll go all the way to the convention floor with you, even if it means I end up destitute.'

The girl relaxed for the first time during the conversation. 'Thank you, Papa. I couldn't have asked for more.'

'No, you certainly couldn't,' he replied. 'Now can I get back to finding out just how the Cubs could possibly have lost the seventh game of the series to the Tigers?'

'They were undoubtedly the weaker team, as the 9–3 score indicates.'

'Young lady, you may imagine you know a thing or two about politics but I can assure you that you know absolutely nothing about baseball,' the man said, as his wife entered the room. He turned his heavy frame towards her. 'Our daughter wants to run for President of the United States. What do you think about that?'

The girl looked up at her eagerly, waiting for a reply.

'I'll tell you what I think,' said the mother. 'I think it's well past her bedtime and I blame you for keeping her up so late.'

'Yes, I suppose you're right,' the husband said. 'Off you go to bed, little one.'

She came to her father's side, kissed him on the cheek and whispered, 'Thank you, Papa.'

The man's eyes followed his eleven-year-old daughter as she left the room and he noticed that the fingers on her right hand were clenched, making a small tight fist, something she always did when she was angry or determined. He suspected she was both on this occasion, but he realised that it would be pointless to try and explain to his wife that their only child was no ordinary mortal. He had long ago abandoned any attempt to involve his wife in his own ambitions, and was at least thankful that she was incapable of dampening their daughter's.

He returned to the Chicago Cubs and had to admit that his daughter's judgment might even be right on that subject.

Florentyna Rosnovski never referred to the conversation again for twenty-two years, but when she did she assumed her father would keep his end of the bargain. After all, the Polish are an honourable race who never go back on their word.

The Past

1934–1968

1

It had not been an easy birth, but then for Abel and Zaphia Rosnovski nothing had ever been easy, and in their own ways they had both become philosophical about that. Abel had wanted a son, an heir who would one day be chairman of the Baron Group. By the time the boy was ready to take over, Abel was confident that his own name would stand alongside those of Ritz and Statler and by then the Baron would be the largest hotel group in the world. Abel had paced up and down the colourless corridor of St. Luke's Hospital waiting for the first cry, his slight limp becoming more pronounced as each hour passed. Occasionally he twisted the silver band that encircled his wrist and stared at the name so neatly engraved on it. He turned and retraced his steps once again, to see Doctor Dodek heading towards him.

'Congratulations, Mr. Rosnovski,' he called.

'Thank you,' said Abel eagerly.

'You have a beautiful girl,' the doctor said as he reached him.

'Thank you,' repeated Abel, quietly, trying not to show his disappointment. He then followed the obstetrician into a little room at the other end of the corridor. Through an observation window Abel was confronted with a row of wrinkled faces. The doctor pointed to the father's first-born. Unlike the others her little fingers were curled into a tight fist. Abel had read somewhere that a child was not expected to do that for at least three weeks. He smiled, proudly.

Mother and daughter remained at St. Luke's for another six days and Abel visited them every morning, leaving his hotel only when the last breakfast had been served, and every afternoon after the last lunch guest had left the dining room. Telegrams, flowers and the recent fashion of greeting cards surrounded Zaphia's iron-framed bed, reassuring evidence that other people too rejoiced in the birth. On the seventh day mother and unnamed child – Abel had considered six boys' names – returned home.

On the anniversary of the second week of their daughter's birth they named her Florentyna, after Abel's sister. Once the infant had been installed in the newly decorated nursery at the top of the house, Abel would spend hours simply staring down at his daughter, watching her sleep and wake, knowing that he must work even harder than he had in the past to ensure the child's future. He was determined that Florentyna would be given a better start in life than he had been. Not for her the dirt and deprivation of his childhood or the humiliation of arriving on the eastern seaboard of America as an immigrant with little more than a few valueless Russian rubles sewn into the jacket of an only suit.

He would ensure that Florentyna was given the formal education he had lacked, not that he had a lot to complain about. Franklin D. Roosevelt lived in the White House and Abel's little group of hotels looked as if they were going to survive the Depression. America had been good to this immigrant.

Whenever he sat alone with his daughter in the upstairs nursery he would reflect on his past, and dream of her future.

When he had first arrived in the United States he had found a job in a little butcher's shop on the lower East Side of New York, where he worked for two long years before filling a vacancy at the Plaza Hotel as a junior waiter. From Abel's first day, Sammy, the old maître d', had treated him as though he was the lowest form of life. After four years, a slave trader would have been impressed by the work and unheard-of overtime that the lowest form of life did in order to reach the exalted position as Sammy's assistant head waiter in the Oak Room. During those early years Abel spent five afternoons a week poring over books at Columbia University, and after dinner had been cleared away read on late into the night.

His rivals wondered when he slept.

Abel was not sure how his newly-acquired degree could advance him while he still only waited on tables in the Oak Room of the Plaza Hotel. The question was answered for him by a well-fed Texan called Mr. Davis Leroy, who had watched Abel serving guests solicitously for a week. Mr. Leroy, the owner of eleven hotels, then offered Abel the position of assistant manager at his flagship, the Richmond Continental in Chicago, with the sole responsibility of running the restaurants.

Abel was brought back to the present when Florentyna turned over and started to thump the side of her crib. He extended a finger which his daughter grabbed like a lifeline thrown from a sinking ship. She started to bite the finger with what she imagined were teeth . . .

When Abel first arrived in Chicago he found the Richmond Continental badly run down. It didn't take him long to discover why. The manager, Desmond Pacey, was cooking the books and as far as Abel could tell probably had been for the past thirty years. The new assistant manager spent his first six months gathering together the proof he needed to nail Pacey and then presented to his employer a dossier containing all the facts. When Davis Leroy realised what had been going on behind his back he immediately sacked Pacey, replacing him with his new protégé. This spurred Abel on to work even harder and he became so convinced that he could turn the fortunes of the Richmond Group around that when Leroy's ageing sister put up for sale her twenty-five per cent of the company's stock Abel cashed everything he owned to purchase them. Davis Leroy was touched by his young manager's personal commitment to the company and proved it by appointing him managing director of the group.

From that moment they became partners, a professional

bond that developed into a close friendship. Abel would have been the first to appreciate how hard it was for a Texan to acknowledge a Pole as an equal. For the first time since he had settled in America, he felt secure – until he found out that the Texans were every bit as proud a clan as the Poles.

Abel still couldn't accept what had happened. If only Davis had confided in him, told him the truth about the extent of the group's financial trouble – who wasn't having problems during the Depression? – between them they could have sorted something out. At the age of sixty-two Davis Leroy had been informed by his bank that his overdraft was no longer covered by the value of the hotels and that they required further security before they would agree to pay next month's wages. In response to the bank's ultimatum, Davis Leroy had had a quiet dinner with his daughter and retired to the Presidential Suite on the twelfth floor with two bottles of bourbon. Then he had opened the window and jumped. Abel would never forget standing on the corner of Michigan Avenue at four in the morning having to identify a body he could recognise only by the jacket his mentor had worn the previous night. The lieutenant investigating the death had remarked that it had been the seventh suicide in Chicago that day. It didn't help. How could the policeman possibly know how much Davis Leroy had done for him, or how much more he had intended to return that friendship in the future? In a hastily composed will Davis had bequeathed the remaining seventy-five per cent of the Richmond Group stock to his managing director, writing to Abel that although the stock was worthless one hundred per cent ownership of the group might give him a better chance to negotiate new terms with the bank.

Florentyna's eyes opened, and she started to howl. Abel picked her up lovingly, immediately regretting the decision as he felt the damp clammy bottom. He changed her nappy quickly, drying the child carefully, before making a triangle of the cloth, not allowing the big pins anywhere near her body: any midwife would have nodded her approval at his deftness. Florentyna closed her eyes and nodded back to sleep on her father's shoulder. 'Ungrateful brat,' he murmured fondly as he kissed her on the cheek.

After Davis Leroy's funeral Abel had visited Kane and Cabot, the Richmond Group's bankers in Boston, and pleaded with one of the directors not to put the eleven hotels up for sale on the open market. He tried to convince the bank that if only they would back him, he could – given time – turn the balance sheet from red into black. The smooth, cold man behind the expensive partner's desk had proved intractable. 'I must act in the bank's best interests,' he had used as an excuse. Abel would never forget the humiliation of having to call a man of his own age 'sir' and still leave empty-handed. The man must have had the soul of a cash register not to realise how many people were affected by his decision. Abel promised himself, for the hundredth time, that one day he would get even with Mr. William 'Ivy League' Kane.

Abel had travelled back to Chicago that night thinking that nothing else could go wrong in his life, only to find the Richmond Continental burned to the ground and the police accusing him of arson. Arson it proved to be, but at the hands of Desmond Pacey, bent on revenge. When arrested, he admitted readily to the crime as his only interest was the downfall of Abel. Pacey would have succeeded if the insurance company had not come to Abel's rescue. Until that moment, he had wondered if he would not have been better off in the Russian prisoner-of-war camp he had escaped from before fleeing to America. But then his luck turned when an anonymous backer who, Abel concluded, must have been Mr. David Maxton of the Stevens Hotel, purchased the Richmond Group and offered Abel his old position as managing director and a chance to prove he could run the company at a profit.

Abel recalled how he had been reunited with Zaphia, the self-assured girl he had first met on board the ship that had brought them to America. How immature she had made him feel then, but not when they re-met and he discovered she was a waitress at the Stevens.

Two years had passed since then and, although the newly named Baron Group had failed to make a profit in 1933, they lost only twenty-three thousand dollars, greatly helped by Chicago's celebration of its centenary when over a million tourists had visited the city to enjoy the World's Fair.

Once Pacey had been convicted of arson, Abel had only to wait for the insurance money to be paid before he could set about rebuilding the hotel in Chicago. He had used the interim period to visit the other ten hotels in the group, sacking staff who showed the same pecuniary tendencies as Desmond Pacey and replacing them from the long lines of unemployed that stretched across America.

Zaphia began to resent Abel's journeys from Charleston to Mobile, from Houston to Memphis, continually checking over his hotels in the south. But Abel realised that if he was to keep his side of the bargain with the anonymous backer there would be little time to sit around at home, however much he adored his daughter. He had been given ten years to repay the bank loan; if he succeeded, a clause in the contract stipulated he would be allowed to purchase the remaining sixty per cent of the company's stock for a further three million dollars. Zaphia thanked God each night for what they already had and pleaded with him to slow down, but nothing was going to stop Abel from trying to fulfil that aim.

'Your dinner's ready,' shouted Zaphia at the top of her voice.

Abel pretended he hadn't heard and continued to stare down at his sleeping daughter.

'Didn't you hear me? Dinner is ready.'

'What? No, dear. Sorry. Just coming.' Abel reluctantly rose to join his wife for dinner. Florentyna's rejected red eiderdown lay on the floor beside her cot. Abel picked up the fluffy quilt and placed it carefully on top of the blanket that covered his daughter. He never wanted her to feel the cold. She smiled in her sleep. Was she having her first dream? Abel wondered, as he switched out the light.

2

FLORENTYNA'S CHRISTENING WAS something everyone present was to remember – except Florentyna, who slept through the entire proceedings. After the ceremony at the Holy Name Cathedral on North Wabash, the guests made their way to the Stevens Hotel. Abel took a private room in the hotel and invited over a hundred guests to celebrate the occasion. His closest friend, George Novak, a fellow Pole who had occupied the bunk above him on the boat coming over from Europe, was to be one Kum while one of Zaphia's cousins, Janina, was to be the other.

The guests devoured a traditional ten-course dinner including pierogi and bigos while Abel sat at the head of the table accepting gifts on behalf of his daughter which included a silver rattle, U.S. savings bonds, a copy of *Huckleberry Finn* and, finest of all, a beautiful antique emerald ring from Abel's unnamed benefactor. He only hoped that the man gained as much pleasure in the giving as his daughter later showed in the receiving. To mark the occasion, Abel presented his daughter with a large brown teddy bear with red eyes.

'It looks like Franklin D. Roosevelt,' said George, holding the bear up for all to see. 'This calls for a second christening – F.D.R.'

Abel raised his glass. 'Mr. President,' he toasted – a name the bear never relinquished.

The party finally came to an end around three o'clock in the morning, when Abel had to requisition a laundry trolley from the hotel to transport all the gifts home. George waved to Abel as he headed up North Michigan Avenue pushing the trolley before him.

The happy father began whistling to himself as he recalled every moment of the wonderful evening. Only when Mr. President fell off the trolley for a third time did he realise how crooked his path down Lake Shore Drive must have been. He picked up the bear and wedged it in the centre of the gifts and was about to attempt a straighter path when a hand touched his shoulder. Abel jumped round, ready to defend with his life anyone who wanted to steal Florentyna's first possessions. He stared up into the face of a young policeman.

'Maybe you can explain why you are pushing a Stevens Hotel laundry trolley down Michigan Avenue at three in the morning?'

'Yes, officer,' replied Abel.

'Well, let's start with what's in the packages.'

'Other than Franklin D. Roosevelt, I can't be certain.'

The policeman immediately arrested Abel on suspicion of theft. While the recipient of the gifts slept soundly under her red eiderdown in the little nursery at the top of their house on Rigg Street, her father spent a sleepless night on an old horsehair mattress in a cell at the local jail. George appeared at the court house first thing in the morning to verify Abel's story.

The next day Abel purchased a four-door maroon Buick from Peter Sosnkowski, who ran a secondhand car lot in the Polish neighbourhood.

Abel began to resent having to leave Chicago and his beloved Florentyna even for a few days, fearing he might miss her first step, her first word or her first anything. From her birth, he had supervised her daily routine, never allowing Polish to be spoken in the house: he was determined there would be no trace of a Polish accent that would make her feel ill at ease in society.

Abel had intently waited for her first word, hoping it would be 'Papa', while Zaphia feared it might be some Polish word that would reveal that she had not been speaking English to her first-born when they were alone.

'My daughter is an American,' Abel had explained to Zaphia, 'and she must therefore speak English. Too many Poles continue to converse in their own language, thus ensuring that their children spend their entire lives in the north-west corner of Chicago being described as "Stupid Polacks" and ridiculed by everyone else they come across.'

'Except our countrymen who still feel some loyalty to the Polish empire,' said Zaphia defensively.

'The Polish empire? What century are you living in, Zaphia?'

'The twentieth century,' she said, her voice rising.

'Along with Dick Tracy and Famous Funnies, no doubt?'

'Hardly the attitude of someone whose ultimate ambition is to return to Warsaw as the first Polish ambassador.'

'I've told you never to mention that, Zaphia. Never.'

Zaphia, whose English remained irredeemably shaky, didn't reply but later grumbled to her cousins on the subject and continued to speak Polish only when Abel was out of the house. She was not impressed by the fact, so often trotted out by Abel, that General Motors's turnover was greater than Poland's budget.

By 1935, Abel was convinced that America had turned the corner and that the Depression was a thing of the past, so he decided the time had come to build the new Chicago Baron on the site of the old Richmond Continental. He appointed an architect and began spending more time in the Windy City and less on the road, as he was determined the hotel would turn out to be the finest in the Mid-West.

The Chicago Baron was completed in May 1936 and opened by the Democratic mayor, Edward J. Kelly. Both Illinois Senators were dancing attendance, only too aware of Abel's burgeoning power.

'Looks like a million dollars,' said J. Hamilton Lewis, the senior Senator.

'You wouldn't be far wrong,' said Abel, as he admired the thickly carpeted public rooms, the high stucco ceilings and the decorations in pastel shades of green. The final touch had been the dark green embossed B that adorned everything from the towels in the bathrooms to the flag that fluttered on the top of the forty-two storey building.

'This hotel already bears the hallmark of success,' said J. Hamilton Lewis, addressing the two thousand assembled guests, 'because, my friends, it is the man and not the building who will always be known as the Chicago Baron.' Abel was delighted by the roar that went up and smiled to himself. His public relations adviser had supplied that line to the Senator's speech writer earlier in the week.

Abel was beginning to feel at ease among big businessmen and senior politicians. Zaphia, however, had not adapted to her husband's change in fortunes and hovered uncertainly in the background, drinking a little too much champagne, and finally crept away before the dinner was served with a lame excuse about wanting to see that Florentyna was safely asleep. Abel accompanied his flushed wife towards the revolving door in silent irritation. Zaphia neither cared for nor understood success on Abel's scale and preferred to ignore his new world. She was only too aware how much this annoyed Abel and couldn't resist saying, 'Don't hurry home', as he bundled her into a cab.

'I won't,' he told the revolving door as he returned, pushing it so hard that it went around three more times after he had left it.

He returned to the hotel foyer to find Alderman Henry Osborne waiting for him.

'This must be the high point in your life,' the alderman remarked.

'High point? I've just turned thirty,' said Abel.

A camera flashed as he placed an arm around the tall, darkly handsome politician. Abel smiled towards the cameraman, enjoying the treatment he was receiving as a celebrity, and said, just loud enough for eavesdroppers to hear, 'I'm going to put Baron hotels right across the globe. I intend to be to America what César Ritz was to Europe. Stick with me, Henry, and you'll enjoy the ride.' The city alderman and Abel walked together into the dining room and once they were out of earshot Abel added: 'Join me for lunch tomorrow, Henry, if you can spare the time. There's something I need to discuss with you.'

'Delighted, Abel. A mere city alderman is always available for the Chicago Baron.'

They both laughed heartily, though neither thought the remark particularly funny.

It turned out to be another late night for Abel. When he returned home he went straight to the spare room, to be sure he didn't wake Zaphia – or that's what he told her the next morning.

When Abel came into the kitchen to join Zaphia for breakfast Florentyna was sitting in her high chair smearing a bowlful of cereal enthusiastically round her mouth and biting at most things that remained within arms' reach – even if they weren't food. He kissed her on the forehead, the only place that seemed to have missed the cereal, and sat down to a plate of waffles and maple syrup. When he had finished, Abel rose from his chair and told Zaphia that he would be having lunch with Henry Osborne.

'I don't like that man,' said Zaphia, with feeling.

'I'm not crazy about him myself,' replied Abel. 'But never forget he's well placed in City Hall to be able to do us a lot of favours.'

'And a lot of harm.'

'Don't lose any sleep over that. You can leave the handling of Alderman Osborne to me,' said Abel as he brushed his wife's cheek and turned to leave.

'Presidunk,' said a voice, and both parents turned to stare at Florentyna, who was gesticulating at the floor where the eight-month-old Franklin D. Roosevelt lay on his furry face.

Abel laughed, picked up the much-loved teddy bear and placed him in the space Florentyna had left for him on the high chair.

'Pres-i-dent,' said Abel slowly and firmly.

'Presidunk,' insisted Florentyna.

Abel laughed again and patted Franklin D. Roosevelt on the head. So F.D.R. was responsible not only for the New Deal but also for Florentyna's first political utterance.

Abel left the house to find his chauffeur waiting for him beside the new Cadillac. Abel's driving had become worse as the car he could afford improved. When he bought a Cadillac, George had advised a driver to go with it. That morning he asked the chauffeur to drive slowly as they approached the Gold Coast. Abel stared up at the gleaming glass of the Chicago Baron and marvelled that there was no other place on earth where a man could achieve so much so quickly. What the Chinese would have been happy to strive for in ten generations, he had achieved in less than fifteen years.

He leaped out of the car before his chauffeur could run around to open the door, walked briskly into the hotel and took the private express elevator to the forty-second floor where he spent the morning checking over every problem with which the new hotel was faced: one of the passenger elevators wasn't functioning properly; two waiters had been involved in a knife fight in the kitchen and had been sacked by George even before Abel had arrived; and the list of damages after the opening looked suspiciously high – Abel would have to check into possible theft by waiters being recorded in the books as breakage. He left nothing to chance in any of his hotels from who was staying in the Presidential Suite to the price of the eight thousand fresh bread rolls the catering department needed every week. He spent the morning dealing with queries, problems and decisions, stopping only when Alderman Osborne was ushered into Abel's office by his secretary.

'Good morning, Baron,' said Henry, patronisingly referring to the Rosnovski family title.

In Abel's younger days as a junior waiter at the Plaza in New York the title had been scornfully mimicked to his face. At the Richmond Continental when he was assistant manager it had figured in whispered jokes behind his back. Lately everyone mouthed the prefix with respect.

'Good morning, Alderman,' said Abel, glancing at the clock on his desk. It was five past one. 'Shall we have lunch?'

Abel guided Henry into the adjoining private dining room. To a casual observer Henry Osborne would hardly have seemed a natural soul-mate for Abel. Educated at Choate and then Harvard, as he continually reminded Abel, he had later served as a young lieutenant with the Marines in the World War. At six feet, with a full head of black hair lightly sprinkled with grey, he looked younger than his history insisted he had to be.

The two men had first met as a result of the fire at the old Richmond Continental. Henry was then working for the Great Western Casualty Insurance Company, which had, for as long as anyone could remember, insured the Richmond Group. Abel had been taken aback when Henry had suggested that a small cash payment would ensure a swifter flow of the claim papers through the head office. Abel did not possess a 'small cash payment' in those days; although the claim eventually found its way through, as Henry also believed in Abel's future.

Abel had learned for the first time about men who could be bought.

By the time Henry Osborne was elected to the Chicago City Council as an alderman, Abel *could* afford a small cash payment, and the building permit for the new Baron proceeded through City Hall as though on roller skates. When Henry later announced that he would be running for the United States House of Representatives for the Ninth District of Illinois, Abel was among the first to send a sizeable cheque for his campaign fund. While Abel remained wary of his new ally personally, he recognised that a tame politician could be of great help to the Baron Group. Abel took care to ensure that none of the small cash payments – he did not think of them as bribes, even to himself – was on the record, and felt confident that he could terminate the arrangement as and when it suited him.

The dining room was decorated in the same delicate shades of green as the rest of the hotel, but there was no sign of the embossed B anywhere in the room. The furniture was nineteenth century, and entirely in oak. Around the walls hung oil portraits from the same period, almost all imported. With the door closed, it was possible to imagine that one was in another world far away from the hectic pace of a modern hotel.

Abel took his place at the head of an ornate table that could have comfortably seated eight guests but that day was laid for only two.

'It's like being in a bit of old England,' said Henry, taking in the room.

'Not to mention Poland,' replied Abel, as a uniformed waiter served smoked salmon, while another poured them both a glass of Bouchard Chablis.

Henry stared down at the full plate in front of him. 'Now I can see why you're putting on so much weight, Baron.'

Abel frowned, and quickly changed the subject. 'Are you going to the Cubs' game tomorrow?'

'What's the point? They have a worse home record than the Republicans. Not that my absence will discourage the *Tribune* from describing the match as a close-fought battle bearing no relation to the score and but for a different set of circumstances, the Cubs would have pulled off a famous victory.'

Abel laughed.

'One thing's for sure,' continued Henry, 'you'll never see a night game at Wrigley Field. That ghastly innovation of playing under floodlights won't catch on in Chicago.'

'That's what you said about beer cans last year.'

It was Henry's turn to frown. 'You didn't ask me to lunch to hear my views on baseball or beer cans, Abel, so what little plan can I assist you with this time?'

'Simple. I want to ask your advice on what I should do about William Kane.'

Henry seemed to choke. I must speak to the chef: there shouldn't be any bones in smoked salmon, thought Abel before he continued.

'You once told me, Henry, in graphic detail what had

happened when your path crossed Mr. Kane's and how he ended up defrauding you of money. Well, Kane did far worse than that to me. During the Depression he put the squeeze on Davis Leroy, my partner and closest friend, and was the direct cause of Leroy's suicide. To make matters worse Kane refused to support me when I wanted to take over the management of the hotels and try to put the group on a sound financial footing.'

'Who did back you in the end?' asked Henry.

'A private investor with the Continental Trust. The manager has never told me in so many words, but I've always suspected it was David Maxton.'

'The owner of the Stevens Hotel?'

'The same.'

'What makes you think it was him?'

'When I had the reception for my wedding and again for Florentyna's christening at the Stevens, the bill was covered by my backer.'

'That's hardly conclusive.'

'Agreed, but I'm certain it's Maxton, because he once offered me the chance to run the Stevens. I told him I was more interested in finding a backer for the Richmond Group, and within a week his bank in Chicago came up with the money from someone who could not reveal their identity because it would clash with their day to day business interests.'

'That's a little more convincing. But tell me what you have in mind for William Kane,' said Henry as he toyed with his wine glass and waited for Abel to continue.

'Something that shouldn't take up a lot of your time, Henry, but might well prove to be rewarding for you both financially and, as you hold Kane in the same high regard as I do, personally.'

'I'm listening,' said Henry, still not looking up from his glass.

'I want to lay my hands on a substantial shareholding in Kane's Boston bank.'

'You won't find that easy,' said Henry. 'Most of the stock is held in a family trust that cannot be sold without his personal concurrence.'

'You seem very well informed,' said Abel.

'Common knowledge,' said Henry.

Abel didn't believe him. 'So let's start by finding out the name of every shareholder in Kane and Cabot and see if any of them are interested in parting with their stock at a price considerably above par.'

Abel watched Henry's eyes light up as he began to work out how much might be in this transaction for him if he could make a deal with both sides.

'If he ever found out he'd play very rough,' said Henry.

'He's not going to find out,' said Abel. 'And even if he did we'd be at least two moves ahead of him. Do you think you are capable of doing the job?'

'I can try. What did you have in mind?'

Abel realised Henry was trying to find out what payment he might expect, but he hadn't finished yet. 'I want a written report the first day of every month showing Kane's shareholdings in any company, his business commitments and all details you can obtain of his private life. I want everything you come up with, however trivial it may seem.'

'I repeat, that won't be easy,' said Henry.

'Will a thousand dollars a month make the task easier?'

'Fifteen hundred certainly would,' replied Henry.

'A thousand dollars a month for the first six months. If you prove yourself, I'll raise the figure to fifteen hundred.'

'It's a deal,' said Henry.

'Good,' said Abel as he took his wallet from his inside pocket and extracted a cheque already made out to cash for one thousand dollars.

Henry studied the cheque. 'You were pretty confident I would fall into line, weren't you?'

'No, not altogether,' said Abel, as he removed a second cheque from his wallet and showed it to Henry. It was made out for fifteen hundred dollars. 'If you come up with some winners in the first six months, you'll only have lost three thousand dollars.'

Both men laughed.

'Now to a more pleasant subject,' said Abel. 'Are we going to win?'

'The Cubs?'

'No, the election.'

'Sure, Landon is in for a whipping. The Kansas Sunflower can't hope to beat F.D.R.' said Henry. 'As the President reminded us, that particular flower is yellow, has a black heart, is useful as parrot food and always dies before November.'

Abel laughed again. 'And how about you personally?'

'No worries. The seat has always been safe for the Democrats. The difficult thing was winning the nomination, not the election.'

'I look forward to your being a Congressman, Henry.'

'I'm sure you do, Abel, and I shall look forward to serving you as well as my other constituents.'

Abel looked at him quizzically. 'Considerably better, I should hope,' he commented as a sirloin steak that almost covered the plate was placed in front of him while another glass was filled with a Côte de Beaune 1929. The rest of the lunch was spent discussing Gabby Hartnett's injury problems, Jesse Owens's four gold medals at the Berlin Olympics, and the possibility that Hitler would invade Poland.

'Never,' said Henry, and started to reminisce about the courage of the Poles at Mons in the Great War.

Abel didn't comment on the fact that no Polish regiment had seen action at Mons.

At two thirty-seven Abel was back at his desk, considering the problems of the Presidential Suite and the eight thousand fresh bread rolls.

He did not arrive home from the Baron that night until nine o'clock, only to find Florentyna already asleep. But she woke immediately as her father entered the nursery and smiled up at him.

'Presidunk, Presidunk, Presidunk.'

Abel smiled. 'Not me. You perhaps, but not me.' He

picked his daughter up and kissed her on the cheek and sat with her while she repeated her one-word vocabulary over and over again.

3

IN NOVEMBER 1936, HENRY OSBORNE was elected to the United States House of Representatives for the Ninth District of Illinois. His majority was slightly smaller than his predecessor's, a fact which could be attributed only to his indolence as Roosevelt had carried every state except Vermont and Maine, and in Congress the Republicans were down to seventeen Senators and one hundred and three Representatives. But all that Abel cared about was that his man had a seat in the House, and he immediately offered him the chairmanship of the Planning Committee of the Baron Group. Henry gratefully accepted.

Abel channelled all his energy into building more and more hotels – with the help of Congressman Osborne, who seemed able to fix building permits wherever the Baron next desired. Abel always paid Henry for these favours with used notes. He had no idea what Henry did with the money, but it was evident that some of it had to be falling into the right hands, and he had no wish to know the details.

Despite his deteriorating relationship with Zaphia, Abel still wanted a son and began to despair when his wife failed to conceive. He initially blamed Zaphia, who longed for a second child, but eventually she nagged him into seeing a doctor. Abel was humiliated to learn that he had a low sperm count: the doctor attributed this to early malnutrition and told him that it was most unlikely he would ever be a father again. From that moment the subject was closed, and Abel lavished all his affections and hopes on Florentyna, who grew like a weed. The only thing in Abel's life that grew faster was the Baron Group. He built a new hotel in the north, and another in the south, while modernising and streamlining the older hotels already in the group.

At the age of four, Florentyna attended her first nursery school. She insisted that Abel and Franklin D. Roosevelt accompany her on the opening day. Most of the other girls were chaperoned by women whom Abel was surprised to discover were not always their mothers but often nannies and, in one case, as he was gently corrected, a governess. That night he told Zaphia that he wanted someone similarly qualified to take charge of Florentyna.

'What for?' asked Zaphia sharply.

'So that no one in that school starts life with an advantage over our daughter.'

'I think it's a stupid waste of money. What would such a person be able to do for her that I can't?'

Abel didn't reply, but the next morning, he placed advertisements in the Chicago *Tribune*, the *New York Times* and the London *Times*, seeking applicants for the post of governess, stating clearly the terms offered. Hundreds of replies came in from all over the country from highly qualified women who wanted to work for the chairman of the Baron Group. Letters arrived from Radcliffe, Vassar and Smith; there was even one from the Federal Reformatory for Women in Alderson, West Virginia. But it was the reply from a lady who had obviously never heard of the Chicago Baron that intrigued him most.

The Old Rectory
Much Hadham
Hertfordshire

12 September 1938

Dear Sir,

In reply to your advertisement in the personal column on the front page of today's issue of *The Times*, I should like to be considered for the post of governess to your daughter.

I am thirty-two years of age, and I am the sixth daughter of The Rev. L. H. Tredgold, and a spinster of the parish of Much Hadham in Hertfordshire. I am at present teaching in the local grammar school and assisting my father in his work as Rural Dean.

I was educated at Cheltenham Ladies' College where I studied Latin, Greek, French and English for my higher matriculation, before taking up a closed scholarship to Newnham College, Cambridge. At the university, I sat my finals gaining first-class awards in all three parts of the Modern Language tripos. I do not hold a Bachelor of Arts degree from the university, as their statutes preclude such awards to women.

I am available for interview at any time and I would welcome the opportunity to work in the New World.

I have the honour to remain, Sir,
Your obedient servant,
W. Tredgold

Abel found it hard to accept that there was such an institution as Cheltenham Ladies' College or indeed such a place as Much Hadham, and he was certainly suspicious of claims of first-class awards without degrees.

He asked his secretary to place a call to Washington. When he was finally put through to the person he wished to speak to he read the letter aloud.

The voice from Washington confirmed that every claim in the letter could be accurate; there was no reason to doubt its credibility.

'Are you sure there really is an establishment called Cheltenham Ladies' College?' Abel insisted.

'Most certainly I am, Mr. Rosnovski. I was educated there myself,' replied the British ambassador's secretary.

That night Abel read the letter over again, this time to Zaphia.

'What do you think?' he asked, although he had already made up his mind.

'I don't like the sound of her,' said Zaphia, not looking up from the magazine she was reading. 'If we must have someone, why can't she be an American?'

'Think of the advantages Florentyna would have if she

were tutored by an English governess.' Abel paused. 'She'd even be company for you.'

This time Zaphia did look up from her magazine. 'Why? Are you hoping she'll educate me as well?'

Abel made no reply.

The following morning he sent a cable to Much Hadham, offering Miss Tredgold the position of governess.

Three weeks later when Abel went to pick up the lady from the Twentieth Century Limited at the La Salle Street Station, he knew immediately he had made the right decision. As she stood alone on the platform, three suitcases of differing sizes and vintages by her side, she could not have been anyone but Miss Tredgold. She was tall, thin and slightly imperious, and the bun that crowned her head gave her fully two inches in height over her employer.

Zaphia, however, treated Miss Tredgold as an intruder who had come to undermine her maternal position, and when she accompanied her to her daughter's room, Florentyna was nowhere to be seen. Two eyes peered suspiciously from under the bed. Miss Tredgold spotted the girl first and fell on her knees.

'I am afraid I won't be able to help you very much if you remain there, child. I'm far too big to live under a bed.'

Florentyna burst out laughing and crawled out.

'What a funny voice you have,' she said. 'Where do you come from?'

'England,' said Miss Tredgold, taking a seat beside her on the bed.

'Where's that?'

'About a week away.'

'Yes, but how far?'

'That would depend on how you travelled during the week. How many ways could I have travelled such a long distance? Can you think of three?'

Florentyna concentrated. 'From my house I'd take a bicycle and when I'd reached the end of America I'd take a . . .'

Neither of them noticed that Zaphia had left the room.

It was only a few days before Florentyna turned Miss Tredgold into the brother and sister she could never have.

Florentyna would spend hours just listening to her new companion, and Abel watched with pride as the middle-aged spinster – he could never think of her as thirty-two, his own age – taught his four-year-old daughter a range of subjects he would have liked to know more about himself.

Abel asked George one morning if he could name Henry VIII's six wives; if he couldn't it might be wise for them to acquire two more governesses from Cheltenham Ladies' College before Florentyna ended up knowing more than they did. Zaphia did not want to know about Henry VIII or his wives, as she still felt Florentyna should be brought up according to simple Polish traditions, but she had long since given up trying to convince Abel on that subject. Zaphia carried out a routine that made it possible for her to avoid the new governess most of the day.

Miss Tredgold's daily routine on the other hand owed as much to the discipline of a Grenadier Guards' officer as to the teachings of Maria Montessori. Florentyna rose at seven o'clock and with a straight spine that never touched the back of the chair received instruction in table manners and posture until she had left the breakfast room. Between seven thirty and seven forty-five Miss Tredgold would pick out two or three items from the Chicago *Tribune*, read and discuss them with her and then question her on them an hour later. Florentyna took an immediate interest in what the President was doing, perhaps because he seemed to be named after her bear. Miss Tredgold found she had to use a considerable amount of her spare time diligently learning the strange American system of government to be certain no question that her ward might ask would go unanswered.

From nine to twelve, Florentyna and F.D.R. attended nursery school where they indulged in the more normal pursuits of her contemporaries. When Miss Tredgold came to pick her up each afternoon it was easy to discern whether Florentyna had selected the clay, the scissors and paste or the finger painting that day. At the end of every play-school session she was taken straight home for a bath and change of clothes with a 'Tut, tut,' and the occasional 'I just don't know'.

In the afternoon, Miss Tredgold and Florentyna would set off on some expedition which Miss Tredgold had carefully planned that morning without Florentyna's knowledge – although this didn't stop Florentyna always trying to find out in advance what her governess had arranged.

'What are we going to do today?' or 'Where are we going?' Florentyna would demand.

'Be patient, child.'

'Can we still do it if it rains?'

'Only time will tell. But if we can't, be assured I shall have a contingency plan.'

'What's a 'tingency plan?' asked Florentyna, puzzled.

'Something you need when everything else you have planned is no longer possible,' Miss Tredgold explained.

Among such afternoon expeditions were walks around the park, visits to the zoo, even the occasional ride on the top of a trolley car, which Florentyna considered a great treat. Miss Tredgold also used the time to give her charge the first introduction to a few words of French, and she was pleasantly surprised to find that her ward showed a natural aptitude for languages. Once they had returned home, there would be half an hour with Mama before tea, followed by another bath before Florentyna was tucked up in bed by seven o'clock. Miss Tredgold would then read a few lines from the Bible or Mark Twain – not that the Americans seemed to know the difference, Miss Tredgold said in a moment of what she imagined was frivolity – and having turned the nursery light out she sat with her charge and F.D.R. until they had both fallen asleep.

This routine was slavishly adhered to and broken only on such rare occasions as birthdays or national holidays when Miss Tredgold allowed Florentyna to accompany her to the United Artists theatre on West Randolph Street to see films such as *Snow White and the Seven Dwarfs* but not before Miss Tredgold had been to the show the previous week in order to ascertain that it was suitable for her ward. Walt Disney met with Miss Tredgold's approval, as did Laurence Olivier playing Heathcliff pursued by Merle Oberon, a film she went to watch three Thursdays running on her afternoon off at a cost of twenty cents a showing. She was able to convince herself it was worth sixty cents; after all, *Wuthering Heights* was a classic.

Miss Tredgold never stopped Florentyna asking questions about the Nazis, the New Deal and even a 'home run', although sometimes she obviously didn't understand the answers. The young girl soon discovered that her mother was not always able to satisfy her curiosity, and on several occasions Miss Tredgold, in order not to render an inaccurate answer, had to disappear into her room and consult the *Encyclopaedia Britannica*.

At the age of five Florentyna attended kindergarten at the Girls Latin School of Chicago where within a week she was moved up a grade because she was so far ahead of her contemporaries. In her world everything looked wonderful. She had Mama and Papa, Miss Tredgold and Franklin D. Roosevelt, and as far as her horizon could reach nothing seemed to be unobtainable.

Only the 'best families', as Abel described them, sent their children to the Latin School, and it came as something of a shock to Miss Tredgold that when she asked some of Florentyna's friends back for tea the invitations were politely declined. Florentyna's best friends, Mary Gill and Susie Jacobson, came regularly; but some of the parents of the other girls would make lame excuses for not accepting and Miss Tredgold soon came to realise that although the Chicago Baron might well have broken the chains of poverty he was still unable to break into some of the better drawing rooms in Chicago. Zaphia did not help, making little effort to get to know the other parents, let alone join any of their charity committees, hospital boards or the clubs to which so many of them seemed to belong.

Miss Tredgold did the best she could to help, but as she was only a servant in the eyes of most of the parents it was not easy for her. She prayed that Florentyna would never learn of these prejudices – but it was not to be.

Florentyna sailed through the first grade, more than holding her own academically with the group, and only her size reminded everyone that she was a year younger.

Abel was too busy building up his own empire to give much thought to his social standing or any problems Miss Tredgold might be facing. The group was showing steady progress with Abel looking well set by 1938 to be on target to repay the loan to his backer. In fact Abel was predicting profits of two hundred and fifty thousand dollars for the year, despite his heavy building programme.

His real worries were not in the nursery or the hotels, but almost five thousand miles away in his beloved homeland. His worst fears were realised when on September 1st, 1939, Hitler marched into Poland, and Britain declared war on Germany two days later. With the outbreak of another war Abel seriously considered leaving control of the Baron Group to George – who was turning out to be a trusty lieutenant – while he sailed off to London to join the Polish army in exile. George and Zaphia managed to talk him out of the idea, so he concentrated instead on raising cash and sending the money to the British Red Cross, while lobbying Democratic politicians to join the war alongside the British.

'F.D.R. needs all the friends he can get,' Florentyna heard her father declare one morning.

By the last quarter of 1939, Abel, with the help of a small loan from the First City Bank of Chicago, became the one hundred per cent owner of the Baron Group. He predicted in the annual report that profits for 1940 would be over half a million dollars.

Franklin D. Roosevelt – the one with the red eyes and the fluffy brown fur – rarely left Florentyna's side even when she progressed to second grade. Miss Tredgold considered that perhaps the time had come to leave F.D.R. at home. In normal circumstances she would have insisted, there might have been a few tears and the matter would have been resolved; but against her better judgment she let the child have her own way. It was a decision that turned out to be one of Miss Tredgold's rare mistakes.

Every Monday, the boys of the Latin School joined the girls to be tutored in French by the modern languages teacher, Mademoiselle Mettinet. For everyone except Florentyna, this was a first, painful introduction to the language. As the class chanted *boucher*, *boulanger*, and *épicier* after Mademoiselle, Florentyna, more out of boredom than bravado, began holding a conversation with F.D.R. in French. Her neighbour, a tall, rather lazy boy named Edward Winchester, who seemed unable to grasp the difference between *le* and *la*, leaned over and told Florentyna to stop showing off. Florentyna reddened. 'I was only trying to explain to F.D.R. the difference between the masculine and the feminine.'

'Were you?' said Edward. 'Well, I'll show you *le différence*, Mademoiselle Know-All,' and in a fit of fury he grabbed F.D.R. and with all the strength he could muster tore one of the bear's arms from its body. Florentyna remained rooted to her seat in shock as Edward then took the inkwell out of his desk and poured the contents over the bear's head.

Mademoiselle Mettinet, who had never approved of having boys in the same class as girls, rushed to the back of the room, but it was too late. F.D.R. was already royal blue from head to toe and sat on the floor in the middle of a circle of stuffing from his severed arm. Florentyna grabbed her favourite friend, tears diluting the puddled ink. Mademoiselle Mettinet marched Edward to the headmaster's office and instructed the other children to sit in silence until she returned.

Florentyna crawled around the floor, trying hopelessly to put the stuffing back into F.D.R., when a fair-haired girl Florentyna had never liked leaned over and hissed, 'Serves you right, stupid Polack.' The class giggled at the girl's remark and some of them started to chant, 'Stupid Polack, stupid Polack, stupid Polack.' Florentyna clung on to F.D.R. and prayed for Mademoiselle Mettinet's return.

It seemed like hours although it was only a few minutes before the French mistress reappeared, with Edward looking suitably crestfallen following in her wake. The chanting stopped the moment Mademoiselle Mettinet entered the room, but Florentyna couldn't even make herself look up. In the unnatural silence, Edward walked up to Florentyna and apologised in a voice that was as loud as it was unconvincing. He returned to his seat and grinned at his classmates.

When Miss Tredgold picked her charge up from school that afternoon she could hardly miss noticing that the child's face was red from crying and that she walked with a bowed head clinging on to a blue-faced F.D.R. by his remaining arm. Miss Tredgold coaxed the whole story out of Florentyna before they reached home. She then gave the child her favourite supper of hamburger and ice cream, two dishes of which she normally disapproved, and put her to bed early, hoping she would quickly fall asleep. After a futile hour with nail brush and soap spent trying to clean up the indelibly stained bear, Miss Tredgold was forced to concede defeat. As she laid the damp animal by Florentyna's side, a small voice from under the bedcovers said, 'Thank you, Miss Tredgold. F.D.R. needs all the friends he can get.'

When Abel returned a little after ten o'clock – he had taken to arriving home late almost every night – Miss Tredgold sought a private meeting with him. Abel was surprised by the request and led her at once through to his study. During the eighteen months she had been in his employ Miss Tredgold had always reported the week's progress to Mr. Rosnovski on Sunday mornings between ten and ten thirty while Florentyna was attending Mass with her mother at the Holy Name Cathedral. Miss Tredgold's reports were always clear and accurate; if anything she had a tendency to underestimate the child's achievements.

'What's the problem, Miss Tredgold?' asked Abel, trying to sound unworried. With such a break in routine he dreaded the thought that she might want to give in her notice. Miss

Tredgold repeated the story of what had happened at school that day.

Abel became redder and redder in the face as the story progressed and was scarlet before Miss Tredgold came to the end.

'Intolerable,' was his first word. 'Florentyna must be removed immediately. I shall personally see Miss Allen tomorrow and tell her exactly what I think of her and her school. I am sure that you will approve of my decision, Miss Tredgold.'

'No, sir, I do not,' came back an unusually sharp reply.

'I beg your pardon?' said Abel in disbelief.

'I believe you are as much to blame as the parents of Edward Winchester.'

'I?' said Abel. 'Why?'

'You should have told your daughter a long time ago the significance of being Polish and how to deal with any problems that might arise because of it. You should have explained the Americans' deep-seated prejudice against the Poles, a prejudice that is in my own opinion every bit as reprehensible as the English attitude towards the Irish, and only a few steps away from the Nazis' barbaric behaviour towards the Jews.'

Abel remained silent. It was a long time since anyone had told him he was wrong about anything.

'Do you have anything else to say?' he asked when he had recovered.

'Yes, Mr. Rosnovski. If you remove Florentyna from Girls Latin, I shall give in my notice immediately. If on the first occasion the child encounters some problem you choose to run away from it, how can I hope to teach her to cope with life? Watching my own country at war because we wanted to go on believing Hitler was a reasonable man, if slightly misguided, I can hardly be expected to pass on the same misconstruction of events to Florentyna. It will be heartbreaking for me to have to leave her, because I could not love Florentyna more if she were my own child, but I cannot approve of disguising the real world because you have enough money to keep the truth conveniently hidden for a few more years. I must apologise for my frankness, Mr. Rosnovski, as I feel I have gone too far, but I cannot condemn other people's prejudices while at the same time condoning yours.'

Abel sank back into his seat before replying. 'Miss Tredgold, you should have been an ambassador, not a governess. Of course you're right. What would you advise me to do?'

Miss Tredgold, who was still standing – she would never have dreamed of sitting in her employer's presence unless she was with Florentyna – hesitated.

'The child should rise thirty minutes earlier each day for the next month and be taught Polish history. She must learn why Poland is a great nation, and why the Poles were willing to challenge the might of Germany when alone they could never have hoped for victory. Then she will be able to face those who goad her about her ancestry with knowledge not ignorance.'

Abel looked her squarely in the eyes. 'I see now what George Bernard Shaw meant when he said that you have to meet the English governess to discover why Britain is great.'

They both laughed.

'I'm surprised you don't want to make more of your life, Miss Tredgold,' said Abel, suddenly aware that what he had said might have sounded offensive. If it had, Miss Tredgold gave no sign of being offended.

'My father had six daughters. He had hoped for a boy, but it was not to be.'

'And what of the other five?'

'They are all married,' she replied without bitterness.

'And you?'

'He once said to me that I was born to be a teacher and that the Lord's plan took us all in its compass so perhaps I might teach someone who does have a destiny.'

'Let us hope so, Miss Tredgold.' Abel would have called her by her first name but he did not know what it was. All he knew was she signed herself 'W. Tredgold' in a way that did not invite further enquiry. He smiled up at her.

'Will you join me in a drink, Miss Tredgold?'

'Thank you, Mr. Rosnovski. A little sherry would be most pleasant.'

Abel poured her a dry sherry and himself a large whisky.

'How bad is F.D.R.?'

'Maimed for life, I fear, which will only make the child love him the more. In the future I have decided that F.D.R. must reside at home and will only travel when accompanied by me.'

'You're beginning to sound like Eleanor Roosevelt talking about the President.'

Miss Tredgold laughed once more and sipped her sherry. 'May I offer one more suggestion concerning Florentyna?'

'Certainly,' said Abel, who proceeded to listen intently to Miss Tredgold's recommendation. By the time they had finished their second drink, Abel had nodded his approval.

'Good,' said Miss Tredgold, 'then, with your permission, I will deal with that at the first possible opportunity.'

'Certainly,' repeated Abel. 'Of course, when it comes to these morning sessions, it may not be practical for me to do a whole month without a break.' Miss Tredgold was about to speak when Abel added, 'There may be appointments that I cannot re-schedule at such short notice, as I am sure you will understand.'

'You must, Mr. Rosnovski, do what you think best, and if you find there is something more important than your daughter's future I am sure it is she who will understand.'

Abel knew when he was beaten. He cancelled all appointments outside Chicago for a full month and rose each morning thirty minutes early. Even Zaphia approved of Miss Tredgold's idea.

The first day Abel started by telling Florentyna how he had been born in a forest in Poland and adopted by a trapper's family, and how later he had been befriended by a great Baron who took him into his castle in Slonim, on the Polish–Russian border. 'He treated me like his own son,' Abel told her.

As the days went by, Abel revealed to his daughter how his

sister Florentyna, after whom she had been named, joined him in the castle and the way he discovered the Baron was his real father.

'I know, I know how you found out,' cried Florentyna.

'How can you know, little one?'

'He only had one nipple,' said Florentyna. 'It must be, it must be. I've seen you in the bath. You only have one nipple, so you had to be his son. All the boys at school have two . . .' Abel and Miss Tredgold stared at the child in disbelief as she continued, '. . . but if I'm your daughter, why have I got two?'

'Because it's only passed from father to son and is almost unknown in daughters.'

'It's not fair. I want only one.'

Abel began laughing. 'Well, perhaps if you have a son, he'll have only one.'

'Time for you to braid your hair and get ready for school,' said Miss Tredgold.

'But it's just getting exciting.'

'Do as you are told, child.'

Florentyna reluctantly left her father and went to the bathroom.

'What do you think is going to happen tomorrow, Miss Tredgold?' she asked, on the way to school.

'I have no idea, child, but as Mr. Asquith once advised, wait and see.'

'Was Mr. Asquith in the castle with Papa?'

In the days that followed Abel explained what life was like in a Russian prison camp and what had caused him to limp. He went on to teach his daughter the stories the Baron had told him in the dungeons over twenty years before. Florentyna followed the stories of the legendary Polish hero Tadeusz Kosciuszko and all the other great figures through to the present day, while Miss Tredgold pointed to a map of Europe she had pinned on the bedroom wall.

He finally explained to his daughter how he had come into possession of the silver band that he wore on his wrist.

'What does it say?' demanded Florentyna, staring at the tiny engraved letters.

'Try to read the words, little one,' said Abel.

'Bar-on Ab-el Ros-nov-ski,' she stuttered out. 'But that's your name,' she insisted.

'And it was my father's.'

After a few more days Florentyna could answer all her father's questions, even if Abel couldn't always answer all of hers.

At school, Florentyna daily expected Edward Winchester to pick on her again, but he seemed to have forgotten the incident, and on one occasion even offered to share an apple with her.

Not everyone in the class, however, had forgotten, and one girl in particular, a fat, rather dull classmate, took special pleasure in whispering the words 'Stupid Polack' within her hearing.

Florentyna did not retaliate immediately, but waited until some weeks later when the girl, having come at the bottom of the class in a history test while Florentyna came top, announced, 'At least I'm not a Polack.' Edward Winchester frowned, but some of the class giggled.

Florentyna waited for total silence before she spoke. 'True. You're not a Polack, you're a third generation American, with a history that goes back about a hundred years. Mine can be traced for a thousand, which is why you are bottom in history and I am top.'

No one in the class ever referred to the subject again. When Miss Tredgold heard the story on the way home she smiled.

'Shall we tell Papa this evening?' asked Florentyna.

'No, my dear. Pride has never been a virtue. There are some occasions on which it is wise to remain silent.'

The six-year-old girl nodded thoughtfully before asking: 'Do you ever think a Pole could be President of the United States?'

'Certainly, if the American people can overcome their own prejudice.'

'And how about a Catholic?'

'That will become irrelevant, even in my lifetime.'
'And a woman?' added Florentyna.
'That might take a little longer, child.'

That night Miss Tredgold reported to Mr. Rosnovski that his lessons had proved worthwhile.

'And when will you carry out the second part of your plan, Miss Tredgold?' Abel asked.

'Tomorrow,' she replied, smiling.

At three thirty the following afternoon Miss Tredgold was standing on the corner of the street, waiting for her ward to finish school. Florentyna came chattering out through the gates and they had walked for several blocks before she noticed that they were not taking their usual route home.

'Where are we going, Miss Tredgold?'

'Patience, child, and all will be revealed.'

Miss Tredgold smiled while Florentyna seemed more concerned with telling her how well she had done in an English test that morning, a monologue which she kept up all the way to Menomonee Street, where Miss Tredgold began to take more interest in the numbers on the doors than in Florentyna's real and imagined achievements.

At last they came to a halt outside a newly painted red door which displayed the number two hundred and eighteen. Miss Tredgold rapped on the door twice with her gloved knuckle. Florentyna stood by her side, silent for the first time since leaving school. A few moments passed before the door opened to reveal a man dressed in a grey sweater and blue jeans.

'I've come in response to your advertisement in the *Sun-Times*,' Miss Tredgold said before the man had a chance to speak.

'Ah, yes,' he replied. 'Will you come in?'

Miss Tredgold entered the house followed by a puzzled Florentyna. They were conducted through a narrow hall covered in photographs and multi-coloured rosettes before reaching the back door which led out to a yard.

Florentyna saw them immediately. They were in a basket

on the far side of the yard and she ran towards them. Six yellow labrador puppies snuggled up close to their mother. One of them left the warmth of the clan and limped out of the basket towards Florentyna.

'This one's lame,' said Florentyna, immediately picking up the puppy and studying the animal's leg.

'Yes, I'm afraid so,' admitted the breeder. 'But there are still five others in perfect condition for you to choose from.'

'What will happen if nobody takes her?'

'I suppose . . .' – the breeder hesitated – 'she will have to be put to sleep.'

Florentyna stared desperately at Miss Tredgold as she clung to the dog, who was busily licking her face.

'I want this one,' said Florentyna without hesitation, fearful of Miss Tredgold's reaction.

'How much will that be?' asked Miss Tredgold, as she opened her purse.

'No charge, ma'am. I'm happy to see that one go to a good home.'

'Thank you,' said Florentyna. 'Thank you.'

The puppy's tail never stopped wagging all the way to its new home while to Miss Tredgold's surprise Florentyna's tongue never wagged once. In fact, she didn't let go of her new pet until she was safely back inside the kitchen. Zaphia and Miss Tredgold watched as the young labrador limped across the kitchen floor towards a bowl of warm milk.

'She reminds me of Papa,' said Florentyna.

'Don't be impertinent, child,' said Miss Tredgold.

Zaphia stifled a smile. 'Well, Florentyna, what are you going to call her?'

'Eleanor.'

4

THE FIRST TIME FLORENTYNA ran for President was in 1940 at the age of six. Miss Evans, her teacher in second grade, decided to hold a mock election. The boys from the Latin School were invited to join the contest, and Edward Winchester, whom Florentyna had never quite forgiven for pouring blue ink over her bear, was chosen to run as the surrogate Wendell Willkie. Florentyna naturally ran as F.D.R.

It was agreed that each candidate would give a five-minute talk to the remaining twenty-seven members of the two classes. Miss Tredgold, without wishing to influence Florentyna, listened to her deliver her oration thirty-one times – or was it thirty-two? – as she remarked to Mr. Rosnovski the Sunday morning before the great election.

Florentyna read the political columns of the Chicago *Tribune* out loud each day to Miss Tredgold searching for any scrap of information she could add to her speech. Kate Smith seemed to be singing 'God Bless America' everywhere and the Dow Jones Index had passed 150 for the first time: whatever that was, it seemed to favour the sitting candidate. Florentyna also read about the progress of the war in Europe, and the launching of a 36,600-ton battleship U.S.S. *Washington*, the first fighting vessel America had built in nineteen years.

'Why are we building a battleship if the President has promised that the American people will never have to go to war?'

'I presume it's in the best interest of our own defence,' suggested Miss Tredgold, who was furiously knitting socks for the boys back home. 'Just in case the Germans decided to attack us.'

'They wouldn't dare,' said Florentyna.

The day that Trotsky was slain with an ice pick in Mexico, Miss Tredgold kept the paper away from her charge, while on another morning she was quite unable to explain what nylons were and why the first 72,000 pairs were sold out in eight hours, the shops limiting the sale to two per customer.

Miss Tredgold, whose legs were habitually clad in beige lisle stockings of a shade optimistically entitled 'Allure', studied the item frowningly. 'I'm sure I shall never wear nylons,' she declared, and indeed she never did.

When election day came, Florentyna's head was crammed with facts and figures, some of which she did not understand but they gave her the confidence to feel she would win. The only problem that still concerned her was that Edward was bigger than her. Florentyna imagined that this was a definite advantage as she had read that twenty-seven of the thirty-two Presidents of the United States had been taller than their rivals.

The two contestants tossed a newly-minted Jefferson nickel to decide the order of speaking. Florentyna won and chose to speak first, a mistake she never made again in her life. She walked to the front of the class, a frail figure, and mindful of Miss Tredgold's final words of advice – 'Stand up straight, child. Remember you're not a question mark' – she stood bolt upright in the centre of the raised wooden platform in front of Miss Evans's desk and waited to be told she could begin. Her first few sentences came choking out. She explained her policies for ensuring the nation's finances remained stable while at the same time promising to keep the United States out of the war. 'There is no need for one American to die because the nations of Europe cannot stay at peace,' she declared – a sentence from one of Mr. Roosevelt's speeches that she had learned by heart. Mary Gill started to applaud, but Florentyna took no notice and went on talking while, at the same time, pushing her dress down nervously with damp hands. Her last few sentences came out in a great rush, and she sat down to a lot of clapping and smiles.

Edward Winchester rose to follow her and a few of the boys from his class cheered him as he walked up to the blackboard. It was the first time Florentyna realised that some of the votes had been decided even before the speeches began. She only hoped that was true for her side as well. Edward told his classmates that winning at kickball was the same as winning for your country, and in any case Willkie stood for all the things that their parents believed in. Did they want to vote against the wishes of their fathers and mothers, because if they did support F.D.R. they would lose everything? This line was greeted with a splutter of applause, so he repeated it. At the end of his speech, Edward was also rewarded with claps and smiles, but Florentyna convinced herself they were no louder or more widespread than hers had been.

After Edward had sat down, Miss Evans congratulated both candidates and asked the twenty-seven voters to take a blank page from their notebooks and write down the name of Edward or Florentyna, according to whom they felt should be President. Pens dipped furiously into inkwells, scratched across paper. Voting slips were blotted, folded, and then passed forward to Miss Evans. When the teacher had received the last one, she began to unfold the little squares and place them in front of her in separate piles, a process that seemed to take hours. The whole classroom remained silent throughout the count which in itself was an unusual event. Once Miss Evans had completed the unfolding she counted the twenty-seven slips of paper slowly and carefully, and then double-checked them.

'The result of the mock election' – Florentyna held her breath – 'for President of the United States is thirteen votes for Edward Winchester' – Florentyna nearly cheered, she had won – '. . . and twelve votes for Florentyna Rosnovski. Two people left their papers blank, which is called abstaining.' Florentyna couldn't believe it. 'I therefore declare Edward Winchester, representing Wendell Willkie, to be the new President.'

It was the only election F.D.R. lost that year, but Florentyna was unable to disguise her disappointment and ran to hide in the girls' locker room to be sure no one could see her crying. When she came out she found Mary Gill and Susie Jacobson waiting for her.

'It doesn't matter,' said Florentyna, trying to put a brave face on the result. 'At least I know both of you supported me.'

'We couldn't.'

'Why couldn't you?' asked Florentyna in disbelief.

'We didn't want Miss Evans to know that we weren't sure how to spell your name,' said Mary.

On the way home, after Miss Tredgold had heard the story seven times, she made so bold as to ask if the child had learned anything from the exercise.

'Oh, yes,' replied Florentyna emphatically. 'I'm going to marry a man with a very simple name.'

Abel laughed when he heard the story that night and repeated it to Henry Osborne over dinner. 'Better keep your eye on her, Henry, because it won't be long before she's after your seat.'

'I've got at least fifteen years before she can vote and by then I'll be ready to hand the constituency over to her.'

'What are you doing about convincing the International Relations Committee that we ought to be in this war?'

'F.D.R. will do nothing until the result of the election is known. Everybody is aware of that, including Hitler.'

'If that's so, I only pray that Britain won't lose before we join in, because America will have to wait until November to confirm F.D.R. as President.'

During the year Abel appointed architects for two more hotels in Washington and San Francisco and had begun his first project in Canada, the Montreal Baron. Although his thoughts were rarely far from the success of the group, something else still remained on his mind.

He wanted to be in Europe, and it wasn't to build hotels.

At the end of the autumn term, Florentyna got her first spanking. In later life she always associated this with snow.

Her classmates decided to build a massive snowman and each member of the class had to bring something with which to decorate him. The snowman ended up with raisin eyes, a carrot nose, potato ears, an old pair of garden gloves, a cigar and a hat supplied by Florentyna. On the last day of the term all the parents were invited to view the snowman and many of them remarked on its hat. Florentyna beamed with pride until her father and mother arrived. Zaphia burst out laughing but Abel was not amused at the sight of his fine silk topper on the head of a grinning snowman. When they arrived home Florentyna was taken to her father's study and given a long lecture on the irresponsibility of taking things that did not belong to her. Abel bent her over his knee and gave her three hard slaps with a hairbrush.

That Saturday night was one she would never forget.

That Sunday morning was one America would always remember.

The Rising Sun appeared over Pearl Harbor on the wings of hostile aircraft and crippled the U.S. battle fleet, virtually wiping out the base and killing 2,403 Americans. The United States declared war on Japan the following day and Germany three days later.

Abel immediately summoned George to inform him that he was going to join the American forces before they sailed for Europe. George protested, Zaphia pleaded and Florentyna cried. Miss Tredgold did not venture an opinion.

Abel knew he only had to settle one final thing before leaving America. He called for Henry.

'Did you spot the announcement in the *Wall Street Journal*, Henry? I nearly missed the item myself because of all the news about Pearl Harbor.'

'You mean the merger of Lester's with Kane and Cabot, which I predicted in last month's report? Yes, I already have the full details.' Henry passed over a file to Abel. 'I guessed that's what you wanted to see me about.'

Abel flipped through the file until he found the relevant article, underlined in red by Henry. He read the paragraph twice and then started to tap his fingers on the table. 'The first mistake Kane has made.'

'I think you might be right,' said Henry.

'You're earning your fifteen hundred dollars a month, Henry.'

'Perhaps it's time to make it two thousand.'

'Why?'

'Because of Article Seven of the new bank's rules.'

'What made him allow the new clause to be inserted in the first place?' said Abel.

'To protect himself. It has obviously never occurred to Mr. Kane that someone might be trying to destroy him, but by exchanging all his shares in Kane and Cabot for the equivalent Lester shares he's lost control of one bank and not gained control of the new one because of Lester's being so much larger. While he only holds eight per cent of the shares in the new venture he has insisted on that clause to be sure that he can stop any transaction for three months, including the appointment of a new chairman.'

'So all we have to do is get hold of eight per cent of Lester's stock and use his own specially inserted clause against him as and when it suits us.' Abel paused. 'I don't imagine that will be easy.'

'That's why I've asked you for a raise.'

Abel found the task of being accepted for service in the armed forces considerably more difficult than he had at first imagined. The army was none too polite about his sight, his weight, his heart or his general physical condition. Only after some string-pulling did he manage to secure a job as a quartermaster with the Fifth Army under General Mark Clark who was waiting to sail to Africa. Abel jumped at the one chance to be involved in the war and disappeared to officers' training school. Miss Tredgold did not realise until he had left Rigg Street how much Florentyna was going to miss her father. She tried to convince the child that the war would not last long but she did not believe her own words. Miss Tredgold had read too much history.

Abel returned from training school as a major, slimmer and younger looking, but Florentyna hated seeing her father in uniform, because everyone else she knew in uniform was going away to somewhere beyond Chicago and they never seemed to come back. In February, Abel waved goodbye and left New York on the S.S. *Borinquen*. Florentyna, who was still only seven, was convinced goodbye meant for ever. Mother assured daughter that Papa would return home very quickly.

Like Miss Tredgold, Zaphia did not believe that – and this time neither did Florentyna.

Florentyna progressed to fourth grade, where she was appointed secretary of her class – which meant she kept weekly minutes of class meetings. When she read her report aloud to the rest of the class each week, no one in the fourth grade showed much interest, but in the heat and dust of Algiers, Abel, torn between laughter and tears, read each line of his daughter's earnest work as if it were the latest best-seller. Florentyna's most recent fad, much approved of by Miss Tredgold, was the Brownies, which allowed her to wear a uniform like her father. Not only did she enjoy dressing up in the smart brown outfit but she soon discovered that she could cover the sleeves with different coloured badges for such enterprises as varied as helping in the kitchen to collecting used stamps. Florentyna was awarded so many badges so quickly that Miss Tredgold was kept busy sewing them on and trying to find a new space for each one. Knots, cooking, gymnastics, animal care, handicrafts, stamps, hiking, followed quickly one after the other. 'It would have been easier if you had been an octopus,' said Miss Tredgold. But final victory was to be hers when her charge won a badge for needlework and had to sew the little yellow triangle on for herself.

When Florentyna progressed to the fifth grade, where the two schools joined together for most classes, Edward Winchester was appointed President of his class, mainly because of his feats on the sports field, while Florentyna held the post of secretary despite having better grades than anyone else including Edward. Her only disasters were in geometry, where she came second, and in the art room. Miss Tredgold always enjoyed rereading Florentyna's reports and positively relished the remarks of the art teacher. 'Perhaps if Florentyna splashed more paint on the paper than on everything that surrounded it, she might hope to become an artist rather than a plasterer and decorator.'

But the line Miss Tredgold quoted whenever she was asked about Florentyna's academic achievements came from her home-room teacher. 'This pupil mustn't cry when she is second.'

As the months passed Florentyna became aware that many of the children in her class had fathers involved in the war. She soon discovered that hers was not the only home that had to face separation. Miss Tredgold enrolled Florentyna in ballet and piano lessons to keep every moment of her spare time occupied. She even allowed her to take Eleanor to the K-9 Corps as a useful pet, but the labrador was sent home because she limped. Florentyna wished they would do the same to her father. When the summer holidays came Miss Tredgold, with the approval of Zaphia, extended their horizons to New York and Washington, despite the travel restrictions imposed by the war. Zaphia took advantage of her daughter's absence to attend charity meetings in aid of Polish soldiers returning from the front.

Florentyna was thrilled by her first trip to New York even though she had to leave Eleanor behind. There were skyscrapers, big department stores, Central Park and more people than she had ever seen before; but despite all the excitement, it was Washington she most wanted to visit. The journey was Florentyna's first in an airplane, and Miss Tredgold's as well, and as the plane followed the line of the Potomac River into Washington's National Airport, Florentyna stared down in awe at the White House, the Washington Monument, the Lincoln Memorial, and the as yet unfinished Jefferson Building. She wondered if it would be a memorial or a monument and asked Miss Tredgold to explain the difference. Miss Tredgold hesitated and said they would have to look the two words up in Webster's Dictionary when they returned to Chicago, as she couldn't be certain there was a difference. It was the first time that Florentyna realised Miss Tredgold didn't know everything.

'It's just like in the pictures,' she said as she stared down out of the tiny airplane window at the Capitol.

'What did you expect?' said Miss Tredgold.

Henry Osborne had organised a special visit to the White House and a chance to watch the Senate and House in session. Once she entered the gallery of the Senate Chamber Florentyna was mesmerised, as each speaker rose at his desk to speak. Miss Tredgold had to drag her away as one might a boy from a football game, but it didn't stop her continually asking Henry Osborne more and more questions. He was surprised by the knowledge the nine-year-old girl already possessed even if she was the daughter of the Chicago Baron.

Florentyna and Miss Tredgold spent the night at the Willard Hotel. Her father had not yet built a Baron in Washington although Congressman Osborne assured them that one was in the pipeline; in fact, he added, the site had already been fixed.

'What does "fixed" mean, Mr. Osborne?'

Florentyna received no satisfactory reply either from Henry Osborne or from Miss Tredgold, and decided to look that up in Webster's Dictionary as well.

That night Miss Tredgold tucked the child up in a large hotel bed and left the room, assuming that after such a long day her charge would quickly fall asleep. Florentyna waited for a few minutes before switching the light back on. She then retrieved her guide to the White House from under the pillow. F.D.R. in a black cloak stared up at her. 'There can be no greater calling than public service' was printed boldly on the line underneath his name. She read the booklet twice through, but it was the final page that fascinated her most. She started to memorise it and fell asleep a few minutes after one, the light still on.

During the return flight home Florentyna studied the back page again carefully while Miss Tredgold read of the progress of the war in the Washington *Times-Herald*. Italy had virtually surrendered, although it was clear that the Germans still believed they could win. Florentyna didn't interrupt Miss Tredgold's reading once between Washington and Chicago, and she wondered as the child was so quiet if she was exhausted from the travel. On returning home she allowed Florentyna to go to bed early, but not before she had written a thank-you letter to Congressman Osborne. When Miss Tredgold came to put the light out, Florentyna was still studying the guide to the White House.

It was exactly ten thirty when Miss Tredgold went down to the kitchen to make her nightly cup of cocoa before retiring to bed. On returning she heard what sounded like a chant. She tiptoed slowly to Florentyna's bedroom door, and stood alert, listening to the firmly whispered words. 'One, Washington; two, Adams; three, Jefferson; four, Madison.' She went through every President without a mistake. 'Thirty-one, Hoover; thirty-two, F.D.R.; thirty-three, Unknown; thirty-four, Unknown; thirty-five, thirty-six, thirty-seven, thirty-eight, thirty-nine, forty, forty-one, Unknown; forty-two . . .' There was a moment's silence then: 'One Washington; two, Adams; three, Jefferson . . .' Miss Tredgold tiptoed back to her room and lay awake for some time staring at the ceiling, her untouched cocoa going cold beside her as she recalled her father's words: 'You were born to be a teacher and the Lord's plan takes us all in its compass: perhaps you will teach someone of destiny.' The President of the United States, Florentyna Rosnovski? No, thought Miss Tredgold, Florentyna was right. She would have to marry someone with a simple name.

Florentyna rose the next morning, bade Miss Tredgold *bonjour* and disappeared into the bathroom. After feeding Eleanor, who now seemed to eat more than she did, Florentyna read in the Chicago *Tribune* that F.D.R. and Churchill had conferred on the unconditional surrender of Italy and told her mother joyfully that meant Papa would be home soon.

Zaphia said she hoped she was right and commented to Miss Tredgold how well she thought Florentyna was looking. 'And how did you enjoy Washington, my dear?'

'Very much, Mama. I think I'll live there one day.'

'Why, Florentyna, what would you do in Washington?'

Florentyna looked up and met Miss Tredgold's eye. She hesitated for a few seconds and then turned back to her mother. 'I don't know. I just thought Washington was a nice city. Would you please pass the marmalade, Miss Tredgold?'

5

FLORENTYNA COULDN'T BE SURE how many of her weekly letters were reaching her father because they had to be mailed to a depot in New York for checking before they were sent on to wherever Major Rosnovski was stationed at the time.

The replies came back spasmodically, and sometimes Florentyna would receive as many as three letters in one week and then no word for three months. If a whole month passed without a letter, she began to believe her father had been killed in action. Miss Tredgold explained that that was not possible since the army always sent a telegram to inform a family if a relative was killed or missing. Each morning, Florentyna would be the first to go downstairs to search through the mail for her father's handwriting or the dreaded telegram. When she did receive a letter from her father she often found some of the words were blocked out with black ink. She tried holding them up to the light over the breakfast table but still she couldn't decipher them. Miss Tredgold told her that this was for her father's own safety, as he might have inadvertently written something that could be useful to the enemy if the letter had fallen into the wrong hands.

'Why would the Germans be interested in the fact that I am second in geometry?' asked Florentyna.

Miss Tredgold ignored the question and asked if she had enough to eat.

'I'd like another bit of toast.'

'A piece, child, a piece. A bit is something you put in a horse's mouth.'

Every six months Miss Tredgold would take her charge, accompanied by Eleanor, to Monroe Street to sit on a high stool with the dog on a box by her side, to smile at a flash bulb so that Major Rosnovski could watch his daughter and the labrador grow up by photograph.

'We can't have him not recognising his only child when he returns home, can we?' she declared.

Florentyna would print her age and Eleanor's age in dog years firmly on the back of each photo and in a letter add the details of her progress at school, how she enjoyed tennis and swimming in the summer and football and basketball in the winter, also how her bookshelves were stacked with his old cigar boxes full of butterflies caught in a wonderful net that Mama had given her for Christmas. She added that Miss Tredgold had carefully chloroformed the butterflies before she pinned them and identified each one with its Latin name; how her mother had joined some charity committee and started taking an interest in the Polish League for Women; how she was growing vegetables in her victory garden, how she and Eleanor didn't like the meat shortage but that she liked bread and butter pudding while Eleanor preferred crunchy biscuits. She always ended each letter in the same way: 'Please come home tomorrow'.

The war stretched into 1944, and Florentyna followed the progress of the Allies in the Chicago *Tribune* and by listening to Edward R. Murrow's reports from London on the radio. Eisenhower became her idol and she nursed a secret admiration for General George Patton because he seemed to be a little bit like her father. On June 6th, the invasion of Western Europe was launched. Florentyna imagined that her father was on the beachhead and she was unable to understand how he could possibly hope to survive. She followed the Allies in their drive towards Paris on the map of Europe that Miss Tredgold had pinned to her playroom wall during the days of her lessons in Polish history. She began to believe that the war was at last coming to an end and that her father would soon return home.

She took to sitting hour after hour on the doorstep of their house on Rigg Street with Eleanor by her side watching the corner of the block. But the hours turned into days, the days into weeks, and Florentyna only became distracted from her vigil by the fact that both Presidential conventions were to be held in Chicago during the summer vacation, which gave her the opportunity to see her political hero in person.

The Republicans chose Thomas E. Dewey as their candidate in June, and later in July the Democrats again selected Roosevelt. Congressman Osborne took Florentyna along to the Amphitheatre to hear the President make his acceptance speech to the Convention. She was puzzled by the fact that whenever she saw Congressman Osborne, he was accompanied by a different woman. She must ask Miss Tredgold about that; she would be sure to have an explanation. After the candidate's speech, Florentyna stood in a long line waiting to shake hands with the President, but she was so nervous that she didn't look up as he was wheeled by.

It was the most exciting day of her life, and on the walk home she confided her interest in politics to Congressman Osborne. He did not point out to her that despite the war there wasn't a woman sitting in the Senate, and there were only two women in Congress.

In November Florentyna wrote to her father to tell him something she imagined he hadn't heard. F.D.R. had won a fourth term. She waited months for his reply.

And then the telegram came.

Miss Tredgold could not extract the missive from the mail before the child spotted the small buff envelope. Her governess immediately carried the telegram to Mrs. Rosnovski in the drawing room with a trembling Florentyna following in her wake, holding on to her skirt, with Eleanor a pace behind them. Zaphia tore the envelope open with nervous fingers, read the contents and burst into hysterical tears. 'No, no,' Florentyna cried. 'It can't be true, Mama. Tell me he's only missing,' and snatched the telegram from her speechless mother to read the contents. It read: MY WAR IS OVER, AM RETURNING HOME SOONEST, LOVE ABEL. Florentyna let out a whoop of joy and jumped on the back of Miss Tredgold, who fell into a chair that normally she would never have sat in. Eleanor, as if aware the usual codes could be broken, also jumped on the chair and started licking both of them while Zaphia burst out laughing.

Miss Tredgold could not convince Florentyna that 'soonest' might turn out to take some time since the army conducted a rigid system in deciding who should come home first, awarding points to those who had served the longest or had been wounded in battle. Florentyna remained optimistic but the weeks passed slowly.

One evening when she was returning home clutching yet another Brownie badge, this time for life-saving, she spotted a light shining through a small window that had not been lit for over three years. She forgot her life-saving achievement immediately, ran all the way down the street and had nearly beaten the door down before Miss Tredgold came to answer it. She dashed upstairs to her father's study, where she found him deep in conversation with her mother. She threw her arms around him and would not let go until finally he pushed her back to take a careful look at his eleven-year-old daughter.

'You're so much more beautiful than your photographs.'

'And you're in one piece, Papa.'

'Yes, and I won't be going away again.'

'Not without me, you won't,' said Florentyna, and clung on to him once more.

For the next few days, she pestered her father to tell her stories of the war. Had he met General Eisenhower? No. General Patton? Yes, for about ten minutes. General Bradley? Yes. Had he seen any Germans? No, but on one occasion he had helped to rescue a platoon that had been ambushed by the enemy at Remagen.

'And what happened –?'

'Enough, enough, young lady. You're worse than a staff sergeant on drill parade.'

Florentyna was so excited by her father's homecoming that she was an hour late for bed that night and still didn't sleep. Miss Tredgold reminded her how lucky she was that her Papa had returned without injury or disfigurement, unlike so many fathers of the children in her class.

When Florentyna heard that Edward Winchester's father had lost an arm at somewhere called Bastogne, she tried to tell him how sorry she was.

Abel quickly returned to the routine of his work. No one had recognised him when he first strode into the Baron: he had lost so much weight and looked so thin that the duty manager asked him who he was. The first decision Abel had to make was to order five new suits from Brooks Brothers because none of his pre-war clothes fitted him.

George Novak, as far as Abel could deduce from the annual reports he had been through, had kept the group on an even keel in his absence, even if he had taken no great strides forward. It was also from George that he learned that Henry Osborne had been re-elected to Congress for a fifth term. He asked his secretary to call Washington.

'Congratulations, Henry. Consider yourself elected to the board.'

'Thank you, Abel. You'll be glad to learn,' said Henry, 'that I have acquired six per cent of Lester's stock while you've been away rustling up gourmet dinners on Primus stoves for our top military brass.'

'Well done, Henry. What hope is there of getting our hands on the magic eight per cent?'

'A very good chance,' replied Henry. 'Peter Parfitt, who expected to be chairman of Lester's before Kane arrived on the scene, has been removed from the board and has about as much affection for Kane as a mongoose has for a cobra.

Parfitt has made it very clear that he is willing to part with his two per cent.'

'Then what's stopping us?'

'He's demanding a million dollars for his holding, because I'm sure he's worked out that his shares are all you need to topple Kane, and there are not many stockholders left for me to buy from. But a million is way above the ten per cent over current stock value that you authorised me to proceed at.'

Abel studied the figures that Henry had left on his desk for him. 'Offer him seven hundred and fifty thousand,' he said.

George was thinking about far smaller sums when he next spoke to Abel. 'I allowed Henry a loan in your absence and he still hasn't paid the money back,' he admitted.

'A loan?'

'Henry's description, not mine,' said George.

'Who's kidding who? How much?' said Abel.

'Five thousand dollars. I'm sorry, Abel.'

'Forget it. If that's the only mistake you've made in the last three years, I'm a lucky man. What do you imagine Henry spends the money on?'

'Wine, women and song. There's nothing particularly original about our Congressman. There's also a rumour around the Chicago bars that he's started gambling quite heavily.'

'That's all I need from the latest member of the board. Keep an eye on him and let me know if the situation gets any worse.'

George nodded.

'And now I want to talk about expansion. With Washington pumping three hundred million dollars a day into the economy we must be prepared for a boom the like of which America has never experienced before. We must also start building Barons in Europe while land is cheap and most people are only thinking about survival. Let's begin with London.'

'For God's sake, Abel, the place is as flat as a pancake.'

'All the better to build on, my dear.'

*

'Miss Tredgold,' said Zaphia, 'I'm going to a fashion show this afternoon in aid of the Chicago Symphony Orchestra and I might not be back before Florentyna's bedtime.'

'Very good, Mrs. Rosnovski,' said Miss Tredgold.

'I'd like to go,' said Florentyna.

Both women stared at the child in surprise.

'But it's only two days before your exams,' said Zaphia, anticipating that Miss Tredgold would thoroughly disapprove of Florentyna attending something as frivolous as a fashion show. 'What are you meant to be doing this afternoon?'

'Medieval history,' replied Miss Tredgold without hesitation. 'Charlemagne through to the Council of Trent.'

Zaphia was sad that her daughter was not being allowed to take an interest in feminine pursuits but rather was expected to act as a surrogate son, filling the gap for her husband's disappointment at not having a boy.

'Then perhaps we'd better leave it for another time,' she said. Zaphia would have liked to put her foot down but realised that if Abel found out both she and Florentyna would suffer for it later.

However, for once Miss Tredgold surprised her.

'I am not sure I agree with you, Mrs. Rosnovski,' she said. 'The occasion might well be the ideal one to introduce the child to the world of fashion and indeed of society.' Turning to Florentyna, she added, 'And a break from your studies a few days before exams can do you no harm.'

Zaphia looked at Miss Tredgold with new respect. 'Perhaps you would like to come yourself?' she added. It was the first time Zaphia had seen Miss Tredgold blush.

'No, thank you, no, I couldn't possibly.' She hesitated. 'I have letters, yes, letters to attend to, and I've set aside this afternoon to pen them.'

That afternoon, Zaphia was waiting by the main school gate dressed in a pink suit in place of Miss Tredgold in her usual sensible navy. Florentyna thought her mother looked extremely smart.

She wanted to run all the way to the fashion show and

when she actually arrived she found it hard to remain still even though her seat was in the front row. She could have touched the haughty models as they picked their way gracefully down the brilliantly lit catwalk. As the pleated skirts swirled and dipped, tight-waisted jackets were taken off to reveal elegantly bare shoulders, and sophisticated ladies in floating yards of pale organza topped with silk hats drifted silently to unknown assignations behind a red velvet curtain. Florentyna sat entranced. When the last model had turned a full circle, signalling the show had ended, a press photographer asked Zaphia if he could take her picture. 'Mama,' said Florentyna urgently as he was setting up his tripod, 'you must wear your hat further forward if you want to be thought chic.'

Mother obeyed child for the first time.

When Miss Tredgold tucked Florentyna into bed that night she asked if she had enjoyed the experience.

'Oh, yes,' said Florentyna. 'I had no idea clothes could make you look so good.'

Miss Tredgold smiled, a little wistfully.

'And did you realise that they raised over eight thousand dollars for the Chicago Symphony Orchestra? Even Papa would have been impressed by that.'

'Indeed he would,' said Miss Tredgold, 'and one day you will have to decide how to use your wealth for the benefit of other people. It is not always easy being born with money.'

The next day, Miss Tredgold pointed out to Florentyna a picture of her mother in *Women's Wear Daily* under the caption, 'Baroness Rosnovski, who enters the fashion scene in Chicago'.

'When can I go to a fashion show again?' asked Florentyna.

'Not until you have been through Charlemagne and the Council of Trent,' said Miss Tredgold.

'I wonder what Charlemagne wore when he was crowned Holy Roman Emperor,' said Florentyna.

That night, locked into her room, with only the light of a

torch to go by, she let down the hem of her school skirt and took two inches in at the waist.

Florentyna was now in her last term of middle school and Abel hoped she might win the coveted Upper School Scholarship. Florentyna was aware that her father could afford to send her to Upper School if she failed to win a scholarship, but she had plans for the money her father would save each year if she was awarded free tuition. She had studied hard that year, but she had no way of knowing how well she had done when the final examination came to an end, as one hundred and twenty-two Illinois children had entered for the examination but only four scholarships were to be awarded. Florentyna had been warned by Miss Tredgold that she would not learn the result for at least a month. 'Patience is a virtue,' Miss Tredgold reminded her, and added with mock horror that she would return to England on the next boat if Florentyna did not come in the first three places.

'Don't be silly, Miss Tredgold, I shall be first,' Florentyna replied confidently, but as the days of the month went by she began to regret her bragging and confided to Eleanor during a long walk that she might have written cosine when she had meant sine in one of the geometry questions, and created an impossible triangle. 'Perhaps I shall come in second,' she ventured over breakfast one morning.

'Then I shall move to the employ of the parents of the child who comes first,' said Miss Tredgold imperturbably.

Abel smiled as he looked up from his copy of the morning paper. 'If you win a scholarship,' he said, 'you will have saved me one thousand dollars a year. If you come top, two thousand dollars.'

'Yes, Papa, and I have plans for that.'

'Oh do you, young lady? And may I enquire what you have in mind?'

'If I win a scholarship, I want you to invest the money in Baron Group shares until I'm twenty-one, and if I'm first I want you to do the same for Miss Tredgold.'

'Good gracious, no,' said Miss Tredgold, stretching to her

full height, 'that would be most improper. I do apologise, Mr. Rosnovski, for Florentyna's impudence.'

'It's not impudence, Papa. If I finish top, half the credit must go to Miss Tredgold.'

'If not more,' said Abel, 'and I'll agree to your demands. But on one condition.' He folded his paper carefully.

'What's that?' said Florentyna.

'How much do you have in your savings account, young lady?'

'Three hundred and twelve dollars,' came back the immediate reply.

'Very well, if you fail to finish in the first four you must sacrifice the three hundred and twelve dollars to help me pay the tuition you haven't saved.'

Florentyna hesitated. Abel waited and Miss Tredgold did not comment.

'I agree,' said Florentyna at last.

'I have never bet in my life,' said Miss Tredgold, 'and I can only hope my dear father does not live to learn of this.'

'It should not concern you, Miss Tredgold.'

'It certainly does, Mr. Rosnovski. If the child is willing to gamble her only three hundred and twelve dollars on the strength of what I have managed to do for her then I must repay in kind and also offer three hundred and twelve dollars towards her education if she fails to win a scholarship.'

'Bravo,' said Florentyna, and threw her arms around her governess.

'A fool and his money are soon parted,' declared Miss Tredgold.

'Agreed,' said Abel, 'for I have lost.'

'What do you mean, Papa?' asked Florentyna. Abel turned over the newspaper to reveal a small headline that read 'The Chicago Baron's Daughter Wins Top Scholarship'.

'Mr. Rosnovski, you knew all the time.'

'True, Miss Tredgold, but it is you who have turned out to be the better poker player.'

Florentyna was overjoyed and spent the last few days of

her life at Middle School as the class heroine. Even Edward Winchester congratulated her.

'Let's go and have a drink to celebrate,' he suggested.

'What?' said Florentyna. 'I've never had a drink before.'

'No time like the present,' said Edward, and led her to a small classroom in the boys' end of the school. Once they were inside, he locked the door. 'Don't want to be caught,' he explained. Florentyna stood in admiring disbelief as Edward lifted the lid of his desk and took out a bottle of beer, which he prised open with a nickel. He poured the flat brown liquid into two dirty glasses, also extracted from the desk, and passed one over to Florentyna.

'Bottoms up,' said Edward.

'What does that mean?' asked Florentyna.

'Just drink the stuff,' he said, but Florentyna watched him take a gulp before she plucked up the courage to try a sip. Edward rummaged around in his jacket pocket and took out a crumpled packet of Lucky Strikes. Florentyna couldn't believe her eyes. The nearest she had been to a cigarette was the advertisement she had heard on the radio which said: 'Lucky Strike means fine tobacco. Yes, Lucky Strike means fine tobacco,' a theme that had driven Miss Tredgold mad. Without speaking, Edward removed one of the cigarettes from the packet, placed it between his lips, lit it and started puffing away. He blew some smoke recklessly into the middle of the room. Florentyna was mesmerised as he extracted a second cigarette and placed it between her lips. She did not dare to move as he struck another match and held the flame to the end of the cigarette. She stood quite still for fear it would catch her hair on fire.

'Inhale, you silly girl,' he said, so she puffed three or four times very quickly and then started coughing.

'You can take the thing out of your mouth, you know,' he said.

'Of course I know,' she said quickly, removing the cigarette the way she remembered Jean Harlow did in *Saratoga*.

'Good,' said Edward, and drank a large draught of his beer.

'Good,' said Florentyna, and did the same. For the next few minutes, she kept in time with Edward as he puffed his cigarette and gulped the beer.

'Great, isn't it?' said Edward.

'Great,' replied Florentyna.

'Like another?'

'No, thank you.' Florentyna coughed. 'But it was great.'

'I've been smoking and drinking for several weeks,' announced Edward.

'Yes, I can tell,' said Florentyna.

A bell sounded in the hall, and Edward quickly returned the beer, cigarettes and two butts to his desk before unlocking the door. Florentyna walked slowly back to her classroom. She felt dizzy and sick when she reached her desk and worse when she returned home an hour later, unaware that the smell of Lucky Strikes was still on her breath. Miss Tredgold did not comment and put her to bed immediately.

The next morning Florentyna woke in terrible discomfort, scabious eruptions on her chest and face. She looked at herself in the mirror and burst into tears.

'Chicken pox,' declared Miss Tredgold to Zaphia.

Chicken pox, the doctor confirmed later, and Miss Tredgold brought Abel to visit Florentyna in her room after the doctor had completed his examination.

'What's wrong with me?' asked Florentyna anxiously.

'I can't imagine,' said her father mendaciously. 'Looks like one of the plagues of Egypt to me. What do you think, Miss Tredgold?'

'I have only seen the like of it once before, and that was with a man in my father's parish who smoked, but of course that doesn't apply in this case.'

Abel kissed his daughter on the cheek, and he and Miss Tredgold both left the room.

'Did we pull it off?' asked Abel when they had reached his study.

'I cannot be certain, Mr. Rosnovski, but I would be willing to wager one dollar that Florentyna never smokes again.'

Abel took out his wallet from an inside pocket, removed a

dollar bill and then replaced it.

'No, I think not, Miss Tredgold. I am too aware what happens when I bet with you.'

Florentyna once heard her headmistress remark that some incidents in history are so powerful in their impact that everyone can tell you exactly where they were when they first heard the news.

On April 12th, 1945, at four forty-seven Abel was talking to a man representing a product called Pepsi-Cola who was pressing him to try out the drink in all the Baron hotels. Zaphia was shopping in Marshall Field's and Miss Tredgold had just come out of the United Artists Theatre where she had seen Humphrey Bogart in *Casablanca* for the third time. Florentyna was in her room looking up the word 'teen-ager' in Webster's Dictionary. The word was not yet acknowledged by Webster's when Franklin D. Roosevelt died in Warm Springs, Georgia.

Of all the tributes to the late President Florentyna read during the next few days, the one she kept for the rest of her life was from the New York *Post*. It read simply:

> Washington, April 19th – Following are the latest casualties in the military services including next of kin.
>
> ARMY – NAVY DEAD
>
> ROOSEVELT, Franklin D., Commander-in-Chief, wife Mrs. Anna Eleanor Roosevelt, The White House.

6

ENTERING UPPER SCHOOL AT Girls Latin prompted Florentyna's second trip to New York, as the only establishments that stocked the official school uniform were Marshall Field's in Chicago and, for shoes, Abercrombie & Fitch in New York. Abel snorted and declared it was inverted snobbery of the worst kind. Nevertheless as he had to travel to New York to check on the newly opened Baron, he agreed as a special treat to accompany Miss Tredgold and his eleven-year-old daughter on their journey to Madison Avenue.

Abel had long considered New York to be the only major city in the world not to boast a first-class hotel. He admired the Plaza, the Pierre and the Carlyle but did not think that any of the three held a candle to Claridge's in London, the George V in Paris or the Danieli in Venice, and only those achieved the standards he was trying to reproduce for the New York Baron.

Florentyna was aware that Papa was spending more and more time in New York, and it saddened her that the affection between her father and mother now seemed to be a thing of the past. The rows were becoming so frequent that she wondered if she was in any way to blame.

Once Miss Tredgold had purchased everything on the list that was available at Marshall Field's – three blue sweaters (navy), three blue skirts (navy), four shirts (white), six blue bloomers (dark), six pairs of grey socks (light), one navy-blue silk dress with white collar and cuffs – she planned the trip to New York.

Florentyna and Miss Tredgold took the train to Grand Central Station and on arrival in New York went straight to Abercrombie & Fitch where they selected two pairs of brown Oxfords.

'Such sensible shoes,' proclaimed Miss Tredgold. 'Nobody who wears Abercrombies needs fear going through life with flat feet.' They then proceeded on to Fifth Avenue. Miss Tredgold had walked several yards before she realised she was on her own. Turning around, she observed Florentyna's nose pressed against the pane of Elizabeth Arden's. She walked quickly back to join her. 'Ten shades of lipstick for the sophisticated woman,' read the sign in the window.

'Rose red is my favourite,' said Florentyna hopefully.

'The school rules are very clear,' said Miss Tredgold authoritatively. 'No lipstick, no nail polish, and no jewelry except a ring and a watch.'

Florentyna reluctantly left the rose-red lipstick and joined her governess on her march up Fifth Avenue towards the Plaza Hotel where her father was expecting them at the Palm Court for tea. Abel could not resist returning to the hotel where he had served his apprenticeship as a junior waiter, and although he recognised no one except Old Sammy, the head waiter in the Oak Room, everyone knew exactly who he was.

After macaroons and ice cream for Florentyna, a cup of coffee for Abel, and lemon tea and a watercress sandwich for Miss Tredgold, Abel returned to work. Miss Tredgold checked her New York itinerary and took Florentyna to the top of the Empire State Building. As the elevator reached the one hundred and second floor Florentyna felt quite giddy and they both burst out laughing when they discovered fog had come in from the East River and they couldn't even see as far as the Chrysler Building. Miss Tredgold checked her list again and decided that their time would be better spent visiting the Metropolitan Museum. Mr. Francis Henry Taylor, the director, had just acquired a large canvas by Pablo Picasso. The oil painting turned out to be a woman with two heads and one breast coming out of her shoulder.

'What do you think of that?' asked Florentyna.

'Not a lot,' said Miss Tredgold. 'I rather suspect that when he was at school he received the same sort of art reports as you do now.'

Florentyna always enjoyed staying in one of her father's hotels when she was on a trip. She would happily spend hours walking around trying to pick up mistakes the hotel was making. After all, she pointed out to Miss Tredgold, they had their investment to consider. Over dinner that night in the Grill Room of the New York Baron, Florentyna told her father that she didn't think much of the hotel shops.

'What's wrong with them?' asked Abel, mouthing questions without paying much attention to the answers.

'Nothing you can point to easily,' said Florentyna, 'except that they are all dreadfully dull compared with real shops like the ones on Fifth Avenue.'

Abel scribbled a note on the back of his menu, 'shops dreadfully dull', and doodled around it carefully before he said: 'I shall not be returning to Chicago with you tomorrow, Florentyna.'

For once Florentyna was silent.

'Some problems have arisen with the hotel at this end and I must stay behind to see they don't get out of hand,' he said, sounding a little too well rehearsed.

Florentyna gripped her father's hand. 'Try and come back tomorrow. Eleanor and I always miss you.'

Once Florentyna had returned to Chicago Miss Tredgold set about preparing her for Upper School. Each day they would spend two hours studying a different subject but Florentyna was allowed to choose whether they should work in the mornings or the afternoons. The only exception to this rule was on Thursdays, when their sessions took place in the morning as it was Miss Tredgold's afternoon off.

At two o'clock promptly every Thursday she would leave the house and not return until seven that night. She never explained where she was going, and Florentyna never summoned up the courage to ask. But as the holiday progressed

Florentyna became more and more curious about where Miss Tredgold spent her time, until finally she resolved to discover for herself.

After a Thursday morning of Latin and a light lunch together in the kitchen, Miss Tredgold said goodbye to Florentyna and retired to her room. As two o'clock struck she opened the front door of the house and headed off down the street carrying a large canvas bag. Florentyna watched her carefully through her bedroom window. Once Miss Tredgold had turned the corner of Rigg Street, Florentyna dashed out and ran all the way to the end of the block. She peered around to see her mentor waiting at a bus stop just ten yards away. She could feel her heart beating at the thought of not being able to follow Miss Tredgold any farther. Within minutes she watched a bus draw up and come to a halt. She was about to turn back for home when she noticed Miss Tredgold disappear up the circular staircase of the double-decker. Without hesitation, Florentyna ran and jumped on to the moving platform, then quickly made her way to the front of the bus.

When the ticket collector asked her where she was going Florentyna suddenly realised she had no idea of her destination.

'How far do you go?' she asked.

The collector looked at her suspiciously. 'The Loop,' he replied.

'One single for the Loop then,' said Florentyna confidently.

'That'll be fifteen cents,' said the conductor.

Florentyna fumbled in her jacket pocket to discover she had only ten cents.

'How far can I go for ten cents?'

'Rylands School,' came back the reply.

Florentyna passed over the money, praying that Miss Tredgold would reach her destination before she would have to get off, while not giving any thought to how she would make the return journey.

She sat low in her seat and watched carefully each time the

bus came to a halt, but even after she had counted twelve stops Miss Tredgold still did not appear as the bus travelled along Lake Front, passing the University of Chicago.

'Your stop is next,' the conductor said firmly.

When the bus next came to a halt at Seventy-first Street, Florentyna knew she was beaten. She stepped down reluctantly on to the pavement thinking about the long walk home and determined that the following week she would have enough money to cover the journey both ways.

She stood unhappily watching the bus as it travelled a few hundred yards farther down the street before coming to a stop once more. A figure stepped out into the road which could only have been Miss Tredgold. She disappeared down a side street, looking as if she knew exactly where she was going.

Florentyna ran as hard as she could, but when she reached the corner, breathless, there was no sign of Miss Tredgold. Florentyna walked slowly down the street wondering where her governess could have gone. Perhaps into one of the houses, or might she have taken another side street? Florentyna decided she would walk to the end of the road and if she failed to spot her quarry then she would have to make her way home.

Just at the point when she was considering turning back she came into an opening that faced a large wrought-iron archway which had embossed on it in gold: South Shore Country Club.

Florentyna didn't consider for a moment that Miss Tredgold could be inside, but out of curiosity she peered through the gates.

'What do you want?' said a uniformed guard standing on the other side.

'I was looking for my governess,' said Florentyna lamely.

'What's her name?'

'Miss Tredgold,' Florentyna said unflinchingly.

'She's already gone into the club house,' said the guard, pointing towards a Victorian building surrounded by trees about a quarter of a mile up a steep rise.

Florentyna marched boldly through, without another word, staying on the path because 'Keep off the grass' signs were displayed every few yards. She kept her eye on the club house and had ample time to leap behind a tree when she saw Miss Tredgold emerge. She hardly recognised the lady dressed in red and yellow check tweed trousers, a heavy Fair Isle sweater and heavy brown brogues. A bag of golf clubs was slung comfortably over one shoulder.

Florentyna stared at her governess, mesmerised.

Miss Tredgold walked towards the first tee where she put down her bag and took out a ball. She placed it on a tee at her feet and selected a club from her bag. After a few practice swings she steadied herself, addressed the ball and hit it firmly down the middle of the fairway. Florentyna couldn't believe her eyes. She wanted to applaud but instead ran forward to hide behind another tree as Miss Tredgold marched off down the fairway.

Miss Tredgold's second shot landed only twenty yards from the edge of the green. Florentyna ran forward to a clump of trees at the side of the fairway and watched Miss Tredgold chip her ball up on to the green and hole it with two putts. Florentyna was left in no doubt that Miss Tredgold had been playing the game for some considerable time.

Miss Tredgold then removed a small white card from her jacket pocket and wrote on it, before heading towards the second tee. As she did so she gazed towards the second green, which was to the left of where Florentyna was hidden. Once again Miss Tredgold steadied herself, addressed the ball and swung, but this time she sliced her shot and the ball ended up only fifteen yards away from Florentyna's hiding place.

Florentyna looked up at the trees but they had not been made for climbing other than by a cat. She held her breath and crouched behind the widest but could not resist watching Miss Tredgold as she studied the lay of her ball. Miss Tredgold muttered something inaudible and then selected a club. Florentyna let out her breath as Miss Tredgold swung. The ball climbed high and straight before landing in the middle of the fairway again.

Florentyna watched Miss Tredgold replace her club in the bag.

'I should have kept a straighter arm on the first shot and then we would never have met.'

Florentyna assumed Miss Tredgold was admonishing herself yet again, and remained behind the tree.

'Come here, child.' Florentyna obediently ran out but said nothing.

Miss Tredgold took another ball from the side pocket of her bag and placed it on the ground in front of her. She selected a club and handed it to her charge.

'Try to hit the ball in that direction,' she said, pointing towards a flag about a hundred yards away.

Florentyna held the club awkwardly before taking several swings at the ball, on each occasion removing what Miss Tredgold called 'divots'. At last she managed to push it twenty yards towards the fairway. She beamed with pleasure.

'I see we are in for a long afternoon,' declared Miss Tredgold resignedly.

'I am sorry,' said Florentyna. 'Can you ever forgive me?'

'For following me, yes. But for the state of your golf, no. We shall have to start with the basics, as it seems in the future I am no longer to have Thursday afternoons to myself, now you have discovered my father's only sin.'

Miss Tredgold taught Florentyna how to play golf with the same energy and application as if it were Latin or Greek. By the end of the summer Florentyna's favourite afternoon was Thursday.

Upper School was very different from Middle School. There was a new teacher for every subject rather than one teacher for everything except gym. The pupils had to move from room to room for their classes, and for many of the activities the girls joined forces with the boys' school. Florentyna's favourite subjects were current affairs, Latin, French and English, although she couldn't wait for her twice-weekly biology classes because they gave her the chance to admire the school's collection of bugs under the microscope.

'Insects, dear child. You must refer to the little creatures as insects,' Miss Tredgold insisted.

'Actually, Miss Tredgold, they're nematodes.'

Florentyna also continued to take an interest in clothes and noticed that the mode for short dresses caused by the enforced economies of war was fast becoming outdated and that once again skirts were nearly reaching the ground. She was unable to do much about experimenting with fashion, as the school uniform was the same year in and year out; the children's department of Marshall Field's, it seemed, was not a great contributor to *Vogue*. However, she studied all the relevant magazines in the library and pestered her mother to take her to more shows. For Miss Tredgold, on the other hand, who had never allowed any man to see her knees, even in the self-denying days of Lend-Lease, the new fashion only proved she had been right all along.

At the end of Florentyna's first year in Upper School the modern languages mistress decided to put on a performance of *Saint Joan* in French. As Florentyna was the only pupil who could think in the language, she was chosen to play the Maid of Orleans and rehearsed for hours in the old nursery with Miss Tredgold playing every other part as well as being prompter and cue reader. Even when Florentyna was word-perfect, Miss Tredgold sat loyally through the daily one-woman shows.

'Only the Pope and I give audiences for one,' she told Florentyna as the phone rang.

'It's for you,' said Miss Tredgold.

Florentyna always enjoyed receiving phone calls, although it was not a practice that Miss Tredgold encouraged.

'Hello, it's Edward. I need your help.'

'Why? Don't tell me you've learnt to read?'

'No hope of that, silly. But I've been given the part of the Dauphin and I can't pronounce all the words.'

Florentyna tried not to laugh. 'Come around at five thirty and you can join the daily rehearsals. Although I must warn you, Miss Tredgold has been making a very good Dauphin up to now.'

Edward came around every night at five thirty and although Miss Tredgold occasionally frowned when 'the boy' lapsed back into an American accent he was 'just about ready' by the day of the dress rehearsal.

When the night of the performance itself came, Miss Tredgold instructed Florentyna and Edward that under no circumstances must they look out into the audience hoping to spot their parents, otherwise those watching the performance would not believe in the characters they were portraying. Most unprofessional, Miss Tredgold considered, and reminded Florentyna that Mr. Noël Coward once left a performance of *Romeo and Juliet* because Mr. John Gielgud looked straight at him during a soliloquy. Florentyna was convinced, though in truth she had no idea who Mr. John Gielgud or Mr. Noël Coward were.

When the curtain went up, Florentyna did not once look beyond the footlights. Miss Tredgold considered her efforts 'most commendable', and during the intermission particularly commented to Florentyna's mother on the scene in which the Maid is alone in the centre of the stage and talks to her voices. 'Moving', was Miss Tredgold's description. 'Unquestionably moving'. When the curtain finally fell, Florentyna received a rapturous ovation, even from those who had not been able to follow every word in French. Edward stood a pace behind her, relieved to have come through the ordeal without too many mistakes. Glowing with excitement, Florentyna removed her make-up, her first experience of lipstick and powder, changed back into her school uniform and joined her mother and Miss Tredgold with the other parents who were having coffee in the dining hall. Several people came over to congratulate her on her performance including the headmaster of the Boys Latin School.

'A remarkable achievement for a girl of her age,' he told Mrs. Rosnovski. 'Though when you think about it she is only a couple of years younger than Saint Joan was when she challenged the entire might of the French establishment.'

'Saint Joan didn't have to learn someone else's lines in a foreign language,' said Zaphia, feeling pleased with herself.

Florentyna did not take in her mother's words as her eyes were searching the crowded hall for her father.

'Where's Papa?' she asked.

'He couldn't make it tonight.'

'But he promised,' said Florentyna. 'He *promised.*' Tears welled up in her eyes as she suddenly realised why Miss Tredgold had told her not to look beyond the footlights.

'You must remember, child, that your father is a very busy man. He has a small empire to run.'

'So did Saint Joan,' said Florentyna.

When Florentyna went to bed that night, Miss Tredgold came to turn out her light.

'Papa doesn't love Mama any more, does he?'

The bluntness of the question took Miss Tredgold by surprise and it was a few moments before she recovered.

'Of only one thing I am certain, child, and that is that they both love you.'

'Then why has Papa stopped coming home?'

'That I cannot explain but whatever his reasons we must be very understanding and grown-up,' said Miss Tredgold, brushing back a lock of hair that had fallen over Florentyna's forehead.

Florentyna felt very ungrown-up and wondered if Saint Joan had been so unhappy when she lost her beloved France. When Miss Tredgold closed the door quietly Florentyna put her hand under the bed to feel the reassuring wet nose of Eleanor. 'At least I'll always have you,' she whispered. Eleanor clambered up from her hiding place on to the bed and settled down next to Florentyna, facing the door: a quick retreat to her basket in the kitchen might prove necessary if Miss Tredgold reappeared.

Florentyna did not see her father during that summer vacation and had long stopped believing the stories that the growing hotel empire was keeping him away from Chicago. Whenever she mentioned him to her mother, Zaphia's replies were often bitter. Florentyna also found out from overheard telephone conversations that she was consulting lawyers.

Each day Florentyna would take Eleanor for a walk down Michigan Avenue in the hope that she might see her father's car drive by. One Wednesday, she decided to make a break in her routine and walk on the west side of the Avenue to study the stores that set the fashions for the Windy City. Eleanor was delighted to be reunited with the magnificent lampposts that had recently been placed for her at twenty-yard intervals. Florentyna had already purchased a wedding dress and a ball gown with her five dollars a week pocket money and was coveting an elegant five-hundred-dollar evening dress in the window of Martha Weathereds' on the corner of Oak Street when she saw her father's reflection in the glass. She turned, overjoyed, to see him coming out of Spaulding's on the opposite side of the street. Without a thought she dashed out into the road not looking either way as she called her father's name. A yellow cab jammed on its brakes and swerved violently, the driver aware of a flash of blue skirt then the heavy thud as the cab made contact. The rest of the traffic came to a screeching halt as the cab driver saw a stout, well-dressed man, followed by a policeman, run out into the middle of the road. A moment later Abel and the taxi driver stood in a state of shock staring down at the lifeless body. 'She's dead,' said the policeman, shaking his head, as he took out his notebook from his top pocket.

Abel fell on his knees, trembling. He looked up at the policeman. 'And the worst thing about it is I am to blame.'

'No, Papa, it was my fault,' wept Florentyna. 'I should never have rushed out into the road. I killed Eleanor by not thinking.'

The driver of the taxi that had hit the labrador explained that he had had no choice, he had to hit the dog to avoid colliding with the girl.

Abel nodded, picked up his daughter and carried her to the side of the road, not letting her look back at Eleanor's mangled body. He placed Florentyna in the back of his car and returned to the policeman.

'My name is Abel Rosno –'

'I know who you are, sir.'

'Can I leave everything to you, officer?'

'Yes, sir,' said the policeman, not looking up from his notebook.

Abel returned to his chauffeur and told him to drive them to the Baron. Abel held his daughter's hand as they walked through the crowded hotel corridor to the private elevator that whisked them to the forty-second floor. George met them when the gates sprang open. He was about to greet his goddaughter with a Polish quip when he saw the look on her face.

'Ask Miss Tredgold to come over immediately, George.'

'Of course,' said George, and disappeared into his own office.

Abel sat and listened to several stories about Eleanor without interrupting before tea and sandwiches arrived but Florentyna managed only a sip of milk. Then without any warning she changed the subject.

'Why don't you ever come home, Papa?' she asked.

Abel poured himself another cup of tea, a little spilling into the saucer. 'I've wanted to come home many times, and I hated missing *Saint Joan*, but your mother and I are going to be divorced.'

'Oh no, it can't be true. Papa . . .'

'It's my fault, little one. I have not been a good husband and . . .'

Florentyna threw her arms around her father. 'Does that mean I will never see you again?'

'No. I have made an agreement with your mother that you shall remain in Chicago while you are at school, but you will spend the rest of the time with me in New York. Of course you can always talk to me on the telephone whenever you want to.'

Florentyna remained silent as Abel gently stroked her hair.

Some time passed before there was a knock on the door and Miss Tredgold entered, her long dress swishing across the carpet as she came quickly to Florentyna's side.

'Can you take her home please, Miss Tredgold?'

'Of course, Mr. Rosnovski.' Florentyna was still tearful. 'Come with me, child,' she said. Bending down, she whispered, 'Try not to show your feelings.'

The twelve-year-old girl kissed her father on the forehead, took Miss Tredgold's hand and left.

When the door closed, Abel, not having been brought up by Miss Tredgold, sat alone and wept.

7

IT WAS AT THE beginning of her second year in Upper School that Florentyna first became aware of Pete Welling. He was sitting in a corner of the music room, playing the latest Broadway hit, 'Almost Like Being in Love' on the piano. He was slightly out of tune but Florentyna assumed it must be the piano. Pete didn't seem to notice her as she passed him, so she turned around and walked back again, but to no avail. He put a hand nonchalantly through his fair wavy hair and continued playing the piano, so she marched off pretending she hadn't seen him. By lunchtime the next day she knew that he was two grades above her, where he lived, that he was vice-captain of the football team, president of his class, and nearly seventeen. Her friend Susie Jacobson warned her that others had trod the same path without a great deal of success.

'But I assure you,' replied Florentyna, 'I have something to offer that will prove irresistible.'

That afternoon she sat down and composed what she imagined to be her first love letter. After much deliberation she chose purple ink and wrote in a bold slanting hand:

My dear Pete,

I knew you were something special the first time I saw

you. I think you play the piano beautifully. Would you like to come and listen to some records at my place?

Very sincerely,
Florentyna (Rosnovski)

Florentyna waited for the break before she crept down the corridor, imagining every eye to be on her as she searched for Pete Welling's hall locker. When she found it, she checked his name against the number on the top of the locker. Forty-two – she felt that was a good omen – and opened his locker door, left her letter on top of a maths book, where he couldn't miss it and returned to her classroom, palms sweating. She checked her own locker, on the hour every hour, expecting his reply, but none was forthcoming. After a week had passed, she began to despair until she saw Pete sitting on the steps of the chapel combing his hair. How daring to break two school rules at once, she thought. Florentyna decided this was her chance to find out if he had ever received her invitation.

She walked boldly towards him, but with only a yard to go she wished he would disappear in a cloud of dust because she couldn't think of anything to say. She stood still like a lamb in the gaze of a python but he saved her by saying, 'Hi.'

'Hi,' she managed. 'Did you ever find my letter?'

'Your letter?'

'Yes, I wrote to you last Monday about coming over to play some records at my place. I've got "Silent Night", and most of Bing Crosby's latest hits. Have you heard him singing "White Christmas"?' she asked, playing her trump card.

'Oh, it was you who wrote that letter,' he said.

'Yes, I saw you play against Francis Parker last week. You were fantastic. Who are you playing next?'

'It's in the school calendar,' he said, putting his comb into an inside pocket and looking over her shoulder.

'I'll be in the stands.'

'I'm sure you will,' he said as a tall blonde from the senior class wearing little white socks that Florentyna felt sure were not official school uniform ran over to Pete and asked if he had been waiting long.

'No, only a couple of minutes,' said Pete, and put his arm around her waist before turning back to Florentyna. 'I'm afraid you'll just have to get in line. But perhaps your time will come,' he said, laughing. 'In any case, I think Crosby's a square. Bix Beiderbecke is my man.'

As they walked away, Florentyna could hear him telling the blonde, 'That was the girl who sent me the note.' The blonde looked back over her shoulder and started laughing. 'She's probably still a virgin,' Pete added.

Florentyna went to the girls' locker room and hid until everyone else had gone home, dreading that they would all laugh at her once the story had gone the rounds. She didn't sleep that night, and the next morning she studied the other girls' faces but couldn't see any signs of sniggers or stares and decided to confide in Susie Jacobson to discover if the news was out. When Florentyna had finished her story, Susie burst out laughing.

'Not you as well,' Susie said.

Florentyna felt a lot better after Susie told her how far down the line she actually was. It gave her the courage to ask Susie if she knew what a virgin was.

'I'm not certain,' said Susie. 'Why do you ask?'

'Because Pete said I was probably one.'

'Then I think I must be one as well. I once overheard Mary Alice Beckman saying it was when a boy made love to you and nine months later you had a baby. Like Miss Horton told us about elephants, but they take two years.'

'I wonder what it feels like?'

'According to all the magazines Mary Alice keeps in her locker, it's dreamy.'

'Do you know anyone who's tried?'

'Margie McCormick claims she has.'

'She would claim anything, and if she has, why hasn't she had a baby?'

'She said she took "precautions", whatever they are.'

'If it's anything like having a period, I can't believe it's worth all the trouble,' said Florentyna.

'Agreed,' said Susie. 'I got mine again yesterday. Do you think men have the same problem?'

'Not a chance,' said Florentyna. 'They always end up with the best of every deal. Obviously we get the periods and the babies and they get shaving and the draft, but I shall have to ask Miss Tredgold about that.'

'I'm not sure she'll know,' said Susie.

'Miss Tredgold,' said Florentyna sounding confident, 'knows everything.'

That evening when Miss Tredgold was approached by a puzzled Florentyna, she did not hesitate to sit the child down and explain the birth process to her in the fullest details, warning her of the consequences of a rash desire to experiment. Florentyna sat and listened to Miss Tredgold in silence. When she had finished Florentyna asked, 'Then why is so much fuss made about the whole thing?'

'Modern society and loose morals make a lot of demands on girls, but always remember that each of us makes our own decision as to what others think of us and, more importantly, what we think of ourselves.'

'She *did* know all about becoming pregnant and having babies,' Florentyna said to Susie the next day with great authority.

'Does that mean you're going to remain a virgin?' asked Susie.

'Oh, yes,' said Florentyna. 'Miss Tredgold is still one.'

'But what about "precautions"?' demanded Susie.

'You don't need them if you remain a virgin,' Florentyna said, passing on her newly acquired knowledge.

The only other event of importance that year for Florentyna was her confirmation. Although Father O'Reilly, a young priest from the Holy Name Cathedral, officially instructed her, Miss Tredgold, resolutely suppressing the Church of England tenets of her youth, studied the Roman Catholic 'Orders in Confirmation' and took Florentyna painstakingly through her preparation, leaving her in no doubt of the obligations that her promises to our dear Lord brought upon her. The Roman Catholic Archbishop of Chicago, assisted by Father O'Reilly, administered the confirmation, and both Abel and Zaphia attended the service. Their divorce having been completed, they sat in separate pews.

Florentyna wore a simple white dress with a high neck, the hem falling a few inches below the knee. She had made the dress herself, with – when she was asleep – a little help from Miss Tredgold. The original design had come from a photograph in *Paris Match* of a dress worn by Princess Elizabeth. Miss Tredgold had brushed Florentyna's long dark hair for over an hour until it shone. She even allowed it to fall to her shoulders. Although she was only thirteen, the young confirmand looked stunning.

'My goddaughter is beautiful,' said George as he stood next to Abel in the front pew of the church.

'I know,' said Abel.

'No, I'm serious,' said George. 'Very soon there is going to be a line of men banging on the Baron's castle door demanding the hand of his only daughter.'

'As long as she's happy, I don't mind who she marries.'

After the service was over the family had a celebration dinner in Abel's private rooms at the Baron. Florentyna received gifts from her family and friends, including a beautiful leather-bound version of the Douai Bible from Miss Tredgold, but the present she treasured most was the one her father had kept safely until he felt she was old enough to appreciate it, the antique ring that had been given to Florentyna on her christening by the man who had put his faith in Papa and backed the Baron Group.

'I must write and thank him,' said Florentyna.

'You can't, my dear, as I am not certain who he is. I honoured my part of the bargain long ago, so now I will probably never discover his true identity.'

She slipped the antique ring on to the third finger of her left hand and throughout the rest of the day her eyes returned again and again to the sparkling little emeralds.

8

'How will you be voting in the Presidential election, madam?' asked the smartly dressed young man.

'I shall not be voting,' said Miss Tredgold, continuing down the street.

'Shall I put you down as "Don't know"?' said the man, running to keep up with her.

'Most certainly not,' said Miss Tredgold. 'I made no such suggestion.'

'Am I to understand you don't wish to state your preference?'

'I am quite happy to state my preference, young man, but as I come from Much Hadham in England it is unlikely to influence either Mr. Truman or Mr. Dewey.'

The man conducting the Gallup Poll retreated, but Florentyna watched him carefully because she had read somewhere that the results of such polls were now being taken seriously by all leading politicians.

It was 1948, and America was in the middle of another election campaign. Unlike the Olympics, the race for the White House was re-run every four years, war or peace. Florentyna remained loyal to the Democrats but did not see how President Truman could possibly hold on to the White House after two such unpopular years as President. The Republican candidate, Thomas E. Dewey, had a lead of over eight per cent in the latest Gallup Poll and looked certain of victory.

Florentyna followed both campaigns closely and was delighted when Margaret Chase Smith beat three men to be chosen as the Republican Senatorial candidate for Maine. For the first time, the American people were able to follow the election on television. Abel had installed an R.C.A. set at Rigg Street only months before he departed, but during term time Miss Tredgold would not allow Florentyna to watch 'that new-fangled machine' for more than one hour a day. 'It can never be a substitute for the written word,' she declared. 'I agree with Professor Chester L. Dawes of Harvard,' she added. 'Too many instant decisions will be made in front of the cameras that will later be regretted.'

Although she did not fully agree with Miss Tredgold's sentiments at the time, Florentyna selected her hour carefully, always choosing the C.B.S. evening news, during which Douglas Edwards would give the campaign round-up, over Ed Sullivan's more popular 'Toast of the Town'. However, she still found time to listen to Ed Murrow on the radio. After all his broadcasts from London during the war, she, like so many other millions of Americans, remained loyal to his every word. She felt it was the least she could do.

During the summer vacation Florentyna parked herself in Congressman Osborne's campaign headquarters and, along with scores of other volunteers of assorted ages and ability, filled envelopes with 'A Message from your Congressman' and a bumper sticker that said in bold print 'Re-elect Osborne'. She and a pale, angular youth who never proffered any opinions would then lick the flap of each envelope and place it on a pile according to district, for hand delivery by another helper. By the end of each day her mouth and lips were covered in gum and she would return home feeling thirsty and sick.

One Thursday the receptionist in charge of the telephone enquiries asked if Florentyna could take her place while she took a break for lunch.

'Of course,' said Florentyna with tremendous excitement, and jumped into the vacated seat before the pale youth could volunteer.

'There shouldn't be any problems,' the receptionist said. 'Just say Congressman Osborne's office, and if you're not sure of anything, look it up in the campaign handbook. Everything you need to know is in there,' she added, pointing to the thick booklet by the side of the phone.

'I'll be just fine,' said Florentyna.

She sat in the exalted chair, staring at the phone, willing it to ring. She didn't have to wait long. The first caller was a man who wanted to know where he voted. That's a strange question, thought Florentyna.

'At the polls,' she said, a little pertly.

'Sure, I know that, you stupid bitch,' came back the reply. 'But where is my polling place?'

Florentyna was speechless for a moment, and then asked, very politely, where he lived.

'In the Seventh Precinct.'

Florentyna flicked through her guide. 'You should vote at Saint Chrysostom's Church on Dearborn Street.'

'Where's that?'

Florentyna studied the map. 'The church is located five blocks from the lake shore and fifteen blocks north of the Loop.' The phone clicked and immediately rang again.

'Is that Osborne's headquarters?'

'Yes, sir,' said Florentyna.

'Well, you can tell that lazy bastard I wouldn't vote for him if he was the only candidate alive.' The phone clicked again and Florentyna felt queasier than she had been when she was licking envelopes. She let the bell ring three times before she could summon up the courage to lift the receiver to answer.

'Hello,' she said nervously. 'This is Congressman Osborne's headquarters. Miss Rosnovski speaking.'

'Hello, my dear, my name is Daisy Bishop, and I will need a car to take my husband to the polls on election day because he lost both his legs in the last war.'

'Oh, I'm so sorry,' said Florentyna.

'Don't worry yourself, young lady. We wouldn't let wonderful Mr. Roosevelt down.'

'But Mr. Roosevelt is . . . Yes, of course you wouldn't. Can I please take down your telephone number and address?'

'Mr. and Mrs. Bishop, 653 West Buena Street, MA4–4816.'

'We will phone you on election morning to let you know what time the car will pick you up. Thank you for supporting the Democratic ticket, Mrs. Bishop,' said Florentyna.

'We always do, my dear. Goodbye and good luck.'

'Goodbye,' said Florentyna, who took a deep breath and felt a little better. She wrote down a '2' in brackets – after the Bishops' name and placed the note in the file marked 'Transportation for Election Day'. Then she waited for the next call.

It was some minutes before the phone sounded again and by then Florentyna had fully regained her confidence.

'Good morning, is this the Osborne office?'

'Yes, sir,' said Florentyna.

'My name is Melvin Crudick and I want to know Congressman Osborne's views on the Marshall Plan.'

'The what plan?' said Florentyna.

'The Marshall Plan,' enunciated the voice authoritatively.

Florentyna frantically flipped the pages of the campaign handbook that she had been promised would reveal everything.

'Are you still there?' barked the voice.

'Yes, sir,' said Florentyna. 'I just wanted to be sure you were given a full and detailed answer on the Congressman's views. If you would be kind enough to wait one moment.'

At last Florentyna found the Marshall Plan and read through Henry Osborne's words on the subject.

'Hello, sir.'

'Yes,' said the voice, and Florentyna started to read it out loud.

' "Congressman Osborne approves of the Marshall Plan." ' There was a long silence.

'Yes, I know he does,' said the voice from the other end.

Florentyna felt weak. 'Yes, he does support the plan,' she repeated.

'*Why* does he?' said the voice.

'Because it will benefit everyone in his district,' said Florentyna firmly, feeling rather pleased with herself.

'Pray tell me, how can giving six billion American dollars to Europe help the Ninth District of Illinois?' Florentyna could feel the perspiration on her forehead. 'Miss, you may inform your Congressman that because of your personal incompetence I shall be voting Republican on this occasion.'

Florentyna put the phone down and was considering running out of the door when the receptionist returned from her lunch. Florentyna did not know what to tell her.

'Anything interesting?' the girl asked as she resumed her place. 'Or was it the usual mixture of weirdos, perverts and cranks who have got nothing better to do with their lunch break?'

'Nothing special,' said Florentyna, nervously, 'except I think I've lost the vote of a Mr. Crudick.'

'Not Mad Mel again? What was it this time, the House Un-American Activities Committee, the Marshall Plan or the slums of Chicago?'

Florentyna returned happily to licking envelopes.

On election day, Florentyna arrived at campaign headquarters at eight o'clock in the morning and spent the day telephoning registered Democrats to be sure they had voted. 'Never forget,' said Henry Osborne in his final pep talk to his voluntary helpers, 'no man has ever lived in the White House who hasn't carried Illinois.'

Florentyna felt very proud to think she was helping to elect a President and didn't take a break all day. At eight o'clock that evening, Miss Tredgold came to collect her. She had worked twelve hours without a rest, but never once did she stop talking all the way home.

'Do you think Mr. Truman will win?' she asked finally.

'Only if he gets more than fifty per cent of the votes cast,' said Miss Tredgold.

'Wrong,' said Florentyna. 'It is possible to win a Presidential election in the United States by winning more electoral college votes than your opponent while failing to secure a majority of the plebiscite.' She then proceeded to give Miss Tredgold a brief lesson on how the American political system worked.

'Such a thing would never have happened if only dear George III had known where America was,' said Miss Tredgold. 'And I daily become aware that it will not be long before you have no further need of me, child.'

It was the first time Florentyna had ever considered that Miss Tredgold would not spend the rest of her life with her.

When they reached home, Florentyna sat down in her father's old chair to watch the early returns, but she was so tired that she dozed off in front of the fire. She, like most of America, went to sleep believing that Thomas Dewey had won the election. When Florentyna woke the next morning, she dashed downstairs to fetch the *Tribune*. Her fears were confirmed: 'Dewey Defeats Truman' ran the headline, and it took half an hour of radio bulletins and confirmation by her mother before Florentyna believed that Truman had been returned to the White House. An eleven o'clock decision had been made by the night editor of the *Tribune* to run a headline that he would not live down for the rest of his life. At least he had been right about Henry Osborne being returned to Congress for a sixth term.

When Florentyna went back to Girls Latin the next day, her home-room teacher called for her and made it quite clear that the election was now over and that the time had come to settle down and do some serious studying. Miss Tredgold agreed, and Florentyna worked with the same enthusiasm for her school exams as she had for President Truman.

During the year, she made the junior varsity hockey team, in which she played right wing without distinction and even managed to squeeze into the school's third tennis VI on one occasion. When the summer term was drawing to a close all the pupils received a note reminding them that if they wished to run for the Student Council their names must be sent to the headmaster of Boys Latin by the first Monday of the new school year. There were six representatives on the Council elected from both schools, and no one could remember a year when they had not all come from the twelfth grade. Nevertheless many of Florentyna's classmates suggested that she should allow her name to be put forward. Edward Winchester, who had years before given up trying to beat Florentyna at anything except arm wrestling, volunteered to help her.

'But anyone who helps me would have to be talented, good looking, popular and charismatic,' she teased.

'For once I agree with you,' said Edward. 'Any fool taking on such a cause will need every advantage possible to overcome the problem of their candidate being stupid, ugly, unapproachable and dull.'

'In which case it might be wise for me to wait another year.'

'Never,' said Edward. 'I can see no hope of improvement in such a short time. In any case, I want you on the council this year.'

'Why?'

'Because if you're the only eleventh grade student elected you'll be a near cert for President next year.'

'Really thought the whole thing through, haven't you?'

'And I would be willing to bet everything in my piggy bank that you have too.'

'Perhaps . . .' said Florentyna quietly.

'Perhaps?'

'Perhaps I'll consider running for the Student Council a year earlier.'

During the summer vacation, which Florentyna spent with her father at the New York Baron, she noticed that many of the big department stores now had millinery departments and wondered why there were not more shops specialising only in clothes. She spent hours in Best's, Saks and in Bonwit Teller's where she bought herself her first strapless evening dress – observing the different customers and comparing their individual preferences with those of shoppers who frequented Bloomingdale's, Altman's and Macy's. In the evening over dinner she would regale her father with all the knowledge she had acquired that day. Abel was so impressed by the speed with which Florentyna assimilated new facts that he began to explain to her in some detail how the Baron Group worked. By the end of her holiday, he was delighted with how much she had picked up about stock control, cash flow, advance reservations, the Employment Act of 1940, and even the cost of eight thousand fresh bread rolls. He warned George that his job as managing director of the group might be in jeopardy in the not-too-distant future.

'I don't think it's my job she's after, Abel.'

'No?' said Abel.

'No,' said George. 'It's yours.'

Abel took Florentyna to the airport on the final day of her holiday and presented her with a black-and-white Polaroid camera.

'Papa, what a fantastic present. Won't I be the neatest thing at school?'

'It's a bribe,' said Abel.

'A bribe?'

'Yes. George tells me you want to be Chairman of the Baron Group.'

'I think I'll start with the Student Council,' said Florentyna.

Abel laughed. 'Make sure you win a *place* on the Council first,' he said, then kissed his daughter on the cheek and waved goodbye as she disappeared up the steps of the waiting plane.

'I've decided to run.'

'Good,' said Edward. 'I have already compiled a list of every student in both schools. You must put a tick by all those who you feel are certain to support you and a cross by those who won't, so that I can work on the don't knows and firm up the backing of your supporters.'

'Very professional. How many people are running?'

'So far fifteen candidates for six places. There are four candidates you can't hope to beat, but it will be a close contest after that. I thought you'd be interested to know that Pete Welling is running.'

'That creep,' said Florentyna.

'Oh, I was led to believe that you were hopelessly in love with him.'

'Don't be so ridiculous, Edward, he's a sap. Let's go through the school lists.'

The election was due to take place at the end of the second week of the new school year, so the candidates had only ten days to gather votes. Many of Florentyna's friends dropped in at Rigg Street to assure her of their support. She was surprised to find some support where she least expected it, while other classmates whom she imagined were friends told Edward they would never back her. Florentyna discussed this problem with Miss Tredgold who warned her that if you ever run for any office which might bring you privilege or profit, it will always be your contemporaries who do not want to see you succeed in your ambitions. You need have no fear of those who are older or younger than yourself; they know you will never be their rival.

All the candidates had to write a mini-election address setting out the reason they wanted to be on the Student Council. Florentyna's was checked over by Abel, who refused to add or subtract anything, and by Miss Tredgold, who only commented on the grammar.

Voting was all day Friday at the end of the second week and the result was always announced by the headmaster after assembly the following Monday morning. It was a terrible weekend for Florentyna, and Miss Tredgold spent the entire time saying, 'Settle down, child.' Even Edward, who played tennis with her on Sunday afternoon, hardly raised a sweat, winning 6–0, 6–0.

'It wouldn't take Jack Kramer to tell you that you're not concentrating – "child".'

'Oh, do be quiet, Edward. I don't care whether I'm elected to the Student Council or not.'

Florentyna woke up at five o'clock on Monday morning and was dressed and ready for breakfast by six. She read the paper through three times from cover to cover and Miss Tredgold did not utter a word to her until it was time to leave for school.

'Remember, my dear, that Lincoln lost more elections than he won but still became President.'

'Yes, but I'd like to start out with a win,' said Florentyna.

The assembly hall was packed by nine o'clock. Morning prayers and the headmaster's announcements seemed to take for ever; Florentyna's eyes stared at the floor.

'And now I shall read the results of the Student Council election,' said the headmaster. 'There were fifteen candidates and six have been elected to the Council:

1st	Jason Morton (President)	109
2nd	Cathy Long	87
3rd	Roger Dingle	85
4th	Eddie Bell	81
5th	Jonathan Lloyd	79

The headmaster coughed and the room remained silent. 'Sixth Florentyna Rosnovski with seventy-six votes. The runner-up was Pete Welling with seventy-five votes. The first Council meeting will be in my office at ten thirty this morning. Assembly dismissed.'

Florentyna was overwhelmed and threw her arms around Edward.

'Don't forget – President next year.'

At the first Council meeting that morning, Florentyna, as junior member, was appointed Secretary.

'That will teach you to come in last,' laughed the new President, Jason Morton.

Back to writing notes that nobody else reads, thought Florentyna. But at least this time I can type them and perhaps next year I will be President. She looked up at the boy whose thin, sensitive face and seemingly shy manner had won him so many votes.

'Now privileges,' said Jason briskly, unaware of her gaze. 'The President is allowed to drive a car, while on one day a week the girls can wear pastel-coloured shirts and the boys can wear loafers instead of Oxfords. Council members are allowed to sign out of study hall when involved in school responsibilities and they can award demerits to any pupil who breaks a school rule.'

So that's what I fought so hard for, thought Florentyna, the chance to wear a pastel-coloured shirt and award demerits.

When she returned home that night Florentyna told Miss Tredgold every detail of what had happened, and she glowed with pride as she repeated the full result along with her new responsibilities.

'Who is poor Peter Welling,' enquired Miss Tredgold, 'who failed to be elected by only one vote?'

'Serves him right,' said Florentyna. 'Do you know what I said to that creep when I passed him in the corridor?'

'No, I'm sure I don't,' said Miss Tredgold apprehensively.

' "Now *you'll* have to get in line, but perhaps your time will come," ' she said, and burst out laughing.

'That was unworthy of you, Florentyna, and indeed of me. Be sure you never in your life express such an opinion again. The hour of triumph is not a time to belittle your rivals, rather it is a time to be magnanimous.'

Miss Tredgold rose from her seat and retired to her room.

When Florentyna went to lunch the next day, Jason Morton took the seat next to her. 'We're going to see a lot of each other now that you've been elected to the Student Council,' he said and smiled. Florentyna didn't smile back because Jason had the same reputation among the pupils of Girls Latin as Pete Welling, and she was determined not to make a fool of herself a second time.

Over lunch, they discussed the problem of the school orchestra's trip to Boston and what to do about the number of boys who had been caught smoking. Student councillors were limited in the punishments they were allowed to impose, and study hall detention on Saturday morning was about the most extreme terror they could evoke. Jason told

Florentyna that if they went so far as to report the smokers to the headmaster, it would undoubtedly mean expulsion for the students involved. A dilemma had arisen among the councillors because no one feared Saturday's detention and equally no one believed they ever would be reported to the headmaster.

'If we allow the smoking to go on,' said Jason, 'very soon we will have no authority at all, unless we're determined to make a positive stand in full Council right from the beginning.'

Florentyna agreed with him and was surprised by his next question.

'Would you be up to a game of tennis on Saturday afternoon?'

Florentyna remained silent for a moment. 'Yes,' she said, trying to sound casual as she remembered that he was captain of the tennis team and her backhand was awful.

'Good, I'll pick you up at three o'clock. Will that be okay?'

'Fine,' said Florentyna, hoping she still sounded uninterested.

'That tennis dress is far too short,' said Miss Tredgold.

'I know,' said Florentyna, 'but it's last year's, and I've grown since then.'

'With whom are you playing?'

'Jason Morton.'

'You really cannot play tennis in a dress like that with a young man.'

'It's either this or the nude,' said Florentyna.

'Don't be cheeky with me, child. I shall allow you to wear the garment on this occasion, but be assured I shall have acquired a new dress for you by Monday afternoon.'

The front doorbell rang. 'He seems to have arrived,' said Miss Tredgold.

Florentyna picked up her racket and ran to the door.

'Don't run, child. Let the young man wait a little. We can't have him knowing how you feel about him, can we?'

Florentyna blushed, tied back her long dark hair with a ribbon and walked slowly to the front door.

'Hi, Jason,' she said, her voice casual again. 'Won't you come in?'

Jason, who was dressed in a smart tennis outfit that looked as if it had been purchased that morning, couldn't take his eyes off Florentyna. 'What a dress,' he ventured, and was about to say more when he saw Miss Tredgold leaving the room. He hadn't realised until that moment what a good figure Florentyna had. The moment he set eyes on Miss Tredgold he knew why he had never been allowed to find out.

'It's last year's, I'm afraid,' continued Florentyna, looking down at her slim legs. 'It's awful, isn't it?'

'No, I think it's swell. Come on, I've reserved a court for three thirty and someone else will grab it if we're a minute late.'

'Good heavens,' said Florentyna as she closed the front door. 'Is that yours?'

'Yes. Don't you think it's fantastic?'

'I would say, if asked to venture an opinion, that it had seen better days.'

'Oh, really,' said Jason. 'I thought it was rather snazzy.'

'If I knew what the word meant I might be able to agree with you. Pray, sir,' she said mockingly, 'am I expected to ride in that machine or help push it?'

'That is a genuine pre-war Packard.'

'Then it deserves an early burial,' said Florentyna as she took her seat in the front, suddenly realising how much of her legs were showing.

'Has anyone taught you how to propel this lump of metal in a forward direction?' she enquired sweetly.

'No, not exactly,' said Jason.

'What?' said Florentyna in disbelief.

'I'm told driving is mostly common sense.'

Florentyna pushed down the handle of her door, opening it slightly, as if to get out. Jason put his hand on her thigh.

'Don't be silly, Tyna. I was taught by my father and I've been driving for nearly a year.'

Florentyna blushed, closed the door again and had to admit to herself that he drove rather well all the way to the tennis club even if the car did rattle and bump a little as it went over the holes in the road.

The tennis match was a desperate affair for Florentyna trying hard to win a point while Jason tried hard to lose one. Somehow Jason managed to win by only 6–2, 6–1.

'What I need is a Coke,' he said at the end of the match.

'What I need is a coach,' said Florentyna.

He laughed and took her hand as they left the court, and even though she felt sweaty and hot, he did not let her hand go until they reached the bar at the back of the club house. He bought one Coke and they sat drinking it from two straws in the corner of the room. When they had finished, Jason drove her home. On reaching Rigg Street, he leaned over and kissed her on the lips. Florentyna did not respond, more out of shock than for any other reason.

'Why don't you come to the movies with me tonight?' he said. '*On the Town* is showing at the United Artists Theatre.'

'Well, I normally . . . Yes, I'd like that,' said Florentyna.

'Good, then I'll pick you up at seven.'

Florentyna watched the car as it chugged away, and tried to think of some reason that would persuade her mother she had to be out that evening. She found Miss Tredgold preparing tea in the kitchen.

'A good game, child?' asked Miss Tredgold.

'Not for him, I'm afraid. By the way he wants to take me to' – she hesitated – 'to Orchestra Hall for a concert this evening so I won't need any dinner.'

'How nice,' said Miss Tredgold. 'Be sure you're back before eleven or your mother will worry.'

Florentyna ran upstairs, sat on the end of the bed and started to think about what she could possibly wear that evening, how awful her hair looked and whether she could steal some of her mother's make-up. She stood in front of the mirror wondering how she could make her breasts look bigger without holding her breath all night.

At seven o'clock Jason returned dressed in a red sloppy Joe sweater and khakis and was met at the door by Miss Tredgold.

'How do you do, young man.'

'How do you do, ma'am,' said Jason.

'Would you like to come into the drawing room?'

'Thank you,' said Jason.

'And what is the concert you're taking Florentyna to?'

'The concert?'

'Yes, I wondered who was playing,' said Miss Tredgold. 'I read a good review of Beethoven's Third in the morning paper.'

'Oh, yeah, Beethoven's Third,' said Jason, as Florentyna appeared on the stairs. Both Miss Tredgold and Jason were stunned. One approved while the other didn't. Florentyna was wearing a green dress that fell just below the knee and revealed the sheerest nylon stockings with dark seams down the back. She walked slowly down the stairs, her long legs unsteady in high-heeled shoes, her small breasts looking larger than usual, her dark shining hair hanging down on her shoulders, reminiscent of Jennifer Jones and making Florentyna appear a lot older than her fifteen years. The only item she wore to which Miss Tredgold could take no exception was the watch she herself had given to Florentyna on her thirteenth birthday.

'Come on, Jason, or we'll be late,' said Florentyna, wanting to avoid any conversation with Miss Tredgold.

'Sure thing,' said Jason. Florentyna did not look back once for fear of being turned into a pillar of salt.

'Be sure she's home before eleven, young man,' commanded Miss Tredgold.

'Sure thing,' repeated Jason as he closed the front door. 'Where did you find her?'

'Miss Tredgold?'

'Yes, she's straight out of a Victorian novel. "Be sure she's home before eleven, young man," ' he mimicked as he opened the car door for her.

'Don't be rude,' said Florentyna, and smiled at him coquettishly.

There was a long line outside the theatre and Florentyna spent most of the time standing beside Jason facing the wall, fearing someone might recognise her. Once inside Jason quickly guided her to the back row with an air of having been there before.

She took her seat and when the lights went down she began to relax for the first time – but not for long. Jason leaned over, put his hand around her shoulder and started kissing her. She began to enjoy the sensation as he forced her lips open and their tongues touched for the first time. Then he broke away and they watched the titles go up on the screen. Florentyna liked Gene Kelly. Jason leaned over again and pressed his mouth against hers. Her lips parted. Almost immediately she felt a hand on her breast. She tried to remove his fingers but once again his backhand was too strong for her. After a few seconds she came up for air and took a quick look at the Statue of Liberty before Jason returned with his other hand and fondled her other breast. This time she managed to push him away but for only a few moments. Annoyed, he took out a packet of Camels and lit one. Florentyna couldn't believe what was happening. After a few puffs he stubbed the cigarette out and placed a hand between her legs. In near panic she stopped any further advance by squeezing her thighs closely together.

'Oh, come on,' said Jason. 'Don't be such a prude or you'll end up like Miss Tredgold,' and he bent over to kiss her once again.

'For heaven's sake, Jason, let's watch the movie.'

'Don't be silly. No one goes to a movie house to watch a film.' He put his hand back on her leg. 'Don't tell me you haven't done it before. Hell, you're nearly sixteen. What are you hoping to be? The oldest virgin in Chicago?'

Florentyna jumped up and pushed her way out, stumbling over several pairs of feet before she reached the aisle. Without straightening her dress she ran out of the theatre as fast as she could. Once outside, she attempted to run, but couldn't manage much more than walking pace in her mother's high heels, so she took the shoes off and ran in her stockinged feet. When she reached the front door of her house she tried to compose herself, hoping she could get up to her room without bumping into Miss Tredgold, but she failed. Miss Tredgold's bedroom door was ajar and as Florentyna tiptoed past, she said, 'Concert over early, my dear?'

'Yes . . . no . . . I mean I didn't feel very well,' said Florentyna, and she ran into her own room before Miss Tredgold could ask any more questions. She went to bed that night still trembling.

She woke early the next morning and although still angry with Jason she found herself laughing at what had taken place and even determined to go and see the film again, on her own this time. She liked Gene Kelly, but it was the first time she had seen her *real* idol on the screen, and she couldn't get over how skinny and vulnerable he looked.

At Student Council the next day, Florentyna could not make herself look at Jason while he was stating in a quiet firm voice that some senior boys who were not members of Council were becoming casual about their dress. He also added that the next person caught smoking would have to be reported to the headmaster or his own reputation as President would be undermined. Everyone except Florentyna nodded their agreement.

'Good, then I'll put a notice on the bulletin board to that effect.'

As soon as the meeting was over, Florentyna slipped off to class before anyone could speak to her. She finished her homework late that evening and did not set off for Rigg Street until a few minutes after six o'clock. As she reached the main school door, it started to rain and she remained under the archway hoping the storm would blow over quickly. As she stood there, Jason walked straight past her with a girl from twelfth grade. She watched them climb into his car and she bit her lip. The rain came down harder, so she decided to return to her classroom and type up the minutes of the Student Council meeting. On her way back into school she passed a small crowd studying a notice on the board confirming the Council's attitude to sloppy dress and smoking.

Florentyna took about an hour to complete the minutes of the Council meeting, partly because her mind wandered continually back to Jason's double standards. The rain had stopped by the time she had finished her typing and she closed her typewriter case and placed the minutes in the top drawer. As she walked back down the corridor, she thought she heard a noise coming from the boys' locker room. No one except members of Student Council was allowed to remain in school after seven o'clock without special permission so she turned back to see who it was. When she was a few yards away from the locker room the light under the door went off. She walked over and opened the door and switched the light back on. It was some time before Florentyna focused on the figure standing in the corner, trying to hide a cigarette behind his back, but he knew she had seen it.

'Pete,' she said in surprise.

'Well, Miss Student Councillor, you've caught me once and for all. Two major offences in one day. In school after hours, and smoking. Bang goes my chance of making Harvard,' Pete Welling said as he ground out the cigarette on the stone floor. The vision returned of the Student Council President stubbing out his cigarette the night before in the back of an unlit cinema.

'Jason Morton is hoping to go to Harvard, isn't he?'

'Yes. What's that got to do with it?' said Pete. 'Nothing will stop him making the Ivy League.'

'I just remembered. No girl is allowed in the boys' locker room at any time.'

'Yes, but you're a member of . . .'

'Good night, Pete.'

Florentyna began to enjoy her new authority and took her duties and responsibilities on the Student Council very seriously, so much so that as the year passed Miss Tredgold feared Florentyna's studies were suffering because of it. She did not comment on the matter to Mrs. Rosnovski, rather she considered it her duty to find a solution. She hoped that Florentyna's attitude might be nothing more than an adolescent phase of misplaced enthusiasm. Even Miss Tredgold, despite past experience of these problems, was surprised by how quickly Florentyna had changed since being entrusted with a little power.

By the middle of the second term Miss Tredgold realised the problem was past that stage and fast becoming out of control. Florentyna was beginning to take herself, and not her work, far too seriously. Her end-of-term report was far from good by her normal high standards, and Florentyna's home-room teacher more than hinted that she was becoming high-handed with some of the other students and giving out demerits a little too freely.

Miss Tredgold could not help noticing that Florentyna had not been receiving as many invitations to parties as she had in the past and her old friends did not seem to visit Rigg Street quite so frequently, except for the loyal Edward Winchester . . . Miss Tredgold liked that boy.

Matters did not improve during the summer term and Florentyna began to be evasive when Miss Tredgold broached the subject of uncompleted homework. Zaphia, who had compensated for the loss of a husband by gaining ten pounds, was uncooperative. 'I haven't noticed anything unusual,' was her only comment when Miss Tredgold tried to discuss the problem.

Miss Tredgold pursed her lips and began to despair when one morning at breakfast Florentyna was downright rude when asked what she had planned to do for the weekend.

'I'll let you know if it concerns you,' she said without looking up from *Vogue*. Mrs. Rosnovski showed no sign of noticing, so Miss Tredgold maintained a stony silence, judging that sooner or later the child was bound to come a cropper.

It came sooner.

9

'THERE'S NO REASON FOR you to be that confident,' said Edward.

'Why? Who's going to beat me? I've been on the Council

for nearly a year and everyone else on it is graduating,' said Florentyna, lounging back in one of the horsehair chairs reserved for members of the Student Council.

Edward remained standing. 'Yes, I realise that, but not everyone likes you.'

'What do you mean?'

'A lot of people think that since you've been on the Council you've become a bit too big for your boots.'

'I hope you're not among them, Edward.'

'No, I'm not. But I am worried that if you don't bother to mix a little more with the students in the lower grades you might be beaten.'

'Don't be silly. Why should I bother to get to know them when they already know me?' she asked, fiddling with some papers on the arm of her chair.

'What's come over you, Florentyna? You didn't act like this a year ago,' said Edward, looking down.

'If you don't like the way I carry out my duties, go and support someone else.'

'It has nothing to do with the way you carry out your duties – everyone acknowledges you've been the best Secretary anyone can remember – but different qualities are needed for President.'

'Thank you for the advice, Edward, but you will discover that I can survive without it.'

'Then you won't want me to help you this year?'

'Edward, you still haven't got the message. It's not a case of not wanting you but simply not needing you.'

'I wish you luck, Florentyna, and I only hope I'm proved wrong.'

'I don't need your luck either. Some things in this life depend on ability.'

Florentyna did not repeat this conversation to Miss Tredgold.

At the end of the academic year, Florentyna was surprised to find that she had finished first in only Latin and French, and overall had fallen to third in the class. Miss Tredgold read her school report carefully and it confirmed her worst fears, but she concluded there was no point in making any adverse comment to the child as she had stopped taking anyone's advice unless it confirmed her own opinions. Once again, Florentyna spent the summer vacation in New York with her father, who allowed her to work as an assistant in one of the hotel shops.

Florentyna rose early each morning and dressed in the pastel green uniform of a junior member of the hotel staff. She threw all her energy into learning how the little fashion shop was run and was soon putting forward new ideas to Miss Parker, the manageress, who was impressed – and not just because she was the Baron's daughter. As the days passed, Florentyna gained more confidence and, conscious of the power of her privileged position, she stopped wearing the shop uniform and even started to order some of the junior sales staff around. She was, however, sufficiently cautious never to do this in front of Miss Parker.

One Friday, when Miss Parker was in her office checking the morning's petty cash, Jessie Kovats, a junior sales assistant, arrived ten minutes late. Florentyna was standing at the door waiting for her.

'You're late again,' said Florentyna, but Jessie didn't bother to reply.

'Did you hear me, Miss Kovats?' demanded Florentyna.

'Sure did,' said Jessie, hanging up her raincoat.

'Then what is your excuse this time?'

'For you, I don't have to have an excuse.'

'We'll see about that,' said Florentyna, starting off towards Miss Parker's office.

'Don't bother yourself, bossy boots, I've had enough of you in any case,' said Jessie, who walked into Miss Parker's office and closed the door behind her. Florentyna pretended to tidy the counter while she waited for Jessie to return. A few minutes later the young assistant came out of the office, put her coat back on and left the shop without another word. Florentyna felt pleased with the result of her admonition. A few minutes later Miss Parker came out of her office.

'Jessie tells me she's leaving the shop because of you.'

'Miss Kovats is hardly a great loss,' volunteered Florentyna. 'She didn't exactly pull her weight.'

'That is not the point, Florentyna. I have to continue to run this shop after you return to school.'

'Perhaps by then we shall have weeded out the Jessie Kovats of this world who shouldn't, after all, be wasting my father's time and money.'

'Miss Rosnovski, this is a team. Not everyone can be clever and bright, or even hard-working, but within their limited abilities they do the best they can, and there have been no complaints in the past.'

'Could that possibly be because my father is too busy to keep a watchful eye on you, Miss Parker?'

Miss Parker visibly flushed and steadied herself on the counter. 'I think the time has come for you to work in another of your father's shops. I have served him for nearly twenty years and he has never once spoken to me in such a discourteous way.'

'Perhaps the time has come for *you* to work in another shop,' said Florentyna, 'and preferably not my father's.' Walking out of the front door, she made straight for the hotel's private elevator and pressed the button marked forty-two. On arrival, Florentyna informed her father's secretary that she needed to speak to him immediately.

'He's chairing a board meeting at the moment, Miss Rosnovski.'

'Then interrupt him and tell him that I wish to see him.'

The secretary hesitated, then buzzed through to Mr. Rosnovski.

'I thought I told you not to disturb me, Miss Deneroff.'

'I apologise, sir, but your daughter is here and insists on seeing you.'

There was a pause. 'All right, send her in.'

'I am sorry, Papa, but this is something that can't wait,' Florentyna said as she entered the room, feeling suddenly less sure of herself as the eight men around the board-room table rose. Abel guided her through to his own office.

'Well, what is it that can't wait, my darling?'

'It's Miss Parker. She's stuffy, incompetent and stupid,' said Florentyna, and she poured out to her father her version of what had happened that morning with Jessie Kovats.

Abel's fingers never stopped tapping on the desk top as he listened to her tale. When she came to the end he flicked a switch on his intercom. 'Please ask Miss Parker in the fashion shop to come up immediately.'

'Thank you, Papa.'

'Florentyna, would you be kind enough to wait next door while I deal with Miss Parker.'

'Of course, Papa.'

A few minutes later, Miss Parker appeared, still looking flushed. Abel asked her what had happened. She gave an accurate account of the altercation, confining her view of Florentyna to the fact that she was a competent assistant but had been the sole reason that Miss Kovats, a long-serving member of her staff, had left. Others, Miss Parker pointed out, might leave too if Florentyna persisted with her attitude. Abel listened, barely controlling his anger. He gave Miss Parker his opinion and told her she would receive a letter by hand confirming his decision.

'If that is what you wish, sir,' said Miss Parker, and left.

Abel buzzed his secretary. 'Would you please ask my daughter to come back in, Miss Deneroff.'

Florentyna strode in. 'Did you tell Miss Parker what you thought, Papa?'

'Yes, I did.'

'She'll find it hard to get another job.'

'She won't need to.'

'Won't need to?'

'No, I gave her a raise and extended her contract,' he said, leaning forward and placing both hands firmly on his desk. 'If you ever treat a member of my staff that way again, I'll put you over my knee and thrash you, and it won't be a gentle tap with a hairbrush. Jessie Kovats has already left because of your insufferable behaviour and it is obvious no one in that shop likes you.'

Florentyna stared at her father in disbelief, then burst into tears.

'And you can save your tears for someone else,' continued Abel remorselessly. 'They don't impress me. I shouldn't have to remind you that I have a company to run. Another week of you and I would have had a crisis on my hands. You will now go down to Miss Parker and apologise for your disgraceful behaviour. You will also stay away from my shops until I decide you are ready to work in them again. And that is the last time you interrupt one of my board meetings. Do you understand?'

'But, Papa –'

'No buts. You will apologise to Miss Parker immediately.'

Florentyna ran out of her father's office and returned to her room in tears, packed her bags, left her green pastel dress on the bedroom floor and took a cab to the airport. Thirty-minutes later she was back in Chicago.

On learning of her departure, Abel phoned Miss Tredgold, who listened to what had taken place with dismay but not with surprise.

When Florentyna arrived home, her mother was still away at a health spa trying to shed a few unwanted pounds. Only Miss Tredgold was there to greet her.

'You're back a week early, I observe.'

'Yes, I got bored with New York.'

'Don't lie, child.'

'Must you pick on me as well?' said Florentyna, and ran upstairs to her room. That weekend she locked herself in and only crept down to the kitchen at odd times for meals. Miss Tredgold made no attempt to see her.

On the first day of school Florentyna put on one of the smart pastel shirts with the new style button-down collar she had bought at Bergdorf Goodman. She knew it would make every other girl at Girls Latin jealous. She was going to show them all how a future President of the Student Council should behave. As no member of Council could be elected for two weeks, she wore a different coloured shirt every day and took upon herself the responsibilities of President. She even started to think about what type of car she would talk her father into buying for her when she had won the election. At all times she avoided Edward Winchester, who had also put his own name forward for the Council, and she laughed openly at any comments made about his popularity. On the Monday of the third week, Florentyna went to morning assembly to hear herself confirmed as the new student President.

When Miss Allen, the headmistress, had read out the full list Florentyna could not believe her ears. She had not even finished in the first six. In fact, she was only barely the runner-up, and of all people Edward Winchester had been elected President. As she left the hall, no one commiserated with her and she spent the day in a silent daze at the back of the classroom. When she returned home that night, she crept up to Miss Tredgold's room and knocked gently on the door.

'Come.'

Florentyna opened the door slowly and looked towards Miss Tredgold who was reading at her desk.

'They didn't make me President,' she said quietly. 'In fact, they didn't even elect me to the Council.'

'I know,' Miss Tredgold replied, closing her Bible.

'How can you have known?' asked Florentyna.

'Because I wouldn't have voted for you myself.' The governess paused. 'But that's an end of the matter, child.'

Florentyna ran across the room and threw her arms around Miss Tredgold, who held her tightly.

'Good, now we shall have to start rebuilding bridges. Dry your tears, my dear, and we shall begin immediately. There is no time to be lost. Pad and pencil are needed.'

Florentyna wrote down the list dictated by Miss Tredgold and did not argue with any of her instructions. That night she wrote long letters to her father, Miss Parker (enclosing another letter for Jessie Kovats), Edward Winchester, and finally, although the name was not on her list, to Miss Tredgold. The next day she went to confession with Father O'Reilly. On returning to school Florentyna helped the newly-appointed Secretary with her first minutes, showing her the system she had found worked most satisfactorily. She wished the new President luck and promised that she would help him and his Council if she was ever needed. She spent the next week answering any queries that came up from the student councillors, but never volunteered advice. When Edward met her in the corridor a few days later he told her that the Council had voted to allow her to keep all her privileges. Miss Tredgold advised her to accept the offer with courtesy but at no time to take advantage of it. Florentyna put all her New York shirts in the bottom drawer and locked them away.

A few days later the headmistress called for her. Florentyna feared it would take longer to regain her respect, however determined she was to do so. When Florentyna arrived at her study the tiny, immaculately dressed woman gave her a friendly smile and motioned to a comfortable seat by her side.

'You must have been very disappointed by the election results.'

'Yes, Miss Allen,' said Florentyna, assuming she was to receive further chastisement.

'But by all accounts you have learned greatly from the experience, and I suspect you will be wanting to make amends.'

'It's too late, Miss Allen, I leave at the end of the year and can now never be President.'

'True, true. So we must look for other mountains to climb. I retire at the end of this year having been headmistress for twenty-five years, and I confess there is little left that I wish to achieve. The boys and girls of Latin have excellent admission records to Harvard, Yale, Radcliffe and Smith and we have always been better than every school in Illinois and as good as any on the east coast. However, there is one achievement that has eluded me.'

'What's that, Miss Allen?'

'The boys have won every major scholarship to the Ivy League universities at least once, Princeton three times, but one scholarship has eluded the girls for a quarter of a century.

That is the James Adams Woolson Prize Scholarship in Classics at Radcliffe. I wish to enter your name for that scholarship. Should you win the prize my cup will be full.'

'I would like to try,' said Florentyna, 'but my record lately . . .'

'Indeed,' said the headmistress, 'but as Mrs. Churchill pointed out to Winston when he was surprisingly beaten in an election, "that may yet turn out to be a blessing in disguise".'

' "Some disguise." ' They both smiled.

That night Florentyna studied the entry form for the James Adams Woolson Prize. The scholarship was open to every girl in America between the ages of sixteen and eighteen on July 1st of that year. There were three papers, one for Latin, one for Greek and a general paper on current affairs.

During the ensuing weeks, Florentyna spoke only Latin and Greek to Miss Tredgold before breakfast, and every weekend Miss Allen assigned her three general questions to be completed by the following Monday morning. As the examination day drew nearer, Florentyna became aware that the hopes of the whole school were with her. She sat awake at night with Cicero, Virgil, Plato and Aristotle, and every morning after breakfast she would write five hundred words on such varied subjects as the Twenty-Second Amendment or the significance of President Truman's power over Congress during the Korean War – even on the impact that television would have by going nationwide.

At the end of each day, Miss Tredgold checked through Florentyna's work, adding footnotes and comments before they would both collapse into bed, only to be up at six thirty the next morning to work their way through further old scholarship examination papers. Far from gaining confidence, Florentyna confided to Miss Tredgold that she became more frightened as each day passed.

The prize exam was set for early March at Radcliffe, and on the eve of the fateful day Florentyna unlocked her bottom drawer and took out her favourite shirt. Miss Tredgold accompanied her to the station and the few words they spoke on the way were in Greek. Her final words were: 'Don't spend the longest time on the easiest question.'

When they reached the platform, Florentyna felt an arm encircle her waist and a rose appeared in front of her.

'Edward, you nut.'

'That is not the way to address the President of the Student Council. Don't bother to come back if you fail to win the Woolson prize,' he said, and kissed her on the cheek.

Neither of them noticed the smile on Miss Tredgold's face.

Florentyna found an empty carriage and remembered very little of the journey, as she rarely looked up from her copy of the *Oresteia*.

When she arrived in Boston, she was met by a Ford 'Woody' station wagon which took her and four other girls who must have been on the same train to the Radcliffe Yard. During the journey spasmodic exchanges of polite conversation punctuated long, tense silences. Florentyna was relieved to find that she had been put in a residential house at 55 Garden Street in a room of her own: she hoped she would be able to conceal how nervous she was.

At six o'clock, the girls all met in Longfellow Hall where the Dean of Instruction, Mrs. Wilma Kirby-Miller, went over the details of the examination.

'Tomorrow, ladies, between nine and twelve, you will write the Latin paper and in the afternoon between three and six the Greek paper. The following morning you will complete the examination with a general paper. It would be foolish to wish everyone success as you cannot all expect to win the Woolson Prize, so I will only express the hope that when you have completed the three papers, each and every one of you will feel that you could not have done better.'

Florentyna returned to her room in Garden Street conscious of how little she knew and feeling very lonely. She went down to the ground floor and called her mother and Miss Tredgold on the pay phone. The next morning she woke at three and read a few pages of Aristotle's *Politics* but nothing would stick. When she came down at seven, she walked around the Radcliffe Yard several times before going to

Agassiz House for breakfast. She found two telegrams awaiting her, one from her father, wishing her luck and inviting her to join him for a trip to Europe during the summer holiday, and the second from Miss Tredgold which read: 'The only thing we have to fear is fear itself.'

After breakfast, she walked once again around the yard, this time with several other silent girls, before taking her place in Longfellow Hall. Two hundred and forty-three girls waited for the clock to chime nine, when the proctors allowed them to open the little brown envelopes placed on the desk in front of them. Florentyna read through the Latin paper once quickly and then again carefully, before selecting those questions that she felt best capable of answering. At twelve, the clock struck again and her blue books were taken away from her. She returned to her room and read Greek for two hours, eating a solitary Hershey bar for lunch. In the afternoon she attempted three more questions in Greek. At six she was still writing amendments when the paper had to be handed in. She walked back to her little room in Garden Street exhausted, fell on to the narrow bed and didn't stir until it was time to eat. Over a late dinner, she listened to the same conversations with different accents from Philadelphia to Houston, and from Detroit to Atlanta: it was comforting to discover that everyone was as nervous about the outcome of the examination as she was. Florentyna knew that almost everyone who took the scholarship examination would be offered a place at Radcliffe, and twenty-two could be awarded scholarships; but only one could win the James Adams Woolson Prize.

On the second day she opened the brown envelope containing the general paper, fearing the worst but relaxed a little when she read the first question: 'What changes do you imagine would have taken place in America if the Twenty-Second Amendment had been passed before Roosevelt became President?' She began to write furiously.

On Florentyna's return to Chicago, Miss Tredgold was standing on the platform waiting for her.

'I shall not ask if you consider you have won the prize, my dear, only if you did as well as you had hoped.'

'Yes,' said Florentyna, after some thought. 'If I don't win a scholarship, it will be because I am not good enough.'

'You can ask for no more, child, and neither can I, so the time has come to tell you that I shall be returning to England in July.'

'Why?' said Florentyna, stunned.

'What do you imagine there is left for me to do for you, now that you're off to university? I have been offered the post of head of the classics department at a girls' school in the West Country, starting in September, and I have accepted.'

' "You could not leave me if you knew how much I loved you." '

Miss Tredgold smiled at the quotation and produced the next line. ' "It is because of how much I love you that I must now leave you, Perdano." '

Florentyna took her hand and Miss Tredgold smiled at the beautiful young woman who could already make men's heads turn as they passed by.

The last three weeks at school were not easy for Florentyna as she waited for the exam results. She tried to assure Edward that at least he was certain to gain a place at Harvard.

'They have more sports fields than lecture halls,' she teased, 'so you can't fail.'

He could fail and she knew it, and as each day passed, the hopes of both turned to fears. Florentyna had been told that the results of the examination would be known on April 14th. On that morning the headmistress called Florentyna to her study and sat her in a corner of the room while she called the registrar at Radcliffe. The registrar already had several people holding to speak to her. At last she took Miss Allen's call.

'Would you be kind enough to let me know if a Miss Florentyna Rosnovski has won a scholarship to Radcliffe?' asked the headmistress.

There was a long pause. 'How do you spell that name?'

'R-O-S-N-O-V-S-K-I.'

Another pause. Florentyna clenched her fist. Then the registrar's voice, audible to them both, came over the line: 'No, I am sorry to tell you that Miss Rosnovski's name is not among the list of scholars but over seventy per cent of those who took the scholarship examination will be offered a place at Radcliffe and will be hearing from us in the next few days.'

Neither Miss Allen nor Florentyna could mask their disappointment. As Florentyna came out of the study she found Edward waiting for her. He threw his arms around her and almost shouted, 'I'm going to Harvard. And how about you? Did you win the Woolson?' But he could see the answer in her face. 'I'm sorry,' he said. 'How thoughtless of me,' and held her in his arms as the tears came. Some younger girls who passed them giggled. Edward took her home and she, Miss Tredgold and her mother ate dinner together in silence.

Two weeks later, on Parents' Day, Miss Allen presented Florentyna with the school Classics Prize, but it was no consolation. Her mother and Miss Tredgold applauded politely but Florentyna had told her father not to come to Chicago as there was nothing particular to celebrate.

After the presentation, Miss Allen tapped the lectern in front of her before she started to speak. 'In all my years at Girls Latin,' said the headmistress in clear, resonant tones, 'it was no secret that I wanted a pupil to win the James Adams Woolson Prize Scholarship to Radcliffe.' Florentyna stared down at the wooden floorboard between her feet. 'And this year,' continued Miss Allen, 'I was convinced that we had produced our finest scholar in twenty-five years and that my dream would be realised. Some weeks ago, I phoned Radcliffe to discover our entrant had not won a scholarship. But today I received a telegram which is nevertheless worth reading to you.'

Florentyna sat back, hoping her father was not responsible for some embarrassing message of congratulation.

Miss Allen put on her reading spectacles. ' "Name of Florentyna Rosnovski not announced among general scholars because happy to inform you she is winner of James Adams Woolson Prize. Please telegraph acceptance." ' The room erupted as pupils and parents cheered. Miss Allen raised a hand, and the hall fell silent. 'After twenty-five years I should have remembered that the Woolson is always announced separately at a later date. You must put it down to old age.' There was a polite ripple of laughter before Miss Allen continued: 'There are those of us here who believe that Florentyna will go on to serve her college and country in a manner that can only reflect well upon this school. I now have only one wish left: that I live long enough to witness it.'

Florentyna stood and looked towards her mother. Large tears were coursing down her cheeks.

No one present would have realised that the lady seated bolt upright next to Zaphia, staring straight in front of her, was revelling in the applause.

So much happiness and sadness now surrounded Florentyna, but nothing was to compare with her farewell to Miss Tredgold. On the train journey from Chicago to New York, during which Florentyna tried to express her love and gratitude, she handed the older woman an envelope.

'What's this, child?' asked Miss Tredgold.

'The four thousand shares of the Baron Group which we have earned over the past four years.'

'But that includes your shares as well as mine, my dear.'

'No,' said Florentyna, 'it doesn't take into account my saving on the Woolson Prize Scholarship.'

Miss Tredgold made no reply.

An hour later, Miss Tredgold stood on the dock in New York harbour waiting to board her ship, finally to release her charge to adult life.

'I shall think of you from time to time, my dear,' she said, 'and hope that my father was right about destiny.' Florentyna kissed Miss Tredgold on both cheeks and watched her mount the gangplank. When she reached the deck, Miss Tredgold turned, waved a gloved hand once and then hailed a porter, who picked up her bags and followed the stern-looking lady towards the private cabins. She did not look back at Florentyna, who stood like a statue on the quayside holding back the tears because she knew Miss Tredgold would not approve.

When Miss Tredgold reached her berth, she tipped the boy fifty cents and locked the door.

Winifred Tredgold sat on the end of the bunk and wept unashamedly.

10

FLORENTYNA HAD NOT BEEN so unsure about anything since her first day at the Girls Latin School. When she returned from her summer holiday in Europe with her father, a thick manila envelope from Radcliffe was awaiting her. It contained all the details of when and where she should report, what to wear, a course catalogue and the 'red book' outlining Radcliffe rules. Florentyna sat in bed studiously taking in page after page of information until she came to Rule 11a: 'If you entertain a man in your room for tea, at all times the door must be kept ajar, and all four feet must always be touching the floor.' Florentyna burst out laughing at the thought that the first time she made love it might be standing up, behind an open door, holding a cup of tea.

As the time drew nearer for her to leave Chicago, she began to realise just how much she had depended on Miss Tredgold. She packed three large suitcases which included all the new clothes she had bought on her European trip. Her mother, looking elegant in the latest Chanel suit, drove Florentyna to the station. When she boarded the train she was suddenly aware it was the first time she had travelled anywhere for any period of time without knowing somebody at the other end.

She arrived in Boston to find New England a beautiful contrast of September greens and browns. An old yellow school bus was waiting to transport students to the campus. As the ancient vehicle crossed the Charles, Florentyna looked through the back window to see the sun glinting off the dome of the State House. A few sails dotted the water and eight enthusiastic students were pulling their oars through the wash while an older man on a bicycle shouted orders through a megaphone as he rode along the towpath. When the bus came to a halt at Radcliffe, a middle-aged woman in academic dress herded the freshmen into Longfellow Hall, where Florentyna had taken the Woolson exam. There they were briefed on which hall they would live in during their first year, and their rooms were allocated to them. Florentyna drew room seven in Whitman Hall. A sophomore helped her carry her bags across to Whitman and then left her to unpack.

The room smelled as if the painters had moved out only the day before. It was clear that she was to share with two other girls: there were three beds, three chests of drawers, three desks, three desk chairs, three desk lamps, three pillows, three bedspreads and three sets of blankets, according to the check list that was left on the inside of the door. As there was no sign of her roommates she chose the bed nearest the window and started to unpack. She was just about to unlock the last suitcase when the door was flung open and a large trunk landed in the middle of the room.

'Hi,' said a voice that sounded to Florentyna more like a foghorn than a freshman from Radcliffe. 'My name is Bella Hellaman. I'm from San Francisco.'

Bella shook hands with Florentyna, who immediately regretted the act as she smiled up at the six-foot giant who must have weighed well over two hundred pounds. Bella looked like a double bass and sounded like a tuba. She began to size up the room.

'I knew they wouldn't have a bed large enough for me,' was her next pronouncement. 'My headmistress did warn me that I should have applied to a man's college.'

Florentyna burst out laughing.

'You won't laugh so loud when I keep you awake all night. I toss and turn so much you'll think you're on board a ship,' Bella warned as she pushed open the window above Florentyna's bed to let in the cold Boston air. 'What time do they serve dinner at this place? I haven't had a decent meal since I left California.'

'I've no idea, but it's all in the red book,' said Florentyna, picking her copy up from the side of her bed. She started flicking through the pages until she reached 'Meals, times of'. 'Dinner, six thirty to seven thirty.'

'Then at the stroke of six thirty,' Bella said, 'I shall be under starter's orders at the dining-room door. Have you found out where the gymnasium is?'

'To be honest, I haven't,' said Florentyna, grinning. 'It wasn't high on my list of priorities for the first day.'

There was a knock on the door, and Bella shouted, 'Come in.' Florentyna later learned that it had not been a shout, just her normal speaking voice. Into the room stepped a Dresden china blonde, dressed in a neat dark blue suit and with not a hair out of place. She smiled, revealing a set of small, even teeth. Bella smiled back at her as though her dinner had arrived early.

'My name is Wendy Brinklow. I think I'm sharing a room with you.' Florentyna wanted to warn her about Bella's handshake but it was too late. She stood and watched Wendy cringe.

'You'll have to sleep over there,' Bella said, pointing to the remaining bed. 'You don't by any chance know where the gymnasium is, do you?'

'Why should Radcliffe need a gymnasium?' said Wendy as Bella helped her in with her suitcases. Bella and Wendy started to unpack and Florentyna fiddled with her books, trying not to make it too obvious that she was fascinated by what came out of Bella's suitcases. First there were goalie pads, a breast pad, and two pairs of cleats, then a face mask which Florentyna tried on, two hockey sticks and finally a pair of hockey gloves. Wendy had all her clothes in neat little piles packed away in her drawer before Bella had even worked out where to put her hockey sticks. Eventually she just threw them under the bed.

When they had finished unpacking, the three girls set off for the dining hall. Bella was the first to reach the cafeteria line and loaded her plate so full with meat and vegetables that she had to balance it on the palm of her hand. Florentyna helped herself to what she considered a normal amount and Wendy managed a couple of spoonfuls of salad. Florentyna was beginning to feel they resembled Goldilocks's three bears.

Two of them had the sleepless night Bella had promised Florentyna, and it was several weeks before either she or Wendy managed eight hours of uninterrupted sleep. Years later Florentyna discovered that she could sleep anywhere, even in a crowded airport lounge, thanks to spending her freshman year with Bella.

Bella was the first freshman to play goalie for the Radcliffe varsity and she spent the year happily terrifying anyone who dared to try to score against her. She always shook hands with the few who did. Wendy spent a lot of the time being chased by men who visited the campus and some of the time being caught. She also passed more hours reading the Kinsey Report than her class notes.

'Darlings,' she said, eyes saucer wide, 'it's a serious piece of academic work written by a distinguished professor.'

'The first academic work to sell over a million copies,' commented Bella, as she picked up her hockey sticks and left the room.

Wendy, seated in front of the one mirror in the room, started checking her lipstick.

'Who's it this time?' asked Florentyna.

'No one in particular,' she replied. 'But Dartmouth has sent their tennis team over to play Harvard and I couldn't think of a more pleasant way to spend the afternoon. Do you want to come along?'

'No thanks, but I would like to know the secret of how you find them,' said Florentyna, looking at herself appraisingly in the mirror. 'I can't remember when anyone other than Edward last asked me out.'

'It doesn't take a lot of research,' said Wendy. 'Perhaps you put them off.'

'How?' asked Florentyna, turning towards her.

Wendy put down her lipstick and picked up a comb. 'You're too obviously bright and intelligent, and not many men can handle that. You frighten them and that's not good for their egos.'

Florentyna laughed.

'I'm serious. How many men would have dared to approach your beloved Miss Tredgold, let alone make a pass at her?'

'So what do you suggest I do about it?' asked Florentyna.

'You're good-looking enough, and I don't know anyone with a better dress sense, so just act dumb and massage their ego; then they feel they have to take care of you. It always works for me.'

'But how do you stop them thinking they have the right to jump into bed with you after one hamburger?'

'Oh, I usually get three or four steaks before I let them try anything. And just occasionally I say yes.'

'That's all very well, but how did you handle it the first time?'

'God knows,' said Wendy. 'I can't remember that far back.'

Florentyna laughed again.

'If you come to the tennis with me you might get lucky. After all, there'll be five other men from Dartmouth, not to mention the six on the Harvard team.'

'No, I can't,' Florentyna said regretfully. 'I still have an essay on Oedipus to complete by six o'clock.'

'And we all know what happened to him,' said Wendy, grinning.

Despite their different interests, the three girls became inseparable, and Florentyna and Wendy would always spend Saturday afternoons watching Bella play hockey. Wendy even learned to scream 'Kill 'em,' from the sidelines, although it didn't sound very convincing. It was a hectic first year and Florentyna enjoyed regaling her father with stories of Radcliffe, Bella and Wendy.

She had to study hard as her adviser, Miss Rose, was quick

to point out that the Woolson Scholarship came up for renewal every year and that it would do neither of their reputations any good if the prize were withdrawn. At the end of the year her grades were more than satisfactory, and she had also found time to join the Debating Society and was made freshman representative for the Radcliffe Democratic Club. But she felt her greatest achievement was trouncing Bella on the Fresh Pond golf course by seven shots.

In the summer vacation of 1952, Florentyna only spent two weeks in New York with her father because she had applied to be a page at the Chicago convention.

Once Florentyna had returned to her mother in Chicago she threw herself back into politics. The Republican Party convention had been held in the city two weeks earlier and the G.O.P. had chosen Dwight D. Eisenhower and Richard Nixon as their candidates. Florentyna couldn't see how the Democrats would come up with anyone to challenge Eisenhower, the biggest national hero since Teddy Roosevelt. 'I like Ike' buttons were everywhere.

When on July 21st the Democratic convention opened, Florentyna was given the job of showing VIPs to their seats on the speakers' platform. During those four days she learned two things of value. The first was the importance of contacts and the second the vanity of politicians. Twice during the four days she placed Senators in the wrong seats, and they could not have made more fuss if she had ushered them into the electric chair. The brightest moment of her week came when a good-looking young Congressman from Massachusetts asked her where she was at college.

'When I was at Harvard,' he said, 'I spent far too much of my time at Radcliffe. They tell me now it's the other way around.'

Florentyna wanted to say something witty and bright that he would remember but nothing came out, and it was many years before she saw John Kennedy again.

The climax of the convention came when she watched the delegates select Adlai Stevenson as their standard-bearer.

She had greatly admired him when he was Governor of Illinois, but Florentyna did not believe that such an academic man could hope to defeat Eisenhower on election day. Despite the shouting, cheering and singing of 'Happy Days Are Here Again', few other people in that hall seemed to believe it either.

Once the convention was over, Florentyna went back to Henry Osborne's headquarters to try to help him retain his seat in Congress. This time she was put in charge of the switchboard enquiries but the responsibility gave her little pleasure as she had known for some time that the Congressman was not respected by his party workers let alone by his constituents. His reputation as a drinker and his second divorce were not helping him with the middle-class voters in his district.

Florentyna found him all too casual and glib about the trust the voters had placed in him, and she began to see why people had so little faith in their elected representatives. That faith took another blow when Eisenhower's Vice-Presidential candidate, Richard Nixon, addressed the nation on September 23rd to explain away an eighteen thousand dollar slush fund which he claimed had been set up for him by a group of millionaire backers as 'necessary political expenses' and for 'exposing Communists'.

On the day of the election, Florentyna and her fellow workers were half-hearted about both of their candidates and those feelings were reflected at the polls. Eisenhower won the election by the largest popular vote in American history, 33,936,234 to 27,314,992. Among the casualties removed in the landslide was Representative Osborne.

Disenchanted with politics, Florentyna returned to Radcliffe for her sophomore year, and put all her energy into her studies. Bella had been elected captain of hockey, the first sophomore to be so honoured. Wendy claimed to have fallen in love with a Dartmouth tennis player named Roger and, taking fashion advice from Florentyna, started studying bridal gowns in *Vogue*. Although they now all had single rooms in Whitman, the three girls still saw each other regularly. Florentyna never missed a hockey game, come rain or snow, both of which Cambridge frequently endured, while Wendy introduced her to several men who never quite seemed worthy of a third or fourth steak.

It was halfway through the spring semester that Florentyna returned to her room to find Wendy sitting on the floor in tears.

'What's the matter?' asked Florentyna. 'Your mid-terms? You haven't flunked them?'

'No, it's much worse than that.'

'What could be worse than that?'

'I'm pregnant.'

'What?' said Florentyna, kneeling down and putting an arm around her. 'How can you be so sure?'

'This is the second month I've missed my period.'

'Well, that's not conclusive, and if the worse comes to the worst, we know Roger wants to marry you.'

'He may not be the father.'

'Oh, my God,' said Florentyna. 'Who is?'

'I think it must have been Bob, the football player from Princeton. You met him, remember?'

Florentyna didn't. There had been quite a few during the year and she wasn't sure what to do next when Wendy couldn't even be certain of the father's name. All three girls sat up late into the night with Bella displaying a gentleness and understanding Florentyna would never have thought possible. It was decided that if Wendy missed her next period she would have to make an appointment to see the university gynaecologist, Doctor MacLeod.

Wendy did miss her next period, and asked Bella and Florentyna to accompany her when she went to Doctor MacLeod's office on Brattle Street. The doctor informed Wendy's class Dean of her pregnancy that night and no one was surprised by her decision. Wendy's father arrived the next day and thanked them both for all they had done before taking his daughter back to Nashville. It all happened so suddenly that neither of them could believe they wouldn't see

Wendy again. Florentyna felt helpless and wondered if she could have done more.

At the end of her sophomore year, Florentyna began to believe she could win a coveted Phi Beta Kappa key. She was fast losing her interest in university politics; a combination of McCarthy and Nixon was not inspiring, and she became even more disillusioned by an incident that occurred at the end of the summer holidays.

Florentyna had returned to work for her father in New York. She had learned a lot since the 'Jessie Kovats' incident. In fact Abel was now happy to leave her in charge of various Baron shops when their managers were on vacation.

During one lunch break she tried to avoid a smartly dressed middle-aged man who was passing through the hotel lobby at the same time, but he spotted her, and shouted:

'Hi, Florentyna.'

'Hello, Henry,' she said with little enthusiasm.

He leaned forward and gripped her on both arms before kissing her on the cheek.

'It's your lucky day, my dear,' he said.

'Why?' asked Florentyna, genuinely puzzled.

'I have been stood up by my date tonight and I'm going to give you the chance to take her place.'

Get lost, is what she would have said if Henry Osborne had not been a director of the Baron Group, and she was about to make some suitable excuse when he added, 'I've got tickets for *Can-Can*.'

Since her arrival in New York Florentyna had been trying to get seats for Broadway's latest smash hit and had been told they were sold out for eight weeks, by which time she would have returned to Radcliffe. She hesitated for a moment and then said, 'Thank you, Henry.'

They agreed to meet at Sardi's, where they had a drink before walking over to the Shubert Theatre. The show lived up to Florentyna's expectation and she realised it would have been churlish of her not to accept Henry's invitation to supper afterwards. He took her to the Rainbow Room and it was there that the trouble started. He had three double scotches before the first course arrived and although he was not the first person to put a hand on her knee he was the first of her father's friends to do so. By the time they came to the end of the meal Henry had drunk so much he was barely coherent.

In the cab on the way back to the Baron, he stubbed out his cigarette and tried to kiss her. She squeezed herself into the corner of the cab, but it didn't deter him. She had no idea how to handle a drunk and didn't know until then how persistent they could be. When they reached the Baron, he insisted on accompanying Florentyna to her room, and she felt unable to refuse his overtures for fear any public row would reflect badly on her father. Once they were in the private elevator he tried to kiss her again and when they reached her small apartment on the forty-first floor Henry forced his way into her room as she opened the door. He immediately went over to the small bar and poured himself another large scotch. Florentyna regretted that her father was in France and that George would have left the hotel to go home long ago. She wasn't quite sure what to do next.

'Don't you think you should leave now, Henry?'

'What?' slurred Henry. 'Before the fun has begun?' He lurched towards her. 'A girl ought to show how grateful she is when a fellow has taken her to the best show in town and given her a first-class meal.'

'I am grateful, Henry, but I am also tired, and I would like to go to bed.'

'Exactly what I had in mind.'

Florentyna felt quite sick as he almost fell on her and ran his hands down her back, stopping only when he reached her buttocks.

'Henry, you had better leave before you do something you'll regret,' Florentyna said, feeling she sounded a little absurd.

'I'm not gonna regret anything,' he said as he tried to force down the zip on the back of her dress. 'And neither will you.'

Florentyna tried to push him away, but he was far too

strong for her, so she began hitting him on the side of the arms.

'Don't put up too much of a fight, my dear,' he panted. 'I know you really want it, and I'll show you a thing or two those college boys won't know about.'

Florentyna's knees gave way and she collapsed on to the carpet with Henry on top of her, knocking the phone from a table on to the floor.

'That's better,' he said, 'I like a bit of spirit.'

He grabbed at her again, pinioning her arms above her head with one hand. He started moving his other hand up her thigh. With all the force she could muster she freed an arm and slapped Henry across the face but it only made him grab her hair tightly and push her dress up above her waist. There was a rip and Henry laughed drunkenly.

'It would have been easier . . . if you had taken the damned thing off . . . in the first place,' he said in breathless grunts as he extended the tear.

Florentyna stared helplessly backwards and saw a heavy crystal vase holding some roses next to where the phone had stood. With her free arm she pulled Henry towards her and started kissing him passionately on the face and neck.

'That's more like it,' he said, releasing her other arm.

Slowly she reached backwards for the vase. When she had it firmly in her hand, she broke away and brought the vase crashing down on the back of his skull. His head slumped forward and it took all her strength to push him off her. Florentyna's first reaction when she saw the blood pouring from his scalp was to fear that she had killed him. There was a loud knock on the door.

Startled, Florentyna tried to stand up, but she felt too weak in the knees. The knock came again, even louder, but this time accompanied by a voice that could belong to only one person. Florentyna staggered to the door and opened it to find Bella taking up the whole space between the jambs.

'You look awful.'

'I feel awful.' Florentyna stared down at her tattered Balenciaga evening dress.

'Who did that to you?'

Florentyna took a pace backwards and pointed to the motionless body of Henry Osborne.

'Now I see why your phone was off the hook,' said Bella as she strode over to the prostrate body. 'Got less than he deserved, I see.'

'Is he still alive?' asked Florentyna weakly.

Bella, knelt over him and checked his pulse, replying, 'Unfortunately, yes. It's only a flesh wound. He wouldn't have lived if I'd hit him. Now all he'll have to show for his trouble is a large bump on his head in the morning, which is not enough for a jerk like that. I think I'll throw him out of the window,' she added, picking Henry up and chucking him over her shoulder as if he were a sack of potatoes.

'No, Bella. We're on the forty-first floor.'

'He won't notice the first forty,' said Bella, and started walking towards the window.

'No, no,' said Florentyna.

Bella grinned before turning back. 'I'll be generous this time and put him in the freight elevator. The management can deal with him as they see fit.' Florentyna did not argue as Bella strode past her with Henry still over her shoulder. She returned a few moments later looking as if she had saved a penalty against Vassar.

'I've sent him to the basement,' she said with glee.

Florentyna was sitting on the floor sipping a Rémy Martin.

'Bella, am I ever going to be wooed romantically?'

'I'm the wrong person to ask. No one has ever tried to rape me, let alone be romantic.'

Florentyna fell into her arms laughing. 'Thank God you came when you did. Why are you here, not that I'm complaining?'

'Little Miss Efficiency has forgotten that I'm being put up in the hotel tonight because I'm playing hockey in New York tomorrow. The Devils against the Angels.'

'But they're both men's teams.'

'That's what they think, and don't interrupt. When I arrived at the desk they had no reservation in my name and the receptionist told me the hotel was packed, so I thought I would come up and complain to the management. Give me a pillow and I'll be happy to sleep in the bath.'

Florentyna held her head in her hands.

'Why are you crying?'

'I'm not, I'm laughing. Bella, you deserve a king-size bed and you shall have one.' Florentyna put the phone back on the hook and then picked up the receiver.

'Yes, Miss Rosnovski?'

'Is the Presidential Suite free tonight?'

'Yes, miss.'

'Please register it in the name of Miss Bella Hellaman and charge it to me. She'll be down to confirm in a minute.'

'Certainly, miss. How will I recognise Miss Hellaman?'

The next morning Henry Osborne called and begged Florentyna not to tell her father what had taken place the night before, pleading with her that it wouldn't have happened if he had not drunk so much and adding plaintively that he could not afford to lose his place on the board. Florentyna stared down at the red bloodstain on the carpet and reluctantly agreed.

11

WHEN ABEL RETURNED FROM Paris he was appalled to learn that one of his directors had been found drunk in a freight elevator, and had needed seventeen stitches in his scalp.

'No doubt Henry is claiming he tripped over a dumb-waiter,' said Abel, before he unlocked his private drawer, took out an unmarked file and added another note to it.

'More likely a dumb blonde,' laughed George.

Abel nodded.

'Are you going to do anything about Henry?' George asked.

'Not at the moment. He's still useful as long as he has contacts in Washington. In any case, I'm up to my eyes with buildings in London and Paris and now I see the board wants me to look at possibilities in Amsterdam, Geneva, Cannes and Edinburgh. Not to mention the fact that Zaphia is threatening to take me to court if I don't increase her alimony.'

'Perhaps the easy way out would be to pension Henry off?' suggested George.

'Not quite yet,' replied Abel. 'There is still a reason why I need him.'

George couldn't think of even one.

'We'll kill 'em,' said Bella. Bella's decision to challenge Harvard's ice hockey team to a field hockey match came as no surprise to anyone except the Harvard team who politely declined the invitation without comment. Bella immediately took out a half-page advertisement in the Harvard *Crimson* which read:

'Harvard Jocks Flunk Radcliffe Challenge.'

The enterprising editor of the *Crimson*, who had seen the advertisement before it went to press, decided to interview Bella so she ended up on the front page as well. A photograph of Bella wearing her mask and pads, and brandishing a hockey stick, ran with the caption: 'She's more frightening when she takes the mask off.' Bella was delighted with the picture and with the caption.

Within a week Harvard had offered to send its third XI team to Radcliffe. Bella refused, demanding varsity players only. A compromise was reached, with Harvard making up a team of four varsity players, four junior varsity players and three third XI players. A date was chosen and the necessary preparations were made. The undergraduates at Radcliffe began to get quite chauvinistic about the challenge, and Bella became a cult figure on campus.

'More figure than cult,' she told Florentyna.

Bella's tactics for trying to win the match were later described by the Harvard *Crimson* as nothing short of diabolical. When the Harvard team arrived in their bus they were met by eleven amazons with hockey sticks slung over their shoulders. The fit young men were immediately whisked off for lunch. Members of the Harvard squad never normally drink a drop before a match but as the girls, without exception, ordered beers, they felt honour-bound to join them. Most of the men managed three cans before lunch and also enjoyed the excellent wine served throughout the meal. None of the Harvard men thought to comment on Radcliffe's generosity or to ask if they were breaking any college rules. All twenty-two ended the lunch with a glass of champagne to toast the fortunes of both colleges.

The eleven Harvard men were then escorted to their locker room, where they found another magnum of champagne awaiting them. The eleven happy ladies left them to change. When the Harvard captain led his team out on to the hockey field he was met by a crowd of over five hundred spectators and eleven strapping girls whom he had never seen before in his life. Eleven other ladies, not unknown to the captain, were finding it hard to remain awake in the stand. Harvard was 3–0 down by half-time and was lucky to lose only 7–0. The Harvard *Crimson* might well have described Bella as a cheat, but the Boston *Globe* declared her to be a woman of great enterprise.

The captain of the Harvard team immediately challenged Bella to a replay against the full varsity squad. 'Exactly what I wanted in the first place,' she told Florentyna. Bella accepted by sending a telegram from one side of Cambridge Common to the other. It read: 'Your place or mine?' Radcliffe had to arrange for several cars to transport their supporters, their ranks swelled by Harvard's decision to put on a dance that evening after the game. Florentyna drove Bella and three other members of the team to the field across the river in her newly acquired 1952 Oldsmobile, with hockey sticks, shin pads and goalie pads piled high in the trunk.

When they arrived, they did not meet up with any of the Harvard team before they reached the playing field. This time they were greeted by a crowd of three thousand, which included President Conant of Harvard and President Jordan of Radcliffe.

Bella's tactics again bordered on the dubious: each of her girls had clearly been instructed to play the man and not to concentrate too much on the ball. Ruthless hacking at vulnerable shins enabled them to hold Harvard to a scoreless first half.

The Radcliffe team nearly scored in the first minute of the second half which inspired them to rise above their normal game and it began to look as if the match might end in a draw when the Harvard centre forward, a man only slightly smaller than Bella, broke through and looked poised to score. He had reached the edge of the circle when Bella came charging out of her cage and hit him flat out with a shoulder charge. That was the last he remembered of the match and he departed a few seconds later on a stretcher. Both referees blew their whistles at once and a penalty was awarded to Harvard with only a minute to go. Their left wing was selected to take the shot. The five-foot-nine, slimly built man waited for the two teams to line up. He cracked the ball sharply to the right inner who lofted a shot straight into Bella's chest-pad. It dropped at her feet, and she kicked it to the right, where it landed back in front of the diminutive left wing. Bella charged at the slight figure, and gentle people in the crowd covered their eyes, but this time she had met her match. The left wing sidestepped deftly leaving the Radcliffe captain spread-eagled on the ground and himself ample time to flick the ball into the back of the net. The whistle blew and Radcliffe had lost 1–0.

It was the only occasion on which Florentyna had seen Bella cry, despite the crowd giving her a standing ovation as she led her team off the field. Although defeated Bella ended up with two compensations: the U.S. Women's Hockey Team selected her to play for her country, and she had met her future husband.

Florentyna was introduced to Claude Lamont at the reception after the match. He looked even smaller in his neat blue blazer and grey flannel trousers than he had on the field.

'Little sweetheart, isn't he?' said Bella, patting him on the head. 'Amazing goal.' Florentyna was surprised that Claude did not seem to object. All he said was, 'Didn't she play a first-class game?'

Bella and Florentyna returned to their rooms in Radcliffe and changed for the dance. Claude accompanied both girls to the hall, which Bella compared with a cattle show as the men swarmed around her old roommate. They all wanted to dance the jitterbug with her, so Claude was dispatched to fetch enough food and drink to feed an army, which Bella disposed of while she watched her friend in a whirl of Trigère silk on the dance floor.

Florentyna first saw him sitting talking to a girl in the corner of the room while she was dancing. He must have been about six feet in height with wavy fair hair and a tan that only proved he did not spend his winter vacations in Cambridge. As she looked he turned towards the dance floor and their eyes met. Florentyna turned quickly away and tried to concentrate on what her partner was saying – something about America moving into the computer age and how he was going to climb on the bandwagon. When the dance ended, the talkative partner took her back to Bella. Florentyna turned to find him by her side.

'Have you had something to eat?' he asked.

'No,' she lied.

'Would you like to join my table?'

'Thank you,' she said, and left Bella and Claude discussing the relative merits of the value of wing to wing passing, comparing field hockey with ice hockey.

For the first few minutes neither of them spoke. He brought some food over from the buffet and then they both tried to speak at once. His name was Scott Forbes and he was majoring in history at Harvard. Florentyna had read about him in Boston's society columns, as the heir to the Forbes family business and one of the most sought-after young men in America. She wished it was otherwise. What's in a name, she said to herself, and she told him hers. It didn't seem to register.

'A pretty name for a beautiful woman,' he said. 'I'm sorry we haven't met before.' Florentyna smiled. He added, 'Actually I was at Radcliffe a few weeks ago, playing in the infamous hockey game when we lost 7–0.'

'You played in that match? I didn't notice you.'

'I'm not surprised. I spent most of the time on the ground feeling sick. I had never drunk so much in my life. Bella Hellaman may look big to you when you're sober, but she looks like a Sherman tank when you're drunk.'

Florentyna laughed and sat happily listening to Scott tell stories of Harvard, his family and his life in Boston. For the rest of the evening she danced only with one man and when the night came to an end he accompanied her back to Radcliffe.

'Can I see you tomorrow?' Scott asked.

'Yes, of course.'

'Why don't we drive out to the country and have lunch together?'

'I'd like that.'

Florentyna and Bella spent most of that night telling each other about their respective partners.

'Do you think it matters that he's straight out of the Social Register?'

'Not if he's a man worth taking seriously,' replied Bella, aware of just how real Florentyna's fears were. 'I have no idea if Claude is on any social register,' she added.

The next morning, Scott Forbes drove Florentyna out into the countryside in his old M.G. She had never been happier in her life. They went to lunch in a little restaurant in Dedham that was full of people whom Scott seemed to know. Florentyna was introduced to a Lowell, a Winthrop, a Cabot and another Forbes. She was relieved to see Edward Winchester coming towards her from a corner table, leading an attractive dark-haired girl by the hand – at least, Florentyna thought, I know someone. She was astonished at how handsome and happy Edward looked and soon found out why, when he introduced his fiancée, Danielle.

'You two ought to get on famously,' said Edward.

'Why?' asked Florentyna, smiling at the girl.

'Danielle is French, and I've been telling her for a long time that I might have been the Dauphin but even when I declared you were a witch, you had to teach me how to pronounce *sorcière*.'

As Florentyna watched them depart hand in hand, Scott said quietly, '*Je n'aurais jamais pensé que je tomberais amoureux d'une sorcière.*'

Florentyna chose a simple meal of sole and agreed with his selection of Muscadet, grateful for her knowledge of food and wine, and was surprised to find at four o'clock that they were the only two left in the restaurant, with a head waiter hinting that the time might have come to prepare for the evening meal. When they returned to Radcliffe Scott kissed her gently on the cheek and said he would call her tomorrow.

He phoned during lunch the next day to ask if she could bear to watch him play ice hockey for the junior varsity against Penn on Saturday and suggested dinner together afterwards.

Florentyna accepted, masking her delight, for she couldn't wait to see him again. It seemed the longest week in her life.

On Saturday morning she made one important decision about her weekend with Scott. She packed a small suitcase and put it in the boot of the car before driving to the rink long before the face-off. She sat in the bleechers, waiting for Scott to arrive. For a moment she feared he might not feel the same way about her when they met for a third time but he dispelled that fear in a moment when he waved and skated across the ice towards her.

'Bella said I can't come home if you lose.'

'Perhaps I don't want you to,' he said, as he glided slantingly away.

She watched the game, becoming colder and colder. Scott hardly seemed to touch the puck all afternoon, but he still managed to get slammed repeatedly into the boards. She decided that it was a stupid sport but that she would not tell him so. After the match was over, she sat in her car waiting for him to change; then another reception and at last they were on their own. He took her to Locke-Ober's where again he seemed to know everyone, but this time she did not recognise anybody other than those she had seen in the fashionable magazines. He didn't notice, as he could not have been more attentive, which helped Florentyna relax. Once more, they were the last to leave, and he drove her back to her car. He kissed her gently on the lips.

'Would you like to come to lunch at Radcliffe tomorrow?'

'I can't,' he said. 'I have a paper to finish in the morning, and I'm not sure I can complete it before two o'clock. You couldn't bear joining me for tea?'

'Of course I will, silly.'

'What a pity. If I had known I would have booked you a room in the guest quarters.'

'What a pity,' echoed Florentyna, thinking of the unopened suitcase lying in the trunk of her car.

The next day, Scott picked her up shortly after three and took her back to his rooms for tea. She smiled as he closed the door, remembering that it was still not allowed at Radcliffe. His room was considerably larger than hers and on his desk was a picture of an aristocratic, slightly severe-looking lady who could only have been his mother. As Florentyna took in the room she realised that none of the furniture belonged to Harvard.

After he had given her tea they listened to America's new singing idol, Elvis Presley, before Scott put on the no longer skinny Sinatra singing 'South of the Border' and they danced, each wondering what was in the other's mind. When they sat down on the sofa, he kissed her at first gently, then with passion. He seemed reluctant to go any further and Florentyna was both too shy and too ignorant to help him. Suddenly he placed a hand over her breast as if waiting for Florentyna's reaction. At last his hand moved to the top of her dress and fumbled with the first button. Florentyna made no attempt to stop him as he continued with the second. Soon he was kissing her, first on the shoulder, then on her breast. Florentyna wanted him so badly that she almost made the next move herself, but quite suddenly he stood up and took off his shirt. In response she quickly slipped out of her dress and let her shoes fall to the floor. They made their way to the bed, clumsily trying to remove what was left of each other's clothing. For a moment they stared at each other before climbing on to the bed. To her surprise the pleasure of making love seemed to be over in seconds.

'I'm sorry, I was awful,' said Florentyna.

'No, no, it was me.' He paused. 'I might as well admit it, that was my first time.'

'Not you as well?' she said, and they both burst out laughing.

They lay in each other's arms for the rest of the evening, and made love twice more, each time with greater pleasure and confidence. When Florentyna woke in the morning, cramped and rather tired but exultantly happy, she felt instinctively they would spend the rest of their lives together. For the remainder of that term they saw one another every weekend, and sometimes during the week as well.

In the spring vacation, they met secretly in New York and Florentyna spent the happiest three days she could remember. *On the Waterfront*, *Limelight* and, on Broadway, *South Pacific* preceded the '21' club, Sardi's and even the Oak Room at the Plaza. In the morning they shopped, visited the Frick and walked through the park. When she returned home at night her arms were laden with presents that ended up by the side of her bed.

The spring term was idyllic and they were rarely out of each other's company. As it drew to a close, Scott invited Florentyna to spend a week in Marblehead during the spring vacation to meet his parents.

'I know they'll love you,' he said, as he put her on the train to Chicago.

'I hope so,' she replied.

Florentyna spent hours telling her mother how wonderful Scott was and how much she was bound to love him. Zaphia was delighted to see her daughter so happy, and genuinely looked forward to meeting Scott's parents. She prayed Florentyna had found someone with whom she could spend the rest of her life and not make an impulsive decision that she would later regret. Florentyna selected yards of different coloured silks from Marshall Field's and passed the evenings designing a dress she felt certain would capture the heart of Scott's mother.

The letter came on a Monday, and Florentyna immediately recognised Scott's handwriting. She tore the envelope open in happy anticipation but it contained only a short note saying that because of a change in his family plans he would have to postpone her trip to Marblehead. Florentyna read the letter again and again, looking for some hidden message. Remembering only how happily they had parted she decided to call his home.

'The Forbes residence,' said a voice that sounded like the butler's.

'May I speak to Mr. Scott Forbes?' Florentyna could hear her voice quiver as she said his name.

'Who is calling him, ma'am?'

'Florentyna Rosnovski.'

'I'll see if he's in, ma'am.'

Florentyna clutched the phone and waited impatiently for Scott's reassuring voice.

'He's not at home at the moment, ma'am, but I will leave a message saying that you called.'

Florentyna didn't believe him and an hour later called again.

The voice said, 'He is still not back ma'am,' so she waited until eight that evening, when the same voice announced that he was at dinner.

'Then please tell him I'm calling.'

'Yes, ma'am.'

The voice returned a few moments later and said perceptibly less politely, 'He cannot be disturbed.'

'I don't believe it. I don't believe you've told him who it is.'

'Madam, I can assure you –'

Another voice came on the line, a lady's, with the ring of habitual authority.

'Who is this calling?'

'My name is Florentyna Rosnovski. I was hoping to speak to Scott as . . .'

'Miss Rosenovski, Scott is having dinner with his fiancée at the moment and cannot be disturbed.'

'His fiancée?' whispered Florentyna, her nails drawing blood from the palm of her hand.

'Yes, Miss Rosenovski.' The phone went dead. It took several seconds for the news to sink in, then Florentyna said out loud, 'Oh, my God, I think I'll die,' and fainted.

She woke to find her mother by the side of her bed.

'Why?' was Florentyna's first word.

'Because he wasn't good enough for you. The right man won't allow his mother to select the person he spends the rest of his life with.'

Once Florentyna returned to Cambridge matters did not improve. She was unable to concentrate on any serious work and often spent hours on her bed in tears. Nothing Bella could do or say seemed to help and she could devise no better tactic than belittlement, 'Not the sort of man I would want on my team.' Other men asked Florentyna for dates but she didn't accept any of them. Her father and mother became so worried for her that they even spoke to each other about the problem.

Finally when Florentyna was near to failing a course, Miss Rose warned her that she had a lot of work to do if she still hoped to win her Phi Beta Kappa key. Florentyna remained indifferent. During the summer vacation she stayed at home in Chicago, accepting no invitations to parties or dinners. She helped her mother choose some new clothes but bought none for herself. She read all the details of the 'society wedding of the year' as the Boston *Globe* referred to the marriage of Scott Forbes to Cynthia Knowles, but it only made her cry again. The arrival of a wedding invitation from Edward Winchester did not help. Later she tried to remove Scott from her thoughts by going to New York and working unheard-of hours for her father at the New York Baron. As the holiday drew to a close she dreaded returning to Radcliffe for her final year. No amount of advice from her father or sympathy from her mother seemed to improve matters. They both began to despair when she showed no interest in the preparations for her twenty-first birthday.

It was a few days before Florentyna was due to return to Radcliffe that she saw Edward across Lake Shore Drive. He looked as unhappy as she felt. Florentyna waved and smiled. He waved back but didn't smile. They stood and stared at each other until Edward crossed the road.

'How's Danielle?' she asked.

He stared at her. 'Haven't you heard?'

'Heard what?' said Florentyna.

He continued to stare at her as if he couldn't get out the words. 'She's dead.'

Florentyna gazed back at him in disbelief.

'She was driving too fast, showing off in my new Austin-Healey, and she turned the car over. I lived, she died.'

'Oh, my God,' Florentyna said, putting her arms around him. 'How selfish I've been.'

'No, I knew you had your own troubles.'

'Nothing compared with yours. Are you going back to Harvard?'

'I have to. Danielle's father insisted, said he would never forgive me if I didn't. So now I have something to work for. Don't cry, Florentyna, because once I start I can't stop.'

Florentyna shuddered. 'Oh, my God, how selfish I've been,' she repeated.

'Come over to Harvard some time. We'll play tennis and you can help me with my French verbs. It will be like old times.'

'Will it?' she said, wistfully. 'I wonder.'

12

When Florentyna returned to Radcliffe, she was greeted by a two-hundred-page course catalogue that took her three evenings to digest. From the catalogue she could choose one elective course outside her major area of study. Miss Rose suggested she ought to take up something new, something she might never have another chance to study in depth.

Florentyna had heard, as every other member of the university had, that Professor Luigi Ferpozzi would be spending a year as guest lecturer at Harvard, and conducting a seminar once a week. Since winning his Nobel Peace Prize he had roamed the world receiving accolades, and when he was awarded an honorary degree from Oxford the citation described him as the only man with whom the Pope and the President were in total agreement, other than God. The world's leading authority on Italian architecture had chosen Baroque Rome for his overall subject. 'City of the Eye and the Mind' was to be the title of his first lecture. The synopsis in the course catalogue was tempting: Gianlorenzo Bernini, the artist aristocrat, and Francesco Borromini, the stone cutter's son, transformed the Eternal City of the Caesars and the Popes into the most recognisable capital in the world. Prerequisites: knowledge of Latin and Italian, with German and French highly recommended. Limited to thirty students.

Miss Rose was not optimistic about Florentyna's chances of being among the chosen few. 'They tell me there is already a line from the Widener Library to Boston Common just to see him, not to mention the fact that he is a well known misogynist.'

'So was Julius Caesar.'

'When I was in the common room last night he didn't treat me like Cleopatra,' said Miss Rose. 'But I do admire the fact that he flew with Bomber Command during the Second World War. He was personally responsible for saving half the churches in Italy by seeing that the planes did not fly over important buildings.'

'Well, I want to be one of his chosen disciples,' said Florentyna.

'Do you?' said Miss Rose, drily. 'Well, if you fail,' she added laughing – as she scribbled a note for Professor Ferpozzi – 'you can always sign up for one of those science survey courses. They seem to have no limit on numbers.'

'Rocks for Jocks,' said Florentyna disparagingly. 'Not me. I'm off to ensnare Professor Ferpozzi.'

The next morning at eight thirty, a full hour before the professor was officially available to see anyone that day, Florentyna climbed the marble steps of the Widener Library. Once in the building, she took the elevator – large enough to hold herself and one book – to the top floor where the senior professors had offices under the eaves. An earlier generation had obviously decided that being far removed from zealous students more than made up for the long climb or the inconvenience of an always occupied elevator.

Once Florentyna had reached the top of the building she found herself standing in front of a frosted door. The name 'Professor Ferpozzi' was newly stencilled in black paint on the glass. She recalled that in 1945 it was this man who had sat with President Conant in Munich and between them they had decided the fate of German architecture: what should be preserved and what should be razed. She was only too aware that she shouldn't bother him for at least another hour. She half turned, intent on retreat, but the elevator was already disappearing to a lower floor. Turning again, she knocked boldly on the door. Then she heard the crash.

'Madonna! Whoever that is, go away. You have caused me

to break my favourite teapot,' said an angry voice whose mother tongue could only have been Italian.

Florentyna stifled the impulse to run and instead slowly turned the door knob. She put her head round the door and looked into a room that must have had walls, but there was no way of knowing because books and periodicals were stacked from floor to ceiling as if they had taken the place of bricks and mortar.

In the middle of the clutter stood a professorial figure who could have been anywhere between forty and seventy. A tall man, he wore an old Harris tweed jacket and grey flannel trousers that looked as though they had been acquired from a secondhand shop or inherited from his grandfather. He was holding a brown china handle that moments before had been attached to a teapot. At his feet lay a teabag surrounded by fragments of brown china.

'I have been in possession of that teapot for over thirty years. I loved it second only to the *Pietà*, young woman. How do you intend to replace it?'

'As Michelangelo is not available to sculpt you another, I will have to go to Woolworth's and buy one.'

The professor smiled despite himself. 'What do you want?' he asked, picking up the teabag but leaving the remains of his teapot on the floor.

'To enroll in your course,' Florentyna replied.

'I do not care for women at the best of times,' he said, not facing her. 'And certainly not for one who causes me to break my teapot before breakfast. Do you possess a name?'

'Rosnovski.'

He stared at her for a moment before sitting at his desk and dropping the teabag into an ashtray. He scribbled briefly. 'Rosnovski, you have the thirtieth place.'

'But you don't know my grades or qualifications.'

'I am quite aware of your qualifications,' he said ominously. 'For next week's group discussion you will prepare a paper on' – he hesitated for a moment – 'on one of Borromini's earlier works, San Carlo alle Quattro Fontane. Good day,' he added, as Florentyna scribbled furiously on her notepad. He returned to the remains of his teapot, without giving her another thought.

Florentyna left, closing the door quietly behind her. She walked slowly down the marble steps trying to compose her thoughts. Why had he accepted her so quickly? How could he have known anything about her?

During the following week she spent long days in the crypts of the Fogg Museum poring over learned journals, making slides of the reproductions of Borromini's plans for San Carlo, even checking his lengthy expense list to see how much the remarkable building had cost. She also found time to visit the china department of Shreve, Crump & Lowe.

When Florentyna had completed the paper, she rehearsed it the night before and felt confident about the outcome, a confidence that evaporated the moment she arrived at Professor Ferpozzi's seminar. The room was already packed with expectant students and when she checked the list pinned to the wall she was horrified to discover that she was the only non-graduate present, the only non-Fine Arts student and the only woman on the course. A projector was placed on his desk facing a large white screen.

'Ah, the home wrecker returns,' the professor said, as Florentyna took the one remaining seat at the front. 'For those of you who have not come across Miss Rosnovski before, do not invite her home for tea.' He smiled at his own remark and tapped his pipe on the corner of the desk, a sign that he wished the class to commence.

'Miss Rosnovski,' he said with confidence, 'is going to give us a talk on Borromini's Oratorio di San Filippo Neri.' Florentyna's heart sank. 'No, no.' He smiled a second time. 'I am mistaken, it was, if I remember correctly, the Church of San Carlo.'

For twenty minutes Florentyna delivered her paper, showing slides and answering questions. Ferpozzi hardly stirred from behind his pipe, other than to correct her occasional mispronunciation of seventeenth-century Roman coins.

When Florentyna finally sat down, he nodded thoughtfully and declared, 'A fine presentation of the work of a genius.' She relaxed for the first time that day as Ferpozzi rose briskly to his feet. 'Now it is my painful duty to show you the contrast, and I want everyone to make notes in preparation for a full discussion next week.' Ferpozzi shuffled over to the projector and flicked his first slide into place. A building shone up on the screen behind the professor's desk.

Florentyna stared in dismay at a ten-year-old picture of the Chicago Baron towering above a cluster of elegant small-scale apartment buildings on Michigan Avenue. There was an eerie silence in the room, and one or two students were staring at her to see how she reacted.

'Barbaric, isn't it?' Ferpozzi's smile returned. 'I am not referring only to the building, which is a worthless piece of plutocratic self-congratulation, but to the overall effect that this edifice has on the city around it. Note the way the tower breaks the eye's sense of symmetry and balance in order to make certain that it's the only building we shall look at.' He flicked a second slide up on to the screen. This time it revealed the San Francisco Baron. 'A slight improvement,' he declared, staring into the darkness at his attentive audience, 'but only because since the earthquake of 1906 the city ordinances in San Francisco do not allow buildings to be more than twenty storeys in height. Now let's travel abroad,' he continued, turning to face the screen again. Up on the screen came the Cairo Baron, its gleaming windows reflecting the chaos and poverty of the slums huddled on top of each other in the distance.

'Who can blame the natives for backing the occasional revolution when such a monument to Mammon is placed in their midst while they try to survive in mud hovels that don't even stretch to electricity?' Inexorably, the professor produced slides of the Barons in London, Johannesburg and Paris, before saying, 'I want your critical opinion on all of these monstrosities by next week. Do they have any architectural value, can they be justified on financial grounds and will they ever be seen by your grandchildren? If so, why? Good day.'

Everyone filed out of the professor's room except Florentyna who unwrapped the brown paper parcel by her side.

'I have brought you a farewell present,' she said, and stood up, holding out an earthenware teapot. Just at the moment Ferpozzi opened his hands, she let go and the teapot fell to the ground at his feet and shattered into several pieces.

He stared at the fragments on the floor. 'I deserved no less,' he said, and smiled at her.

'That,' she rejoined, determined to say her piece, 'was unworthy of a man of your reputation.'

'Absolutely right,' he said, 'but I had to discover if you had backbone. So many women don't, you know.'

'Do you imagine your position allows you . . .'

He waved a dismissive hand. 'Next week I shall read your defence of your father's empire with interest, young woman, and I shall be only too happy to be found wanting.'

'Did you imagine I would be returning?' she said.

'Oh yes, Miss Rosnovski. If you are half the woman my colleagues claim you are, I shall have a battle on my hands next week.'

Florentyna left, just stopping herself from slamming the door behind her.

For seven days she talked with architecture professors, Boston's city planners and international urban conservationists. She telephoned her father, mother and George Novak before coming to the reluctant conclusion that, although they all had different excuses, Professor Ferpozzi had not exaggerated. She returned to the top of the library a week later and sat at the back of the room, dreading what her fellow students would have come up with.

Professor Ferpozzi stared at her as she sank into her seat. He then tapped his pipe into an ashtray and addressed the class. 'You will leave your essays on the corner of my desk at the end of this session, but today I want to discuss the influence of Borromini's work on European churches during the century after his death.' Ferpozzi then delivered a lecture of such colour and authority that his thirty students hung on every word. When he had finished he selected a sandy-haired young man in the front row to prepare next week's paper on Borromini's first meeting with Bernini.

Once again, Florentyna remained seated while all the other students filed out, leaving their essays on the corner of Ferpozzi's desk. When they were alone, she handed him a brown paper parcel. He unwrapped it to find a Royal Worcester 'Viceroy' teapot in bone china, dated 1912. 'Magnificent,' he said. 'And it will remain so as long as no one drops it.' They both laughed. 'Thank you, young lady.'

'Thank you,' Florentyna replied, 'for not putting me through any further humiliation.'

'Your admirable restraint, unusual in a woman, made it clear that it was unnecessary. I hope you will forgive me, but it would have been equally reprehensible not to try and influence someone who will one day control the largest hotel empire in the world.' Such a thought had never crossed Florentyna's mind until that moment. 'Please assure your father that I always stay in a Baron whenever I have to travel. The rooms, the food and the service are quite the most acceptable of any of the major groups, and there is never anything to complain about once you are *inside* the hotel looking out. Be sure you learn as much about the stonecutter's son as I know about the empire-builder from Slonim. Being an immigrant is something your father and I will always be proud to have in common. Good day, young lady.'

Florentyna left the office below the eaves of Widener sadly aware of how little she knew of the workings of her father's empire.

During that year she concentrated hard on her modern language studies, but she could always be found on Tuesday afternoons sitting on a pile of books listening intently to Professor Ferpozzi's lectures. It was President Conant who remarked at dinner one night that it was sad that his learned colleague was having the kind of friendship with Florentyna that he really should have had thirty years before.

Graduation day at Radcliffe was a colourful affair. Proud, smartly dressed parents mingled with professors swathed in the scarlet, purple and multi-coloured hoods appropriate to their degrees. The academics glided about, resembling a convocation of bishops, informing the visitors how well their offspring had done, sometimes with a little considerate licence. In the case of Florentyna there was no need for exaggeration, for she had graduated summa cum laude and had been elected to Phi Beta Kappa earlier in the year.

It was a day of celebration and sadness for Florentyna and Bella, who were to live on opposite sides of America, one in New York and the other in San Francisco. Bella had proposed to Claude on February 28th of their junior year – 'Couldn't wait for Leap Year,' she explained – and they had been married in the Houghton chapel at Harvard during the spring vacation. Claude had insisted on, and Bella had agreed to, 'Love, honour and obey'. Florentyna had realised then how lucky they both were when Claude said to her at the reception, 'Isn't Bella beautiful?'

Florentyna smiled and turned to Bella who was saying that it was sad Wendy was not with them. 'Not that she ever did a day's work,' added Bella, grinning.

'Florentyna could not have worked harder in her final year, and frankly no one will be surprised by her achievements,' said Miss Rose.

'I am sure she owes a great deal to you, Miss Rose,' Abel replied.

'No, no, but I was hoping to convince Florentyna to return to Cambridge and carry out some research work for a Ph.D. and then join the faculty, but she seems to have other ideas.'

'We certainly do,' said Abel. 'Florentyna will be joining the Baron Group as a director, with special responsibilities for the leasing of the shops in the hotels. They have grown out of control in the last few years and I fear I have been neglecting them.'

'You didn't tell me that was what you had in mind, Florentyna,' boomed Bella. 'I thought you said . . .'

'Shhhhh, Bella,' said Florentyna, putting a finger to her lips.

'Now what's this, young lady? Have you been keeping a secret from me?'

'Now's not the time or place, Papa.'

'Oh, come on, don't keep us in suspense,' said Edward. 'Is it the United Nations or General Motors who feel they cannot survive without you?'

'I must confess,' said Miss Rose, 'now that you have gained the highest qualifications this university can award I should be fascinated to know how you intend to use them.'

'Hoping to be a Rockette, perhaps,' said Claude.

'That's the nearest anyone has been yet,' said Florentyna.

Everyone laughed except Florentyna's mother.

'Well, if you can't find a job in New York, you can always come and work in San Francisco,' said Bella.

'I'll bear the offer in mind,' said Florentyna lightly.

To her relief, further discussion of her future was impossible because the graduation ceremony was about to begin. George Kennan, the former U.S. ambassador to Russia, delivered the address. His speech was received enthusiastically. Florentyna particularly enjoyed the quotation from Bismarck which ended his peroration: 'Let us leave just a few tasks for our children to perform.'

'You'll deliver that address one day,' said Edward, as they passed Tricentennial Hall.

'And pray, sir, what will be my chosen subject?'

'The problems of being the first woman President.'

Florentyna laughed. 'You still believe it, don't you?'

'And so do you, even if it will always fall upon me to remind you.'

Edward had been seen regularly with Florentyna during the year, and friends hoped they might soon announce their engagement, but Edward knew that would never be. This was one woman who would always be unattainable, he thought. They were destined to be close friends, never lovers.

After Florentyna had packed her last few belongings and said goodbye to her mother, she checked that she had left nothing in her room and sat on the end of her bed reflecting on her time at Radcliffe. All she had to show for it was that she had arrived with three suitcases and was leaving with six and a Bachelor of Arts degree. A crimson ice hockey pennant once given to her by Scott was all that remained on the wall. Florentyna unpinned the pennant, held it for a moment, then dropped it into a waste-paper basket.

She sat in the back of the car with her father as the chauffeur drove out of the campus for the last time.

'Could you drive a little slower?' she asked.

'Certainly, ma'am.'

Florentyna turned and stared out of the rear window until the spires of Cambridge were no longer visible above the trees, and there was nothing left of her past to see.

13

THE CHAUFFEUR BROUGHT THE Rolls-Royce to a halt at the traffic lights on Arlington Street on the west side of the Public Garden. He waited for the lights to turn green while Florentyna chatted with her father about their forthcoming trip to Europe.

Just as the lights changed, another Rolls passed in front of them, turning off Commonwealth Avenue. Another graduate and parent were deep in conversation in the back.

'I sometimes think it would have been better for you to have gone to Yale, Richard,' she said.

Richard's mother looked at him approvingly. He already had the fine aristocratic looks that had attracted her to his father over twenty years before, and now he had made it five generations of the family who had graduated from Harvard.

'Why Yale?' he asked gently, pulling his mother back from her reminiscences.

'Well, it might have been more healthy for you to get away from the introverted air of Boston.'

'Don't let father hear you say that. He would consider such a suggestion nothing less than treason.'

'But do you have to return to Harvard Business School, Richard? Surely there must be other business schools?'

'Like father, I want to be a banker. If I'm going to follow in his footsteps, Yale isn't equipped to tie Harvard's laces,' he said mockingly.

A few minutes later the Rolls came to a halt outside a large house on Beacon Hill. The front door opened and a butler stood in the doorway.

'We have about an hour before the guests arrive,' said Richard, checking his watch. 'I'll go and change immediately. Mother, perhaps we could meet up a little before seven thirty in the West Room?' He even sounded like his father, she thought.

Richard bounded up the stairs two at a time; in most houses he could have managed three. His mother followed behind at a more leisurely pace, her hand never once touching the banister rail.

The butler watched them disappear before returning to the pantry. Mrs. Kane's cousin, Henry Cabot Lodge, would be joining them for dinner, so he needed to double-check that everything below stairs was perfect.

Richard stood in the shower smiling at the thought of his mother's concern. He had always wanted to graduate from Harvard and improve on his father's achievements. He couldn't wait to enroll at the business school next fall, although he had to admit he was looking forward to taking Mary Bigelow to Barbados that summer. He had met Mary in the rehearsal rooms of the music society and later they were both invited to play in the university string quartet. The pert little lady from Vassar played the violin far better than he performed on the cello. When he eventually serenaded the reluctant Mary into bed he found she was again the better tuned, despite her pretence at inexperience. Since those days he had also discovered she was highly-strung.

Richard turned the dial to 'cold' for a brief moment before leaping out, drying and changing into evening dress. He checked himself in the mirror: double-breasted. Richard suspected he would be the only person that night wearing the latest fashion – not that it mattered when you were a little over six feet, slim and dark. Mary had once said that he looked good in everything from jock strap to morning coat.

He went downstairs and waited in the West Room for his mother to join him. When she appeared the butler served them both with a drink.

'Good heavens, are double-breasted suits back in fashion?' she enquired.

'You had better believe it. The very latest thing, Mother.'

'I can't believe it,' she said. 'I remember . . .'

The butler coughed. They both looked around. 'The Honourable Henry Cabot Lodge,' he announced.

'Henry,' said Richard's mother.

'Kate, my dear,' he replied, before kissing her on the cheek. Kate smiled; her cousin was wearing a double-breasted jacket.

Richard smiled, because it looked twenty years old.

Richard and Mary Bigelow returned from Barbados almost as brown as the natives. They stopped off in New York to have dinner with Richard's parents, who thoroughly approved of his choice. After all, she was the great-niece of Alan Lloyd, who had succeeded Richard's grandfather as chairman of the family bank.

As soon as Richard had returned to the Red House, their Boston residence on Beacon Hill, he quickly settled down and prepared himself for the business school. Everyone had warned him it was the most demanding course at the university with the largest drop-out rate, but once the term had started even he was surprised by how little free time he had to enjoy other pursuits. Mary began to despair when he had to relinquish his place in the string quartet and could manage to see her only at weekends.

At the end of his first year she suggested they take another vacation in Barbados and was disappointed to find he intended to stay put in Boston and continue studying.

When Richard returned for his final year he was determined to finish at or near the top of his class, and his father warned him not to relax until after the last exam paper had been completed. His father had added that if he did not make the top ten per cent he needn't apply for a position at the bank. He would not be accused of nepotism.

At Christmas, Richard rejoined his parents in New York, but remained for only three days before returning to Boston. His mother became quite anxious about the pressure he was putting himself under, but Richard's father pointed out that it was only for another six months. Then he could relax for the rest of his life. Kate reserved her opinion; she hadn't seen her husband relax in twenty-five years.

At Easter, Richard called his mother to say he ought to remain in Boston during the brief spring vacation, but she managed to convince him he should come down for his father's birthday. He agreed but added that he would have to return to Harvard the next morning.

Richard arrived at the family home on East Sixty-eighth Street just after four o'clock on the afternoon of his father's birthday. His mother was there to greet him as were his sisters, Virginia and Lucy. His mother thought he looked drawn and tired, and she longed for his exams to be over. Richard knew that his father would not break his routine at the bank for anyone's birthday. He would arrive home a few minutes after seven.

'What have you bought for Daddy's birthday?' enquired Virginia.

'I was waiting to seek your advice,' said Richard flatteringly, having quite forgotten about a present.

'That's what I call leaving it until the last moment,' said Lucy. 'I bought my present for him three weeks ago.'

'I know the very thing he needs,' said his mother. 'A pair of gloves. His old ones are nearly worn out.'

'Dark blue, leather, with no pattern,' said Richard laughing. 'I'll go to Bloomingdale's and choose a pair right now.'

He strode down Lexington Avenue, falling in with the pace

of the city. He was already looking forward to joining his father in the fall, and felt confident that if there were no distractions in the last few months he would come out in that top ten per cent. He would emulate his father and one day be chairman of the bank. He smiled at the thought. He pushed open the doors of Bloomingdale's, strode up the steps and asked an assistant where he could buy some gloves. As he began making his way through the crowded store, he glanced at his watch. There would be plenty of time to change for dinner before his father returned. He looked up at the two girls behind the glove counter. He smiled; the wrong one smiled back.

The smiling girl came quickly forward. She was a honey blonde with a little too much lipstick and one more button undone than Bloomingdale's could possibly have approved of. Richard couldn't help but admire such confidence. A small name tag pinned over her left breast read 'Maisie Bates'.

'Can I help you, sir?' she asked.

'Yes,' said Richard. He glanced towards the dark-haired girl. 'I need a pair of gloves, dark blue, leather and no pattern,' he said without letting his eyes return to the blonde.

Maisie selected a pair and put them on Richard's hands, pushing the leather slowly down each finger and then holding them up for him to admire.

'If they don't suit you, you could try another pair.'

'No, that's just fine,' he said. 'Do I pay you or the other girl?'

'I can take care of you.'

'Damn,' said Richard under his breath. He left reluctantly, determined he would return the next day. Until that afternoon he had considered love at first sight the most ridiculous cliché, fit only for readers of women's magazines.

His father was delighted with the 'sensible' present, as he referred to the gloves over dinner that night, and even more delighted with Richard's progress at business school.

'If you are in the top ten per cent I shall be happy to

consider offering you a position of trainee at the bank,' he said for the thousandth time.

Virginia and Lucy grinned. 'What if Richard comes out number one, Daddy? Will you make him chairman?' asked Lucy.

'Don't be frivolous, my girl. If Richard ever becomes chairman it will be because he will have earned the position after years of dedicated, hard work.' He turned to his son. 'Now, when are you returning to Harvard?'

Richard was about to say tomorrow, when he said, 'I think tomorrow.'

'Quite right,' was all his father commented.

The next day Richard returned not to Harvard, but to Bloomingdale's where he headed straight for the glove counter. Before he had any chance of letting the other girl serve him, Maisie pounced; he could do nothing about it, except purchase another pair of gloves and return home.

The following morning, Richard returned to Bloomingdale's for a third time and studied ties on the next counter until Maisie was busy serving a customer and the other girl was free. He then marched confidently up to the counter and waited for her to serve him. To Richard's horror, Maisie disengaged herself in mid-sentence from her customer and rushed over while the other girl took her place.

'Another pair of gloves?' giggled the blonde.

'Yes . . . Yes,' he said lamely.

Richard left Bloomingdale's with yet another pair of gloves – dark blue, leather with no pattern.

The following day, he told his father he was still in New York because he had to gather some data from Wall Street to complete a paper. As soon as his father had left for the bank, he headed off to Bloomingdale's. This time he had a plan for ensuring he spoke to the other girl. He marched up to the glove counter fully expecting Maisie to rush up, when the other assistant came forward to serve him.

'Good morning, sir,' she said.

'Oh, good morning,' said Richard, suddenly at a loss for words.

'Can I help you?'

'No – I mean yes. I would like a pair of gloves,' he added unconvincingly.

'Yes, sir. Have you considered dark blue? In leather? I'm sure we have your size – unless we're sold out.'

Richard looked at the name on her lapel badge: Jessie Kovats. She passed him the gloves. He tried them on. They didn't fit. He tried another pair and looked towards Maisie. She grinned at him encouragingly. He grinned nervously back. Miss Kovats handed him another pair of gloves. This time they fitted perfectly.

'I think that's what you're looking for,' said Jessie.

'No, not really,' said Richard.

Jessie lowered her voice and said, 'I'll go and rescue Maisie. Why don't you ask her out? I'm sure she'll say yes.'

'Oh, no,' said Richard. 'You don't understand. It's not her I want to take out – it's you.'

Jessie looked totally surprised.

'Will you have dinner with me tonight?'

'Yes,' she said shyly.

'Shall I pick you up at your home?'

'No. Let's meet at the restaurant.'

'Where would you like to go?'

Jessie didn't reply.

'Allen's at Seventy-third and Third?' Richard suggested.

'Yes, fine,' was all Jessie said.

'Around eight suit you?'

'Around eight,' said Jessie.

Richard left Bloomingdale's with what he wanted – and it wasn't a pair of gloves.

Richard couldn't remember a time when he had spent all day thinking about a girl, but from the moment Jessie had said 'Yes', he had thought of nothing else.

Richard's mother was delighted that he had decided to spend another day in New York and wondered if Mary

Bigelow was in town. Yes, she decided, when she passed the bathroom and heard Richard singing 'Once I had a secret love'.

Richard gave an unusual amount of thought to what he should wear that evening. He decided against a suit, finally selecting a dark blue blazer and a pair of grey flannel slacks. He also spent a little longer looking at himself in the mirror. Too Ivy League, he feared, but there wasn't much he could do about that at short notice.

He left the house on Sixty-eighth Street just before seven to avoid having to explain to his father why he was still in town. It was a crisp, clear evening and he arrived at Allen's a few minutes after seven thirty and ordered himself a Budweiser. Every few moments he checked his watch as the minute hand climbed up towards eight, and then every few seconds once it had passed the agreed hour, wondering if he would be disappointed when he saw her again.

He wasn't.

She stood in the doorway looking radiant in a simple blue dress that he assumed had come from Bloomingdale's, though any woman would have known it was a Ben Zuckerman. Her eyes searched the room. At last she saw Richard walking towards her.

'I am sorry to be late . . .' she began.

'It's not important. What's important is that you came.'

'You thought I wouldn't?'

'I wasn't sure,' Richard said, smiling. They stood staring at each other. 'I'm sorry, I don't know your name,' he said, not wanting to admit he had seen it every day at Bloomingdale's.

She hesitated. 'Jessie Kovats. And yours?'

'Richard Kane,' he said, offering her his hand. She took it, and he found himself not wanting to let go.

'And what do you do when you're not buying gloves at Bloomingdale's?' asked Jessie.

'I'm at Harvard Business School.'

'I'm surprised they didn't teach you that most people only have two hands.'

He laughed, already delighted that it wasn't going to be her looks alone that would make the evening memorable.

'Shall we sit down?' suggested Richard, taking her arm and leading her to his table.

Jessie began to study the menu on the blackboard.

'Salisbury steak?' she enquired.

'A hamburger by any other name,' said Richard.

She laughed and he was surprised that she had picked up his out of context quotation so quickly, and then felt guilty, because as the evening progressed it became obvious that she had seen more plays, read more novels and even attended more concerts than he had. It was the first time in his life he regretted his single-minded dedication to studying.

'Do you live in New York?' he asked.

'Yes,' she said, as she sipped the third coffee Richard had allowed the waiter to pour. 'With my parents.'

'Which part of town?' he asked.

'East Fifty-seventh Street,' Jessie replied.

'Then let's walk,' he said, taking her hand.

Jessie smiled her agreement and they zigzagged back across the city together. To make the journey take longer Richard stopped to gaze at shop windows which he would normally have passed on the trot. Jessie's knowledge of fashion and shop management was daunting. Richard felt sorry that she had left school at sixteen to work in the Baron Hotel before going to Bloomingdale's.

It took them nearly an hour to cover the sixteen blocks. When they reached Fifty-seventh Street, Jessie stopped outside a small old apartment house.

'This is where my parents live,' she said. He held on to her hand.

'I hope you will see me again,' said Richard.

'I'd like that,' said Jessie, not sounding very enthusiastic.

'Tomorrow?' asked Richard diffidently.

'Tomorrow?' queried Jessie.

'Yes. Why don't we go to the Blue Angel and see Bobby Short?' He took her hand again. 'It's a little more romantic than Allen's.'

Jessie seemed uncertain, as if the request was causing her a problem.

'Not if you don't want to,' he added.

'I'd love to,' she said in a whisper.

'I'm having dinner with my father, so why don't I pick you up around ten o'clock?'

'No, no,' said Jessie. 'I'll meet you there. It's only two blocks away.'

'Ten o'clock then.' He leaned forward and kissed her on the cheek. It was the first time he was aware of a delicate perfume. 'Goodnight, Jessie,' he said, and walked away.

Richard began to whistle Dvorak's *Cello Concerto* and by the time he arrived home, had reached the end of the first movement. He couldn't recall an evening he had enjoyed more. He fell asleep thinking about Jessie instead of Galbraith or Freedman. The next morning he accompanied his father down to Wall Street and spent a day in the *Journal*'s library, taking only a short break for lunch. In the evening, over dinner, he told his father about the research he had been doing on reverse take-over bids and feared he might have sounded a little too enthusiastic.

After dinner, he went off to his room. He made sure that no one noticed him slip out of the front door a few minutes before ten. Once he had reached the Blue Angel he checked his table and returned to the foyer to wait for Jessie.

He could feel his heart beating and wondered why that had never happened with Mary Bigelow. When Jessie arrived, he kissed her on the cheek and led her into the lounge. Bobby Short's voice came floating through the air: 'Are you telling me the truth or am I just another lie?'

As Richard and Jessie walked in, Short raised his arm. Richard found himself acknowledging the wave although he had seen the artist only once before and had never been introduced to him.

They were guided to a table in the centre of the room where to Richard's surprise Jessie chose the seat with her back to the piano.

Richard ordered a bottle of Chablis and asked Jessie about her day.

'Richard, there is something I must –'

'Hi, Richard.' He looked away.

Standing by the table was another man dressed in dark blue blazer and grey flannel slacks.

'Hi, Steve. May I introduce Jessie Kovats – Steve Mellon. Steve and I were at Harvard together.'

'Seen the Yankees lately?' asked Steve.

'No,' said Richard. 'I only follow winners.'

'Like Eisenhower. With his handicap you would have thought he had been to Yale.' They chatted on for a few minutes. Jessie made no effort to interrupt them. 'Ah, she's arrived at last,' said Steve, looking towards the door. 'See you, Richard. Nice to have met you, Jessie.'

During the evening Richard told Jessie about his plans to come to New York and work at Lester's, his father's bank. She was such an intent listener he only hoped he hadn't been boring her. He enjoyed himself even more than the previous night and when they left he waved to Bobby Short as if they had grown up together. When they reached Jessie's home he kissed her on the lips for the first time. For a moment she responded, but then she said, 'Good night' and disappeared into the old apartment building.

The next morning he returned to Boston. As soon as he arrived back at the Red House he phoned Jessie: was she free to go to a concert on Friday? She said she was and for the first time in his life he crossed days off a calendar. Mary phoned him later in the week and he tried to explain to her as gently as possible why he was no longer available.

When the weekend came it was memorable. The New York Philharmonic, *Dial M for Murder* – Jessie even seemed to enjoy the New York Knicks. Richard reluctantly returned to Harvard on Sunday night. The next four months were going to be long weeks and short weekends. He phoned Jessie every day and they were rarely apart at weekends.

He began to dread Mondays.

*

During one Monday morning lecture, on the '29 crash, Richard found he couldn't concentrate. How was he going to explain to his father that he had fallen in love with a girl who worked behind the gloves, scarves and woollen hats counter at Bloomingdale's? Even to himself, Richard couldn't understand why such a bright, attractive girl could be so unambitious. If only Jessie had been given the opportunities he had had . . . He scribbled her name on the top of his class notes. His father was going to have to learn to live with it. He stared at what he had written: Jessie Kane.

When Richard arrived back in New York that weekend, he made an excuse to his mother about running out of razor blades. His mother suggested that he use his father's.

'No, no, it's all right,' said Richard. 'I need some of my own. In any case, we don't use the same brand.'

Kate Kane thought this was strange because she knew they did.

Richard had to run the eight blocks to Bloomingdale's to be sure he would make the store before it closed. When he reached the glove counter, Jessie was nowhere to be seen. Maisie was standing in a corner filing her fingernails.

'Is Jessie around?' he asked her breathlessly.

'No, she's already gone home – she left a few minutes ago. She can't have gone far. Aren't you . . .?'

Richard ran out on to Lexington Avenue. He searched for Jessie's face among the figures hurrying home. He would have given up if he hadn't recognised the flash of red, a scarf he had given her. She was on the other side of the street, walking towards Fifth Avenue. Her apartment was in the opposite direction; somewhat guiltily he decided to follow her. When she reached Scribner's on Forty-eighth Street, he stopped and watched her go into the bookshop. If she wanted something to read, surely she could have picked it up at Bloomingdale's? He was puzzled. He peered through the window as Jessie talked to a sales clerk, who left her for a few moments and then returned with two books. He could just make out their titles: *The Affluent Society* by John Kenneth Galbraith and *Inside Russia Today* by John Gunther. Jessie signed for them – which surprised Richard – and left as he ducked around the corner.

'Who *is* she?' said Richard out loud as he watched her double back and enter Bendel's. The doorman saluted respectfully, leaving a distinct impression of recognition. Once again Richard peered through the window to see sales ladies fluttering around Jessie with more than casual respect. An older lady appeared with a package, which Jessie had obviously been expecting. She opened it to reveal a full-length evening dress in red. Jessie smiled and nodded as the sales lady placed the dress in a brown and white box. Then, mouthing the words 'Thank you', Jessie turned towards the door without even signing for her purchase. Richard barely managed to avoid colliding with her as she hastened out of the store to jump into a cab.

He grabbed a taxi that an old lady had originally thought was hers, and told the driver to follow Jessie's cab. 'Like the movies, isn't it?' said the cab driver. Richard didn't reply. When the cab passed the small apartment house outside of which they normally parted, he began to feel queasy. The taxi in front continued for another hundred yards and came to a halt outside a dazzling new apartment house complete with a uniformed doorman, who was quick to open the door for Jessie. With astonishment and anger, Richard jumped out of his cab and started to make his way up to the door through which she had disappeared.

'That'll be ninety-five cents, fella,' said a voice behind him.

'Oh, sorry,' said Richard. He thrust his hand into his pocket and took out a note, hurriedly pushing it at the cab driver, not thinking about the change.

'Thanks, buddy,' said the driver, clutching on to the five-dollar bill. 'Someone sure is happy today.'

Richard hurried through the door of the building and managed to catch Jessie as she stepped into the elevator. She stared at him but didn't speak.

'Who are you?' demanded Richard as the elevator door closed. The other two occupants stared in front of them with a look of studied indifference as the elevator glided up to the second floor.

'Richard,' she stammered. 'I was going to tell you everything this evening. I never seemed to find the right opportunity.'

'Like hell you were going to tell me,' he said, following her out of the elevator and into an apartment. 'Stringing me along with a pack of lies for nearly three months. Well, now the time has come for the truth.'

He pushed his way past her brusquely as she opened the door. He looked beyond her into the apartment while she stood helplessly in the passageway. At the end of the entrance hall there was a large living room with a fine oriental rug and a magnificent Georgian bureau. A handsome grandfather clock stood opposite a side table on which there was a bowl of fresh anemones. The room was impressive even by the standards of Richard's own home.

'Nice place you've got yourself for a salesgirl,' he said sharply. 'I wonder which of your lovers pays for this?'

Jessie took a pace towards him and slapped him so hard that her own palm stung. 'How dare you?' she said. 'Get out of my home.'

As she said the words, she started to cry. Richard took her in his arms.

'Oh, God, I'm sorry,' he said. 'That was a terrible thing to suggest. Please forgive me. It's just that I love you so much and imagined I knew you so well, and now I find I don't know a thing about you.'

'Richard, I love you too and I'm sorry I hit you. I didn't want to deceive you, but there's no one else – I promise you that.' She touched his cheek.

'It was the least I deserved,' he said as he kissed her.

Clasped tightly in one another's arms, they sank on to the sofa and for some moments remained almost motionless. Gently he stroked her hair until her tears subsided. Jessie slipped her fingers through the gap between his top two shirt buttons.

'Do you want to sleep with me?' she asked quietly.

'No,' he replied. 'I want to stay awake with you all night.'

Without speaking further, they undressed and made love, gently and shyly at first, afraid to hurt each other, desperately trying to please. Finally, with her head on his shoulder, they talked.

'I love you,' said Richard. 'I have since the first moment I saw you. Will you marry me? Because I don't give a damn who you are, Jessie, or what you do, but I know I must spend the rest of my life with you.'

'I want to marry you too, Richard, but first I have to tell you the truth.'

She pulled Richard's jacket over her naked body as he lay silent waiting for her to speak.

'My name is Florentyna Rosnovski,' she began, and then told Richard everything about herself. Florentyna explained why she had taken the name of Jessie Kovats – so that she would be treated like any other sales girl while she learned the trade, and not like the daughter of the Chicago Baron. Richard never spoke once during her revelation and remained silent when she came to the end.

'Have you stopped loving me already?' she asked. 'Now that you know who I really am?'

'Darling,' said Richard very quietly. 'My father hates your father.'

'What do you mean?'

'Just that the only time I ever heard your father's name mentioned in his presence, he flew completely off the handle, saying your father's sole purpose in life seemed to be a desire to ruin the Kane family.'

'What? Why?' said Florentyna, shocked. 'I've never heard of your father. How do they even know each other? You must be mistaken.'

'I wish I were,' said Richard, and repeated the little his mother had once told him about the quarrel with her father.

'Oh, my God. That must have been the "Judas" my father referred to when he changed banks after twenty-five years,' she said. 'What shall we do?'

'Tell them the truth,' said Richard. 'That we met innocently, fell in love and now we're going to be married. And that nothing they can do will stop us.'

'Let's wait for a few weeks,' said Florentyna.

'Why?' asked Richard. 'Do you think your father can talk you out of marrying me?'

'No, Richard,' she said, touching him gently as she placed her head back on his shoulder. 'Never, my darling. But let's find out if we can do anything to break the news gently before we present them both with a *fait accompli*. Anyway, maybe they won't feel as strongly as you imagine. After all, you said the problem with the Richmond Group was over twenty years ago.'

'They still feel every bit as strongly, I promise you that. My father would be outraged if he saw us together, let alone thought we were considering marriage.'

'All the more reason to leave it for a little before we break the news to them. That will give us time to consider the best way to go about it.'

He kissed her again. 'I love you, Jessie.'

'Florentyna.'

'That's something else I'm going to have to get used to,' he said.

To begin, Richard allocated one afternoon a week to researching the feud between the two fathers, but after a time it became an obsession, biting heavily into his attendance at lectures. The Chicago Baron's attempt to get Richard's father removed from his own board would have made a good case study for the Harvard Business School. The more he discovered the more Richard realised that his father and Florentyna's were formidable rivals. Richard's mother spoke of the feud as if she had needed to discuss it with someone for years.

'Why are you taking such an interest in Mr. Rosnovski?' she asked.

'I came across his name when I was going through some back copies of the *Wall Street Journal*.' The truth, he thought, but a lie.

Florentyna took a day off from Bloomingdale's and flew to Chicago to tell her mother what had happened. When Florentyna pressed her as to what she knew of the row she spoke for almost an hour without interruption. Florentyna hoped her mother was exaggerating but a few carefully worded questions over dinner with George Novak made it painfully obvious that she hadn't been.

Every weekend the two lovers exchanged their knowledge, which only added to the catalogue of hate.

'It all seems so petty,' said Florentyna. 'Why don't they just meet and talk it over? I think they would get on rather well together.'

'I agree,' said Richard. 'But which one of us is going to try telling them that?'

'Both of us are going to have to, sooner or later.'

As the weeks passed Richard could not have been more attentive and kind. Although he tried to take Florentyna's mind off 'sooner or later' with regular visits to the theatre, the New York Philharmonic and long walks through the park, their conversation always drifted back to their parents.

Even during a cello recital which Richard gave her in her flat, Florentyna's mind was occupied by her father – how could be so obdurate? As the Brahms sonata came to an end Richard put down his bow and stared into her grey eyes.

'We have got to tell them soon,' he said, taking her in his arms.

'I know we must. I just don't want to hurt my father.'

'I know.'

She looked down at the floor. 'Next Friday, Papa will be back from Washington.'

'Then it's next Friday,' said Richard quietly, not letting her go.

As Florentyna watched Richard drive away that night she wondered if she would be strong enough to keep her resolve.

On the Friday, Richard ducked his morning lecture and travelled down to New York in time to spend the rest of the day with Florentyna.

They spent that afternoon going over what they would say when they respectively faced their parents. At seven o'clock the two left Florentyna's apartment on Fifty-seventh Street. They walked without talking. When they reached Park Avenue they stopped at the light.

'Will you marry me?'

It was the last question on Florentyna's mind as she braced herself to meet her father. A tear trickled down her cheek, a tear that she felt had no right to be there on the happiest moment of her life. Richard took a ring out of a little red box – a sapphire set in diamonds. He placed it on the third finger of her left hand. He tried to stop the tears by kissing her. They broke and stared at each other for a moment, then he turned and strode away.

They had agreed to meet again at the apartment as soon as their ordeal was over. She stared at the ring on her finger, next to the antique one, her favourite of the past.

As Richard walked up Park Avenue he went over the sentences he had so carefully composed in his mind and found himself on Sixty-eighth Street long before he felt he had completed the rehearsal.

He found his father in the drawing room drinking the usual Teacher's and soda before changing for dinner. His mother was complaining that his sister didn't eat enough. 'I think Virginia plans to be the thinnest thing in New York.' Richard wanted to laugh.

'Hello, Richard, I was expecting you earlier.'

'Yes,' said Richard. 'I had to see someone before I came home.'

'Who?' said his mother, not sounding particularly interested.

'The woman I am going to marry.'

They both looked at him astonished; it certainly wasn't the opening sentence Richard had planned so carefully.

His father was the first to recover. 'Don't you think you're a bit young? I feel sure you and Mary can afford to wait a little longer.'

'It's not Mary I intend to marry.'

'Not Mary?' said his mother.

'No,' said Richard. 'Her name is Florentyna Rosnovski.'

Kate Kane turned white.

'The daughter of Abel Rosnovski?' William Kane said without expression.

'Yes, Father,' said Richard firmly.

'Is this some sort of joke, Richard?'

'No, Father. We met in unusual circumstances and fell in love without either of us realising there was a misunderstanding between our parents.'

'Misunderstanding? Misunderstanding?' he repeated. 'Don't you realise that jumped-up Polish immigrant spends most of his life trying to get me thrown off my own board – and once nearly succeeded? And you describe that as a "misunderstanding"? Richard, you will never see the daughter of that crook again if you hope to sit on the board of Lester's Bank. Have you thought about that?'

'Yes, Father, I have, and it will make no difference to my decision. I have met the woman with whom I intend to spend the rest of my life and I am proud that she would even consider being my wife.'

'She has tricked and ensnared you so that she and her father can finally take the bank away from me. Can't you see through their plan?'

'Even you can't believe something as preposterous as that, Father.'

'Preposterous? He once accused me of being responsible for killing his partner, Davis Leroy, when I . . .'

'Father, Florentyna knew nothing of the circumstances surrounding your quarrel until she met me. How can you be so irrational?'

'She has told you she's pregnant, so you will have to marry her.'

'Father, that was unworthy of you. Florentyna has never put the slightest pressure on me from the moment we met. On the contrary.' Richard turned to his mother. 'Won't you both meet her and then you'll understand how it came about?'

Kate was going to reply when Richard's father shouted, 'No. Never,' and turning to his wife, he asked her to leave them alone. As she left, Richard could see that his mother was weeping.

'Now listen to me, Richard. If you marry the Rosnovski girl I will cut you off without a penny.'

'You suffer like generations of our family, Father, from imagining money can buy everything. Your son is not for sale.'

'But you could marry Mary Bigelow – such a respectable girl, and from our own background.'

Richard laughed. 'Someone as wonderful as Florentyna couldn't be replaced by a suitable Brahmin family friend.'

'Don't you mention our heritage in the same breath as that stupid Polack.'

'Father, I never thought I would have to listen to such pathetic prejudice from a normally sober person.'

William Kane took a pace towards his son. Richard never flinched. His father stopped in his tracks. 'Get out,' he said. 'You're no longer a member of my family. Never . . .'

Richard left the room. As he walked across the hall he became aware that his mother was leaning hunched against the banister. He went to her and took her in his arms. She whispered, 'I'll always love you,' and released him when she heard her husband come into the corridor.

Richard closed the front door gently behind him. He was back on Sixty-eighth Street. His only thought was how Florentyna had managed to face her own encounter. He hailed a cab and without looking back directed it to Florentyna's apartment.

He had never felt so free in his life.

When he reached Fifty-seventh Street he asked the doorman if Florentyna had returned. She hadn't, so he waited under the canopy, beginning to fear she might not have been able to get away. He was deep in thought and didn't notice when another cab came to a halt at the kerb and the frail figure of Florentyna stepped out. She was holding a tissue to a bleeding lip. She rushed towards him and they quickly went upstairs to the privacy of the apartment.

'I love you, Richard,' were her first words.

'I love you, too,' said Richard, and took her in his arms, holding her tightly as if it would solve their problems.

Florentyna didn't let go of Richard as he spoke.

'He threatened to cut me off without a penny if I married you,' he told her. 'When will they understand we don't care a damn about their money? I tried appealing to my mother for support, but even she couldn't control my father's temper. He insisted that she leave the room. I've never seen him treat my mother that way before. She was weeping, which only made my resolve stronger. I left him in mid-sentence. God knows, I hope he doesn't take it out on Virginia and Lucy. What happened when you told your father?'

'He hit me,' said Florentyna very quietly. 'For the first time in my life. I think he'll kill you if he finds us together. Richard darling, we must get out of here before he discovers where we are, and he's bound to try the apartment first. I'm so frightened.'

'No need for you to be frightened. We'll leave tonight and go as far away as possible and to hell with them both.'

'How quickly can you pack?' asked Florentyna.

'I can't,' said Richard. 'I can never return home now. You pack your things and then we'll go. I've got about a hundred dollars with me and my cello which is still in the bedroom. How do you feel about marrying a hundred-dollar man?'

'As much as a sales girl can hope for, I suppose – and to think I dreamed of being a kept woman. Next you'll be wanting a dowry.' Florentyna rummaged in her bag. 'Well, I've got two hundred and twelve dollars and an American Express card. You owe me fifty-six dollars, Richard Kane, but I'll consider repayment at a dollar a year.'

'I think I like the idea of a dowry better,' said Richard.

In thirty minutes Florentyna was packed. Then she sat down at her desk, scrawled a note to her father explaining she would never be willing to see him again unless he would accept Richard. She left the envelope on the table by the side of her bed.

Richard hailed a cab. 'Idlewild,' he said after placing Florentyna's three suitcases and his cello in the boot.

Once they had reached the airport Florentyna made a phone call. She was relieved when it was answered. When she told Richard the news he booked a flight.

At seven thirty the American Airlines Super Constellation 1049 taxied out on to the runway to start its seven-hour flight.

Richard helped Florentyna with her seatbelt. She smiled at him.

'Do you know how much I love you, Mr. Kane?'

'Yes, I think so – Mrs. Kane,' he replied.

'You'll live to regret your actions tonight.'

He didn't reply immediately, but just sat motionless, staring in front of him. Then all he said was, 'You will never contact him again.'

She left the room without replying.

He sat alone in the crimson leather chair; time was suspended. He didn't hear the phone ring several times. The butler knocked quietly on the door and entered the room.

'A Mr. Abel Rosnovski on the line, sir. Are you in?'

William Kane felt a sharp pain in the pit of his stomach. He knew he had to take the call. He rose from his chair and only by a supreme effort stopped himself from collapsing back into it. He walked over to the phone and picked it up.

'William Kane speaking.'

'This is Abel Rosnovski.'

'Indeed, and when exactly did you think of setting up your daughter with my son? At the time, no doubt, when you failed so conspicuously to cause the downfall of my bank.'

'Don't be such a damn . . .' Abel checked himself before continuing. 'I want this marriage stopped every bit as much as you do. I never tried to take away your son. I only learned of his existence today. I love my daughter even more than I hate you and I don't want to lose her. Can't we get together and work something out between us?'

'No,' said William Kane.

'What's the good of raking over the past now, Kane? If you

know where they are, perhaps we can stop them. That's what you want too. Or are you so goddam proud that you'll stand by and watch your son marry my girl rather than help?'

William Kane hung up the phone and walked back to the leather chair.

The butler returned. 'Dinner is served, sir.'

'No dinner, and I'm not at home.'

'Yes, sir,' said the butler and left the room.

William Kane sat alone. No one disturbed him until eight o'clock the next morning.

14

WHEN FLIGHT 1049 LANDED at San Francisco's International Airport, Florentyna hoped it hadn't been too short notice. Richard had hardly placed a foot on the tarmac when he saw a massive woman charge towards them and throw her arms around Florentyna. Florentyna still couldn't get her arms around Bella.

'You don't give a girl much time, do you? Calling just as you're boarding the plane.'

'I'm sorry, Bella, I didn't know until . . .'

'Don't be silly. Claude and I had been grumbling that we didn't have anything to do this evening.'

Florentyna laughed and introduced the two of them to Richard.

'Is that all the luggage you have?' queried Bella, staring down at the three suitcases and the cello.

'We had to leave in rather a hurry,' explained Florentyna.

'Well, there's always been a home for you here,' said Bella, immediately picking up two of the suitcases.

'Thank God for you, Bella. You haven't changed a bit,' said Florentyna.

'I have in one respect. I'm six months pregnant. It's just

that I'm like a giant panda – nobody's noticed.'

The two girls dodged in and out of the airport traffic to the parking lot with Richard carrying the cello and Claude following in their wake. During the journey into San Francisco, Bella revealed that Claude had become an associate in the law firm of Pillsbury, Madison and Sutro.

'Hasn't he done well?' she said.

'And Bella's the senior physical education teacher at the local high school, and they haven't lost a hockey game since she joined them,' said Claude with equal pride.

'And what do you do?' said Bella, prodding a finger into Richard's chest. 'From your luggage I can only assume that you're an out-of-work musician.'

'Not exactly,' said Richard, laughing. 'I'm a would-be banker, and I shall be looking for a job tomorrow.'

'When are you getting married?'

'Not for three weeks at least,' said Florentyna. 'I want to be married in a church, and they'll have to read the banns first.'

'So you'll be living in sin,' declared Claude as he drove past the 'San Francisco Welcomes Careful Drivers' sign. 'Quite the modern couple. I always wanted to, but Bella wouldn't hear of it.'

'And why did you leave New York so suddenly?' asked Bella, ignoring Claude's comment.

Florentyna explained how she had met Richard and the historic feud that existed between their fathers. Bella and Claude listened incredulously to the story, both remaining unusually silent, until the car came to a halt.

'This is our home,' said Claude, putting on the brakes firmly and leaving the car in first gear.

Florentyna got out on the side of a steep hill not quite overlooking the bay.

'We go higher up the hill when Claude becomes a partner,' said Bella. 'But this will have to do for now.'

'It's fantastic,' said Florentyna as they entered the little house. She smiled when she saw hockey sticks in the umbrella stand.

'I'll take you straight to your room so you can unpack.'

Bella led the two guests up a small winding staircase to the spare room on the top floor. 'It may not be the Presidential Suite at the Baron, but it's better than joining the communes on the streets.'

It was some weeks before Florentyna discovered that Bella and Claude had spent the afternoon lugging their double bed up the stairs to the spare room and carrying the two singles back down so that Richard and Florentyna could spend their first night together.

It was four a.m. in New York when they finally climbed into bed.

'Well, now that Grace Kelly is no longer available, I suppose I'm stuck with you. Although I think Claude may be right. Perhaps we should live in sin.'

'If you and Claude lived together in sin, no one in San Francisco would even notice.'

'Any regrets so far?'

'Yes. I always hoped I'd end up with a man who slept on the left-hand side of the bed.'

In the morning, after a Bella-type breakfast, Florentyna and Richard scoured the papers for jobs.

'We must try and find something quickly. I don't think our money will last for more than a month,' said Florentyna.

'It may be easier for you. I can't believe that many banks will offer me a job without a degree or at least a reference from my father.'

'Don't worry,' said Florentyna, ruffling his hair. 'We can beat both our fathers.'

Richard turned out to be right. It took Florentyna only three days and her prospective employers one phone call to the personnel director at Bloomingdale's before she was offered a position at a young fashion shop called 'Wayout Columbus' which had advertised for a 'bright sales assistant' in the *Chronicle*. It was only another week before the manager realised what a bargain they had picked up.

Richard, on the other hand, plodded around San Francisco from bank to bank. The personnel director always asked him to call back and when he did there suddenly 'wasn't a position available at the present time' for someone with his qualifications. As the day of the wedding drew nearer Richard became increasingly anxious.

'You can't blame them,' he told Florentyna. 'They all do a lot of business with my father and they don't want to upset him.'

'Bunch of cowards. Can you think of anyone who has had a row with Lester's Bank and therefore refuses to deal with them?'

Richard buried his head in his hands and considered the question for a few moments. 'Only the Bank of America. My father had a quarrel with them once over a stop-loss guarantee which they took rather a long time to honour and it resulted in a considerable loss in interest. He swore he would never do business with them again. It's worth a try – I'll give them a call tomorrow.'

When the manager interviewed him the next day he asked if the reason Richard had applied to work at the Bank of America was the well known disagreement with his father.

'Yes, sir,' replied Richard.

'Good, then we both have something in common. You will start on Monday as a junior teller, and if you are indeed the son of William Kane I don't imagine you will stay in that position for long.'

On the Saturday of their third week in San Francisco, Richard and Florentyna were married in a simple ceremony at St. Edward's Church on California Street. Father O'Reilly – accompanied by Florentyna's mother – flew in from Chicago to conduct the service. Claude gave the bride away and then ran round to Richard's side to be best man while Bella was the matron of honour, gargantuan in a pink maternity smock. The six celebrated that night with a dinner at DiMaggio's on Fisherman's Wharf. Richard and Florentyna's combined weekly salaries didn't cover the final bill, so Zaphia came to the rescue.

'If you four want to eat out again,' added Zaphia, 'just give me a call and I'll be out on the next plane.'

Bride and groom crept into bed at one o'clock in the morning.

'I never thought I would end up married to a bank teller.'

'I never thought I would end up married to a shop assistant, but sociologically it ought to make an ideal partnership.'

'Let's hope it doesn't end with sociology,' said Florentyna, turning off the light.

Abel tried every means at his disposal to discover where Florentyna had disappeared. After days of phone calls, telegrams, and even efforts to involve the police, he realised there was only one lead left open. He dialled a number in Chicago.

'Hello,' said a voice every bit as cold as William Kane's.

'You must know why I'm ringing.'

'I can guess.'

'How long have you known about Florentyna and Richard Kane?'

'About three months. Florentyna flew up to Chicago and told me all about him. Later I met Richard at the wedding. She didn't exaggerate. He's a rare man.'

'Do you know where they are right now?' demanded Abel.

'Yes.'

'Where?'

'Find out for yourself.' The line went dead. Someone else who didn't want to help.

On the desk in front of him lay an unopened file containing details of his forthcoming trip to Europe. He flicked over the pages. Two airplane tickets, two reservations in London, Edinburgh and Cannes. Two opera tickets, two theatre tickets, but now only one person was going. Florentyna would not be opening the Edinburgh Baron or the Cannes Baron.

He sank into a fitful sleep from which he didn't want to be woken. George found him slumped at his desk at eight o'clock the next morning.

He promised Abel by the time he had returned from Europe he would have located Florentyna, but Abel now realised after reading Florentyna's letter again and again that even if he did she wouldn't agree to see him.

15

'I WOULD LIKE TO borrow thirty-four thousand dollars,' said Florentyna.

'What do you need the money for?' said Richard coldly.

'I want to take over the lease for a building on Nob Hill to open a fashion shop.'

'What are the terms of the lease?'

'Ten years, with an option to renew.'

'What security can you offer against the loan?'

'I own three thousand shares in the Baron Group.'

'But that's a private company,' said Richard, 'and the shares are in effect worthless as they can't be traded over the counter.'

'But the Baron Group is worth fifty million of anybody's money and my shares represent one per cent of the company.'

'How did you come into possession of these shares?'

'My father is the chairman of the company and he gave them to me on my twenty-first birthday.'

'Then why don't you borrow the money direct from him?'

'Oh, hell,' said Florentyna. 'Will they be that demanding?'

'I'm afraid so, Jessie.'

'Are all bank managers going to be as tough as you? They never treated me like this in Chicago.'

'That's because they had the security of your father's account. Anyone who doesn't know you is not going to be as accommodating. A loan manager has to consider that every new transaction will *not* be repaid, so unless his risk is covered twice over it's his job that will be on the line. When you borrow money you must always look across the table and consider the other person's point of view. Everyone who wants to borrow money is sure they are on to a winner, but the manager knows that over fifty per cent of deals put up to him will eventually fail, or at best break even. So the manager has to pick and choose carefully to be certain he can always see a way of retrieving his money. My father used to say that most financial deals saw a return of one per cent for the bank, which didn't allow you the opportunity to make a one hundred per cent loss more than once every five years.'

'That all makes sense, so how do I answer, "Why don't you go to your father"?'

'Tell the truth. Remember, banking is based on trust, and if they know you're always being straight with them, they'll stand by you when you are going through hard times.'

'You still haven't answered the question.'

'You simply say: my father and I quarrelled over a family matter and now I wish to succeed in my own right.'

'Do you think that will work?'

'I don't know, but if it does, at least you'll have started with all your cards on the table. Right, let's go back over it again.'

'Must we?'

'Yes. No one owes you money, Jessie.'

'I would like to borrow thirty-four thousand dollars.'

'What do you need the money for?'

'I would like to take over –'

'Supper's ready,' roared Bella.

'Rescued,' said Florentyna.

'Only until after we've eaten. How many banks are you seeing on Monday?'

'Three. Bank of California, Wells Fargo and Crocker. Why don't I pop along to the Bank of America and you can simply pass the thirty-four thousand over the counter?'

'Because there are no mixed prisons in America.'

Claude put his head around the door. 'Hurry up, you two, or there won't be any left.'

*

George spent as much of his time following up leads on Florentyna as he did being managing director of the Baron Group. He was determined to come up with some concrete results before Abel returned from Europe.

George had a little more success in one quarter than Abel. Zaphia was pleased to inform him that she was making regular trips to the coast to see the happily married couple. It took George only one phone call to a travel agent in Chicago to discover that these trips had been to San Francisco. Within twenty-four hours he had Florentyna's address and phone number. On one occasion, George even managed a brief conversation with his goddaughter, but she was fairly reticent with him.

Henry Osborne made a pretext at wanting to help, but it soon became obvious that he only wished to know what was going on in Abel's life. He even tried to press George into lending him some more money.

'You'll have to wait until Abel returns,' George told him sharply.

'I am not sure I can last that long.'

'I'm sorry, Henry, but I don't have the authority to sanction personal loans.'

'Not even to a board member? You may live to regret that decision, George. After all, I know a lot more about how the group got started than you do, and I am sure there are others who would be willing to pay me for such information.'

George always arrived at Idlewild Airport thirty minutes early whenever Abel was returning from Europe. He knew the Baron, like a newly appointed director, would be impatient to learn of any developments within the group. But this time he felt certain Abel's opening question would be on a different subject.

As always Abel was one of the first through Customs and once he and George were seated in the back of the company Cadillac, he wasted no time on small talk.

'What news?' demanded Abel, only too aware that George would know to what he was referring.

'Some good, some bad,' said George as he pressed a button by the side window. Abel watched a sheet of glass glide up between the driver and the passenger section of the car. He tapped his finger on the side pane impatiently as he waited. 'Florentyna continues to be in touch with her mother. She's living in a small apartment in San Francisco with some old friends from Radcliffe days.'

'Married?'

'Yes.'

Abel didn't speak for some moments as if taking in the finality of the statement.

'And the Kane boy?' he asked.

'He's found a job in a bank. It seems a lot of people turned him down because word got around that he didn't complete Harvard Business School and his father wouldn't supply a reference. Not many people were willing to employ him if as a consequence they antagonised William Kane. He was finally hired as a junior teller with the Bank of America, at a salary way below what he might have expected with his qualifications.'

'And Florentyna?'

'She's working as the assistant manager in a fashion shop called "Wayout Columbus" near Golden Gate Park. She's also been trying to borrow money from several banks.'

'Why?' said Abel, sounding worried. 'Is she in any sort of trouble?'

'No, she's looking for capital to open her own shop.'

'How much is she hoping to raise?'

'She needs thirty-four thousand dollars for the lease on a small building that's become vacant on Nob Hill.'

Abel considered the information for a moment. 'See that she gets the money. Make it look as if the transaction is an ordinary bank loan and be sure that it's not traceable back to me.' He started tapping on the window again. 'This must always remain between the two of us, George.'

'Anything you say, Abel.'

'And keep me informed of every move she makes, however trivial.'

'What about Richard Kane?'

'I'm not interested in him,' said Abel. 'Now, what's the bad news?'

'Trouble with Henry Osborne again. It seems he owes money everywhere, and I'm fairly certain his only source of income is you. He's still making threats – about revealing that you condoned bribes in the early days when you had taken over the group. Says he's kept all the papers from the first day he met you, when he claims he fixed an extra payment after the fire at the old Richmond in Chicago. He's telling everyong that he now has a file on you three inches thick.'

'I'll deal with Henry in the morning,' said Abel.

Abel was fully up to date on the group's activities when Henry arrived for his private meeting. Abel looked up at him: the heavy drinking and the debts were beginning to take their toll. For the first time, Abel thought Henry looked older than his years.

'I need a little money to get me through a tricky period,' said Henry even before they had shaken hands. 'I've been a bit unlucky.'

'Again, Henry? You should know better at your age. How much do you need this time?'

'Ten thousand would see me through,' said Henry.

'Ten thousand,' said Abel, spitting out the words. 'What do you think I am, a gold mine? It was only five thousand last time.'

'Inflation,' said Henry, trying to laugh.

'This is the last time, do you understand me?' said Abel as he took out his cheque book. 'Come begging once more and I'll remove you from the board and turn you out without a penny.'

'You're a real friend, Abel. I swear I'll never come back again – I promise you that. Never again.' Abel watched Henry take a cigar from the humidor on the table in front of him and light it. George hadn't done that in twenty years. 'Thanks, Abel. You'll never regret your decision.'

Henry sauntered out of the office drawing on the cigar. Abel waited for the door to be closed, then buzzed for George. He appeared moments later.

'What happened?'

'I gave in for the last time,' said Abel. 'I don't know why – it cost me ten thousand.'

'Ten thousand?' said George, sighing. 'You can be sure he'll be back again. I'd be willing to put money on that.'

'He'd better not,' said Abel, 'because I'm through with him. Whatever he's done for me in the past it's now quits. Anything new about my girl?'

'I've set up a facility for Florentyna with the Crocker National Bank of San Francisco,' said George. 'She has an appointment next Monday with the loan officer. The agreement will appear to her as one of the bank's ordinary loan transactions, with no special favours. In fact, they're charging her half a per cent more than usual so there can be no reason for her to be suspicious. What she doesn't know is that the money is covered by your guarantee.'

'Thanks, George, that's perfect. I'll bet you ten dollars she pays off the loan within two years and never needs to go back for another. Keep me briefed on everything she's up to. Everything.'

Florentyna visited three banks the following Monday. The Bank of California showed some interest, Wells Fargo none and Crocker asked her to call back. Richard was surprised and delighted.

'What terms did they discuss?'

'The Bank of California say they would want eight per cent and require to hold the deeds of the lease. Crocker wants eight and a half per cent, the deeds *and* my shares in the Baron Group.'

'Fair terms considering you have no banking history with them, but it will mean you must make a twenty-five per cent profit before taxes, just to break even.'

'I've worked it all out on paper, Richard, and I think I'll make thirty-two per cent in the first year.'

'I studied those figures last night, Jessie, and you're being overly optimistic. You have no hope of achieving that. In fact, I think the company will lose between seven and ten thousand dollars in the first year – so you'll just have to hope they believe in your long-term future.'

'That's exactly what the loan officer said.'

'When are they going to let you know their decision?'

'By the end of the week. It's worse than waiting for exam results.'

'You've done well, Kane,' said the manager. 'And I am advising head office to promote you. What I have in mind . . .'

The phone buzzed on the manager's desk. He picked it up and listened.

'It's for you,' he said, surprised, before passing it to Richard.

'The Bank of California said their loans committee had turned me down, but Crocker said yes. Oh, Richard, isn't that wonderful?'

'Yes, ma'am, it's good news indeed,' said Richard avoiding the manager's eye.

'Well, that's very kind of you to say so, Mr. Kane. Now I also have this sociological problem and I was wondering if you could help in some way.'

'Perhaps if you were to come around to the bank, ma'am, we could discuss it in greater detail.'

'What a great idea. I've always had this fantasy of making love in a bank vault surrounded by money. Lots and lots of Benjamin Franklins staring at me.'

'I agree with your proposition, ma'am, and I'll call you and confirm at the first possible opportunity.'

'Don't leave it too long or I may decide to move my account.'

'We always try to be of service at the Bank of America, ma'am.'

'If you look at my account, there's not much sign of it.'

The phone clicked.

*

'Where are we having the celebration?' asked Richard.

'I told you over the phone – in the bank vaults.'

'Darling, when you called I was in private conference with the manager, and he was offering me the number three post in the overseas department.'

'That's fantastic. Then it's a double celebration. Let's go to Chinatown and have five takeaways and five giant Cokes.'

'Why five, Jessie?'

'Because Bella will be joining us. Incidentally, Mr. Kane, I prefer it when you call me "ma'am".'

'No, I think I'll stick with Jessie. It reminds me how far you've come since we met.'

Claude arrived that evening carrying a bottle of champagne under each arm. 'Let's open one immediately and celebrate,' said Bella.

'Agreed,' said Florentyna. 'But what about the other one?'

'It's to be saved for some special occasion that none of us could have anticipated,' Claude said firmly.

Richard opened the first bottle and poured out four glasses while Florentyna put the second in the corner of the fridge.

She signed the lease on the tiny building on Nob Hill the next day and the Kanes moved into the small apartment above the shop. Florentyna, Bella and Richard spent their weekends painting and cleaning while Claude, the most artistic of the four, printed the name 'Florentyna's' in royal blue above the shop window. A month later they were ready to open.

During her first week as owner, manageress and clerk, Florentyna contacted all the main wholesalers who had dealt with her father in New York. In no time she had a shop full of goods and ninety days' credit.

Florentyna opened the little shop on August 1st, 1958. She always remembered the date because just after midnight Bella produced a twelve-pound baby.

Florentyna had sent out a large mailing announcing the opening of the store, choosing the day before the government raised postage stamps from three cents to four. She had also stolen an assistant named Nancy Ching – who had Maisie's charm but fortunately not Maisie's I.Q. – from her old employers, 'Wayout Columbus'. On the morning of the opening, the two girls stood by the door in hopeful anticipation but only one person came into the shop the whole day and all he wanted to know was the way to the Mark Hopkins. The next morning, a young woman came in and spent an hour looking at all the shirts they had in from New York. She tried on several but left without purchasing anything. In the afternoon a middle-aged lady fussed about for a long time and finally bought a pair of gloves.

'How much will that be?' she asked.

'Nothing,' said Florentyna.

'Nothing?' queried the lady.

'That's correct. You are the first customer to make a purchase at Florentyna's and there will be no charge.'

'How kind of you,' said the lady. 'I shall tell all my friends.'

'You never gave me any gloves when I shopped at Bloomingdale's, Miss Kovats,' said Richard that evening. 'You'll be bankrupt by the end of the month if you go on like that.'

But this time his judgment proved wrong. The lady turned out to be President of the Junior League in San Francisco and one word from her was worth more than a full-page advertisement in the San Francisco *Chronicle*.

For the first few weeks Florentyna seemed to be working an eighteen-hour day, for as soon as the doors closed she would check the inventory while Richard went over the books. As the months passed she began to wonder how the little shop could ever hope to make a profit.

At the end of her first year they invited Bella and Claude to join in celebrating the loss of seven thousand three hundred and eighty dollars.

'We've got to achieve better results next year,' said Florentyna firmly.

'Why?' said Richard.

'Because our grocery bills are going to be larger.'

'Is Bella coming to live with us?'

'No. I'm pregnant.'

Richard was overjoyed and his only anxiety was that he couldn't stop Florentyna from working right up until the day she went into hospital. They celebrated the end of their second year with a small profit of two thousand dollars and a large son of nine pounds three ounces. He only had one nipple.

The decision on what they would call their first born, if it was a boy, had been decided weeks before.

George Novak was both shocked and delighted to be chosen as a godfather for Florentyna's son. Although he didn't admit as much, Abel was also pleased, for he welcomed any opportunity to find out what was happening in his daughter's life.

The day before the christening, George flew out to Los Angeles to check on the progress of the new Baron. Abel was determined to have the building complete by the middle of September in order that John Kennedy could open it while he was on the campaign trail. George then flew on to San Francisco confident that Abel's deadline would be met.

By nature, George took a long time to like people and even longer to trust them. It was not so with Richard Kane. George took to him immediately, and once he was able to see for himself what Florentyna had achieved in such a short time it became obvious that she could not have done it without her husband's common sense and cautious approach. George intended to leave Abel in no doubt how he felt about the boy when he returned to New York.

After a quiet dinner the two men played backgammon at a dollar a point, and discussed the christening. 'Not at all like Florentyna's,' George confided to Richard, who laughed at the thought of his reluctant father-in-law spending a night in jail.

'You seem to throw doubles all the time,' said George, sipping the Rémy Martin Richard had poured for him.

'My father . . .' said Richard, and then hesitated for a moment, 'always accused me of being a bad loser if I made any mention of doubles.'

George laughed. 'And how is your father?'

'I've no idea. There's been no contact with him since Jessie and I were married.' George still couldn't get used to hearing his goddaughter being referred to as Jessie. When he was told the reason why, he knew it would amuse Abel.

'I'm sorry your father seems to be reacting the same way as Abel,' said George.

'I remain in touch with my mother,' continued Richard sipping his brandy, 'but I can see no end to my father's attitude, especially while Abel continues to try and increase his holding in Lester's.'

'Are you sure of that?' asked George, sounding surprised.

'Two years ago every banker on Wall Street knew what he was up to.'

'Abel is now so set in his ways,' said George, 'I can't make him listen to reason. But I don't believe he will cause any more trouble at the moment,' he added, before returning to his brandy. Richard didn't enquire why: he realised that if George wanted to explain he would.

'You see, if Kennedy wins the election,' George continued, once he had put the glass down, 'Abel has an outside chance of a minor appointment in the new administration. I put it no higher than that.'

'Our ambassador to Poland, no doubt,' said Florentyna as she came into the room carrying a tray laden with coffee cups. 'He would be the first Polish immigrant to be so honoured. I've known about that ambition ever since our trip to Europe.'

George didn't reply.

'Is Henry Osborne behind this?' asked Florentyna.

'No, he doesn't even know about it,' said George, relaxing back in his chair. 'Your father no longer places any trust in him. Since Henry lost his seat in Congress he has proved unreliable, to say the least, and your father is even considering removing him from the board.'

'At last Papa has woken up to what a nasty piece of work Henry really is.'

'I think he has always known, but there's no denying Henry was useful to your father when he was in Washington. Personally I think he is still dangerous despite being removed from Congress.'

'Why?' asked Florentyna from her seat in the corner of the room.

'Because I suspect he knows too much about the enmity between Abel and Richard's father, and if he gets into any more debt I fear he may trade that information with Mr. Kane direct.'

'Never,' said Richard.

'How can you be so sure?' asked George.

'You mean after all these years you don't know?' Richard asked.

George stared from one to the other. 'Know what?'

'Obviously not,' said Florentyna.

'You'll need a double,' said Richard, and poured George another large brandy before continuing.

'Henry Osborne hates my father even more than Abel does.'

'What? Why?' said George, leaning forward.

'Henry was married to my grandmother, after my grandfather died.' Richard poured himself another coffee before continuing. 'Many years ago when he was a young man, he tried to part my grandmother from a small family fortune. Osborne didn't succeed because *my* father, aged only seventeen, discovered that his Harvard military background was nothing more than a front and proceeded to throw him out of his own home.'

'Omój Jezu!' said George. 'I wonder if Abel knows any of this.' He hadn't noticed it was his turn to throw the dice.

'Of course he does,' said Florentyna. 'It must have been the deciding factor for employing Henry in the first place. He needed someone on his side who he could be certain would never open his mouth to Kane.'

'How did you find out?'

'Pieced it together when Richard discovered I wasn't Jessie Kovats. Most of the stuff on Henry is in a file locked in the bottom of Papa's desk.'

'I thought I was too old to learn so much in one day,' said George.

'Your day's learning hasn't begun,' said Richard. 'Henry Osborne never went to Harvard, never served in the war, and his real name is Vittorio Togna.'

George didn't speak, just opened his mouth.

'We also know that Papa has six per cent of Lester's Bank. Just imagine the problems he would cause if he could lay his hands on another two per cent,' said Florentyna.

'We think he's trying to buy that two per cent from Peter Parfitt, the deposed chairman of Lester's, with the final aim of removing my father from his own board,' Richard added.

'That may have been right in the past.'

'Why not now?' queried Florentyna.

'Abel won't become involved with anything as silly as removing your father from the bank while Kennedy has him in mind for Warsaw. So you need have no fear in that direction. And perhaps that might make you consider coming as my guest to see the candidate open the new Baron in Los Angeles?'

'Is there any hope of Richard being invited as well?'

'You know the answer to that, Florentyna.'

'Another game, George?' said Richard, changing the subject.

'No, thank you. I know a winner when I see one.' He removed his wallet from an inside pocket and handed over eleven dollars. 'Mind you, I still blame the doubles.'

16

NANCY CHING HAD RUN the shop well while Florentyna was away in the hospital, but with Kane junior safely parked in a crib in the back room Florentyna was only too happy to return to work. She explained to Miss Tredgold when she sent the first photos of them together that she was hoping to be a responsible mother until it became impossible not to employ someone. 'Not that I'll find anyone like you outside of Much Hadham,' she added.

During the first two years of their marriage, both she and Richard had concentrated on building their careers. When Florentyna acquired her second shop, Richard also advanced another rung on the bank ladder.

Florentyna would have liked to spend more time concentrating on fashion trends rather than the day-to-day finances but she felt unable to ask Richard to spend every night on her books after he had returned from the bank. She discussed her bold ideas for the future with Nancy, who was a little sceptical about placing so many orders for small sizes.

'It may suit me' – the petite Chinese girl grinned – 'but not most American women.'

'I don't agree. Small is going to be beautiful and we must be the first to anticipate it. If American women think it's the trend, we are going to witness a skinny revolution the like of which will even make you look fat.'

Nancy laughed. 'Looking at your future orders for 4s and 6s, you'd better be right.'

Neither Richard nor Florentyna brought up the vexed subject of their families after George's visit since they both despaired of any reconciliation. They both spoke to their mothers on the phone from time to time, and although Richard received letters from his two sisters, he was particularly sad that he was not invited to attend Virginia's wedding. This unhappy state of affairs might have drifted on indefinitely had it not been for two events. The first was hard to avoid, while the second was caused by the wrong person picking up the phone.

The first occurred because it was Los Angeles's turn to open a Baron. Florentyna followed its progress with great interest while she was preparing to open her third shop. The new hotel was completed in September 1960 and Florentyna took the afternoon off to watch Senator John Kennedy perform the opening ceremony. She stood at the back of a large crowd that had come to see the candidate while she kept an eye on her father. He seemed to her a lot older and had certainly put on weight. From those who were surrounding him it was obvious that he was now well connected in Democratic circles. She wondered if Kennedy were elected would her father be offered 'the chance to serve under him'. Florentyna was impressed by the competent speech of welcome Abel made, but she was mesmerised by the young Presidential candidate who seemed to her to embody the new America. After she had heard him she passionately wanted John Kennedy to be the next President. As soon as the speech in San Francisco was over, she left the newly opened Baron resolved to give time and send money to the Ninth District of Illinois for the Kennedy campaign, although she suspected her father had already contributed a sum that would make her own efforts appear minuscule. Richard remained unshakeably Republican and a supporter of Nixon.

'No doubt you remember what Eisenhower said when he was asked about your standard-bearer?' Florentyna teased.

'Something unflattering, I'm sure.'

'A journalist asked him "What major decisions has the Vice-President participated in?" '

'And what was Ike's reply?'

'If you give me a week, I might think of one.'

During the remaining weeks of the campaign, Florentyna spent what free time she had addressing envelopes and answering phone calls at the Party's headquarters in San Francisco. Unlike the past two elections, she was convinced the Democrats had found a man in whom she could place unreserved support. The final television debate between the candidates re-awakened in her the political ambitions so nearly buried by Henry Osborne. Kennedy's charisma and political insight were dazzling, while Florentyna was left to wonder how anyone who had followed the campaign could possibly vote Republican. Richard pointed out to her that charisma and good looks were not to be traded for a future policy and a proven record, even if it had to include a five o'clock shadow.

All through the election night Richard and Florentyna sat up watching the results. The twists, the turns and the upsets lasted all the way to California, where by the smallest margin in American electoral history Kennedy became President. Florentyna was ecstatic about the final outcome, while Richard maintained that Kennedy would never have made it without Mayor Daley and the Cook County ballot boxes – or lack of them.

'Would you vote the Democratic ticket if I were running for office?'

'It would depend on your policies. I'm a banker, not a sentimentalist.'

'Well, unsentimental banker, I want to open a fourth shop.'

'What?' said Richard.

'There's a bargain going in San Diego, a building with a lease of only two years to run but it could be renewable.'

'How much?'

'Thirty thousand dollars.'

'You're mad, Jessie. That's your projected profits for this year gone in expansion.'

'And while you're on the subject of expansion, I'm pregnant again.'

When the thirty-fifth President delivered his Inaugural Address Florentyna and Richard watched the ceremony on television in the apartment above the main shop.

'*Let the word go forth, from this time and place, to friend and foe alike, that the torch has been passed to a new generation of Americans, born in this century, tempered by war, disciplined by a hard and bitter peace*' – Florentyna's eyes never once left the man in whom so many people had placed their trust. When President Kennedy concluded his speech with the words, '*Ask not what your country can do for you. Ask what you can do for your country*,' Florentyna watched the crowd rise and found herself joining in the applause. She wondered how many people were clapping in other homes throughout America. She turned to Richard.

'Not bad for a Democrat,' he said, aware he was also clapping.

Florentyna smiled. 'Do you think my father is there?'

'Undoubtedly.'

'So now we sit and wait for the appointment.'

George wrote the next day to confirm that Abel had been in Washington for the celebrations. He ended on the words: 'Your father seems confident about going to Warsaw, and I am equally sure that if he is offered the position, it will be easier to get him to meet Richard.'

'What a friend George has turned out to be,' said Florentyna.

'To Abel as well as to us,' said Richard thoughtfully.

Each day Florentyna checked the new appointments as they were released by Press Secretary Pierre Salinger. But no announcement concerning the Polish ambassador was forthcoming.

17

WHEN FLORENTYNA DID SEE her father's name in the paper, she could hardly miss it: the banner headline was all across the front page:

THE CHICAGO BARON ARRESTED

Florentyna read the story in disbelief.

> NEW YORK–Abel Rosnovski, the international hotelier, known as the Chicago Baron, was arrested at eight thirty this morning at an apartment on East Fifty-seventh Street by agents of the FBI. The arrest took place after his return the previous night from a business trip to Turkey where he had opened the Istanbul Baron, the latest in his chain of hotels. Rosnovski was charged by the FBI with bribery and corruption of government officials in fourteen different states. The FBI also wants to question ex-Congressman Henry Osborne who has not been seen in Chicago for the past fortnight.
>
> Rosnovski's defence attorney, H. Trafford Jilks, made a statement denying the charges and added that his client had a full explanation which would exonerate him completely. Rosnovski was granted bail in his own recognisance of ten thousand dollars.

The news story went on to report that rumours had been

circulating in Washington for some time that the White House had been considering Mr. Rosnovski as America's next ambassador to Poland.

That night Florentyna lay awake wondering how it could have all happened, and what her father must be going through. She assumed Henry was involved in some way, and decided to follow every scrap of information that was reported in the papers. Richard tried to comfort her by saying there were very few businessmen alive who had not at some stage in their careers been involved in a little bribery.

Three days before the trial was due to begin the Justice Department found Henry Osborne in New Orleans. He was arrested, charged and immediately turned State's evidence. The FBI asked Judge Prescott for a postponement to discuss with ex-Congressman Osborne the contents of a dossier on Rosnovski that had recently come into their possession. Judge Prescott granted the FBI a further four weeks to prepare their case.

The press soon discovered that Osborne, in order to clear his considerable debts, had sold the file that he had compiled over ten years while serving as a director of the Baron Group, to a firm of private investigators in Chicago. How the file had then come into the hands of the FBI remained a mystery.

Florentyna was fearful that with Henry Osborne as star witness for the prosecution her father might have to serve a long jail sentence. After another sleepless night, Richard suggested she ought to contact her father. She agreed, and wrote him a long letter assuring him of her support and her belief in his innocence. She was about to lick the envelope when she walked over to her desk, took out her favourite picture of her son and sent it to his grandfather.

Four hours before the trial was due to begin Henry Osborne was found hanging in his cell by a guard bringing in his breakfast. He had used a Harvard tie.

'Why did Henry commit suicide?' Florentyna asked her mother on the phone later that morning.

'Oh, that's easy to explain,' replied Zaphia. 'Henry

thought the private investigator who cleared his debts wanted the file for the sole purpose of blackmailing your father.'

'And what was the real reason?' asked Florentyna.

'The file had been purchased anonymously in Chicago on behalf of William Kane, who then passed it on to the FBI.'

Florentyna could only feel hatred whenever she thought about William Kane; she couldn't stop herself from taking it out on Richard. But it was obvious that Richard was every bit as angry about his father's behaviour, which Florentyna discovered when she overheard a phone conversation between him and his mother.

'That was pretty tough,' said Florentyna when he finally put the phone down.

'Yes it was. My poor mother's getting it from both sides.'

'We haven't reached the last act of this tragedy,' said Florentyna. 'Papa has wanted to return to Warsaw for as long as I can remember. Now he will never forgive your father.'

Once the trial began, Florentyna followed the proceedings each day by phoning her mother in the evening after Zaphia had returned from the courtroom. When she listened to her mother's view on the day's happenings she wasn't always convinced they both wanted the same outcome.

'The trial is beginning to go in your father's favour,' she said in the middle of the week.

'How can you be so sure?' asked Florentyna.

'Since the FBI has lost its star witness their case hasn't stood up to much cross-examination. H. Trafford Jilks is making Henry Osborne sound like Pinocchio with a nose that is just about touching the ground.'

'Does that mean Papa will be proved innocent?'

'I wouldn't have thought so, but the courtroom officials are predicting that the FBI will end up having to make a deal.'

'What sort of deal?'

'Well, if your father pleads guilty to some minor offences, they will drop the main charges.'

'Will he get away with a fine?' asked Florentyna anxiously.

'If he's lucky. But Judge Prescott is tough, so he may still end up in jail.'

'Let's hope it's just a fine.'

Zaphia made no comment.

'Six months' suspended sentence for the Chicago Baron,' Florentyna heard the newscaster say on her car radio as she was driving to pick up Richard from the bank. She nearly collided with the Buick in front of her and pulled over into a 'no parking' zone so that she could concentrate on what the newscaster had to say.

'The FBI has dropped all the main indictments of bribery against Abel Rosnovski – known as the Chicago Baron – and the defendant pleaded guilty to misdemeanours on two minor counts of attempting to improperly influence a public official. The jury was dismissed. In his summing up Judge Prescott said: "The right to do business does not include the right to suborn public officials. Bribery is a crime and a worse crime when condoned by an intelligent and competent man, who should not need to stoop to such levels.

' "In other countries," the Judge added, "bribery might be an accepted way of life, but that is not the case in the United States." Judge Prescott gave Rosnovski a six months' suspended sentence and a twenty-five thousand dollar fine.

'In other news, President Kennedy has agreed to accompany the Vice-President to Dallas this fall . . .' Florentyna turned off the radio to find someone tapping on the side window. She wound it down.

'Do you know that you're in a restricted area, ma'am?'

'Yes,' replied Florentyna.

'I'm afraid it's going to cost you ten dollars.'

*

'Twenty-five thousand dollars and a six months' suspended sentence. It could have been worse,' said George in the car on the way back to the Baron.

'Don't forget that I lost Poland,' said Abel, 'but that's all history now. Purchase the two per cent of the Lester's shares we need from Parfitt, even if it costs a million. That will make up the eight per cent of Lester's that I need to invoke Article Seven of their by-laws and then I can slaughter William Kane in his own board room.'

George nodded sadly.

A few days later the State Department announced that the next American ambassador to Warsaw would be John Moors Cabot.

18

THE MORNING AFTER JUDGE PRESCOTT'S verdict the second event occurred. The extension of the apartment phone rang in the shop and because Nancy was removing the light summer clothes from the window, replacing them with the new autumn collection, Florentyna answered it.

'Oh, I wondered if Mr. Kane was in,' said a lady's voice. She sounded a long way off.

'No, I'm sorry, he has already left for the bank. Would you like to leave a message? It's Florentyna Kane speaking.'

There was no immediate reply and then a voice said: 'It's Katherine Kane – please don't hang up.'

'Why should I do that, Mrs. Kane?' said Florentyna, her knees feeling so weak that she sank into a chair beside the phone.

'Because you must hate me, my dear, and I can't blame you,' Richard's mother said quickly.

'No, of course I don't hate you. Would you like Richard to call you back when he comes home?'

'Oh, no. My husband doesn't realise that I'm in touch with him. He would be very angry if he ever found out. No, what I was really hoping for will finally depend on you.'

'On me?'

'Yes. I desperately want to visit you and Richard and see my grandson – if you'll allow me.'

'I'd like that very much, Mrs. Kane,' said Florentyna, not sure how she could sound more welcoming.

'Oh, how understanding of you. My husband is going to a conference in Mexico in three weeks' time and I could fly out on the Friday. Only I would have to be back first thing on Monday morning.'

When Richard heard the news he went straight to the refrigerator. Florentyna followed, bewildered. She smiled as he stripped the gold foil from Claude's bottle of Krug and began pouring.

Three weeks later Florentyna accompanied Richard to the airport to welcome his mother.

'But you're beautiful,' were Florentyna's first words as she greeted the elegant, slim lady who showed not the slightest sign of having spent the last six hours on a plane. 'And you make me feel terribly pregnant.'

'What were you expecting, my dear? An ogre with red horns and a long black tail?'

Florentyna laughed as Katherine Kane put an arm through hers and they walked off together, temporarily forgetting her son.

Richard was relieved to see how quickly the two of them became friends. When they arrived back at the flat Katherine reacted in the time-honoured way when she set eyes on her first grandchild.

'I do wish your father could see his grandson,' she said. 'But I fear it's now reached a stage where he won't even allow the subject to be discussed.'

'Do you know any more than we do about what is happening between the two men?' asked Richard.

'I wouldn't have thought so. Your father refused to let the bank support Davis Leroy when his hotel group collapsed, and Florentyna's father therefore blames my husband for the subsequent suicide of Mr. Leroy. The whole unfortunate episode might have ended there if Henry Osborne hadn't come on to the scene.' She sighed. 'I pray to God the problem will be sorted out in my lifetime.'

'I fear one of them will have to die before the other comes to his senses,' said Richard. 'They are both so confoundedly obstinate.'

The four of them had a wonderful weekend together even if Kate's grandson did spend most of his time throwing his toys on to the floor. When they drove Katherine back to the airport on Sunday night she agreed to come and see them the next time her husband was away on business. Katherine's last words to Florentyna were, 'If only you and my husband could meet, he would be in no doubt why Richard fell in love with you.'

As she turned to wave goodbye, her grandson repeated his one-word vocabulary: 'Dada'. Katherine Kane laughed, 'What chauvinists men are. That was also Richard's first word. Has anyone ever told you what yours was, Florentyna?'

Annabel came screaming into this world a few weeks later, and Richard and Florentyna had a double celebration at the end of the year when Florentyna delivered a nineteen thousand one hundred and seventy-four dollar profit. Richard decided to mark the occasion by spending a small part of those profits on a golf membership of the Olympic Club.

Richard was given more responsibility in the overseas department of the bank, and started coming home an hour later. Florentyna decided the time had come to employ a full-time nanny so that she could concentrate on her work in the shops. She realised that she would never find a Miss Tredgold but Bella recommended a black girl called Carol who had graduated from high school the year before and was finding it hard to secure employment. Their son threw his arms around Carol the moment he met her. It brought home to Florentyna that prejudice was something children learn from their elders.

19

'I CAN'T BELIEVE IT,' said Florentyna. 'I never thought it would happen. What wonderful news. But what made him change his mind?'

'He's not getting any younger,' said Katherine Kane, her voice crackling down the phone, 'and he's frightened that if he and Richard don't patch up their differences soon he will retire from Lester's without a son on the board. He also believes that the man most likely to succeed him in the chair is Jake Thomas, and as Mr. Thomas is only two years older than Richard, he certainly won't want a younger Kane in the board room.'

'I wish Richard was at home so I could tell him the news, but since he's been promoted to head of the overseas department he rarely gets back before seven. He'll be so pleased. I'll try not to show how nervous I am about meeting your husband,' said Florentyna.

'Not half as nervous as he is about meeting you. But have no fears, my dear, he's preparing the fatted calf for his prodigal son. Have you heard anything from your father since I last spoke to you?'

'No, nothing. I fear there's never going to be a fatted calf for the prodigal daughter.'

'Don't give up. Something may yet arise that makes him see the light. We'll all put our heads together when you come to New York.'

'I would love to believe it was still possible for Papa to be reconciled, but I've almost given up hope.'

'Well, let's be thankful that one father has at least come to his senses,' said Katherine. 'I'll fly out to see you and fix up all the details.'

'How soon can you come?'

'I could get away this weekend.'

When Richard came home that evening he was overjoyed by the news, and once he had finished reading the next chapter of *Winnie the Pooh* to his son, he settled down to listen to the details of his mother's news.

'We could go to New York around November,' said Richard.

'I'm not sure I can wait that long.'

'You've waited for over three years.'

'Yes, but that's different.'

'You always want everything to have happened yesterday, Jessie. That reminds me, I read your proposal for the new shop in San Diego.'

'And?'

'Basically the idea makes a lot of sense and I approve.'

'Good heavens. What next? I never thought I would hear such words from you, Mr. Kane.'

'Now hold on, Jessie, it doesn't get my whole-hearted support because the one part of your expansion programme I don't understand is the necessity to employ your own designer.'

'That's easy enough to explain,' said Florentyna. 'Although we now have five shops my expenditure on buying clothes remains as high as forty per cent of turnover. If my own garments were designed for me, I would have two obvious advantages. First, I could cut down my immediate expenditure, and second we would be continually advertising our own product.'

'It also has a major disadvantage,' suggested Richard.

'What's that?'

'There can be no rebate on clothes returned within ninety days if we already own them.'

'Agreed,' said Florentyna. 'But the more we expand the more that problem will diminish. And if I choose the right designer we'll end up with our trade-mark clothes also being sold by our rivals.'

'Has that proved worthwhile for other designers?'

'In the case of Pierre Cardin, the designer became more famous than the shops.'

'Finding such a man won't be easy.'

'Didn't I find you, Mr. Kane?'

'No, Jessie, I found you.'

Florentyna smiled. 'Two children, a sixth shop, and you're going to be invited to join the board of Lester's. Most important of all I have a chance to meet your father. What more could we want?'

'It hasn't happened yet.'

'Typical banker. Whatever the forecast, you expect it to rain by mid-afternoon.'

Annabel started to cry.

'See what I mean?' said Richard. 'Your daughter's at it again.'

'Why is it always my daughter who is bad and your son who is good?'

Despite Florentyna's desire to travel to New York immediately after Kate had returned to the east coast, she was more than fully occupied with opening the new shop in San Diego, keeping an eye on the other five shops, and somehow looking for the right designer, while still trying to be a mother. As the day for their journey to New York grew nearer she became more and more nervous. She selected her own wardrobe carefully and bought several new outfits for the children. She even purchased a new shirt with a thin red stripe running through it for Richard, but she doubted that he would wear it except at weekends. Florentyna lay awake each night anxious that Richard's father might not approve of her, but Richard kept reminding her of Katherine's words: 'Not half as nervous as he is.'

To celebrate the opening of the sixth shop and the imminent reconciliation with his father, Richard took Florentyna to a performance of *The Nutcracker* by the Italian State Ballet

Company at the War Memorial Opera House. Richard didn't care much for the ballet himself but he was surprised to find Florentyna equally as restless during the performance. As soon as the house lights went up for the intermission he asked if anything was wrong.

'Yes. I've been waiting over an hour to find out who designed those fabulous costumes.' Florentyna started to thumb through her programme.

'I would have described them as outrageous,' said Richard.

'That's because you're colour-blind,' said Florentyna. Having found what she was looking for she started reading the programme notes to Richard. 'His name is Gianni di Ferranti. His biography says he was born in Milan in 1931 and that this is his first tour with the Italian State Ballet Company since leaving the Institute of Modern Art in Florence. I wonder if he would consider resigning from the company and working for me?'

'I wouldn't, with the inside information I have on the company,' said Richard, helpfully.

'Perhaps he's more adventurous than you, darling.'

'Or just mad. After all, he is Italian.'

'Well, there's only one way to find out,' said Florentyna, standing up.

'And how do you propose doing that?'

'By going backstage.'

'But you'll miss the second half of the performance.'

'The second half might not change my whole life,' said Florentyna, stepping into the aisle.

Richard followed her out of the building and they made their way around the outside to the stage door. A young security guard pushed open his window.

'Can I help you?' he asked, sounding as if it were the last thing he wanted to do.

'Yes,' Florentyna said confidently. 'I have an appointment with Gianni di Ferranti.'

Richard looked at his wife disapprovingly.

'Your name, please,' said the guard, picking up a phone.

'Florentyna Kane.'

The guard repeated the name into the mouthpiece, listened for a moment, then replaced the receiver.

'He says he's never heard of you.'

Florentyna was taken aback for a moment but Richard took out his wallet and placed a twenty-dollar bill on the ledge in front of the guard.

'Perhaps he has heard of me,' said Richard.

'You better go and find out,' said the guard, casually removing the note. 'Through the door, take the corridor to your right, second door on the left,' he added before slamming down the window.

Richard led Florentyna through the entrance.

'Most businessmen are involved in a little bribery at some stage in their careers,' she teased.

'Now don't get annoyed just because your lie failed,' said Richard, grinning.

When they reached the room, Florentyna knocked firmly and peered around the door.

A tall, dark-haired Italian was seated in one corner of the room eating spaghetti with a fork. Florentyna's first reaction was one of admiration. He was wearing a pair of tailored jeans and blue blazer over a casual open-necked shirt. But the thing that struck her most was the young man's long, artistic fingers. The moment he saw Florentyna he rose gracefully to his feet.

'Gianni,' she began expansively. 'What a privilege –'

'No,' said the man in a soft Italian accent. 'He's in the washroom.'

Richard smirked and received a sharp kick on the ankle. Florentyna was about to speak again when the door opened and in walked a man no more than five feet five, nearly bald, and from the programme notes she knew he was not yet thirty. His clothes were beautifully cut, but the pasta had had a greater effect on his waistline than it had had on his friend.

'Who are these people, Valerio?'

'Mrs. Florentyna Kane,' said Florentyna before the young man could speak. 'And this is my husband, Richard.'

'What do you want?' he asked, not looking at her while taking the seat opposite his companion.

'To offer you a job as my designer.'

'Not another one,' he said, throwing his hands in the air.

Florentyna took a deep breath. 'Who else has spoken to you?'

'In New York, Yves Saint Laurent. In Los Angeles, Pierre Cardin. In Chicago, Balmain. Need I go on?'

'But did they offer you a percentage of the profits?'

'What profits?' Richard wanted to ask, but remembered the kick on the ankle.

'I already have six shops and we have plans for another six in the pipeline,' Florentyna continued impulsively. She hoped that Gianni di Ferranti hadn't noticed her husband's eyebrows rise dramatically at her words.

'The turnover could be millions within a few years,' she continued.

'Saint Laurent's turnover already is,' said di Ferranti, still not turning to face her.

'Yes, but what did they offer you?'

'Twenty-five thousand dollars a year, and one per cent of the profits.'

'I'll offer you twenty thousand and five per cent.'

The Italian waved a dismissive hand.

'Twenty-five thousand dollars and ten per cent?' she said.

The Italian laughed, rose from his chair and opened the door for Florentyna and Richard to leave. She stood firm.

'You are the sort of person who would expect Zeffirelli to be available to design your next shop while still hoping to retain Luigi Ferpozzi as honorary adviser. Not that I could expect you to understand what I'm talking about,' he added.

'Luigi,' said Florentyna, haughtily, 'is a dear friend of mine.'

The Italian placed his hands on his hips and roared with laughter. 'You Americans are all the same. Next you'll be saying you designed the Pope's vestments.'

Richard had some sympathy with him.

'Your bluff is called, signora. Ferpozzi came to see the show in Los Angeles only last week and spoke to me at length about my work. Now at least I have found a way to be rid of you.' Di Ferranti left the door open and picked up the phone on his dressing table and without another word dialled a 213 number.

No one spoke while they waited for the call to be answered. Eventually Florentyna heard a voice which she thought she recognised.

'Luigi?' said di Ferranti. 'It's Gianni. I have an American lady with me called Mrs. Kane who claims she is a friend of yours.'

He listened for a few moments, his smile becoming broader.

He turned to Florentyna. 'He says he doesn't know anyone called Mrs. Kane, and perhaps you would feel more at home on Alcatraz?'

'No, I wouldn't care for Alcatraz,' said Florentyna. 'But tell him he thinks my father built it.'

Gianni di Ferranti repeated Florentyna's sentiments over the phone. As he listened to the reply his face became puzzled. He finally looked back at her. 'Luigi says to offer you a cup of tea. But only if you've brought your own pot.'

It took Florentyna two lunches, one dinner with Richard, one with her bankers, and an advance big enough to move Gianni and his friend Valerio from Milan to a new home in San Francisco to persuade the little Italian to join her as the company's new in-house designer. Florentyna was confident that this was the breakthrough she had been looking for. In the excitement of convincing Gianni she quite forgot they were only six days away from going to New York to meet Richard's father.

Florentyna and Richard were having breakfast that Monday morning when his face turned so white that she thought he was going to faint.

'What's the matter, darling?'

He pointed to the front page of the *Wall Street Journal* as if unable to speak. Florentyna read the bald announcement and silently handed the paper back to her husband. He read the statement slowly for a second time to be certain he understood the full implications. The brevity and force of the words were stunning. 'William Lowell Kane, the President and Chairman of Lester's Bank, resigned after Friday's board meeting.'

Richard knew that the city would put the worst interpretation possible on such a sudden departure, made without explanation or any suggestion of illness, especially as his only son, a banker, had not been invited to take his place on the board. He put his arms around Florentyna and held her close to his chest.

'Does it mean our trip to New York will be cancelled?'

'Not unless your father was the cause.'

'It can't happen – I won't *let* it happen. Not after waiting so long.'

The phone rang and Richard leaned over to answer it, not letting go of Florentyna.

'Hello?'

'Richard, it's mother. I've been trying to get away from the house. Have you heard the news?'

'Yes, I've just read it in the *Wall Street Journal*. What in heaven's name made father resign?'

'I'm not certain of all the details myself, but as far as I can gather, Mr. Rosnovski has held six per cent of the bank's shares for the past ten years, and for some reason he only needed eight per cent to be able to remove your father from the chair.'

'To invoke Article Seven,' said Richard.

'Yes, that's right. But I'm still not sure what that means.'

'Well, father had the clause put into the bank's by-laws to protect himself from ever being taken over. He considered the clause was foolproof because only someone in possession of eight per cent or more could challenge his authority. He never imagined anyone other than the family could ever get their hands on such a large stake in the company. Father would never have given up his fifty-one per cent of Kane and

Cabot to become chairman of Lester's if he had felt an outsider could remove him.'

'But that still doesn't explain why he had to resign.'

'I suppose Florentyna's father somehow got hold of another two per cent. That would have given him the same powers as father and made life at the bank impossible for him as chairman.'

'But how could he make life impossible?' It was now obvious to Richard that his father had not even confided in Kate about what was happening at the bank.

'Among the safeguards that Article Seven stipulates, if I remember correctly,' Richard continued, 'is that anyone in possession of eight per cent of the shares can hold up any transaction the bank is involved in for three months. I know from the bank's audit that Mr. Rosnovski held six per cent. I suppose he obtained the other two per cent from Peter Parfitt.'

'No, he didn't get the shares from Parfitt,' said Kate. 'I know your father managed to secure those shares by getting an old friend to purchase them for considerably more than they were worth, which is why he has felt so relaxed and confident about the future lately.'

'Then the real mystery is how Mr. Rosnovski got hold of the other two per cent. I know no one on the board who would have parted with their own shares unless . . .'

'Your three minutes are up, ma'am.'

'Where are you, Mother?'

'I'm in a pay phone. Your father has forbidden any of us to contact you ever again, and he never wants to set eyes on Florentyna.'

'But this has nothing to do with her, she's . . .'

'I'm sorry, ma'am, but your three minutes are up.'

'I'll pay for the call, operator.'

'I'm sorry, sir, but the call has been disconnected.'

Richard replaced the phone reluctantly.

Florentyna looked up. 'Can you forgive me, darling, for having a father who was involved in such a terrible thing? I know I will never forgive him.'

'Never prejudge anyone, Jessie,' said Richard, as he stroked her hair. 'I suspect that if we ever discover the whole truth we shall find that the blame is fairly evenly distributed on both sides. Now, young lady, you have two children and six stores to worry about and I, no doubt, have irate customers waiting for me at the bank. Put this whole incident behind you because I am convinced that the worst is now over.'

Florentyna continued to cling to her husband, thankful for the strength of his words, even if she did not believe them.

Abel read the announcement of William Kane's resignation in the *Wall Street Journal* the same day. He picked up the phone, dialled Lester's Bank and asked to speak to the new chairman. A few seconds later Jake Thomas came on the line. 'Good morning, Mr. Rosnovski.'

'Good morning, Mr. Thomas. I'm just phoning to confirm that I shall release this morning my eight per cent holding in Lester's to you personally for two million dollars.'

'Thank you, Mr. Rosnovski, that's most generous of you.'

'No need to thank me, Mr. Chairman. It's no more than we agreed on when you sold me your two per cent.'

Florentyna realised that it would take a considerable time to recover from the blow inflicted by her father. She wondered how it was still possible to love him and to hate him at the same time. She tried to concentrate on her fast-growing empire and to put the thought of never seeing her father again out of her mind.

Another blow, not as personal, but every bit as tragic for Florentyna was delivered on November 22nd, 1963. Richard called her from the bank, something he had never done before, to tell her that President Kennedy had been shot in Dallas, and early reports feared he might die.

20

FLORENTYNA'S NEWLY ACQUIRED ITALIAN designer Gianni di Ferranti, had come up with the idea of putting a small entwined double F on the collar or hem of all his garments. It looked most impressive and only added to the company's reputation. Although Gianni was the first to admit that it was nothing more than a copy of an idea that Yves Saint Laurent had used, nevertheless it worked.

Florentyna found time to fly to Los Angeles to check on a property that was up for sale on Rodeo Drive in Beverly Hills. Once she had seen it, she told Richard she had plans for a seventh Florentyna's. He said he would need to study the figures carefully before he could advise her if she should take up the offer, but he was under such pressure at the bank that it might have to wait a few days.

Not for the first time Florentyna felt the need of a partner or at least a financial director, now that Richard was so overworked. She would have liked to ask him to join her but she felt diffident about suggesting it.

'You'll have to put an advertisement in the *Chronicle* and see how many replies you get,' said Richard. 'I'll help you screen them and we can interview the short list together.'

Florentyna followed Richard's instructions, and within days the letters had flooded in from bankers, lawyers and accountants, all of whom showed considerable interest in the appointment. Richard helped Florentyna sift through the replies. Halfway through the evening he paused over a particular letter and said: 'I'm crazy.'

'I know, my darling, that's why I married you.'

'We've wasted four hundred dollars.'

'Why? You felt sure the advertisement would turn out to be a worthwhile investment.'

Richard handed her the letter he had been reading.

'Seems well qualified,' said Florentyna, after she had read it through. 'Since he's at the Bank of America, you must have your own opinion as to whether he's a suitable man to be my financial director.'

'He's eminently suitable. But who do you imagine will fill his position if he leaves the bank to join you?'

'I've no idea.'

'Well, since he's my boss, it might be me,' said Richard.

Florentyna burst out laughing. 'And to think I didn't have the courage to ask you. Still, I consider it four hundred dollars well spent – partner.'

Richard Kane left the Bank of America four weeks later and joined his wife as a fifty per cent partner and the Financial Director of Florentyna Inc. of San Francisco, Los Angeles and San Diego.

Another election went by. Florentyna didn't become involved because she was so overworked with her expanding empire. She admitted to Richard that she couldn't trust Johnson while she despised Goldwater. Richard put a bumper sticker on their car which Florentyna immediately tore off:

$$Au + H^2O = 1964$$

They agreed not to discuss the subject again, although Florentyna did gloat over the Democratic landslide that followed in November.

During the next year, their two children grew more quickly than the company, and on their son's fifth birthday they opened two more Florentyna's: in Chicago and Boston. Richard remained cautious about the speed at which the shops were springing up but Florentyna's pace never faltered. With so many new customers wanting to wear Gianni di Ferranti's clothes, she spent most of her spare time combing cities for prime sites.

By 1966 there was only one important city that did not boast a Florentyna's. She realised it might be years before a site fell vacant on the only avenue fit for the Florentyna's of New York.

21

'You're a stubborn old fool, Abel.'

'I know, but I can't turn the clock back now.'

'Well, I can tell you, nothing's going to stop me accepting the invitation.'

Abel looked up from his bed. He had hardly left the penthouse since that severe bout of 'flu six months before. After he had returned from an extensive trip to Poland, George was almost his only contact with the outside world. He knew his oldest friend was right, and he had to admit that it was tempting. He wondered if Kane would be going. He found himself hoping so, but he doubted it. The man was every bit as stubborn as he was . . .

George voiced Abel's thoughts. 'I bet William Kane will be there.'

Abel made no comment. 'Have you the final run-down on Warsaw?'

'Yes,' said George sharply, angry that Abel had changed the subject. 'All the agreements are signed and John Gronowski couldn't have been more cooperative.'

John Gronowski, the first Polish ambassador to Warsaw, reflected Abel. *He would never recover from . . .*

'Your trip to Poland last year has achieved everything you could have hoped for. You will live to open the Warsaw Baron.'

'I always wanted Florentyna to open it,' said Abel quietly.

'Then invite her, but don't expect any sympathy from me. All you have to do is acknowledge Richard's existence. And even you must have woken up to the fact that their marriage is a success, otherwise *that* wouldn't be on the mantelpiece.' George stared across the room. There, propped up in front of a vase, stood an unanswered invitation.

Everyone in New York seemed to be there when Florentyna Kane opened her new boutique on Fifth Avenue. Florentyna, wearing a green dress that had been specially designed for her with the now famous double F on the high collar, stood near the entrance of the shop, greeting each of her guests and offering them a glass of champagne. Katherine Kane, accompanied by her daughter Lucy, was among the first to arrive and very quickly the floor was crowded with people whom Florentyna either knew very well or had never seen before. George Novak arrived a little later and delighted Florentyna by his first request – to be introduced to the Kanes.

'Will Mr. Rosnovski be coming later?' Lucy asked innocently.

'I'm afraid not,' said George. 'I told him that he was a stubborn old fool to miss such a good party. Is Mr. Kane here?'

'No, he's not been well lately and rarely leaves the house nowadays,' said Kate, and she then confided to George a piece of news that delighted him.

'How is my father?' Florentyna whispered into George's ear.

'Not well. I left him in bed in the penthouse. Perhaps when he hears that tonight you're going to . . .'

'Perhaps,' said Florentyna. She took Kate by the arm and introduced her to Zaphia. For a moment, neither of the old ladies spoke. Then Zaphia said, 'It's wonderful to meet you at last. Is your husband with you?'

The room became so crowded that it was almost impossible to move, and the ringing laughter and chatter left Florentyna in no doubt how well the opening was going, but now she had only one thing on her mind: dinner that evening.

*

Outside, a large crowd had gathered on the corner of Fifty-sixth Street to stare at what was going on and the traffic on Fifth Avenue had nearly come to a standstill as men and women, young and old, peered through the large plate glass windows.

A man stood in a doorway on the far side of the road. He wore a black coat, a scarf around his neck and a hat pulled well down on his head. It was a cold evening and the wind was whistling down Fifth Avenue. Not a day for old men, he thought, and wondered if after all it had been wise to leave the warmth of his bed. But he was determined that nothing would prevent his witnessing the opening of this shop. He fiddled with the silver band around his wrist and remembered the new will he had made, not leaving the heirloom to his daughter as he had originally promised.

He smiled as he watched young people surge in and out of the splendid shop. Through the window he could just make out his ex-wife talking to George, and then he saw Florentyna and a tear trickled down his lined cheek. She was even more beautiful than he remembered her. He wanted to cross the road that divided them and say, 'George was right, I've been a stubborn old fool for far too long. Can you possibly forgive me?' but instead he just stood and stared, his feet remaining fixed to the ground. He saw a young man by his daughter's side, tall, self-assured and aristocratic; he could only be the son of William Kane. A fine man, George had told him. How had he described him? Florentyna's strength. Abel wondered if Richard hated him and feared that he must. The old man turned up his collar, took one last look at his beloved daughter and turned to retrace his steps back to the Baron.

As he walked away from the shop he saw another man heading slowly along the pavement. He was taller than Abel, but his walk was just as unsteady. Their eyes met, but only for a moment, and as they passed each other the taller of the old men raised his hat. Abel returned the compliment and they continued on their separate ways without a word.

*

'Thank heavens, the last one has gone,' said Florentyna. 'And only just enough time for a bath before changing for dinner.'

Katherine Kane kissed her and said, 'See you in an hour.'

Florentyna locked the front door of the shop and, holding her children's hands tightly, she walked with them towards the Pierre. It would be the first time since her childhood she had stayed in a hotel in New York other than the Baron.

'Another day of triumph for you, my darling,' said Richard.

'To be followed by a night?'

'Oh, stop fussing, Jessie. Father will adore you.'

'It's been such a long time, Richard.'

Richard followed her through the front door of the Pierre, then caught up with his wife and put his arm around her. 'Ten wasted years, but now we have the chance to make up for the past.' Richard guided his family towards the elevator. 'I'll make sure that the children are washed and dressed while you have your bath.'

Florentyna lay in the bath, wondering how the evening would turn out. From the moment Kate Kane had told her of Richard's father's desire to see them all, she had feared he would change his mind once again; but now the meeting was only an hour away. She wondered if Richard was having the same misgivings. She stepped out of the bath, dried herself before putting on a hint of Joy, her favourite perfume, and a long blue dress especially chosen for the occasion: Kate had told her that her husband's favourite colour was blue. She hunted through her jewelry for something simple and slipped on the antique ring given to her so long ago by her father's backer. When she was fully dressed she stared at herself critically in the mirror: thirty-three, no longer young enough to wear mini skirts, nor old enough to be elegant.

Richard came in from the adjoining room. 'You look stunning,' he said. 'The old man will fall in love with you on sight.' Florentyna smiled and brushed the children's hair while Richard changed. Their son, now seven, was wearing his first suit and looked quite grown-up; Annabel had on a red dress with a white ribbon around the hem: she had no problem with the latest mini fashion.

'I think we're all ready,' said Florentyna when Richard reappeared. She couldn't believe her eyes: he was wearing a shirt with a thin red stripe running through it.

The chauffeur opened the door of their hired Lincoln and Florentyna followed her children into the back. Richard sat in front. As the car drove slowly through the crowded New York streets Florentyna sat in silence. Richard leaned over and touched her hand. The chauffeur brought the car to a stop outside a small elegant brownstone apartment on Sixty-eighth Street.

'Now, children, remember you must be on your best behaviour,' said Florentyna.

'Yes, Mummy,' they said in unison, unawed by the thought of at last meeting one of their grandfathers.

Before they had even stepped out of the car the front door of the house was opened by an elderly man in a morning coat who bowed slightly.

'Good evening, ma'am,' he said. 'And how nice to see you again, Mr. Richard.'

Kate was waiting in the hall to greet them. Florentyna's eyes were immediately drawn to an oil painting of a beautiful woman who sat in a crimson leather chair, hands resting in her lap.

'Richard's grandmother,' said Kate. 'I never knew her, but it's easy to see why she was considered one of the beauties of her day.'

Florentyna continued to stare.

'Is something wrong, my dear?' Kate asked.

'The ring,' she said, barely in a whisper.

'Yes, it's beautiful, isn't it?' said Kate, holding up her hand to display a diamond and sapphire ring. 'William gave it to me when he asked me to be his wife.'

'No, the other one in the portrait,' said Florentyna.

'The antique one, yes, quite magnificent. It had been in the family for generations but I fear it's been lost for some years. When I remarked on its disappearance to William he said he knew nothing of it.'

Florentyna raised her right hand and Kate stared down at the antique ring in disbelief. They all looked at the oil painting – there was absolutely no doubt.

'It was a christening present,' said Florentyna. 'Only I never knew who gave it to me.'

'Oh, my God,' said Richard. 'It never crossed my mind . . .'

'And my father still doesn't know,' said Florentyna.

A maid bustled into the hall. 'Excuse me, ma'am, I've told Mr. Kane that everybody has arrived. He asked if Richard and his wife would be kind enough to go up on their own.'

'You go on up,' said Kate. 'I'll join you in a few minutes with the children.'

Florentyna took her husband's arm and climbed the stairs, nervously fingering the antique ring. They entered the room to find William Lowell Kane sitting in the crimson leather chair by the fire. Such a fine-looking man, thought Florentyna, realising for the first time what her husband would look like when he was old.

'Father,' said Richard, 'I would like you to meet my wife.'

Florentyna stepped forward, to be greeted by a warm and gentle smile on William Kane's face.

Richard waited for his father's response but Florentyna knew that the old man would never speak to her now.

22

ABEL PICKED UP THE phone by the side of his bed. 'Find George for me. I need to get dressed.' Abel read the letter again. He couldn't believe William Kane had been his backer.

When George arrived, Abel didn't speak. He just handed

over the letter. George read it slowly. 'Oh, my God,' he said.
'I must attend the funeral.'

George and Abel arrived at Trinity Church in Boston a few minutes after the service had begun. They stood behind the last row of respectful mourners. Richard and Florentyna stood on each side of Kate. Three senators, five congressmen, two bishops, most of the chairmen of the leading banks and the publisher of the *Wall Street Journal* were all there. The chairman and every director of the Lester's board were also present.

'Do you think they can forgive me?' asked Abel.

George did not reply.

'Will you go and see them?'

'Yes, of course.'

'Thank you, George. I hope William Kane had a friend as good as you.'

Abel sat up in bed looking towards the door every few moments. When it eventually opened he hardly recognised the beautiful lady who had once been his 'little one'. He smiled defiantly as he stared over the top of his half-moon spectacles. George remained by the door as Florentyna ran to the side of the bed and threw her arms around her father – a long hug that couldn't make up for ten wasted years, he told her.

'So much to talk about,' he continued. 'Chicago, Poland, politics, the shops . . . But first, Richard. Can he ever believe I didn't know until yesterday that his father was my backer?'

'Yes, Papa, because he only discovered it himself a day before you, and we are still not sure how you found out.'

'A letter from the lawyers of the First National Bank of Chicago who had been instructed not to inform me until after his death. What a fool I've been,' Abel added. 'Will Richard see me?' he asked, his voice sounding very frail.

'He wants to meet you so much, he and the children are waiting downstairs.'

'Send for them, send for them,' Abel said, his voice rising. George smiled and disappeared.

'And do you still want to be President?' Abel asked.

'Of the Baron Group?'

'No, of the United States. Because if you do, I well remember my end of the bargain. All the way to the convention floor even if it means I end up destitute.'

Florentyna smiled, but made no comment.

A few moments later there was a knock at the door. Abel tried to push himself up as Richard came into the room, followed by the children. The head of the Kane family walked forward and shook hands warmly with his father-in-law.

'Good morning, sir,' he said. 'It's an honour to meet you.'

Abel couldn't get any words out so Florentyna introduced him to Annabel and his grandson.

'And what is your name?' demanded the old man.

'William Abel Kane.'

Abel gripped the boy's hand. 'I am proud to have my name linked with that of your other grandfather.

'You will never begin to know how sad I am about your father,' he said turning to Richard. 'I never realised. So many mistakes over so many years. It didn't cross my mind, even for a moment, that your father could have been my benefactor. God knows, I wish I could be given one chance to thank him personally.'

'He would have understood,' said Richard. 'But there was a clause in the deeds of the family trust which didn't allow him to reveal his identity because of the potential conflict between his professional and private interests. He would never have considered making an exception to any rule. That's why his customers trusted him with their life savings.'

'Even if it resulted in his own death?' asked Florentyna.

'I've been just as obdurate,' said Abel.

'That's hindsight,' said Richard. 'None of us could have known that Henry Osborne would cross our paths.'

'Your father and I met, you know, the day he died,' said Abel.

Florentyna and Richard stared at him in disbelief.

'Oh, yes,' said Abel. 'We passed each other on Fifth Avenue – he had come to watch the opening of your new shop. He raised his hat to me. It was enough, quite enough.'

Soon they were talking of happier days; both laughed a little and cried a lot.

'You must forgive us, Richard,' said Abel. 'The Polish are a sentimental race.'

'I know,' he replied. 'My children are half Polish.'

'Can you join me for dinner tonight?'

'Of course,' said Richard.

'Have you ever experienced a real Polish feast, my boy?'

'Every Christmas for the past ten years,' Richard replied.

Abel laughed, then talked of the future and how he saw the progress of his group. 'We ought to have one of your shops in every hotel,' he told Florentyna.

She agreed.

Abel had only one other request of Florentyna: that she and Richard would accompany him on his journey to Warsaw in nine months' time for the opening of the latest Baron. Richard assured him both of them would be there.

During the following months Abel was reunited with his daughter and quickly grew to respect his son-in-law. George had been right about the boy all along – why *had* he been so stubborn?

He confided in Richard that he wanted their return to Poland to be one Florentyna would never forget. Abel had asked his daughter to open the Baron Warsaw but she had insisted that only the President of the group could perform such a task, although she was anxious about her father's health.

Every week Florentyna and her father would follow the progress of the new hotel. As the time drew nearer for the opening the old man even practised his speech in front of her.

The whole family travelled to Warsaw together. They inspected the first Western hotel to be built behind the Iron

Curtain, to be reassured that it was everything Abel had promised.

The opening ceremony took place in the massive gardens in front of the hotel. The Polish Minister of Tourism made the opening speech welcoming the guests. He then called upon the President of the Baron Group to say a few words before performing the opening ceremony.

Abel's speech was delivered exactly as he had written it and at its conclusion the thousand guests on the lawn rose and cheered.

The Minister of Tourism then handed a large pair of scissors to the President of the Baron Group. Florentyna cut the ribbon that ran across the entrance of the hotel and said, 'I declare the Baron Warsaw open.'

Florentyna had travelled to Slonim to scatter the ashes of her father in his birthplace. As she stood on the land where her father had been born she vowed never to forget her family's origins.

Richard tried to comfort her, but in the short time he had come to know his father-in-law he had recognised the many qualities he had passed on to his daughter.

Florentyna realised that she could never come to terms with their short reconciliation. She still had so much to tell her father and even more to learn from him. She continually thanked George for the time they had been allowed to share as a family, knowing the loss was every bit as deep for him. The last Baron Rosnovski was left on his native soil while his only child and oldest friend returned to America.

The Present

1968–1982

23

Florentyna Kane's appointment as chairman of the Baron Group was confirmed at the board meeting the day she returned from Warsaw. Richard's first piece of advice was that they should transfer the head office of Florentyna's from San Francisco to New York. A few days later the two of them flew back to stay in their little home on Nob Hill for the last time. They spent the next four weeks in California, making the necessary arrangements for their move, which included leaving the west coast operation in the competent hands of their senior manager and putting Nancy Ching in overall charge of the two shops in San Francisco. When it came to saying goodbye to Bella and Claude, Florentyna assured her closest friends that she would be flying back to the coast on a regular basis.

'Going as suddenly as you came,' said Bella.

It was only the second time she had seen Bella cry.

Once they had settled down in New York, Richard recommended that Florentyna should make the shops a subsidiary of the Baron Group so that the companies could be consolidated for tax purposes. Florentyna agreed and made George Novak President for life on his sixty-fifth birthday, giving him a salary that even Abel would have considered generous. Florentyna became chairman of the group and Richard its chief executive.

Richard found them a magnificent new home on East Sixty-fourth Street. They continued to live on the forty-second floor of the New York Baron while their new home was being decorated. William was enrolled at the fashionable Buckley school like his father before him, while Annabel went to Spence. Carol thought perhaps the time had come to look for another job, but at the mere mention of the subject, Annabel would burst into tears.

Florentyna spent every waking hour learning from George how the Baron Group was run. At the end of her first year as chairman, George Novak's private qualms as to whether his goddaughter would have the toughness necessary to run such a huge empire were entirely allayed, especially after her stand in the south on equal pay for Baron Group employees whatever their colour.

'She has inherited her father's genius,' George told Richard. 'All she lacks now is experience.'

'Time will take care of that,' Richard predicted.

Richard made a full report to the board on the state of the company after Florentyna's first year as chairman. The group declared a profit of over twenty-seven million dollars despite a heavy worldwide building schedule and the drop in the value of the dollar caused by the escalating war in Vietnam. Richard then presented his ideas to the board for a comprehensive investment programme for the seventies. He ended his report by recommending that this sort of exercise should be taken over by a bank.

'Agreed,' said Florentyna, 'but I still look upon you as a banker.'

'Don't remind me,' said Richard. 'Only with the turnover we now generate in more than fifty currencies and the fees we pay to the many financial institutions we employ, perhaps the time has come for us to control our own bank.'

'Isn't it nearly impossible nowadays to buy a bank outright?' asked Florentyna. 'And almost as hard to fulfil the government requirements for a licence to run one?'

'Yes it is, but we already own eight per cent of Lester's and we know what problems that created for my father. This time let's turn it to our advantage. What I should like to recommend to the board is . . .'

The following day Richard wrote to Jake Thomas, the chairman of Lester's, seeking a private interview. The letter he received in reply was guarded to the point of hostility. Their secretaries agreed on a time and place for the meeting.

When Richard entered the chairman's office Jake Thomas rose from behind his desk and ushered him into a seat before returning to the leather chair that had been occupied by Richard's father for more than twenty years. The bookcases were not as full or the flowers as fresh as Richard remembered. The chairman's greeting was formal and short but Richard was not cowed by Thomas's approach as he knew that he was bargaining from strength. There was no small talk.

'Mr. Thomas, I feel that as I hold eight per cent of Lester's stock and have now moved to New York, the time has come for me to take my rightful place on the board of the bank.'

It was obvious from Jake Thomas's first words that he had anticipated what was on Richard's mind. 'I think in normal circumstances that might have been a good idea, Mr. Kane, but as the board has quite recently filled its last place perhaps the alternative would be for you to sell your stock in the bank.'

It was exactly the answer Richard had expected. 'Under no circumstances would I part with my family shares, Mr. Thomas. My father built this bank up to be one of the most respected financial institutions in America, and I intend to be closely involved in its future.'

'That's a pity, Mr. Kane, because I am sure you are aware that your father did not leave the bank in the happiest of circumstances and I feel certain we could have offered you a reasonable price for your shares.'

'Better than the price my father-in-law offered you for yours?' said Richard.

Jake Thomas's cheeks flushed brick-red. 'I see you have only come here to be destructive,' he said.

'I have often found in the past that construction must be preceded by a little destruction, Mr. Thomas.'

'I don't think you hold enough cards to make this house tumble,' the chairman retorted.

'No one knows better than you that two per cent may suffice,' said Richard.

'I can see no point in prolonging this conversation, Mr. Kane.'

'For the time being, I agree with you, but you can be sure that it will be continued in the not too distant future,' said Richard.

He rose to leave. Jake Thomas did not accept his outstretched hand.

'If that's his attitude, we must declare war,' said Florentyna.

'Brave words,' said Richard, 'but before we make our next move I want to consult my father's old lawyer, Thaddeus Cohen. There's nothing he doesn't know about Lester's bank. Perhaps if we combine our knowledge we can come up with something.'

Florentyna agreed. 'George once told me something my father thought of doing if he failed to remove your father even when he had eight per cent.'

Richard listened intently as Florentyna outlined the plan.

'Do you think that might work in this case?' she asked her husband.

'We just might pull it off, but it would be one hell of a risk.'

'The only thing we have to fear is fear itself,' said Florentyna.

'Jessie, when will you learn that F.D.R. was a politician, not a banker?'

Richard spent most of the next four days locked in consultation with Thaddeus Cohen at the city office of Cohen, Cohen, Yablons and Cohen.

'The only person who now holds eight per cent of Lester's stock is you,' he assured Richard from behind his desk. 'Even Jake Thomas has only two per cent. If your father had known that Thomas could only afford to hold on to Abel Rosnovski's stock for a few days, he might well have called his bluff and held on to the chair.'

The old family lawyer leaned back, placing both hands on top of his bald head.

'That piece of information will make victory even sweeter,' said Richard. 'Do you have the names of all the shareholders?'

'I'm still in possession of the names of the registered stockholders at the time that your father was the bank's chief executive. But by now it may be so out-of-date as to be rendered virtually useless. I don't have to remind someone with your training that you are entitled under state law to demand a formal inspection of the shareholders' list.'

'And I can imagine how long Thomas would take to release that.'

'Around Christmas would be my guess,' said Thaddeus Cohen, allowing himself a thin smile.

'What do you imagine would happen if I called an extraordinary meeting and gave a full account of how Jake Thomas sold his own stock in order to remove my father from the board?'

'You wouldn't gain a great deal from such an exercise, apart from embarrassing a few people. Jake Thomas would see that the meeting was held on an inconvenient day and badly attended. He would also undoubtedly obtain a fifty-one per cent proxy vote against any resolution you put forward. Into the bargain I suspect Mr. Thomas would use such a move by you to re-wash dirty linen in public which would only add a further stain to your father's reputation. No, I think Mrs. Kane has come up with the best idea so far and, if I may be permitted to say so, it is typical of her father's boldness in such matters.'

'But if we should fail?'

'I am not a betting man, but I'd back a Kane and Rosnovski against Jake Thomas any day.'

'If I agree, when should we launch the bid?' asked Richard.

'April 1st,' Thaddeus Cohen said unhesitatingly.

'Why that date in particular?'

'Because it's the right length of time before everyone has to file their tax returns to be fairly certain that quite a number of people will be in need of some spare cash.'

Richard went over the detailed plan with Thaddeus Cohen again, and that night he explained it in full to Florentyna.

'How much do we stand to lose if we fail?' was her first question.

'Roughly?'

'Roughly.'

'Thirty-seven million dollars.'

'That's pretty rough,' said Florentyna.

'We don't exactly lose the money, but all our capital will be locked up in Lester's stock and that would put a severe restriction on the cash flow for the rest of the group, if we didn't control the bank.'

'What does Mr. Cohen think of our chances of pulling that off?'

'Better than fifty-fifty. My father would never have considered going ahead with such odds,' added Richard.

'But my father would have,' said Florentyna. 'He always considered a glass to be half full, never half empty.'

'Thaddeus Cohen was right.'

'About what?'

'About you. He warned me that if you were anything like your father, prepare for battle.'

During the next three months Richard spent most of his time with accountants, lawyers and tax consultants, who had all the paperwork completed for him by March 15th. That afternoon, he booked space on every major financial page in America for April 1st and informed the advertising departments that the copy would arrive by hand twenty-four hours prior to publication. He couldn't help reflecting on the date, and wondered if it would be he or Jake Thomas who would end up the fool. During the final two weeks Richard and Thaddeus Cohen checked over the plan again and again to be certain they hadn't overlooked anything and could be confident that the details of 'Operation Bust a Gut' remained known to only three people.

On the morning of April 1st, Richard sat in his office and studied the full-page advertisement in the *Wall Street Journal*:

> The Baron Group announces that it will offer fourteen dollars for every Lester's Bank share. The current market value of Lester's shares is eleven dollars and a quarter. Any persons wishing to take advantage of this offer should contact their broker or write direct for details to Mr. Robin Oakley, Chase Manhattan Bank, One Chase Manhattan Plaza, New York, N.Y. 10005. This offer remains open until July 15th.

In his article on the facing page, Vermont Royster pointed out that this bold bid to take over Lester's must have had the support of Chase Manhattan, which would be holding the stock of the Baron Group as security. The columnist went on to predict that if the bid succeeded Richard Kane would undoubtedly be appointed the new chairman, a position his father had held for more than twenty years. If, on the other hand, the move failed, the Baron Group might find themselves with severe cash restrictions placed on their reserves for several years as the group would be encumbered with a large minority shareholding without actually controlling the bank. Richard could not have summed up the situation more accurately himself.

Florentyna called Richard's office to congratulate her husband on the way he had carried out 'Operation Bust a Gut'. 'Like Napoleon, you have remembered that the first rule of war is surprise.'

'Well, let's hope Jake Thomas is not my Waterloo.'

'You're such a pessimist, Mr. Kane. Just remember, Mr. Thomas is probably sitting in the nearest men's room at this moment, and he doesn't have a secret weapon and you do.'

'I do?' said Richard.

'Yes. Me.' The phone clicked and rang again immediately.

'Mr. Thomas of Lester's Bank on the line for you, Mr. Kane.'

I wonder if he has a phone in the men's room, thought Richard. 'Put him through,' he said, understanding for the first time a little of what the confrontation between his father and Abel Rosnovski must have been like.

'Mr. Kane, I thought we ought to see if we can sort out our differences. Perhaps I was a little over-cautious in not offering you a place on the board immediately.'

'I'm no longer interested in a place on the board, Mr. Thomas.'

'No? But I thought that –'

'No. I am now interested only in the chair.'

'You do realise that if you fail to secure fifty-one per cent of Lester's stock by July 15th, we could institute immediate changes in the allocation of bearers' stock and voting shares that will diminish the value of the stock you already hold? And I feel I should add that the members of the board already control between them forty per cent of Lester's stock, and I intend to contact all the other shareholders by telegram today with a recommendation not to take up your offer. Once I am in possession of another eleven per cent, you will have lost a small fortune.'

'That's a risk I'm willing to take,' said Richard.

'Well, if that's your attitude, Kane, I shall call a full shareholders' meeting for July 23rd. If you haven't obtained your fifty-one per cent by then I shall personally see to it that you are kept out of any dealing with this bank for as long as I am chairman.' Without warning Thomas's tone changed from bullying to ingratiating. 'Now perhaps you might like to reconsider your position.'

'When I left your office, Mr. Thomas, I made it clear what I had in mind. Nothing has changed.' Richard put the phone down, opened his diary to July 23rd and put a line through the page, writing across it: *Stockholders meeting, Lester's Bank*, with a large question mark. He received Jake Thomas's telegram to all stockholders that afternoon.

Every morning Richard followed the response to his advertisement with calls to Thaddeus Cohen and Chase Manhattan. By the end of the first week they had picked up thirty-one per cent of the shares, which with Richard's own eight per cent meant that they held thirty-nine per cent in all. If Thomas had in fact started with forty per cent, it was going to be a tight finish.

Two days later Richard received a detailed letter sent by Jake Thomas to all shareholders in which he advised strongly against consideration of the offer from the Baron Group. 'Your interests would be transferred into the hands of a company which until recently was controlled by a man convicted of bribery and corruption,' stated the final paragraph. Richard was disgusted by Jake Thomas's personal attack on Abel and he had never seen anything make Florentyna so angry.

'We are going to beat him, aren't we?' she asked, her fingers clenched into a tight fist.

'It will be close. I know they have over forty per cent among the directors and their friends. As of four o'clock this afternoon we have forty-one per cent, so it's a battle for the last nineteen per cent that will decide who wins on July 23rd.'

By the end of the month Richard heard nothing from Jake Thomas, which made him wonder if he had already captured fifty-one per cent, but with only eight weeks left until the stockholders' meeting it was Richard's turn to read over breakfast a full-page advertisement that made his heartbeat hit one hundred and twenty. On page thirty-seven of the *Wall Street Journal* Jake Thomas had made an announcement on behalf of Lester's. They were offering two million shares of authorised but previously unoffered stock to be sold for a newly set-up pension fund on behalf of the bank's employees.

In an interview with the *Journal*'s chief reporter, Thomas explained that this was a major step in profit sharing and that the funding of retirement income would be a model to the nation both inside and outside the banking community.

Richard swore uncharacteristically as he left the table and walked towards the phone, leaving his coffee to go cold.

'What did you say?' asked Florentyna.

'Balls,' he repeated, and passed over the paper. She read the news while Richard was dialling.

'What does it mean?'

'It means that, even if we do acquire fifty-one per cent of the present stock, with Thomas's authorised issue of a further two million new shares – which you can be sure would be sold only to the institutions – it'll be impossible to defeat the bastard on July 23rd.'

'Is it legal?' enquired Florentyna.

'That's what I'm about to find out,' said Richard.

Thaddeus Cohen gave him an immediate reply. 'It's legal, unless you succeed in getting a judge to stop them. I'm having the necessary papers drawn up now, but I warn you, if we are not granted a preliminary injunction you will never be chairman of Lester's.'

During the next twenty-four hours Richard found himself rushing in and out of lawyers' offices and courtrooms. He signed three affidavits and a judge in chambers heard the case for an injunction. This was followed by a special expedited appeal in front of a three-judge panel which, after a day of deliberation, decided by two to one in favour of holding up the share offering until the day after the extraordinary general meeting. Richard had won the battle but not the war; when he returned to his office the next morning he found he still had only forty-six per cent of the stock needed to defeat Jake Thomas.

'He must have the rest,' said Florentyna forlornly.

'I don't think so,' replied Richard.

'Why not?' she asked.

'Because he would not have bothered with that smoke screen exercise of the pension fund shares if he already had fifty-one per cent.'

'Good thinking, Mr. Kane.'

'The truth is,' said Richard, 'that he believes *we* have fifty-one per cent. So where is the missing five per cent?'

During the last few days of June, Richard had to be stopped from phoning Chase Manhattan every hour to discover if they had received any more shares. When July

15th came he had forty-nine per cent, and was acutely aware that in exactly eight days Thomas would be able to issue new voting shares that would make it virtually impossible for him ever to gain control of Lester's. Because of the cash flow requirements of the Baron Group, he would have to dump some of his Lester's shares immediately – no doubt, as Jake Thomas had predicted, at a considerable loss. He found himself mumbling 'two per cent, only two per cent', several times during the day.

With only a week to go Richard found it hard to concentrate on the new hotel fire regulations pending before Congress when Mary Preston rang.

'I don't know a Mary Preston,' Richard told his secretary.

'She says you would remember her as Mary Bigelow.'

Richard smiled, wondering what she could possibly want. He hadn't seen her since leaving Harvard. He picked up his phone. 'Mary, what a surprise. Or are you only phoning to complain about bad service at one of the Baron hotels?'

'No, no complaints, although we once spent a night at a Baron if you can remember that far back.'

'How could I forget?' he said, not remembering.

'No, I was only calling to seek your advice. Some years ago my great-uncle, Alan Lloyd, left me three per cent of Lester's. I received a letter from a Mr. Jake Thomas last week asking me to pledge those shares to the board and not to deal with you.'

Richard held his breath and could hear his heart beat.

'Are you still there, Richard?'

'Yes, Mary. I was just thinking. Well, the truth is . . .'

'Now don't start a long speech, Richard. Why don't you and your wife come and spend a night in Florida with my husband and me and then you can advise us.'

'Florentyna doesn't return from San Francisco until Sunday . . .'

'Then come on your own. I know Max would love to meet you.'

'Let me see if I can re-arrange a couple of things and then I will call you back within the hour.'

Richard phoned Florentyna who told him to drop everything and go on his own. 'On Monday morning we will be able to wave goodbye to Jake Thomas once and for all.'

Richard then informed Thaddeus Cohen of the news, who was delighted. 'On my list the stock is still under the name of Alan Lloyd.'

'Well, it's now in the name of Mrs. Max Preston.'

'I don't give a damn what her name is, just go and get it.'

Richard flew down on Saturday afternoon and was met at the West Palm beach airport by Mary's chauffeur who drove him out to the Prestons. When Richard first saw the house Mary was living in he wondered how they could fill it without about twenty children. The vast mansion stood on the far side of a golf course on the Inter-coastal Waterway. It took six minutes to drive from the Lion Lodge gates to the imposing forty steps in front of the house. Mary was standing on the top step waiting to greet him. She was dressed in a well-cut riding outfit. Her fair hair still touched her shoulders. As Richard looked up at her he recalled what had first attracted him nearly fifteen years before.

The butler whisked away Richard's overnight bag and ushered him into a bedroom large enough to hold a small convention. On the end of the bed was a riding outfit.

Mary and Richard rode around the grounds before dinner, and although there was no sign of Max she said he was expected about seven. Richard was thankful that Mary never went beyond a canter. It had been a long time since he had ridden with her and he knew he was going to be stiff in the morning. When they returned to the house Richard had a bath and changed into a dark suit before going down to the drawing room a little after seven. The butler poured him a sherry. When Mary floated into the room in a delicate off-the-shoulder evening dress the butler handed her a large whisky without waiting to be asked.

'I am sorry, Richard, but Max has just phoned to say he has been held up in Dallas and won't be back until late tomorrow afternoon. He will be very disappointed not to meet you.' Before Richard could comment, she added: 'Now let's go and have dinner and you can explain to me why the Baron Group needs my three per cent.'

Richard took her slowly through the story of what had happened since his father had taken over from her great-uncle. He hardly noticed the first two courses of dinner, he became so intent.

'So with my three per cent,' said Mary, 'the bank can return safely into the hands of the Kanes?'

'Yes,' said Richard. 'Five per cent is still missing, but as we already have forty-nine per cent, you can put us over the top.'

'That's simple enough,' said Mary, as the soufflé dish was whisked away. 'I shall speak to my broker on Monday and arrange everything. Let's go and have a celebration brandy in the library.'

'You don't know what a relief that will be,' said Richard, rising from his chair and following his hostess down a long corridor.

The library turned out to be the size of a basketball court with almost as many seats. Mary poured Richard a coffee while the butler offered him a Hine. She told the butler that that was all she needed for the rest of the evening and sat down next to Richard on the sofa.

'Quite like old times,' said Mary, edging towards him.

Richard agreed as he came back from his daydreams of being chairman of Lester's. He was enjoying the brandy and hardly noticed Mary rest her head on his shoulder. After she had poured him a second brandy he couldn't miss that her hand had shifted on to his leg. He took another sip of cognac. Suddenly and without warning she threw her arms around Richard and kissed him on the lips. When she eventually released him, he laughed and said, 'Just like old times.' He stood up and poured himself a large black coffee. 'What's keeping Max in Dallas?'

'Gas piping,' said Mary, without much enthusiasm. Richard remained standing by the mantelpiece.

During the next hour he learned all about gas piping and a little about Max. When the clock struck twelve he suggested it might be time to turn in. She made no comment, just rose from her seat and accompanied him up the vast staircase to his room. She walked away before he could kiss her good night.

Richard found it hard to sleep as his mind was a mixture of elation at having secured Mary's three per cent of Lester's coupled with his plans for how the take-over of the bank would be carried out with a minimum of disruption. He realised that, even as ex-chairman, Jake Thomas could still be a nuisance and was considering ways of controlling Thomas's anger at losing the take-over battle when he heard a slight click from the bedroom door. He glanced towards it to see the handle turning, and then the door itself pushed slowly open. Mary stood silhouetted, wearing a see-through pink negligee.

'Are you still awake?'

Richard lay motionless, wondering if he could get away with pretending to be asleep. But he was aware she might have seen him move, so he said, sleepily, 'Yes.' He was amused by the thought that this was not a time for thinking on his feet.

Mary padded over to the edge of the bed and sat down. 'Would you like anything?'

'A good night's sleep,' said Richard.

'I can think of two ways of helping you achieve that,' said Mary, leaning forward and stroking the back of his head. 'You could take a sleeping pill, or we could make love.'

'That's a nice idea, but I've already taken the sleeping pill,' said Richard, drowsily.

'It doesn't seem to have had the desired effect, so perhaps we should try the second remedy,' said Mary. She lifted the negligee over her head, allowing it to fall to the floor. Then without another word she slipped under the covers, drawing herself close to Richard. Richard could feel that her firm figure was that of a woman who did a lot of exercise and had had no children.

'Hell, I wish I hadn't taken that pill,' said Richard, 'or at least I could stay another night.'

Mary started kissing Richard's neck while running a hand down his back until she reached between his legs.

Christ, thought Richard, I'm only human. And then a door slammed. Mary threw back the covers, grabbed her negligee, ran across the room, and disappeared faster than a thief when a hall light is turned on. Richard pulled the sheets back over his body and listened to a murmur of conversation which he couldn't make out. He spent the rest of the night in a fitful sleep.

When he came down to breakfast the next morning, he found Mary chatting to an elderly man who must once have been very handsome.

The man rose and shook Richard by the hand. 'Allow me to introduce myself. I'm Max Preston,' he said. 'Although I hadn't planned to be with you this weekend, my business finished early and I managed to catch the last flight out of Dallas. I certainly wouldn't have wanted you to leave my home without having experienced true southern hospitality.' Max and Richard chatted over breakfast about the problems they were both facing on Wall Street. They were deep into the effects of Nixon's new tax regulations when the butler announced that the chauffeur was waiting to take Mr. Kane to the airport.

The Prestons accompanied Richard down the forty steps to the waiting car, where Richard turned and kissed Mary on the cheek, thanked her for all she had done and shook Max warmly by the hand.

'I hope we shall meet again,' said Max.

'That's a nice idea. Why don't you give me a call when you're next in New York?' Mary smiled at him gently.

Mary and Max Preston waved as the Rolls-Royce glided down the long drive. Once his plane had taken off, Richard felt a tremendous sense of relief. The stewardess served him a cocktail and he began to think about his plans for Monday. To his delight Florentyna was waiting for him on his return to Sixty-fourth Street.

'The shares are ours,' he told her triumphantly and went over the full details during dinner. They fell asleep on the sofa by the fire a little before midnight, Florentyna's hand resting on his leg.

The next morning Richard placed a call through to Jake Thomas to inform him he was now in possession of fifty-one per cent.

Richard could hear an intake of breath.

'As soon as the certificates are in my lawyer's hands, I shall come over to the bank and let you know how I expect the transition to be carried out.'

'Of course,' said Thomas resignedly. 'May I ask from whom you obtained the last two per cent?'

'Yes, from an old friend of mine, Mary Preston.'

There was a pause at the other end. 'Not Mrs. Max Preston of Florida?' asked Jake Thomas.

'Yes,' said Richard triumphantly.

'Then you needn't bother to come over, Mr. Kane, because Mrs. Preston lodged her three per cent of Lester's with us four weeks ago and we have been in possession of the stock certificates for some time.' The phone clicked. It was Richard's turn to gasp.

When Richard told Florentyna about the new development all she could say was: 'You should have slept with the damned woman. I bet Jake Thomas would have.'

'Would you have slept with Scott Forbes in the same circumstances?'

'Good God, no, Mr. Kane.'

'Precisely, Jessie.'

Richard spent another sleepless night thinking of how that final two per cent might still be acquired. It was obvious that both sides now had forty-nine per cent of the stock. Thaddeus Cohen had already warned him that he must face reality and start thinking of ways to recoup the maximum amount of cash for the shares he already had. Perhaps he should take a leaf out of Abel's book and sell heavily the day before the meeting. Richard continued to toss and turn as useless ideas rushed through his mind. He turned over once again and tried to catch some sleep precisely when Florentyna woke with a start.

'Are you awake?' she asked quietly.

'Yes, chasing two per cent.'

'So am I. Do you remember your mother telling us that someone had purchased two per cent from a Mr. Peter Parfitt on behalf of your father to stop my father getting his hands on it?'

'Yes, I do,' said Richard.

'Well, perhaps they haven't heard about our offer.'

'My darling, it's been in every paper in the United States.'

'So have the Beatles, but not everyone has heard of them.'

'I suppose it's worth a try,' said Richard, picking up the phone by the side of his bed.

'Who are you calling? The Beatles?'

'No, my mother.'

'At four o'clock in the morning? You can't ring your mother in the middle of the night.'

'I can and I must.'

'I wouldn't have told you if I'd known you might do that.'

'Darling, there are only two and a half days to go before I lose you thirty-seven million dollars, and the owner of the shares we need so badly might live in Australia.'

'Good point, Mr Kane.'

Richard dialled the number and waited. A sleepy voice answered the phone.

'Mother?'

'Yes, Richard. What time is it?'

'Four o'clock in the morning. I'm sorry to bother you, but there is no one else I can turn to. Now please listen carefully. You once said that a friend of father's bought two per cent of Lester's shares from Peter Parfitt to keep the stock from falling into the hands of Florentyna's father. Can you remember who it was?'

There was a pause. 'Yes, I think so. It will come back to me if you hold on a minute. Yes, it was an old friend from England, a banker who had been at Harvard with your father. The name will come in a moment.' Richard held his breath. Florentyna sat up in bed.

'Dudley, Colin Dudley, the chairman of . . . oh dear, I can't remember.'

'Don't worry, Mother, that's enough to be getting on with. You go back to sleep.'

'What a thoughtful and considerate son you are,' said Kate Kane as she put the phone down.

'Now what, Richard?'

'Just make breakfast.'

Florentyna kissed him on the forehead and disappeared.

Richard picked up the phone. 'International operator, please. What time is it in London?'

'Seven minutes past nine.'

Richard flicked through his personal phone book and said, 'Please connect me to 01-735-7227.'

He waited impatiently. A voice came on the line.

'Bank of America.'

'Put me through to Jonathan Coleman, please.'

Another wait.

'Jonathan Coleman.'

'Good morning, Jonathan, it's Richard Kane.'

'Nice to hear from you, Richard. What are you up to?'

'I need some information urgently. Which bank is Colin Dudley chairman of?'

'Hold on a minute, Richard, and I'll look him up in the *Bankers' Year Book*.' Richard could hear the pages turning. 'Robert Fraser and Company,' came back the reply. 'Only now he's Sir Colin Dudley.'

'What's his number?'

'493-3211.'

'Thank you, Jonathan. I'll give you a call when I'm next in London.'

Richard wrote the number on the corner of an envelope and dialled the international operator again as Florentyna came into the bedroom.

'Getting anywhere?'

'I'm about to find out. Operator, can you please get me a number in London, 493-3211.' Florentyna sat on the end of the bed while Richard waited.

'Robert Fraser and Company.'

'May I speak to Sir Colin Dudley, please.'

'Who shall I say is calling, sir?'

'Richard Kane of the Baron Group, New York.'

'Hold on please, sir.'

Richard waited again.

'Good morning. Dudley here.'

'Good morning, Sir Colin. My name is Richard Kane. I think you knew my father?'

'Of course. We were at Harvard together. Good chap, your old man. I was very sad to read about his death. Wrote to your mother at the time. Where are you calling from?'

'New York.'

'Get up early, you Americans, don't you? So what can I do for you?'

'Do you still own two per cent of Lester's Bank shares?' Richard held his breath again.

'Yes, I do. Paid a bloody king's ransom for them. Still, can't complain. Your father did me a few favours in his time.'

'Would you consider selling them, Sir Colin?'

'If you're willing to offer me a sensible price.'

'How much would you consider sensible?'

There was a long pause. 'Eight hundred thousand dollars.'

'I accept,' said Richard, without hesitation, 'but I must be able to pick them up tomorrow, and I'm not risking a courier service. If I bank-transfer the money, can you have all the paperwork done by the time I arrive?'

'Simple, dear boy,' Dudley said without demur. 'I'll also have a car meet you at the airport and put at your disposal while you're in London.'

'Thank you, Sir Colin.'

'Go easy with the "Sir", young fellow. I've reached that age when I prefer to be called by my Christian name. Just let me know when you expect to arrive and everything will be ready for you.'

'Thank you . . . Colin.'

Richard put the phone down.

'You're not getting dressed, are you?'

'I certainly am. I won't get any more sleep tonight. Now where's my breakfast?'

By six o'clock, Richard was booked on the nine fifteen flight from Kennedy Airport. He had also booked himself on a return flight the following morning at eleven arriving back in New York by one thirty-five the following afternoon, giving him twenty-four hours to spare before the stockholders' meeting at two o'clock on Wednesday.

'Running things a bit close, aren't we?' said Florentyna, 'but, fear not, I believe in you. By the way, William is expecting you to bring him back a model of a red London bus.'

'You're always making these major commitments on my behalf. It's a heavy load I carry as the chief executive of your group.'

'I know, dear, and to think it's only because you sleep with the chairman.'

By seven Richard was seated at his office desk writing explicit instructions for the transfer of the eight hundred thousand dollars by telex to Robert Fraser and Company, Albemarle Street, London W.1. Richard knew the money would be in Sir Colin Dudley's bank long before he was. At seven thirty he was driven to the airport and he checked in. The 747 took off on time and he arrived at London's Heathrow at ten o'clock that night. Sir Colin Dudley had been as good as his word. A driver was waiting to pick him up and whisk him off to the Baron. The manager had put him in the Davis Leroy Suite. The Presidential Suite, he explained, was already occupied by Mr. Jagger. The rest of his group had taken over the ninth floor.

'I don't think I know the group,' said Richard. 'What area do they specialise in?'

'Singing,' said the manager.

When Richard checked at the reception desk, there was a message waiting for him from Sir Colin suggesting they meet at the bank at nine the following morning.

Richard dined quietly in his rooms and called Florentyna to bring her up to date before going to bed.

'Hang in there, Mr. Kane. We're all depending on you.'

Richard woke at seven and packed before going down to breakfast. His father had always gone on about the kippers in London, so he ordered them with some anticipation. When he had finished the last morsel, he realised that they were so good that he would undoubtedly bore his own son with the same story for many years to come. After breakfast, he walked round Hyde Park to kill the hour before the bank opened. The park was green and the flowerbeds a mass of untouched roses. He couldn't help but compare its beauty to Central Park, and recalled that London still had five royal parks of a similar size.

As nine o'clock struck, Richard walked in the front door of Robert Fraser and Company in Albemarle Street only a few hundred yards from the Baron. A secretary ushered him through to Sir Colin Dudley's office.

'Had a feeling you'd be on time, old fellow, so I have everything prepared for you. I once remember finding your father sitting on the doorstep with the milk bottles. Everybody drank black coffee that day.'

Richard laughed.

'Your eight hundred thousand dollars arrived before close of business yesterday so all I have to do is sign the share certificates over to you in the presence of a witness.' Sir Colin flicked a switch. 'Can you come in, Margaret?' Sir Colin's private secretary watched the chairman of one bank sign the transfer certificates so that the recipient could become the chairman of another bank.

Richard checked over the documents, carefully signed his part of the agreement and was handed a receipt for eight hundred thousand dollars.

'Well, I hope that all the trouble you've taken in coming yourself will ensure that you become the chairman of Lester's, old chap.'

Richard stared at the elderly man with the white walrus

moustache, bald head and military bearing. 'I had no idea you realised . . .'

'Wouldn't want you Americans to think we're altogether asleep over here. Now you bustle off and catch the eleven o'clock from Heathrow and you'll make your meeting easily: not many of my customers pay as promptly as you do. By the way, congratulations on that moon chappie.'

'What?' said Richard.

'You've put a man on the moon.'

'Good heavens,' said Richard.

'No, not quite,' said Sir Colin, 'but I'm sure that's what NASA has planned next.'

Richard laughed and thanked Sir Colin again. He walked quickly back to the Baron, literally humming. He knew exactly what it felt like to be the man on the moon. He had left his overnight bag with the porter so he was able to check out quickly, and Sir Colin's chauffeur drove him back to Heathrow. Richard entered Terminal Three well in time to check in for the eleven o'clock flight. He was going to be back in New York with twenty-four hours to spare: if his father had had to make the same transaction before he became chairman the process would have taken at least two weeks.

Richard sat in the Clipper Club lounge toying with a Martini while reading in *The Times* about Rod Laver's fourth Wimbledon triumph, unable to see the fog descending outside. It wasn't until thirty minutes later that an announcement warned passengers that there would be a short delay on all flights. An hour later, they called Richard's flight, but as he walked across the tarmac he could see the fog growing denser by the minute. He sat in his seat, belt fastened, reading a copy of the previous week's *Time* magazine, willing himself not to look outside, waiting to feel the plane move. Nixon, he read, had named the first women generals, Colonel Elizabeth Hoisington and Colonel Anne Mae Hays; no doubt the first Nixon initiative that Florentyna would approve of, he thought.

'We are sorry to announce that this flight has been delayed until further notice because of fog.' A groan went up inside the first-class cabin. 'Passengers should return to the terminal where they will be issued with luncheon vouchers and advised when to reboard the aircraft. Pan American apologises for the delay and hopes it will not cause any great inconvenience.' Richard had to smile, despite himself. Back inside the terminal, he went around to every ticket counter to discover who had the first plane out. It turned out to be an Air Canada flight to Montreal. He reserved a seat, after being told that his Pan Am flight to New York was now the twenty-seventh in line for departure. He then checked the flights out of Montreal to New York. There was one every two hours and the flying time was just over an hour. He pestered Pan American and Air Canada every thirty minutes but the polite bland reply remained unvaried: 'I'm sorry, sir, we can do nothing until the fog lifts.'

At two in the afternoon, he called Florentyna to warn her about the delay.

'Not impressive, Mr. Kane. While you're on the phone, did you manage to pick up a red London bus for William?'

'Damn. I completely forgot.'

'Not doing very well today, Mr. Kane. Better try the duty-free gift shop, hadn't we?'

Richard found an airport shop that sold several sizes of London buses. He selected a large plastic one and paid for it with the last of his English money. With the bus safely under his arm he decided to use his luncheon voucher. He sat down to the worst airport lunch he had ever had: one thin piece of beef about an inch square that had been misleadingly described as a minute steak on the menu, along with three tired lettuce leaves posing as a side salad. He checked his watch. It was already three o'clock. For two hours, he tried to read a copy of *The French Lieutenant's Woman* but he was so anxious listening to every radio announcement that he never got past page four.

At seven o'clock, after Richard had walked around Terminal Three several times, he began to think it would soon be too late for planes to take off whatever the weather. The loudspeaker forbodingly warned of an important announcement to follow shortly. He stood like a statue as the words came out. 'We are sorry to announce that all flights out of Heathrow have been cancelled until tomorrow morning with the exception of Iran Air Flight 006 to Jeddah and Air Canada flight 009 to Montreal.' Richard had been saved by his foresight: he knew the Air Canada flight would be completely sold out within minutes. Once again he sat in a first-class lounge. Although the flight was further delayed it was eventually called a few minutes after eight. Richard almost cheered when the 747 took off a little after nine o'clock. Thereafter he found himself checking his watch every few minutes. The flight was uneventful except for more appalling food and the plane eventually landed at Montreal airport shortly before eleven.

Richard sprinted to the American Airlines counter to discover that he had missed the last flight to New York by a few minutes. He swore out loud.

'Don't worry, sir, there is a flight at ten twenty-five tomorrow morning.'

'What time does it arrive in New York?'

'Eleven thirty.'

'Two hours and thirty minutes to spare,' he said out loud. 'It's a bit tight. Can I hire a private plane?' The clerk looked at his watch, 'Not at this time of night, sir.'

Richard thumped the desk and reserved a seat and took a room in the Airport Baron and phoned Florentyna.

'Where are you now?' she asked.

'The Airport Baron, Montreal.'

'Curiouser and curiouser.'

Richard explained what had happened.

'Poor darling. Did you remember the red London bus?'

'Yes, I'm clinging on to it, but my overnight bag is still on the Pam Am flight to New York.'

'And the stock certificates?'

'They are in my briefcase and have never left my side.'

'Well done, Mr. Kane. I'll have a car waiting for you at the airport and Mr. Cohen and I will be at the stockholders' meeting at Lester's clutching on to our forty-nine per cent. So if you're in possession of your two per cent, Jake Thomas will be on the dole by this time tomorrow.'

'How can you be so cool about it?'

'You've never let me down yet. Sleep well.'

Richard did not sleep well, and was back at the American Airlines terminal hours before the plane was due for boarding. There was a slight delay but the captain was still anticipating that he could land at Kennedy by eleven thirty. Richard had no baggage and felt confident he could now make the meeting with at least half an hour to spare. For the first time in over twenty-four hours he began to relax, and even made some notes for his first speech as Lester's chairman.

When the 707 arrived at Kennedy it began to circle the airport. Richard looked out of his little window and could clearly see the building in Wall Street that he had to be at within two hours. He thumped his knee in anger. At last the plane descended a few hundred feet, only to start circling again.

'This is Captain James McEwen speaking. I am sorry for this delay, but we have been put into a holding pattern because of traffic congestion. It seems there are some delayed flights from London now arriving into New York.' Richard wondered if the Pan American flight from Heathrow would land before he did.

Five minutes, ten minutes, fifteen minutes. Richard checked the agenda. Item number one – a motion to reject the take-over bid by the Baron Group. Item number two – the issue of new voting shares. If they couldn't prove they had fifty-one per cent, Jake Thomas would close the proceedings within minutes of the meeting starting. The plane began to descend and the wheels touched the ground at twelve twenty-seven. Richard sprinted through the terminal. He passed his chauffeur on the run, who quickly followed him to the car park, where Richard once again checked his watch. An hour and twenty minutes to spare. He was going to make the meeting comfortably.

'Step on it,' said Richard.

'Yes, sir,' said the chauffeur as he moved into the left-hand lane of the Van Wyck Expressway. Richard heard the siren a few minutes later and a policeman on a motorcycle overtook the car and waved them on to the hard shoulder. The policeman parked and walked slowly towards Richard who had already leaped out of the car. Richard tried to explain it was a matter of life and death.

'It always is,' said the officer. 'Either that or "My wife is having a baby".' Richard left his chauffeur to deal with the policeman while he tried to hail a passing cab: but they were all full. Sixteen minutes later the policeman let them go. It was one twenty-nine as they crossed the Brooklyn Bridge and turned on to F.D.R. Drive. Richard could see the giant skyscrapers of Wall Street in the distance but the cars were bumper to bumper all the way. It was six minutes to two before they reached Wall Street when Richard could bear it no longer and jumped out of the car, briefcase under one arm, a red London bus under the other, and sprinted the last three blocks, dodging slow pedestrians and fast honking cab drivers. He heard the clock at Trinity Church chime two as he reached Bowling Green and prayed that it was fast as he raced up the steps of the Lester's building, suddenly realising he didn't know where the meeting was being held.

'Fifty-first floor, sir,' the doorman informed him.

The 30 to 60 elevator was full with the post-lunch hour crowd and it stopped at 31 – 33 – 34 – 42 – 44 – 47 – 50 – 51. Richard jumped out of the elevator and ran down the corridor following the red arrow that indicated where the meeting was taking place. As he arrived in the crowded room, one or two faces turned to look at him. There must have been over five hundred people seated listening to the chairman, but he was the only shareholder sweating from head to toe. He was greeted by the sight of a cool Jake Thomas, who gave him a knowing smile from the platform. Richard realised he was too late. Florentyna was sitting in the front row, her head bowed. He took a seat at the back of the room and listened to the chairman of Lester's.

'All of us believe that the decision that has been made

today is in the best interests of the bank. In the circumstances that your board of directors faced, no one will have been surprised by my request, and Lester's will now continue its traditional role as one of America's great financial institutions. Item number two,' said Jake Thomas. Richard felt sick. 'My final task as chairman of Lester's is to propose that the new chairman be Mr. Richard Kane.'

Richard could not believe his ears. A little old lady rose from her seat in the front row and said that she would like to second the motion because she felt that Mr. Kane's father had been one of the finest chairmen the bank had ever had. There was a round of applause as the old lady sat down.

'Thank you,' said Jake Thomas. 'Those in favour of the resolution?' Richard stared into the body of the hall as hands shot into the air.

'Those against.' Jake Thomas looked down from the platform. 'Good, the resolution is carried unanimously. I am now happy to invite your new chairman to address you. Ladies and gentlemen, Mr. Richard Kane.' Richard walked forward and everyone stood up and applauded. As he passed Florentyna he handed her the red bus.

'Glad you accomplished *something* on your trip to London,' she whispered.

Richard walked, dazed, on to the platform. Jake Thomas shook his hand warmly and then took a seat on the end of the row.

'I have little to say on this occasion,' began Richard, 'other than to assure you that I wish Lester's to carry on in the same tradition as it did under my father and that I will dedicate myself to that end.' Unable to think of anything else to add, he smiled and said, 'I thank you for your attendance today and look forward to seeing you all at the annual meeting.' There followed another round of applause and the shareholders began to disperse chattering.

As soon as they could escape from those who wished to talk to Richard, either to congratulate him or tell him how they felt Lester's should be run, Florentyna led him away to the chairman's office. He stood and stared at the portrait of his father that hung over the fireplace and turned to his wife.

'How did you manage it, Jessie?'

'Well, I remembered a piece of advice my governess taught me when I was younger. Contingency, Miss Tredgold used to say. Always have a contingency plan ready in case it rains. When you called from Montreal I was afraid there might be an outside chance it would pour, and you wouldn't make the meeting. So I rang Thaddeus Cohen and explained what my contingency plan was, and he spent the morning drawing up the necessary documents.'

'What documents?' said Richard.

'Patience, Mr. Kane. I do feel after my triumph that I have the right to spin out this tale a little longer.'

Richard remained impatiently silent.

'When I had the vital document in my hand, I phoned Jake Thomas and asked if he could see me twenty minutes before the stockholders' meeting was due to start. Had you arrived in time, I would have cancelled the confrontation with Mr. Thomas, but you didn't.'

'But your plan . . .'

'My father – no fool – told me once a skunk, always a skunk, and he turned out to be right. At the meeting with Thomas I informed him that we were in possession of fifty-one per cent of Lester's stock. He was disbelieving until I mentioned the name of Sir Colin Dudley and then he turned quite pale. I placed the whole bundle of certificates on the table in front of him and, before he could check them, told him that if he sold me his two per cent before two o'clock I would still pay him the full fourteen dollars per share. I added that he must also sign a document saying he would resign as chairman and make no attempt to interfere in any future dealings involving Lester's Bank. For good measure, although it was not in the contract, he must propose you for chairman.'

'My God, Jessie, you have the nerve of ten men.'

'No. One woman.'

Richard laughed. 'What was Thomas's response?'

'Asked what I would do if he refused. If you refuse, I told

him, we'll sack you publicly without compensation for loss of office. Then I pointed out to him that he would have to sell his stock for the best price he could get on the open market because as long as we had fifty-one per cent of Lester's he would play no part in the future of the bank.'

'And then?'

'He signed there and then without even consulting his fellow directors.'

'Brilliant, Jessie, both in conception and execution.'

'Thank you, Mr. Kane. I do hope that now you are chairman of a bank you won't be running all over the world getting yourself delayed, missing meetings and having nothing to show for your troubles other than a model of a red London bus. By the way, did you remember to bring a present for Annabel?'

Richard looked embarrassed. Florentyna bent down and handed him an F.A.O. Schwarz shopping bag. He lifted out a package that showed a picture of a toy typewriter on the outside with 'Made in England' printed all along the bottom of the box.

'Just not your day is it, Mr. Kane? By the way, Neil Armstrong got back quicker than you did. Perhaps we should invite him to join the board?'

Richard read Vermont Royster's article in the *Wall Street Journal* the next morning:

> Mr. Richard Kane seems to have won a bloodless coup in his bid to become chairman of Lester's. There was no vote taken by shareholders at the extraordinary meeting, and his succession to the chair was proposed by the retiring incumbent, Jake Thomas, and carried unanimously.
>
> Many stockholders present at the meeting referred to the traditions and standards set by the late William Lowell Kane, the present chairman's father. Lester's stock ended the day up two points on the New York Exchange.

'That's the last we'll hear of Jake Thomas,' said Florentyna.

24

Richard had never heard of Major Abanjo before that morning. Neither had anyone else in America other than those who took an over-zealous interest in the affairs of Nambawe, Central Africa's smallest state. Nevertheless, it was Major Abanjo who caused Richard to run late for his most important appointment that day, the eleventh birthday party of his only son.

When Richard arrived back at the apartment on Sixty-fourth Street, Major Abanjo was driven from his mind by Annabel, who had a few minutes earlier poured a pot of tea over William's hand because she wasn't receiving enough attention. She hadn't realised that it was boiling hot. It seemed that Carol had been in the kitchen fussing over the birthday cake at the time. Annabel was getting even less attention now that William was screaming at the top of his voice and all the other children had to be sent home. A few minutes later Annabel was also screaming, after Richard had placed her across his knee and administered six hard whacks with his slipper before both children were put to bed – William with two aspirins and an ice pack to help him sleep and Annabel as a further punishment. Eleven candles – and one to grow on – had burned themselves down to the icing on the large cake that remained untouched on the dining-room table.

'I'm afraid William will have a scar on his right hand for the rest of his life,' said Florentyna after she had checked to see that her son was at last asleep.

'Still, he took it like a man.'

'I don't agree,' said Florentyna. 'He never once grumbled.'

'It probably wouldn't have happened if I had been on time,' said Richard, ignoring her comment. 'Damn Major Abanjo.'

'Who is Major Abanjo?' asked Florentyna.

'A young army officer who was behind the coup in Nambawe today.'

'Why should a little African state stop you being on time for William's birthday party?'

'That little African state has an outstanding five-year loan agreement of three hundred million dollars that Lester's led on in 1966 and the repayment date is due in three months' time.'

'We are in for three hundred million dollars?' said Florentyna, flabbergasted.

'No, no,' said Richard. 'We covered the first fifteen per cent of the loan, and the remaining eighty-five million was divided among thirty-seven other financial institutions.'

'Can we survive a loss of forty-five million dollars?'

'Yes we can, as long as the Baron Group remains our friend,' said Richard, smiling at his wife. 'It's three years' profits down the drain, not to mention a severe blow to our reputation with the other thirty-seven banks involved and the inevitable drop in our stock price tomorrow.'

Lester's stock price dropped the next day by more than Richard had anticipated, for two reasons. The newly self-appointed President of Nambawe, General Abanjo, announced that he had no intention of honouring previous government commitments made with any 'fascist regime' including America, Britain, France, Germany and Japan. Richard wondered how many Russian bankers were boarding planes to Central Africa at that moment.

The second reason became apparent when a reporter from the *Wall Street Journal* called Richard and asked him if he had any statement to make about the coup.

'I really have nothing to say,' said Richard, trying to sound as if the whole episode were about as troublesome to him as brushing a fly off his sleeve. 'I feel sure the problem will sort itself out during the next few days. After all, the loan is only one of many that Lester's is involved with at the present time.'

'Mr. Jake Thomas might not agree with that opinion,' said the journalist.

'You have spoken to Mr. Thomas?' said Richard in disbelief.

'Yes, he called the *Journal* earlier today and had an off-the-record conversation with our publisher, leaving us in no doubt that he would be surprised if Lester's could survive such a demand on cash flow.'

'No comment,' said Richard curtly, and put the phone down.

At Richard's request, Florentyna called a board meeting of the Baron Group to ensure enough financial backing to see that Lester's could survive a run on its stock. To their surprise, George was not at all convinced that the Baron Group should enmesh itself in Lester's problems. He told them that he had never approved of using the Baron shares as security for the take-over of the bank in the first place.

'I remained silent at the time but I'm not willing to do so on a second occasion,' he said, his hands resting on the board-room table. 'Abel never liked throwing good money after bad whatever his personal involvement. He used to say that anyone could *talk* about future profits and start spending money they hadn't yet earned. Have you considered that we might both end up going bankrupt?'

'The sum involved is not that large to the Baron Group,' said Richard.

'Abel always considered any loss caused ten times the problem of any profit,' George told him. 'And what outstanding loans do you have to other countries around the world which could be taken over while we are asleep in bed?'

'Only one outside the E.E.C., and that's a loan of two hundred million to the Shah of Iran. Again we are the lead bank with a commitment of thirty million, but Iran has never missed an interest payment by so much as an hour.'

'When is their final payment due?' asked George.

Richard flicked through a bulky file that lay on the table in front of him and ran his forefinger down a column of figures. Although nettled by George's attitude, he was pleased to be well-prepared for any query that might arise.

'June 19th, 1978.'

'Then I want an assurance you won't involve the bank again when the loan comes up for renewal,' said George firmly.

'What?' said Richard. 'The Shah is as safe as the Bank of England –'

'Which hasn't proved to be so solid lately.'

Richard was beginning to look angry and was about to respond when Florentyna interrupted.

'Hold on, Richard. If Lester's agrees not to renew its loan with the Shah in 1978, or involve itself in any further Third World commitments, George, will you in turn agree to the Baron Group's underwriting the forty-five million loss on the African contract?'

'No, I'd still need some more convincing.'

'Like what?' said Richard.

'Richard, you don't have to raise your voice. I am still the President of the Baron Group and have given thirty years of my life to building the company up to its present position. I don't intend at this late stage to watch that achievement demolished in thirty minutes.'

'I'm sorry,' said Richard. 'I haven't had much sleep for the last four days. What would you like to know, George?'

'Other than the agreement with the Shah, is Lester's committed to any other loans over ten million?'

'No,' said Richard. 'Most major country to country loans are serviced by the prime banks like Chase or Chemical and we end up with only a tiny percentage of the capital sum. Obviously Jake Thomas felt that Nambawe, which is rich in copper and manganite, was as sure a bet as he could hope to find.'

'We already know, to our cost, that Mr. Thomas is fallible,' said George. 'So, what other loans above five million remain outstanding to the bank?'

'Two,' replied Richard. 'One with General Electricity in Australia for seven million, which is secured by the government, and one with ICI in London. Both are five-year loans with set payment dates and so far repayments have been met on schedule.'

'So if the group wrote off the forty-five million, how long would it take Lester's to recoup the loss?'

'That would depend on the percentage any lender required and over what period of time the money was loaned.'

'Fifteen per cent over five years.'

'Fifteen per cent?' repeated Richard, shocked.

'The Baron Group is not a charity, Richard, and as long as I am President it is not in business to prop up ailing banks. We are hoteliers by trade and have shown a seventeen per cent return on our money over the past thirty years. If we loaned you forty-five million, could you pay it back in five years at fifteen per cent?'

Richard hesitated, scribbled some figures on the pad in front of him and checked his file before he spoke. 'Yes, I am confident we could repay every penny in five years, even assuming the African contract is a total write-off,' he said quietly.

'I think we must treat the contract precisely that way,' said George. 'My informants tell me that the former head of state, King Erobo, has escaped to London, taken up residence at Claridge's and is looking at a house which is for sale in Chelsea Square. It appears he has more money stashed away in Switzerland than anyone other than the Shah, so I feel he is unlikely to return to Africa in a hurry – and I can't say I blame him.' Richard tried to smile as George continued. 'Subject to all you have told us being confirmed by the Baron's auditors, I agree to covering the African loan on the terms stated, and I wish you luck, Richard. I'll also let you in on a little secret: Abel didn't like Jake Thomas any more than you do, which is what tipped the balance for me.' George closed his file. 'I hope you will both excuse me now as I have a lunch appointment with Conrad Hilton and he has never once been late in thirty years.'

When George had closed the door behind him, Richard turned to Florentyna. 'Jesus, whose side does he think he's on?'

'Ours,' replied Florentyna. 'Now I know why my father happily trusted him to run the group while he went off to fight the Germans.'

A statement in the *Wall Street Journal* the following day, confirming that the Baron Group had underwritten Lester's loans, caused the bank's stocks to rise again and Richard settled down to what he called 'my five years of drudgery'.

'What are you going to do about Jake Thomas?'

'Ignore him,' said Richard. 'Time is on my side. No bank in New York will employ him once it's known that he is willing to run to the press whenever he has a disagreement with his past employers.'

'But how will anyone ever find out?'

'Darling, if the *Wall Street Journal* knows, everybody knows.'

Richard turned out to be right; the whole story was repeated back to him over a lunch he had with a director of Bankers Trust only a week later. The director went on to remark, 'That man's broken the golden rule of banking. From now on, he'll even find it hard to open a current account.'

William recovered from his burns far more quickly than Florentyna had expected and returned to school a few days later with a scar on his hand too small even to impress his friends. For the first few days after the accident Annabel looked away every time she saw the scar and seemed genuinely contrite.

'Do you think he's forgiven me?' she asked her mother.

'Of course, my darling. William is just like his father – forgets any quarrel by the next morning.'

*

Florentyna considered that the time had come for her to make a tour of the Baron hotels in Europe. Her staff worked out a detailed itinerary which took in Rome, Paris, Madrid, Lisbon, Berlin, Amsterdam, Stockholm, London and even Warsaw. She felt a new confidence in leaving George in control, she told Richard as they were driven to the airport. He agreed and then reminded her that they had never been apart for as long as three weeks since the day they had met.

'You'll survive, darling.'

'I'll miss you, Jessie.'

'Now, don't you get all sentimental. You know that I have to work for the rest of my life to make sure that my husband can continue posing as chairman of a New York bank.'

'I love you,' said Richard.

'I love you too,' said Florentyna. 'But you still owe me fifteen million and fifty-six dollars.'

'Where does the fifty-six come from?' said Richard.

'From our days in San Francisco. You've never repaid me that fifty-six dollars I lent you before we were married.'

'*You* said it was a dowry.'

'No, you said it was a dowry. I said it was a loan. I think I shall have to take George's advice about how it should be repaid as soon as I return. Perhaps fifteen per cent over five years would seem reasonable, Mr. Kane, which means you must now owe me around four hundred dollars.' She leaned up and kissed him goodbye.

Richard was driven back to New York by the chauffeur and on arrival at his office he immediately phoned Cartier's in London. He gave clear instructions what he required and said it had to be ready in eighteen days.

The time had come for Richard to prepare his annual general report for the bank. The red African figure maddened him. Without it, Lester's would have shown a healthy profit: so much for hoping he would beat Jake Thomas's figures in his first year. All that the stockholders would remember was a thumping loss compared with 1970.

Richard followed Florentyna's detailed schedule with interest every day and made sure that he caught up with her by phone at least once in every capital. She seemed pleased by most of what she had seen, and although she had a few ideas for changes she had to admit that the hotels on the Continent were well run by the group's European directors. Any excess expenditure had been caused by her own demands for higher standards of architecture. When she phoned from Paris Richard passed on the news that William had won the class mathematics prize and that he was now confident that his son would be accepted by St. Paul's. And since the hot water incident Annabel had tried a little harder at school and had even scraped herself off the bottom of the class. She considered it the best news Richard had given her.

'Where's your next stop?' Richard asked.

'London,' she replied.

'Great. I've got a feeling I know someone you'll want to call when you're there,' he said with a chuckle, and went to bed feeling better than he had for some days.

He heard from Florentyna a lot earlier than he had expected. Around six o'clock the next morning Richard was in a deep sleep, dreaming that he and General Abanjo were having a shoot-out; Richard pulled the trigger, the bullet fired. Then the phone rang. He woke up and lifted the receiver, expecting to hear General Abanjo's last words.

'I love you.'

'What?' he said.

'I love you.'

'Jessie, do you know what time it is?'

'A few minutes after twelve.'

'It's eight minutes past six in New York.'

'I only wanted to tell you how much I love my diamond brooch.'

Richard smiled.

'I'm going to wear it to lunch with Sir Colin and Lady Dudley. They are due to arrive any minute to take me to the Mirabelle, so I must say goodbye. Talk to you tomorrow – my today.'

'You're a nut.'

'By the way, I don't know if it's of any interest to you, but there's a reporter on the midday news here in England saying something about a certain General Abanjo being killed in a counter-coup in some Central African state and the old king will be returning home tomorrow to a hero's welcome.'

'What?'

'The king is just being interviewed now so I'll repeat what he's saying. "My government intends to honour all the debts it has incurred with our friends in the western world."'

'What?' repeated Richard, once again.

'He looks such a nice fellow now that he's got the crown back on his head. Good night, Mr. Kane. Sleep well.'

As Richard was leaping up and down on his bed, there was a knock on Florentyna's door, and Sir Colin and Lady Dudley came into her suite.

'Are you ready, young lady?' asked Sir Colin.

'I certainly am,' said Florentyna.

'You look very pleased with yourself. No doubt the reinstatement of King Erobo has brought the roses back to your cheeks.'

'Well informed as you are, Sir Colin, that is not the reason,' said Florentyna as she glanced down at the card that lay on the table in front of her and read the words again.

> I hope that this will be acceptable security until I can return the fifty-six dollars, plus interest.
>
> Mr. Kane

'What a lovely brooch you're wearing,' said Lady Dudley. 'It's a donkey, isn't it? Does that signify anything in particular?'

'It certainly does, Lady Dudley. It means the giver intends to vote for Nixon again.'

'Then you have to give him elephant cuff-links in return,' said Sir Colin.

'You know, Richard was right: it doesn't pay to underestimate the British,' said Florentyna.

*

After lunch Florentyna phoned Miss Tredgold at her school. The school secretary put her through to the staff room. Miss Tredgold, it turned out, did not need to be informed about the late General Abanjo, but seemed more interested in all the news about William and Annabel. Florentyna's second call was to Sotheby's – this time in person. On arrival she asked to see one of the heads of department.

'It may be many years before such a collector's item comes under the hammer, Mrs. Kane,' the expert told her.

'I understand,' said Florentyna. 'But please let me know the moment it does.'

'Certainly, madam,' said the expert as he wrote down Florentyna's name and address.

When Florentyna returned to New York three weeks later she settled down to institute the changes she had been considering on her European tour. By the end of 1972, with her energy, George's wisdom and Gianni di Ferranti's genius, she was able to show an increased profit. Thanks to King Erobo being as good as his word, Richard also declared a handsome profit.

On the night of the annual stockholders' meeting, Richard, Florentyna and George went out for a celebration dinner. Even though George had officially retired on his sixty-fifth birthday, he still came into his office every morning at eight o'clock. It had taken only twenty-four hours for everyone at the Baron to realise his retirement party had been a misnomer. Florentyna began to appreciate how lonely George must be now that he had lost most of his contemporaries and how close he had been to her father. She never once suggested that he should slow down, because she knew it was pointless, and it gave her particular happiness whenever George took Annabel and William on outings. Both the children called him 'Grandpapa' which brought tears to his eyes and always guaranteed them a large ice cream.

Florentyna thought she knew how much George did for the group but the truth only came home to her after his retirement could no longer be postponed. George died peacefully in his sleep in October 1972. In his will, he left everything to the Polish Red Cross. A short note addressed to Richard asked him to act as his executor.

Richard carried out George's every wish to the letter and even travelled to Warsaw accompanied by Florentyna to meet the President of the Polish Red Cross to discuss how George's donation could best be put to use. When they returned to New York Florentyna sent a directive to all managers in the group that the finest suite in each hotel was no longer to be the Presidential Suite but was to be renamed the 'George Novak Suite'.

When Richard woke the morning after they had returned from Warsaw, Florentyna, who had been waiting impatiently for him to open his eyes, told her husband that although George had taught her so much in life, he had now added to her learning even in death.

'What are you talking about?'

'George left everything he possessed to charity, but never once referred to the fact that my father rarely made charitable contributions other than the occasional gift to Polish or political causes. I'm every bit as remiss myself, and if you hadn't added a footnote to the group's annual general report concerning tax relief for charitable donations, I would never have given the matter a second thought.'

'As I'm sure you're not planning for something after your death, what do you have in mind?'

'Why don't we set up a foundation in memory of both our fathers? Let's bring the two families together. What they failed to do in their lifetime, let us do in ours.'

Richard sat up and stared at his wife as she got out of bed and continued to talk as she walked towards the bathroom.

'The Baron Group should donate one million dollars a year to the foundation,' she said.

'Spending only the income, never the capital,' he interjected.

Florentyna closed the bathroom door, which gave Richard a few moments to consider her proposal. He could still be surprised by her bold, sweeping approach to any new venture, even if, as he suspected, she had not thought through who would run the day-to-day administration of such an enterprise once it had taken off. He smiled to himself when the bathroom door reopened.

'We could spend the income derived from such a trust on first-generation immigrants who are not getting the chance of a decent education.'

'And also create scholarships for exceptionally gifted children whatever their background,' said Richard, getting out of bed.

'Brilliant, Mr. Kane, and let us hope that occasionally the same person will qualify for both.'

'Your father would have,' said Richard as he disappeared into the bathroom.

Thaddeus Cohen insisted on coming out of retirement to draw up the deeds of the foundation to cover the wishes of both Kanes. It took him over a month. When the trust fund was launched, the national press welcomed the financial commitment as another example of how Richard and Florentyna Kane were able to combine bold originality with common sense.

A reporter from the Chicago *Sun-Times* phoned Thaddeus Cohen to enquire why the foundation was so named. Cohen explained that 'Remagen' had been chosen because it was the battlefield on which Colonel Rosnovski had unknowingly saved the life of Captain Kane.

'I had no idea they had met on a battlefield,' said a young voice.

'Neither did they,' replied Thaddeus Cohen. 'It was only discovered after their deaths.'

'Fascinating. Tell me, Mr. Cohen, who is going to be the first trustee of the Remagen Foundation?'

'Professor Luigi Ferpozzi.'

Both Lester's Bank and the Baron Group set new records for the following year as Richard established himself as a force on Wall Street and Florentyna visited her hotels in the

Middle East and Africa. King Erobo held a banquet in Florentyna's honour when she arrived in Nambawe, and although she promised to build a hotel in the capital city she wouldn't be drawn into an explanation why Lester's had not been among the banks involved with the king's latest international loan.

William had a good first year at St. Paul's, showing the same flair for maths which his father had before him. As they had been taught by the same master, both father and son avoided asking for any comparison. Annabel did not progress as quickly as William, although her teacher had to admit she had improved, even if she had fallen in love with Bob Dylan.

'Who's he?' asked Florentyna.

'I don't know,' said Richard, 'but I'm told he's doing for Annabel what Sinatra did for you twenty-five years ago.'

When Florentyna started her sixth year as chairman of the group she found she was beginning to repeat herself. Richard seemed to find new challenges all the time, while Gianni di Ferranti appeared to be well in control of the chain of shops without bothering to ask her anything other than where to send the cheques. The Baron Group was now so efficient, and her management team so competent, that no one showed a great deal of concern one morning when Florentyna didn't come into the office.

That evening, when Richard was sitting in the crimson leather chair by the fire reading *The Billion Dollar Killing*, she expressed her thoughts out loud.

'I'm bored.'

Richard made no comment.

'It's time I did something with my life other than build on my father's achievements,' she added.

Richard smiled but didn't look up from his book.

25

'YOU'RE ALLOWED THREE GUESSES as to who this is.'

'Am I given any clues?' asked Florentyna, annoyed that she knew the voice but couldn't quite place it.

'Good-looking, intelligent and a national idol.'

'Paul Newman.'

'Feeble. Try again.'

'Robert Redford.'

'Worse still. One more chance.'

'I need another clue.'

'Appalling at French, not much better at English and still in love with you.'

'Edward. Edward Winchester. A voice from the past – only you don't sound as if you've changed a bit.'

'Wishful thinking. I'm over forty, and by the way so will you be next year.'

'How can I be when I'm only twenty-four this year?'

'What, again?'

'No, I have been on ice for the last fifteen years.'

'Not from what I've read about you. You go from strength to strength.'

'And how about you?'

'I'm a partner in a law firm in Chicago: Winston and Strawn.'

'Married?'

'No, I've decided to wait for you.'

Florentyna laughed. 'If you've taken this long to phone and propose, I should warn you that I've been married for over fifteen years and I have a son of fourteen and a daughter of twelve.'

'All right then, I won't propose, but I would like to see you. It's a private matter.'

'A private matter? Sounds intriguing.'

'If I were to fly to New York one day next week, would you have lunch with me?'

'I'd enjoy that.' Florentyna flicked over the pages of her calendar. 'How about next Tuesday?'

'Suits me. Shall we say the Four Seasons, one o'clock?'

'I'll be there.'

Florentyna put down the phone and sat back in her chair. Other than Christmas cards and the odd letter, she had had very little contact with Edward for sixteen years. She walked across to the mirror and studied herself. A few small lines were beginning to appear around the eyes and mouth. She turned sideways to confirm that she had kept her slim figure. She didn't feel old. There was no denying that she had a daughter who could already make young men stop in the street for a second glance, and a teenage son she now had to look up to. It wasn't fair. Richard didn't look forty: a few white tufts appearing at the sides of the temples and the hair perhaps a shade thinner than it had been, but he was every bit as slim and vigorous as the day they had met. She admired the fact that he still found time to play squash at the Harvard Club twice a week and practise the cello most weekends. Edward's phone call made her think of middle age for the first time; how morbid. She would be thinking of death next. Thaddeus Cohen had died the previous year; only her mother and Kate Kane remained of that generation.

Florentyna tried to touch her toes and couldn't, so she returned to the monthly statements of the Baron Group for reassurance. London was still not paying its way, even though the hotel occupied one of the finest sites in Mayfair. Somehow the English seemed to combine impossible wage demands with high unemployment and staff shortages all at the same time. In Riyadh they had had to clear out almost the entire management because of theft, and in Poland the government would still not allow the group to take any exchangeable currency out of the country. But despite these minor problems, all of which could be sorted out by her management team, the company was in good shape.

Florentyna had confidently assured Richard that the Baron Group profits would be over forty-one million for 1974, whereas Lester's would be lucky to touch eighteen million. Richard, however, had predicted that Lester's profits would pass the Baron Group's by 1974. She feigned disdain but knew when it came to financial forecasts he was rarely wrong.

Her thoughts floated back to Edward when the phone rang. Gianni di Ferranti wondered if she would like to see his new collection for the Paris show, which put her old classmate out of her mind until one o'clock the following Tuesday.

Florentyna arrived at the Four Seasons a few minutes after one, wearing one of Gianni's new dresses in midi-length bottle-green silk with a sleeveless jacket over it. She wondered if she would still recognise Edward. She walked up the wide staircase to find him waiting for her on the top step. She privately hoped she had aged as well as he had.

'Edward,' she cried, 'you haven't changed a bit.' He laughed. 'No, no,' mocked Florentyna, 'I've always liked grey hair and the extra weight suits you. I wouldn't expect anything less of a distinguished lawyer from my home town.'

He kissed her on both cheeks like a French general and then she put her arm through his as they followed the maître d' through to their table. A bottle of champagne awaited them.

'Champagne. How lovely. What are we celebrating?'

'Just being with you again, my dear.' Edward noticed that Florentyna seemed to be lost in thought. 'Is something wrong?' he enquired.

'No. I was just remembering myself sitting on the floor at Girls Latin, crying, while you tore the arm off Franklin D. Roosevelt and then poured royal-blue ink over his head.'

'You deserved it, you were a dreadful little show-off. F.D.R. didn't. Poor little bear. Is he still around?'

'Oh, yes. He's taken up residence in my daughter's bedroom and as she has managed to keep his remaining arm and both legs I can only reluctantly conclude that Annabel handles young men better than I did.'

Edward laughed. 'Shall we order? I have so much to talk to you about. It's been fun following your career on the television and in the papers but I want to see if you've changed.'

Florentyna ordered salmon and a side salad while Edward chose the prime rib with asparagus.

'I'm intrigued.'

'By what?' asked Edward.

'Why a Chicago lawyer would fly all the way to New York just to see an hotelier.'

'I do not come as a Chicago lawyer and I have no interest in talking to an hotelier. I come as treasurer of the Cook County Democratic Party.'

'I gave one hundred thousand dollars to the Chicago Democrats last year,' said Florentyna. 'Mind you, Richard donated one hundred thousand to the New York Republicans.'

'I don't want your money, Florentyna, although I know you have supported the Ninth District financially at every election. It's you I want.'

'That's a new line,' she said, grinning. 'Men have stopped saying that to me lately. You know, Edward,' she continued, her tone changing, 'I've been so overworked during the last few years, I barely have had the time to vote, let alone become personally involved. What's more, since Watergate I found Nixon detestable, Agnew worse, and with Muskie a non-runner I was only left with George McGovern, who didn't exactly inspire me.'

'But surely . . .'

'I also have a husband, two young children, and a two hundred million dollar company to run.'

'And what are you going to do for the next twenty years?'

She smiled to herself. 'Turn it into a billion dollar company.'

'In other words, just repeat yourself. Now I agree with you about McGovern and Nixon – one was too good and the other too bad – and I don't see anyone on the horizon who excites me.'

'So now you want me to run for President in '76?'

'No, I want you to run for Congress as the representative of the Ninth District of Illinois.'

Florentyna dropped her fork. 'If I remember the job specification correctly, it's an eighteen-hour day, forty-two thousand five hundred dollars a year, no family life, and your constituents are allowed to be as rude to you as they like. Worst of all, you are required to live in the Ninth District of Illinois.'

'That wouldn't be so bad. The Baron is in the Ninth District, and besides, it's just a stepping-stone.'

'To what?'

'To the Senate.'

'When the whole state can be rude to you.'

'And then the Presidency.'

'When the rest of the world can join in. Edward, this is not Girls Latin and I don't have two lives, one which can run my hotels and one . . .'

'And one in which you can give back some of what you have taken from others.'

'That was a bit rough, Edward.'

'Yes, it certainly was. I apologise. But I have always believed you could play a role in national politics, as you did once yourself, and I feel the time is right, especially as I am now convinced you haven't changed.'

'But I haven't been involved in politics at a grass-roots level, let alone a national level, for years.'

'Florentyna, you know as well as I do that most people in Congress have neither your experience nor your intelligence. That goes for most Presidents, come to think of it.'

'I'm flattered, Edward, but not convinced.'

'Well, I can tell you that a group of us in Chicago are convinced you should come home and run for the Ninth District.'

'Henry Osborne's old seat?'

'Yes. The Democrat who won back Osborne's seat in '54 is retiring this session and Mayor Daley wants a strong candidate to ward off any Republican challenger.'

'A Polish woman?'

'With the woman *Time* said ran behind only Jackie Kennedy and Margaret Mead in the nation's esteem.'

'You're mad, Edward. Who needs it?'

'I suspect you do, Florentyna. Just give me one day in your life, come to Chicago and meet the people who want you. Express in your own words how you feel about the future of our country. Won't you at least do that for me?'

'All right, I'll think about it and call you in a few days. But I warn you, Richard will think I'm nuts.'

On that count Florentyna turned out to be wrong. Richard had arrived home late that night after a trip to Boston, and told her over breakfast that she had been talking in her sleep.

'What did I say?'

Richard stared at her. 'Something I have always suspected,' he replied.

'And what was that?'

'Can I afford to run?'

Florentyna made no reply.

'Why did Edward want to see you for lunch so urgently?'

'He wants me to return to Chicago and stand for Congress.'

'So that's what brought it on. Well, I think you should consider the offer seriously, Jessie. For a long time you have been critical of the fact that competent women don't go into politics. And you have always been outspoken about the abilities of those who do enter public life. Now you can stop complaining and do something about it.'

'But what about the Baron Group?'

'The Rockefeller family managed to survive when Nelson became Governor; no doubt the Kane family will survive somehow. In any case, the group now employs twenty-seven thousand people, so I imagine we can find ten men to take your place.'

'Thank you, Mr. Kane. But how do I live in Illinois while you're in New York?'

'That's easily solved. I'll fly to Chicago every weekend. Wednesday nights you can fly to New York and now that Carol has agreed to stay it shouldn't be too unsettling for the children. When you're elected, I'll take the shuttle down to Washington Wednesday nights.'

'You sound as though you've been thinking about this for some time, Mr. Kane.'

Florentyna flew out to Chicago a week later and was met at O'Hare airport by Edward. It was pouring, and the wind was blowing so hard that even Edward, tightly clutching a large umbrella with both hands, could only just protect her from the rain.

'Now I know why I wanted to come back to Chicago,' she said as she scampered into the car, cold and wet. They were driven into the city while Edward briefed her on the people she would meet.

'They're all party workers and faithful stalwarts who have only read about you or have seen you on television. They'll be surprised to find that you only have two arms, two legs, and a head like any one of them.'

'How many do you expect to be at the meeting?'

'Around sixty. Seventy would be exceptional.'

'And all you want me to do is meet them, and then say a few words about my feelings on national affairs?'

'Yes.'

'Then I can return home?'

'If that's what you want to do.'

The car came to a halt outside the Cook County Democratic headquarters on Randolph Street where Florentyna was greeted by a Mrs. Kalamich, a fat homely woman who led her through to the main hall. Florentyna was shocked to find it was packed with people, some standing at the back. As she walked in, they began to applaud.

'You told me there would only be a few people, Edward,' she whispered.

'I am as surprised as you are. I expected about seventy, not over three hundred.'

Florentyna suddenly felt nervous as she was introduced to the members of the selection committee, and then led on to the stage. She sat next to Edward, aware of how cold the room was and how the hall was full of people with hope in their eyes, people who enjoyed so few of the privileges she took for granted. How different this room was from her own board room, full of men in Brooks Brothers suits who ordered Martinis before dinner. For the first time in her life she felt embarrassed by her wealth and hoped it didn't show.

Edward rose from his chair in the centre of the platform.

'Ladies and gentlemen, it is my privilege tonight to introduce a woman who has gained the respect and admiration of the American people. She has built up one of the largest financial empires in the world, and I believe she could now build a political career of the same dimensions. I hope she will launch that career in this room tonight. Ladies and gentlemen, Mrs. Florentyna Kane.'

Florentyna rose nervously to her feet. She wished she had spent more time preparing her speech.

'Thank you, Mr. Winchester, for your kind words. It's wonderful to be back in Chicago, my home town, and I appreciate so many of you turning out for me on this cold, wet night.

'I, like you, feel let down by the political leaders of the day. I believe in a strong America, and if I were to enter the political arena I would dedicate myself to those words Franklin D. Roosevelt said in this city over thirty years ago:

"There can be no greater calling than public service."

'My father came to Chicago as an immigrant from Poland and only in America could he have achieved the success he did. Each of us must play our role in the destiny of the country we love, and I shall always remember your kindness in inviting me to be considered as your candidate. Be assured that I shall not make my final decision lightly. I have not come with a long prepared speech as I would prefer to answer the questions you consider important.'

She sat down and three hundred people applauded enthusiastically. When the noise had died down, Florentyna answered questions on subjects ranging from the U.S. bombing of Cambodia to legalised abortion, from Watergate to the energy crisis. It was the first time she had attended any meeting without all the facts and figures at her fingertips, and she was surprised to find how strongly she felt on so many issues. After she had answered the final question, over an hour later, the crowd rose and started chanting 'Kane for Congress', refusing to stop until she left the platform. It was one of those rare moments in her life when she wasn't sure what to do next. Edward came to her rescue.

'I knew they would love you,' said Edward, obviously delighted.

'But I was awful,' she shouted back, above the noise.

'Then I can't wait to find out what you're like when you're good.'

Edward led her off the platform as the crowd surged forward. A pale man in a wheelchair managed to touch her arm. She turned.

'This is Sam,' said Edward. 'Sam Hendrick. He lost both his legs in Vietnam.'

'Mrs. Kane,' he said. 'You won't remember me; we once licked envelopes together in this hall for Stevenson. If you decide to run for Congress, my wife and I will work night and day to see you are elected. Many of us in Chicago have always believed you would come home and represent us.' His wife, who stood behind the chair, nodded and smiled.

'Thank you,' said Florentyna. She turned and tried to walk to the exit, but it was blocked by outstretched hands and well-wishers. She was stopped again at the door, this time by a girl of about twenty-five who told her, 'I lived in your old room in Whitman and Radcliffe and, like you, once stood in Soldier Field and listened to President Kennedy. America needs another Kennedy. Why shouldn't it be a woman?'

Florentyna stared at the eager, intense young face. 'I've graduated and work in Chicago now,' the girl continued, 'but the day you run, a thousand students from Illinois will be on the streets to see that you are elected.'

Florentyna tried to catch her name but was pushed on by the crowd. At last Edward managed to bustle her through the throng and into a waiting car which drove them back to the airport. She didn't speak during the journey. When they arrived at O'Hare, the black chauffeur jumped out and opened the door for her. She thanked him.

'It's a pleasure, Mrs. Kane. I want to thank you for the stand you took for my people in the south. We won't forget that you led our struggle for equal pay and all the hotels in the country had to follow. I hope I'll have a chance to vote for you.'

'Thank you again,' said Florentyna, smiling.

Edward took her to the terminal and guided her to the departure gate.

'Made your flight in good time. Thank you for coming, Florentyna. Please let me know when you have made up your mind.' He paused. 'If you feel you can't go ahead with the nomination, I shall always understand.' He kissed her lightly on the cheek and left.

On the flight back, Florentyna sat alone thinking about what had happened that night and how unprepared she had been for such a demonstration. She wished her father could have been in the hall to witness it.

A stewardess asked for her drink order.

'Nothing, thank you.'

'Is there anything else I can do for you, Mrs. Kane?'

Florentyna looked up, surprised that the young girl knew her name.

'I used to work in one of your hotels.'

'Which one?' asked Florentyna.

'The Detroit Baron. Barons would always be the first choice for stewardesses for a stop-over. If only America was governed the way you run your hotels, we wouldn't be in the trouble we're in now,' she said before moving on down the aisle.

Florentyna flicked through a copy of *Newsweek*. Under the headline 'How far does Watergate reach?' she studied the faces of Ehrlichman, Haldeman and Dean before closing the magazine. On the cover was a picture of Richard Nixon and the caption: 'When was the President told?'

A little after midnight, she arrived back at East Sixty-fourth Street. Richard was sitting up in the crimson chair by the fire. He rose to greet her.

'Well, did they ask you to run for President of the United States?'

'No. But how do you feel about Congresswoman Kane?'

Florentyna phoned Edward the next day. 'I am willing to put my name forward as the Democratic candidate for Congress,' she said.

'Thank you. I ought to try and express my thoughts more fully, but for now – thank you.'

'Edward, may I know who would have been the candidate if I had said no?'

'They were pressing me to run myself. But I told them I had a better candidate in mind. As I'm certain this time round you'll take advice, even if you became President.'

'I never did become Class President.'

'I did, and I've still ended up serving you.'

'Where do I start, coach?'

'The Primary will be in March, so you'd better reserve every weekend between now and the fall.'

'I already have, starting this weekend – and can you tell

me who was the young woman from Radcliffe who stopped me at the door and talked about Kennedy?'

'Janet Brown. In spite of her age, she's already one of the most respected case workers in the city's Human Services department.'

'Do you have her phone number?'

During the week Florentyna informed the Baron board of directors of her decision. They appointed Richard co-chairman of the group and elected two new directors.

Florentyna called Janet Brown and offered her a job as her full-time political assistant and was delighted by Janet's immediate acceptance. She then added two new secretaries to her staff for political work only. Finally she called the Chicago Baron and instructed them to leave the thirty-eighth floor free, warning them she would need the entire floor left at her disposal for at least a year.

'Taking it seriously, aren't we?' said Richard later that evening.

'Indeed I am, because I'm going to have to work very hard if you're ever going to be the First Gentleman.'

26

'ARE YOU EXPECTING MUCH opposition?'

'Nothing of real consequence,' said Edward. 'There may be a protest candidate or two, but as the committee is fully behind you, the real fight should be with the Republicans.'

'Do we know who their candidate is likely to be?'

'Not yet. My spies tell me it's between two men, Ray Buck, who seems to be the choice of the retiring member, and Stewart Lyle, who's served on the City Council for the past eight years. They'll both run a good campaign, but that's not our immediate problem. With so little time left, we must concentrate on the Democratic Primary.'

'How many people do you think will vote in the Primary?' asked Florentyna.

'Can't be certain. All we do know is that there are roughly one hundred and fifty thousand registered Democrats and that the turnout is usually between forty-five and fifty per cent. So that would point to around seventy or eighty thousand.'

Edward unfolded a large map of Chicago and placed it in front of Florentyna.

'The boundaries of the constituency are marked in red and run from Chicago Avenue in the south to the Evanston border in the north, from Ravenswood and Western Highway in the west to the lake in the east.'

'The district hasn't changed since the days of Henry Osborne,' said Florentyna, 'so it should all come back to me very quickly.'

'Let's hope so, because our main task is to see that as many Democrats in that area are aware of who you are through the press, advertising, television and public appearances. Whenever they open their newspaper, turn on the radio or watch TV Florentyna Kane must be with them. The voters must feel you are everywhere and they must believe your only interest is in them. In fact, there can be no major function in Chicago between now and March 19th at which you are not present.'

'Suits me,' said Florentyna. 'I've already set up my campaign headquarters in the Chicago Baron, which my father had the foresight to build in the heart of the district. I propose to spend weekends here and any free days during the week at home with my family, so where do you want me to start?'

'I've called a press conference for next Monday, to be held at Democratic headquarters. A short speech followed by a question-and-answer session, and then we'll serve them coffee so you can meet all the key people individually. As you enjoy thinking fast on your feet, you should relish meeting the press.'

'Any particular advice?'

'No, just be yourself.'

'You may live to regret that.'

Edward's judgment turned out to be right. After Florentyna had made a short opening statement the questions came thick and fast. Under his breath, Edward whispered the names of the various journalists as each rose to his feet.

The first was Mike Royko, of the Chicago *Daily News*.

'Why do you think it appropriate that a New York millionairess should run for the Ninth District of Illinois?'

'In this context,' said Florentyna standing to take the questions, 'I am not a New York millionairess. I was born in St. Luke's Hospital and brought up on Rigg Street. My father, who came to this country with nothing but the clothes he stood in, founded the Baron Group right here in the Ninth District. I believe we must always fight to ensure that any immigrant arriving on our shores today, whether he be from Vietnam or Poland, has the opportunity to achieve the same goals as my father did.'

Edward pointed to another journalist for the next question.

'Do you consider it a disadvantage to be a woman when seeking public office?'

'Perhaps to a limited or ill-informed person I would have to answer yes, but not with any intelligent voter who puts the issues before outdated prejudices. Which of you if involved in a traffic accident on the way home today would think twice if the first doctor on the scene turned out to be a woman? I hope the issue of sex will soon be as irrelevant as that of religion. It seems a century ago that people asked John F. Kennedy if he thought the Presidency might change because he was a Roman Catholic. I notice nowadays the question never arises with Teddy Kennedy. Women are already playing leading roles in other nations. Golda Meir in Israel and Indira Gandhi in India are just two examples. I consider it sad that in a nation of two hundred and thirty million people women number not one of the hundred Senators and only sixteen out of the four hundred and thirty-four members of Congress.'

'What does your husband feel about you wearing the trousers in your family?' demanded an unsolicited questioner. Laughter broke out in certain parts of the room and Florentyna waited for complete silence.

'He's far too intelligent and successful for such a pathetic question to occur to him.'

'What is your attitude on Watergate?'

'A sad episode in American political history which I hope will be behind us before too long, but not forgotten.'

'Do you feel President Nixon should resign?'

'That's a moral decision and one for the President to make himself.'

'Would you resign if you were President?'

'I wouldn't have to break into any hotels. I already own one hundred and forty-three.' A burst of laughter followed by applause gave Florentyna a little more confidence.

'Do you think the President should be impeached?'

'That's a question Congress will have to decide based on the evidence the Judiciary Committee is considering, including the White House tapes, if and when President Nixon releases them. But the resignation of the Attorney-General, Elliot Richardson, a man whose integrity has never been in question, should ring warning bells for the general public.'

'Where do you stand on abortion?'

'I shall not fall into the trap that Senator Mason did only last week when asked the same question, to which he replied, "Gentlemen, that one's below the belt".' Florentyna waited for the laughter to die down before saying in a more serious tone. 'I am a Roman Catholic by birth and upbringing, so I feel strongly about the protection of the unborn child. However, I also believe there are situations in which it is both necessary and indeed morally correct for a qualified doctor to carry out an abortion.'

'Can you give an example?'

'Rape would be an obvious one, and also in a case where the mother's health is in danger.'

'Isn't that against the teachings of your church?'

'That is correct, but I have always believed in the separation of church and state. Any person who runs for public office must be willing to take stands on certain issues that will not please all of the people all of the time. I think Edmund Burke summed it up better than I could hope to do when he said, "Your representative owes you, not his industry only, but his judgment, and he betrays instead of serving you, if he sacrifices it to your opinion."'

Edward sensed the effect of the last statement and promptly rose from his chair. 'Well, ladies and gentlemen of the press, I think the time has come to adjourn for coffee, which will give you the opportunity to meet Florentyna Kane personally – although I am sure by now you know why we feel she is the right person to represent the Ninth District in Congress.'

For the next hour, Florentyna faced a further barrage of personal and political questions, some of which, had they been put to her in the privacy of her own home, she would have found objectionable, but she was quickly learning that one cannot be a public figure and hope to maintain a private stance on anything. When the last journalist had left, she collapsed into a chair, not even having had the time to drink one cup of coffee.

'You were great,' said Janet Brown. 'Didn't you think so, Mr. Winchester?'

Edward smiled. 'Good, not great, but I blame myself for not warning you about the difference between being chairman of a private company and running for public office.'

'What are you getting at?' asked Florentyna, surprised.

'Some of those journalists are very powerful and they talk to hundreds of thousands of people every day through their columns. They want to tell their readers that they know you personally and once or twice you were a little too aloof, and with the man from the *Tribune* you were just plain rude.'

'Was that the man who asked about who wore the trousers?'

'Yes.'

'What was I supposed to say?'

'Turn it into a joke.'

'It wasn't funny, Edward, and it was he who was rude.'

'Possibly, but he's not the one who's running for public office and you are, so he can say what he likes. And don't ever forget his column is read by more than five hundred thousand people in Chicago every day including most of your constituents.'

'So you want me to compromise myself?'

'No, I want you to get elected. When you're in the House, you can prove to everyone that they were right in voting for you. But just now you're an unknown commodity with a lot going against you. You're a woman, you're Polish and you're a millionairess. That combination is going to arouse just about every form of prejudice or jealousy in most ordinary people. The way to counter those feelings is always to appear humorous, kind and interested in people who do not share the privileges you have.'

'Edward, it's not me who should be running for public office, it's you.'

Edward shook his head. 'I know you're the right person, Florentyna, but I realise now that it will take a little time for you to adjust to your new environment. Thank God you've always been a quick learner. By the way, I don't disagree with the sentiments you voiced so vociferously, but as you seem to like quoting statesmen of the past, don't forget Jefferson's comment to Adams: "You can't lose votes with a speech you didn't make."'

Again Edward turned out to be right: the press the next day gave Florentyna a mixed reception, and the *Tribune* reporter called her the worst sort of opportunistic carpet-bagger he had ever had the misfortune to come across on the political trail – surely Chicago could find a local person? Otherwise he would have to recommend for the first time that his readers vote Republican. Florentyna was horrified and adjusted quickly to the fact that a journalist's ego was sometimes even more sensitive than a politician's. She settled down to working five days a week in Chicago, meeting people, talking to the press, appearing on television, fund raising and then going over it all again whenever she saw Richard. Even Edward was beginning to feel confident that the tide was turning her way, when the first blow came.

'Ralph Brooks? Who on earth is Ralph Brooks?' asked Florentyna.

'A local lawyer, very bright and very ambitious. I'd always thought his sights were set on the State's Attorney's office en route to the federal bench, but it seems I'm wrong. I wonder who put him up to this?'

'Is he a serious candidate?' Florentyna asked.

'He certainly is. A local boy, educated at the University of Chicago before going on to Yale Law School.'

'Age?' asked Florentyna.

'Late thirties.'

'And of course he's good-looking?'

'Very,' said Edward. 'When he rises in court every woman on the jury wants him to win. I always avoid opposing him if I can.'

'Does this Olympian have any disadvantages?'

'Naturally. Any man who has been a lawyer in this city is bound to have made a few enemies, and I know for certain Mayor Daley won't be overjoyed about his entry into the race, since Ralph Brooks is an obvious rival for his son.'

'What am I expected to do about him?'

'Nothing,' said Edward. 'When asked, you simply give the standard answer: say it's democracy at work and may the best man – or woman – win.'

'He's left himself with only five weeks before the Primary.'

'Sometimes that's a clever tactic; he'll hope you've run out of steam. The one good thing to come out of this is that Mr. Brooks will have killed any complacency among our workers. Everyone will now know they have a fight on their hands, which will be good training for when we face the Republicans.'

Florentyna was reassured that Edward still sounded confident, although he confided in Janet Brown later that it was going to be one hell of a fight. During the next five weeks Florentyna learned just how much of a fight. Everywhere she went, Ralph Brooks seemed to have been there just before her. Every time she made a press statement on a major issue, Brooks had given his opinion the night before. But as the day of the Primary drew nearer, she learned to play Brooks at his own game, and beat him at it. However, just at the point when the opinion polls showed she was holding her lead he played an ace that Florentyna hadn't foreseen. She read the details on the front page of the Chicago *Tribune*.

'Brooks Challenges Kane to Debate' ran the headline. She knew that with all his court experience and practice at cross-examination he was bound to be a formidable opponent. Within minutes of the paper hitting the streets, the phone in her headquarters was besieged with queries from the press. Would she accept the challenge? Was she avoiding him? Didn't the people of Chicago have the right to see both candidates debate the issues? Janet held them off while Florentyna held a hasty conference with Edward. It lasted for three minutes, during which Florentyna wrote out a statement for Janet to read to all enquirers.

'Florentyna Kane is delighted to accept the invitation to debate Ralph Brooks and looks forward to the encounter.'

During the week Edward appointed a representative to consult with Brooks's campaign manager in determining the time and place for the debate.

The Thursday before the Primary was the date agreed by both sides; the venue was to be the Bernard Horwich Jewish Community Centre on West Touhy. Once the local C.B.S.-TV affiliate had agreed to cover the debate, both candidates knew that the outcome of the election might well depend on the confrontation. Florentyna spent days preparing her speech and answering questions shot at her by Edward, Janet and Richard. It brought back memories of Miss Tredgold and their preparation for the Woolson Prize Scholarship.

On the night of the debate every seat in the Community Centre was taken. People were standing at the back while others sat on window sills. Richard had flown in from New York for the occasion, and he and Florentyna arrived a half hour before the debate was due to begin. She went through the usual ordeal of television make-up while Richard found himself a seat in the front row.

She was greeted by warm applause as she entered the hall and took her seat on the stage. Ralph Brooks arrived moments later to an equally tumultuous applause. He pushed back his hair rather self-consciously as he strode across the floor. No woman in the room took her eyes from him, including Florentyna. The chairman of the Ninth District Democratic Congressional Committee welcomed them both before taking them to one side to remind them that they would each make an opening speech, which would be followed by a question-and-answer session, and then they would be invited to make a closing statement. They both nodded; the chairman was only repeating what had been agreed to by their representatives days before. He then took a new half-dollar from his pocket and Florentyna stared at the head of John Kennedy. The chairman spun the coin, and she called heads. Kennedy looked up at her again.

'I'll speak second,' she said, not even hesitating.

Without another word, they walked back on to the stage. Florentyna took a seat on the right of Edward while Ralph Brooks sat on his left. At eight o'clock, the moderator banged the gavel and called the meeting to order. 'Mr. Brooks will address you first and then Mrs. Kane will speak. The speeches will be followed by a question-and-answer session.'

Ralph Brooks rose and Florentyna stared up at the tall, handsome man. She had to admit it: if a film director had been casting for the role of President, Ralph Brooks would be given the part. From the moment he started to speak, Florentyna was in no doubt that she would not have to travel beyond Chicago to face a more formidable rival. Brooks was relaxed and assured, his delivery was professional without sounding glib.

'Ladies and gentlemen, fellow Democrats,' he began. 'I stand before you tonight, a local man who has made his way in life right here in Chicago. My great-grandfather was born in this city and for four generations the Brooks family has practised law from our offices on La Salle Street, always serving this community to the best of our ability. I offer myself today as your candidate for Congress in the belief that representatives of the people should always come from the grass-roots of their community. I do not have the vast wealth that is at the disposal of my opponent, but I bring a dedication to and care for this district that I hope you will feel surpasses wealth.' There was an outburst of applause, but Florentyna could see several people who were not joining in. 'On the issues of crime prevention, housing, public transportation and health, I have for several years sought to promote public good in the courts of Chicago. I now seek the opportunity to promote your interests in the United States House of Representatives.'

Florentyna listened intently to each well delivered phrase and was not surprised when Brooks sat down to applause that was loud and sustained. Edward rose to make Florentyna's introduction. When he had finished, she stood up – and wanted to run out of the hall. Richard smiled up at her from the front row and she regained her confidence.

'My father came to America over fifty years ago,' she began, 'having escaped first from the Germans and then from the Russians. After educating himself in New York he came to Chicago where he founded the hotel group of which I have the privilege of being chairman, right here in the Ninth District. A group that now employs twenty-seven thousand people in every state of America. When my father's career was at its zenith, he left this country to fight the Germans again and he returned to America with a Bronze Star. I was born in this city and went to high school not a mile from this hall, a Chicago education that made it possible for me to go to college. Now I have returned home wishing to represent the people who made my American dream possible.'

Loud applause greeted Florentyna's words, but she noticed once again that several people did not join in. 'I hope I will not be prevented from holding office because I was born with wealth. If that were to be a disqualification, Jefferson, Roosevelt and Kennedy would never have held office. I hope I will not be prevented because my father was an immigrant. If that were the case, then one of the greatest mayors this community has ever known, Anton Cermak, would never have worked in City Hall, and if I am to be prevented because I am a woman, then half the population of America must be disqualified along with me.' This was greeted with loud applause from all parts of the hall. Florentyna drew a deep breath.

'I do not apologise for being the daughter of an immigrant. I do not apologise for being wealthy. I do not apologise for being a woman, and I will never be apologetic about wanting to represent the people of Chicago in the United States Congress.' The applause was deafening. 'If it is not my destiny to represent you, I shall support Mr. Brooks. If, on the other hand, I have the honour of being selected to be your candidate, you can be assured that I shall tackle the problems that Chicago faces with the same dedication and energy I put into making my company one of the most successful hotel groups in the world.'

Florentyna sat down to continuing applause and looked towards her husband, who was smiling. She relaxed for the first time and stared into the hall where some people even stood to applaud although she was only too aware most of them were on her staff. She checked her watch: eight twenty-eight. She had timed it perfectly. 'Laugh-In' was almost due on TV and the Chicago Black Hawks would be warming up on channel nine. There would be a lot of changing of channels in the next few minutes. Judging by the frown on Ralph Brooks's face he was equally aware of the scheduling.

After questions – which brought no surprises – and the closing statements, Florentyna and Richard left the hall surrounded by well-wishers and returned to their room at the Baron. They waited nervously for a bellboy to deliver the first edition of the papers. The overall verdict was in favour of Florentyna. Even the *Tribune* said it had been a very close-run affair.

During the last three days of the campaign before the Primary, Florentyna pounded pavement, pressed flesh and walked the entire route of the St. Patrick's Day Parade before literally collapsing into a hot bath every night. She was woken by Richard each morning with a cup of hot coffee, after which she started the whole mad process again.

'The great day has at last arrived,' said Richard.

'Not a moment too soon,' said Florentyna. 'I am not sure my legs can go through anything like this ever again.'

'Have no fear. All will be revealed tonight,' said Richard from behind a copy of *Fortune*.

Florentyna rose and dressed in a simple blue suit of a crease-resistant fabric: although she still felt crumpled at the end of each day. She put on what Miss Tredgold would have called sensible shoes, having already worn out two pairs on the campaign trail. After breakfast, she and Richard walked down to the local school. She cast her vote for Florentyna Kane. It felt strange. Richard as a registered New York Republican remained outside.

In a heavier turnout than Edward had predicted, 49,312 other people voted for Florentyna that day, while 42,972 voted for Ralph Brooks.

Florentyna Kane had won her first election.

The Grand Old Party candidate turned out to be Stewart Lyle, who was an easier opponent than Ralph Brooks. He was an old-fashioned Republican who was always charming and courteous and who did not believe in personal confrontation. Florentyna liked him from the day they met and had no doubt that, if elected, he would have represented the district with compassion, but after Nixon had resigned on August 9th and Ford had pardoned the ex-President, the Democrats looked set for a landslide win.

Florentyna was among those elected on the bandwagon. She captured the Ninth District of Illinois with a majority over the Republican candidate of more than 27,000. Richard was the first to congratulate her.

'I am so proud of you, my darling,' he smiled mischievously. 'Mind you, I'm sure Mark Twain would have been as well.'

'Why Mark Twain?' asked Florentyna, puzzled.

'Because it was he who said: "Suppose you were an idiot and suppose you were a member of Congress. But I repeat myself."'

27

WILLIAM AND Annabel joined their father and mother for Christmas at the Kane family house on Cape Cod. Florentyna enjoyed having the children around her for the festivities, and they soon recharged all her human batteries.

William, nearly fifteen, was already talking about going to Harvard and spent every afternoon poring over maths books that even Richard didn't understand. Annabel spent most of her holiday on the phone talking long distance about boys to different school friends until Richard finally had to explain to her how the Bell Telephone Company made its money. Florentyna read Michener's *Centennial* and under pressure from her daughter listened to Roberta Flack singing 'Killing Me Softly With His Song' loudly, again and again. Richard got so sick of the record he begged Annabel to turn the damn thing over. She did, and for the first time Richard listened to a popular record he knew he would enjoy for the rest of his life. Annabel was puzzled when she saw her mother smile at the lyrics her father seemed entranced by:

> Jessie come home, there's a hole in the bed
> where you slept, and now it's getting cold.
> Jessie, the blues . . .

When the Christmas vacation came to an end Florentyna flew back to New York with Richard. It took her a week of going over reports on the Baron Group and being briefed by the heads of each department before she felt she had covered everything that had happened in her absence.

During the year they had completed hotels in Brisbane and Johannesburg, and were refurbishing old Barons in Nashville and Cleveland. In Florentyna's absence, Richard had slowed the forward planning programme down a little but had still managed to increase the profits to a record forty-five million dollars for the year ending 1974. Florentyna was in no position to complain, as Lester's was on target to show a massive increase in the credit column that year.

Florentyna's only anxiety was that Richard, for the first time in his life, was beginning to look his age: lines were appearing on his forehead and around his eyes that could only have resulted from continual and considerable stress. When she taxed him with working uncivilised hours (even his cello practice seemed less frequent) he chided her that it was a hard road to toil when one wanted to be First Gentleman.

Congresswoman Kane flew into Washington in early January. She had sent Janet Brown on to the capital in December to head up her Congressional staff and work out the transition with her predecessor's office. When Florentyna joined her, everything seemed to be organised, down to the George Novak Suite at the Washington Baron. Janet had made herself indispensable during the previous six months, and Florentyna was well prepared when the first session of the 94th Congress was ready to open. Janet had allocated the $227,270 a year each House member is permitted to staff the office. She did this with stringent care, placing the emphasis on competence in her selection whatever the age of any applicant. She had appointed a personal secretary to Florentyna named Louise Drummond, a legislative assistant, a press secretary, four legislative correspondents to research issues as well as to handle mail, two further secretaries and a receptionist. In addition, Florentyna had left three case workers in her district office under a capable Polish field representative.

Florentyna had been assigned rooms on the seventh floor

of the Longworth Building, the oldest and middle of the three House buildings. Janet told her that her office had been occupied in the past by Lyndon Johnson, John Lindsay and Pete McCloskey. '"Hear no evil, see no evil, speak no evil,"' she commented. Florentyna's new office suite was only two hundred yards from the Capitol, and she could always go directly to the chamber on the little subway if the weather was inclement or if she wished to avoid the ubiquitous herded groups of Washington sightseers.

Florentyna's personal office was a modest-sized room already cluttered with massive brown congressional furniture, a wooden desk, a large brown leather sofa, several dark, uncomfortable chairs and two glass-fronted cabinets. From the way the office had been left, it was easy to believe that the previous occupant had been male.

Florentyna quickly filled the bookcases with a copy of the U.S. Code, the Rules of the House, the Hurd Annotated Illinois Revised Statutes, and Carl Sandburg's six-volume biography of Lincoln, one of her favourite works despite his party. She then hung some water colours of her own choice on the drab cream walls in an effort to cover the nail holes left by the previous tenant. On her desk she placed a family photograph taken outside their first shop in San Francisco and when she discovered that each member of Congress was entitled to plants from the botanical gardens, she instructed Janet to claim their maximum allocation as well as arranging for fresh flowers on her desk every Monday.

She also asked Janet to decorate the front office in a way that was both welcoming and dignified; under no circumstances were there to be any portraits of her on view. Florentyna disliked the way most her colleagues filled their reception areas with self-laudatory memorabilia.

She reluctantly agreed to place the flag of Illinois and the United States flag behind her desk.

On the afternoon before Congress convened she held a reception for her family and campaign workers. Richard and Kate flew down with the children, and Edward accompanied Florentyna's mother and Father O'Reilly from Chicago.

Florentyna had sent out nearly one hundred invitations to friends and supporters all across the country, and to her surprise over seventy people turned up.

During the celebrations she took Edward aside and invited him to join the board of the Baron Group; full of champagne, he accepted and then forgot about the offer until he received a letter from Richard confirming the appointment and adding that it would be valuable for Florentyna to have two boardroom views to consider while she concentrated on her political career.

When Richard and Florentyna climbed into yet another Baron king-size bed that night, he told her once more how proud he was of her achievement.

'I couldn't have done it without your support, Mr. Kane.'

'There was no suggestion that I supported you, Jessie, though I reluctantly admit to considerable pleasure at your victory. Now I must catch up with the group's European forecasts before I switch off the light on my side of the bed.'

'I do wish you would slow down a bit, Richard.'

'I can't, my darling. Neither of us can. That's why we're so good for each other.'

'Am I good for you?' asked Florentyna.

'In a word, no. If I could have it all back, I would have married Maisie and saved the money on several pairs of gloves.'

'Good God, I wonder what Maisie is up to nowadays.'

'Still in Bloomingdale's. Having given up any hope of me, she's married a travelling salesman, so I suppose I am stuck with you. Now can I get down to reading this report?'

She took the report out of his hand and dropped it on the floor.

'No, darling.'

When the first session of the 94th Congress opened Speaker Carl Albert, dressed sombrely in a dark suit, took his place on the podium and banged his gavel as he gazed down into the semi-circle of members seated in their green leather chairs. Florentyna turned in her place and smiled up at Richard and her family, who had been allocated places in the gallery above. When she looked around the chamber at her colleagues, she couldn't help thinking that they were the worst-dressed group of people she had ever seen in her life. Her bright-red wool suit, in the latest midi fashion, made her conspicuous by exception.

The Speaker asked the House chaplain, the Reverend Edward Latch, to pronounce the benediction. This was followed by an opening speech by the leaders of both parties and an address by the Speaker. Mr. Albert reminded Congressmen that they should keep their speeches brief and to refrain from making too much noise in the chamber while others were at the podium. He then adjourned the session and everyone left the chamber to attend some of the dozens of receptions given on the opening day.

'Is that all you have to do, Mummy?' asked Annabel.

Florentyna laughed. 'No, darling, that's just the opening session; the real work starts tomorrow.'

Even Florentyna was surprised the next morning. Her mail contained one hundred and sixty-one items, including two out-of-date Chicago papers, six 'Dear Colleague' letters, from Congressmen she had yet to meet, fourteen invitations to trade association receptions, seven letters from special interest groups; several invitations to address meetings – some out of Chicago and Washington – three dozen letters from constituents, two requests to be placed on her mailing list, fifteen résumés from hopeful job-seekers, and a note from Carl Albert to say that she had been placed on the Appropriations and Small Businesses committees.

The mail looked manageable compared with the ceaseless telephone demands for everything from Florentyna's official photograph to press interviews. The Washington reporters from the Chicago papers called regularly, but Florentyna was also contacted by the local Washington press, who were always intrigued by new female additions to Congress, especially those who did not resemble all-in wrestlers. Florentyna quickly learned the names she should know, including those of Maxine Cheshire and Betty Beale, as well as David Broder and Joe Alsop. Before the end of March, she had been the subject of a front-page 'Style' interview in the *Post* and had appeared in Washingtonian Magazine's 'New Stars on the Hill'. She turned down the continual invitations to appear on 'Panorama', and began to question where the proper balance lay between gaining visibility, which would be of use in influencing issues, and losing all her free time to the media.

During those first few weeks, Florentyna seemed to do nothing except run very fast trying to remain on the same spot. She considered herself fortunate to be the Illinois delegation's choice for a vacancy on the powerful Appropriations Committee, the first freshman in years to be so honoured, but discovered nothing had been left to chance when she opened a scrawled note from Mayor Daley which simply read, 'You owe me one'.

Florentyna found her new world fascinating but it felt rather like being back at school as she searched the corridors for committee rooms, sprinted through the underground to the Capitol to record her vote, met with lobbyists, studied briefing books and signed hundreds of letters. The idea of getting a signature machine grew increasingly appealing.

An elderly Democratic colleague from Chicago advised her on the wisdom of sending out a constituent newsletter to her one hundred and eighty thousand households every two months. 'Remember, my dear,' he added, 'it may appear as though you are doing nothing more than papering the Ninth District, but there are only three ways of assuring your re-election: the frank, the frank and the frank.'

He also advised Florentyna to assign two of her district staffers to clip every article from the local newspapers that referred to a constituent. Voters began receiving congratulations on their weddings, births, community achievements – and even basketball victories now that eighteen-year-olds had the vote. Florentyna always added a personal word or two in Polish where appropriate, quietly thanking her mother for disobeying her father's orders over the teaching of Polish.

With the help of Janet, who was always in the office before her and still there when she left, Florentyna slowly got on top of the paperwork, and by the July 4th recess she was almost in control. She had not yet spoken on the floor and had said very little in any committee hearings. Sandra Read, a House colleague from New York, had advised her to spend the first six months listening, the second six months thinking and the third six months speaking occasionally.

'What about the fourth six months?' asked Florentyna.

'You'll be campaigning for re-election,' came the reply.

On weekends she would regale Richard with stories of the bureaucratic waste of the taxpayers' money and the lunacy with which America's democratic system was conducted.

'I thought you had been elected to change all that?' he said, looking down at his wife, who was sitting cross-legged on the floor in front of him, clutching her knees.

'It will take twenty years to change anything. Are you aware that committees make decisions involving millions of dollars, but half the members haven't the slightest idea what they're voting on and the other half don't even attend but vote by proxy.'

'Then you will have to become chairman of a committee, and see to it that your members do their homework and attend hearings.'

'I can't.'

'What do you mean, you can't?' asked Richard, finally folding his morning newspaper.

'You can only become the chairman of a committee by seniority, so it's irrelevant when you reach the peak of your mental prowess. If there is someone who has been on the committee longer than you, he automatically gets the job. At this moment, of twenty-two standing committees there are three committee chairmen in their seventies, and thirteen in their sixties, which leaves only six under sixty. I've worked out that I will become chairman of the Appropriations Committee on my sixty-eighth birthday, having served twenty-eight years in the House. That is if I win the thirteen elections in between, because if you lose one, you start again. It's taken me only a few weeks to work out why so many southern states elect freshmen to Congress who are under thirty. If we ran the Baron Group the way Congress is run we'd have been bankrupt long ago.'

Florentyna was slowly coming to accept the fact that it would take years to reach the top of the political tree, and the truth was that the climb consisted of a long hard grind, known as 'serving your time'. 'Go along and get along', was the way her committee chairman put it. She decided that if it was going to be any different for her, she would have to turn the disadvantage of being a freshman into the advantage of being a woman.

It happened in a way she could never have planned. She did not speak on the House floor for the first six months, although she had sat in her seat for hours watching how the debates were conducted and learning from those who used their limited speaking time with skill. When a distinguished Republican, Robert C. L. Buchanan, announced he would be proposing an anti-abortion amendment to the Defence Appropriations Bill, Florentyna felt the time had come to deliver her maiden speech.

She wrote to the chairman and asked for permission to speak against the motion. He sent back a courteous reply, reminding her she would only be allowed five minutes and wishing her luck.

Buchanan spoke with great emotion to a silent chamber and used his five minutes with the skill of a professional House man. Florentyna thought him the worst sort of back-woodsman, and as he spoke, added some notes to her carefully prepared speech. When Buchanan sat down, Sandra Read was recognised, and she made a powerful case against the amendment although she was regularly interrupted by noisy comments from the floor. A third speaker added nothing to the debate, simply reiterating the words of Robert Buchanan, to be sure his views were on the record and would be in his local newspaper. Speaker Albert then recognised 'the distinguished gentle lady from Illinois'. Florentyna rose with some trepidation and made her way to the speaking rostrum in the well of the House, trying to keep her hands from trembling too noticeably.

'Mr. Speaker, I must apologise to the House for rising for the first time to address members on a note of controversy, but I cannot support the amendment for several reasons.' Florentyna started by talking about the role of a mother who wanted to continue a professional career. She then proceeded to outline the reasons why Congress should not adopt the amendment. She was aware of being nervous and unusually inarticulate, and after a minute or so noticed that Buchanan and the other Republican who had spoken before her were now holding a heated discussion which only encouraged some of the members in the chamber to talk among themselves while others left their seats to chat to colleagues. Soon the noise reached such a pitch that Florentyna could hardly hear the sound of her own voice. Suddenly in the middle of a sentence, she stopped speaking and stood in silence.

The Speaker banged his gavel and asked if she had yielded her time to anyone.

She turned to Carl Albert and said, 'No, Mr. Speaker, I do not intend to continue.'

'But the distinguished member was in the middle of a sentence.'

'Indeed I was, Mr. Speaker, but it has become obvious to me that there are some in this august chamber who are more interested in the sound of their own voices than in anyone else's views.' Buchanan rose to object, but was gavelled down as out of order by the Speaker. Uproar broke out, and members who had never noticed her before stared at Florentyna.

She remained at the rostrum as the Speaker went on to bang his gavel continually. When the noise died down, Florentyna continued. 'I am aware, Mr. Speaker, that it takes several years in this place before one can hope to get anything done, but I had not realised that it might take as many years before anyone would have the good manners to listen to what one had to say.'

Once again pandemonium broke out while Florentyna remained silently clutching on to the rostrum. She was now trembling from head to toe. Eventually the Speaker brought the chamber to order.

'The Honourable Member's point is well taken,' he said, staring down at the two offenders, who looked more than a little embarrassed. 'I have mentioned this habit to the House on several occasions in the past. It has taken a new member to remind us how discourteous we have become. Perhaps the distinguished gentle lady from Illinois would now like to resume.' Florentyna checked the point she had reached in her notes. The House waited in expectant silence.

She was about to continue when a hand rested firmly on her shoulder. She turned to see a smiling Sandra Read by her side. 'Sit down. You've beaten them all. If you speak now it can only spoil the effect you've created. As soon as the next speaker rises, leave the chamber immediately.' Florentyna nodded, yielded the remainder of her time, before returning to her seat.

Speaker Albert recognised the next speaker and Florentyna walked towards the Speaker's gallery exit with Sandra Read. When they reached the doors Sandra left her with the words, 'Well done. Now you're on your own.'

Florentyna did not understand what Sandra had meant until she walked into the lobby and found herself surrounded by reporters.

'Can you step outside?' asked an interviewer from C.B.S. Florentyna followed him where she was met by television cameras, reporters and flash bulbs.

'Do you think that Congress is a disgrace?'

'Will your stand help the pro-choice advocates?'

'How would you change the procedure?'

'Did you plan the whole exercise?'

Question after question came flying at Florentyna, and before the evening was out Senator Mike Mansfield, the Democratic Majority Leader in the Senate, had called to congratulate her and she had been asked by Barbara Walters to appear on the 'Today' show.

The following morning the *Washington Post*'s version of events in the chamber made it sound as though Florentyna had single-handedly caused a declaration of war. Richard called to read the caption underneath her photograph on the front page of the *New York Times*: 'Woman of courage arrives in Congress', and as the morning wore on it became obvious that Congresswoman Kane had become famous overnight because she *hadn't* made a speech. Phyllis Mills, a Representative from Pennsylvania, warned her the following day that she had better choose her next subject carefully because the Republicans would be lying in wait for her with sharpened knives.

'Perhaps I should quit while I'm ahead,' said Florentyna.

When the initial furore had subsided and her mail had dropped from one thousand letters per week back to the usual three hundred, Florentyna began to settle down to building a serious reputation. In Chicago that reputation was already growing as she found from her twice-monthly visits. Her constituents were coming to believe that she could actually influence the course of events. This worried Florentyna because she was quickly discovering how little room a politician has for manoeuvre outside the established guidelines. At a local level, however, she felt that she could help people who were often simply overwhelmed by the bureaucratic system. She decided to add another staff member to the Chicago office to handle the extra case work.

Richard was delighted to see how rewarding Florentyna found her new career, and tried to take as much pressure off her as possible when it came to the day-to-day business of the Baron Group. Edward Winchester helped considerably by taking on some of the responsibilities, both in New York and Chicago. In Chicago, Edward had gained considerable sway in the smoke-filled rooms as Mayor Daley recognised the need for a new breed of political operative in the wake of the 1972 Presidential election. It seemed Daley's old supporters were coming to terms with Florentyna's future. Richard was full of praise for Edward's contribution as a member of the board and was already considering inviting him to join Lester's as well.

No sooner had Florentyna completed her first year in Congress than she complained to Richard that she would soon have to start campaigning again.

'What a crazy system that sends you to the House for only two years; no sooner have you settled into the place than you have to recycle the campaign bumper stickers.'

'How would you change it?' asked Richard

'Well, senators are in a far better position, coming up for election only every six years, so I think I would make Congressional terms at least four years in length.'

When she repeated her grouse to Edward in Chicago he was sympathetic but pointed out that in her case she didn't look as if she would have any real opposition from the Democrats or the Republicans.

'What about Ralph Brooks?'

'He seems to have his eye firmly set on the State's Attorney's office since his recent marriage. Perhaps with his wife's social background she doesn't want to see him in Washington politics.'

'Don't believe it,' said Florentyna. 'He'll be back.'

In September, Florentyna flew to New York and, together with Richard, drove William up to Concord, New Hampshire, to start his fifth-form year at St. Paul's. The car was packed with more stereo equipment, Rolling Stones records and athletic gear than books. Annabel was now in her first year at the Madeira so she could be near her mother, but she still showed no signs of wanting to follow Florentyna to Radcliffe.

Florentyna was disappointed that Annabel's sole interests always seemed to centre on boys and parties. Not once during the holidays did she discuss her progress at school or even open a book. She avoided her brother's company and would even change the subject whenever William's name came up in conversation. It became more obvious every day that she was jealous of her brother's achievements.

Carol did the best she could to keep her occupied but on two occasions Annabel disobeyed her father and once returned home from a date hours after she had agreed.

Florentyna was relieved when the time came for Annabel to return to school as she had decided not to overreact to her daughter's holiday escapades. She hoped it was nothing more than an adolescent stage she was passing through.

Struggling to survive in a man's world was nothing new for Florentyna and she began her second year in Congress with considerably more confidence. Life at the Baron had been a little sheltered in comparison with politics. After all, she had been the chairman of the group and Richard had always been there by her side. Edward was quick to point out that perhaps having to fight a little harder than any man was no bad preparation for the time when she would have to face new rivals. When Richard asked her how many of her colleagues she considered capable of holding down a place on the board of the Baron Group, she had to admit that there were very few.

Florentyna enjoyed her second year far more than her first, and there were many highlights: in February she successfully sponsored an amendment to a Bill which exempted from any taxation scientific publications selling under ten thousand copies per issue. In April she fought several provisions in Reagan's budget proposal. In May, she and Richard received an invitation to a reception at the White House for Queen Elizabeth II. But the most pleasing aspect of the whole year was the feeling that for the first time she was actually influencing issues that affected her constituents' lives.

The invitation that gave her the most pleasure that year came from Transportation Secretary William Coleman to view the tall ships enter New York Harbour in honour of the Bicentennial. It reminded her that America also had a history she could be proud of.

In all, it was a memorable year for Florentyna, and the only sad event that occurred was the death of her mother who had been afflicted with respiratory trouble for many months. For over a year Zaphia had dropped out of Chicago life at the very moment when she had been dominating the society columns. She had told Florentyna as far back as 1968, when she had brought the revolutionary Saint Laurent show to the Windy City, 'These new fashions simply don't compliment a woman of my age.' After that she was rarely seen at any of the major charity events and her name soon began to disappear from the embossed notepaper used for such occasions. She was happy to spend hours listening to stories about her grandchildren, and she often offered a word of motherly advice that her daughter had grown to respect.

Florentyna had wanted a quiet funeral. As she stood by the grave – with her son and daughter on each side of her – listening to the words of Father O'Reilly, she realised that she could no longer hope for privacy, even in death. As the coffin was lowered into the grave the flash bulbs continued to pop until the earth had completely covered the wooden casket and the last of the Rosnovskis was buried.

During the final few weeks before the Presidential election, Florentyna spent more of her time in Chicago, leaving Janet in Washington to run the office. After Representative Wayne Hayes admitted paying a member of his staff fourteen thousand dollars a year salary even though she could not type a word or answer the phone, Janet and Louise put in for a rise.

'Yes, but Miss Ray is supplying a service for Mr. Hayes that I have not yet found necessary in my office,' said Florentyna.

'But the problem in this office is the other way around,' said Louise.

'What do you mean?' asked Florentyna.

'We spend our life being propositioned by members who think we're a Capitol Hill perk.'

'How many members have propositioned you, Louise?' said Florentyna, laughing.

'Over a couple of dozen,' said Louise.

'And how many have you accepted?'

'Three,' said Louise, grinning.

'And how many have propositioned you?' said Florentyna, turning to Janet.

'Three,' said Janet.

'And how many did you accept?'

'Three,' said Janet.

When they had stopped laughing, Florentyna said, 'Well, perhaps Joan Mondale was right. What the Democrats do to their secretaries, the Republicans do to the country. You both get a rise.'

Edward turned out to be accurate about her selection. She was unopposed as the Democratic candidate, and the Primary for the Ninth District was virtually a walkover. Stewart Lyle, who ran again as the Republican candidate, admitted privately to her that he now had little chance. 'Re-elect Kane' stickers seemed to be everywhere.

Florentyna looked forward to a new session of Congress with a Democratic President in the White House. The Republicans had selected Jerry Ford after a tough battle with Governor Reagan, while the Democrats had chosen Jimmy Carter, a man she had barely heard of until the New Hampshire Primary.

Ford's Primary battle against Ronald Reagan did not enhance the President's cause and the American people had still not forgiven him for pardoning Nixon. On the personal front, Ford seemed incapable of avoiding naïve mistakes such as bumping his head on helicopter doors and falling down airplane steps. And during a television debate with Carter, Florentyna sat horrified when he suggested that there was no Soviet domination of Eastern Europe. 'Tell the Polish people that,' she said indignantly to the small screen.

The Democratic candidate committed his share of mistakes as well, but in the end it seemed to Richard that

Carter's image as an anti-Washington, evangelical Christian, when viewed against the problems Ford had inherited from his links with Nixon, would be enough to give Carter the election by a small margin.

'Then why was I returned with an increased majority?' Florentyna demanded.

'Because many Republicans voted for you but not for Carter.'

'Were you among them?'

'I plead the Fifth Amendment.'

28

RICHARD WORE A SMART dark suit on the day of the Inauguration but was sorry the President had insisted that no one wear morning dress. The Kane family watched the new President deliver a speech that lacked the charisma of Kennedy or the wisdom of Roosevelt but its simple message of Christian honesty above all else captured the mood of the moment. America wanted a decent, homespun man in the White House and everyone was willing him to succeed. President Ford sat on his immediate left; President Nixon was conspicuously absent. Florentyna felt the tone for Carter's Administration was set with the words:

'I have no dream to set forth today, but rather urge a fresh faith in the old dream. We have learned that "more" is not necessarily "better"; that even our great nation has recognised limits, and that we can neither answer all questions nor solve all problems.'

The Washington crowds were delighted when the new President, the First Lady and their daughter Amy walked down Pennsylvania Avenue hand in hand to the White House, and it was obvious that the Secret Service were quite unprepared for such a break with tradition.

'Dancer is on the move,' said one of them over his two-way radio. 'God help us if we are going to have four years of spontaneous gestures.'

That evening the Kanes attended one of the seven 'People's Parties', as Carter had named them, to commemorate the Inauguration. Florentyna was dressed in a new Gianni di Ferranti gown of white with a faint trace of gold thread which kept the camera bulbs flashing all night. During the evening they were both introduced to the President, who seemed to Florentyna to be as shy in person as he was in public.

When Florentyna took her seat on the floor of the chamber for the start of the 95th Congress it felt like returning to school, with all the back-slapping, hand shaking, hugging and noisy discussion about what members had been up to during the recess.

'Glad to see you won again.'

'Was it a hard campaign?'

'Don't imagine you'll be able to select your own committee now that Mayor Daley is dead.'

'What did you think of Jimmy's address?'

The new Speaker, Tip O'Neill, took his place in the centre of the podium, banged his gavel, called everyone to order and the whole process began again.

Florentyna had moved up two places on the Appropriations Committee, following one retirement and one defeat since the last election. She now understood how the committee system worked but still feared it would be many years and several elections before she made any real headway for the causes she espoused. Richard had suggested she concentrate on a field in which she could gain more public recognition and she had wavered between abortion and tax reform. Richard counselled against too close an association with abortion and reminded her of how her colleagues referred to Elizabeth Holtzman as 'Congressperson Holzperson'. Florentyna agreed in principle but was no nearer deciding what her special subject should be when the subject chose itself.

A debate of the Defence Appropriations Bill was taking

place on the floor of the House, and Florentyna sat listening as members casually discussed the allocation of billions of dollars on defence spending. She did not sit on the Defence Sub-Committee on which Robert C. L. Buchanan was the ranking Republican, but she was deeply interested in his opinions. Buchanan was reminding the House that Defence Secretary Brown had recently asserted that the Russians now had the capability to destroy American satellites in space. Buchanan went on to demand that the new President spend more money on defence and less in other areas. Florentyna still considered Buchanan the worst sort of conservative fool and in a moment of anger rose to challenge him. Everyone in the chamber remembered their last confrontation and knew that Buchanan would have to allow her to state her case.

'Would the Congressman yield for a question?'

'I yield to the gentle lady from Illinois.'

'I am grateful to the distinguished gentleman and would like to enquire where the extra money for these grandiose military schemes will come from?'

Buchanan rose slowly to his feet. He wore a three-piece tweed suit and his silver hair was parted neatly to the right. He rocked from leg to leg like a cavalry officer on a cold parade ground. 'These "grandiose schemes" are no more and no less than those requested by the committee on which I serve and, if I remember correctly, that committee still has a majority from the party which the distinguished member from Illinois represents.' Loud laughter greeted Buchanan's remarks. Florentyna stood up a second time; Buchanan immediately gave way again.

'I am still bound to enquire of the distinguished gentleman from Tennessee where he intends to get this money. From education, hospitals, welfare perhaps?' The chamber was silent.

'I would not take it from anyone, ma'am, but I would warn the gentle lady from Illinois that if there is not enough money for defence we may not need any money for education, hospitals or welfare.'

Buchanan picked up a document from his table and

informed the House of the exact figures spent in the previous year's budget in all the departments Florentyna had mentioned. They showed that in real terms defence spending had dropped more than all the others. 'It's members like the gentle lady who come to the chamber without facts, equipped with nothing more than a vague feeling that defence spending is too high, that make the Kremlin leaders rub their hands with glee while the reputation of the House is at the same time diminished. It is the type of ill-informed attitude that tied the hands of President Roosevelt and left us so little time to come to terms with the menace of Hitler.'

Florentyna wished she had never entered the chamber that afternoon as members from both sides echoed their agreement. As soon as Buchanan had finished his remarks she left the floor and returned quickly to her office.

'Janet, I want all the committee reports from the Appropriations Sub-Committee on Defence for the last ten years, and ask my legislative researchers to join us immediately,' she said even before she reached her desk.

'Yes, ma'am,' said Janet, somewhat surprised, as Florentyna had never mentioned defence in the three years she had known her. The staffers filed in and sank on to Florentyna's old sofa.

'For the next few months I plan to concentrate on defence matters. I need you to go over the reports of the subcommittee during the last ten years and mark up any relevant passages. I am trying to get a realistic appraisal of America's military strength, if we were called upon to defend ourselves against an attack from the Soviets.' The four assistants were writing furiously. 'I want all the major works on the subject including the CIA Team A and Team B evaluations, and I want to be briefed when lectures or seminars on defence or related matters take place in Washington. I want all press comments from the *Washington Post*, the *New York Times*, *Newsweek* and *Time* put in a file for me every Friday night. No one must be able to quote something I haven't had a chance to consider.'

The assistants were as surprised as Janet because they had

been concentrating their efforts on small business and tax reform for over two years. They were not going to have many free weekends during the coming months. Once they had departed Florentyna picked up the phone and dialled five digits. When a secretary answered, she requested an appointment with the Majority Leader.

'Of course, Mrs. Kane. I will ask Mr. Chadwick to call you later today.'

Florentyna was ushered into the Majority Leader's office at ten o'clock the next morning.

'Mark, I want to be put on the Appropriations Sub-Committee on Defence.'

'I wish it were that easy, Florentyna.'

'I know, Mark. But this is the first favour I've asked for in three years.'

'There is only one slot open on that sub-committee and so many members are twisting my arm it's amazing that I'm not permanently in splints. Nevertheless, I'll give your request my serious consideration.' He made a note on the pad in front of him. 'By the way, Florentyna, the League of Women Voters is holding its annual meeting in my district, and they've invited me to make the key speech on the opening day. Now I know how popular you are with the League and I was hoping you might find it possible to fly up and do the speech of introduction.'

'I'll give your request my serious consideration,' said Florentyna, smiling.

She received a note from the Speaker's office two days later informing her of her appointment as the junior member of the Appropriations Sub-Committee on Defence. Three weeks later she flew to Texas and told the League of Women Voters that as long as there were men like Mark Chadwick in Congress they need have no fears for America's well-being. The women applauded loudly while Florentyna turned to find Mark grinning – with one arm behind his back.

During the summer vacation the whole family went to California. They spent the first ten days in San Francisco with Bella and her family in their new home, high up on the hill, now overlooking the bay.

Claude had become a partner in the law firm, and Bella had been appointed an assistant headmistress. If anything, Richard decided, Claude was a little thinner and Bella a little larger than when they had last seen them.

The holiday would have been enjoyed by everyone if Annabel hadn't frequently disappeared off on her own. Bella gripping a hockey stick firmly in her hand left Florentyna in no doubt how she would have dealt with the girl.

Florentyna tried to keep harmony between the two families, but a confrontation was unavoidable when Bella found Annabel in the attic smoking pot and asked what she thought she was doing.

'Mind your own business,' she said, as she inhaled once more.

When Florentyna lost her temper with Annabel she informed her mother that if she took more interest in *her* welfare and less in that of her constituents perhaps she could have expected a little more from her.

When Richard heard the story he immediately ordered Annabel to pack and accompanied her back to the east coast while Florentyna and William travelled on to Los Angeles for the rest of their holiday.

Florentyna spent an unhappy time phoning Richard twice a day to find out how Annabel was. She and William returned home a week early.

In September, William entered his freshman year at Harvard, taking up residence in the Yard, on the top floor of Gray's Hall, making the fifth generation of Kanes that had been educated at Cambridge. Annabel returned to the Madeira School, where she seemed to make little progress despite the fact that she started spending most weekends under her parents' watchful eyes in Washington.

During the next session of Congress Florentyna allocated all her spare time to reading the defence papers and books her staffers put in front of her. She became engrossed in the problems the nation faced if it wished to remain strategically safe. She read papers by experts, spoke to Assistant Secretaries at the Defence Department, and studied the major U.S. treaties with her NATO allies. She visited the Air Force SAC headquarters, toured U.S. bases in Europe and the Far East, observed army manoeuvres in North Carolina and California, even spent a weekend submerged in a nuclear submarine. She sought meetings with admirals and generals, as well as having discussions with privates and non-commissioned officers, but she never once raised her voice in the House chamber and only asked questions in committee hearings, where she was often struck by the fact that the most expensive weapons were not always the most effective. She began to realise that the military had a long way to go in improving its readiness, which had not been fully tested since the Cuba confrontation. After a year of listening and studying she came to the conclusion that Buchanan had been right and it was she who had been the fool. America had no choice but to increase defence spending while Russia remained so openly aggressive. She was surprised to find how much she enjoyed her new discipline and realised much how her views had been changed when a colleague openly referred to her as a hawk.

She studied all the papers on the M-X missile system, when it came under the jurisdiction of the House Armed Services Committee. As soon as the so-called Simon Amendment to hold up the authorisation of the system appeared on the calendar she asked Chairman Galloway to be recognised during the debate.

Florentyna listened intently as other members gave their views for and against the amendment. Robert Buchanan gave a considered speech against it. When he took his seat Florentyna was surprised the Speaker called on her next. She rose to a packed house. Representative Buchanan said in a voice loud enough to carry, 'We are now about to hear the views of an expert.' One or two Republicans seated near him laughed as Florentyna walked to the front of the podium. She placed her notes on the lectern in front of her.

'Mr. Speaker, I address the House as a convinced supporter of the M-X missile. America cannot afford to delay any further the defence of this country because a group of Congressmen claim they want more time to read the relevant documents. Those papers have been available to every member of the House for over a year. It hardly needs a course in speed reading for members to have done their homework before today. The truth is that this amendment is nothing more than a delaying tactic for members who are opposed to the M-X missile system. I condemn those members as men with their heads in the sand, heads that will remain in the sand until the Russians have made their first pre-emptive strike. Don't they realise America must also have a first-strike capability?

'I approve of the Polaris submarine system but we cannot hope to push all our nuclear problems out to sea, especially now that navy intelligence informs us that the Russians have a submarine that can travel at a speed of forty knots and remain below the ocean for four years – four years, Mr. Speaker – without returning to base. The argument that the citizens of Nevada and Utah are in more danger from the M-X system than anyone else is spurious. The land where the missiles would be deployed is already owned by the government and is at present occupied by one thousand nine hundred and eighty sheep and three hundred and seventy cows. I do not believe the American people need to be mollycoddled on the subject of the nation's safety. They have elected us to carry out long-term decisions, not to go on talking while we become weaker by the minute. Some members of Congress would make Nero appear to the American people as a man who was giving a violin concert in aid of the Rome fire brigade.'

When the laughter had diminished, Florentyna became verv grave. 'Have members so quickly forgotten that in 1935 more people worked for the Ford Motor Company than served in the United States armed forces? Have we also forgotten that in the same year we had a smaller army than

Czechoslovakia, a country since trampled on by Germany and Russia in turn? We had a navy half the size of that of France, a country humiliated by the Germans while we sat and watched, and an air force that even Hollywood didn't bother to hire for war movies. When the threat of Hitler first arose we could not have rattled a sabre at him. We must be certain such a situation can never arise again.

'The American people have never seen the enemy on the beaches of California or on the docksides of New York, but that does not mean that the enemy does not exist. As late as 1950, Russia had as many combat planes as the United States, four times as many troops and thirty tank divisions to America's one. We must never allow ourselves to be at such a disadvantage again. Equally I pray that our great nation will never be involved in another débâcle such as Vietnam, and that none of us will live to see another American die in combat. But our enemies must always be aware that we will meet aggression head on. Like the eagle that bestrides our standard, we will hover always alert to the defence of our friends and the protection of our citizens.'

Some members on the floor of the House started to applaud.

'To each American who says our defence expenditure is too costly, I reply let them look to the countries behind the Iron Curtain and see that no price is too high to pay for the democratic freedom we take for granted in this country. The Iron Curtain is drawn across East Germany, Czechoslovakia, Hungary and Poland, with Afghanistan and Yugoslavia guarding their borders in daily expectation of that curtain being drawn still further, perhaps even reaching the Middle East. After that the Soviets will not be satisfied until it encircles the entire globe.' The House was so silent that Florentyna dropped her voice before she continued. 'Many nations have through history played their role in the protection of the free world. That responsibility has now been passed to the leaders of this commonwealth. Let our grandchildren never say we shirked that responsibility in a cheap exchange for popularity. Let us assure America's freedom by being willing to make a sacrifice now. Let us be able to say to every American that we did not shirk our duty in the face of danger. Let there be in this House no Nero, no fiddler, no fire and no victory for our enemies.'

Members in the chamber cheered while Florentyna remained standing. The Speaker repeated his attempts to gavel the meeting to order. When the last cheer had died she spoke almost in a whisper.

'Let that sacrifice never again be the lives of America's youth, or replaced by the dangerous illusion that we can keep peace in the world without providing for its defence against aggression. Adequately protected, America can exert her influence without fear, govern without terror and still remain the bastion of the free world. Mr. Speaker, I oppose the Simon Amendment as irrelevant, and worse, irresponsible.'

Florentyna took her seat and she was quickly surrounded by colleagues from both sides who praised her speech. The press heaped further praise on her the next day and all the networks included passages from her speech in their evening bulletins. Florentyna was shocked at how glibly they described her as an expert on defence. Two papers even talked of her as a future Vice-President.

Once again Florentyna's mail rose to over a thousand letters a week, but there were three letters that particularly moved her. The first was a dinner invitation from an ailing Hubert Humphrey. She accepted but, like the other guests, did not attend. The second came from Robert Buchanan, simply written in a bold hand:

'I salute you, madam.'

The third was an anonymous scrawled note from Ohio:

> 'You are a commie traitor bent on destroying America with impossible defence commitments. The gas chamber is too good a place for people like you. You should be strung up with that dummy Ford and that pimp Carter. Why don't you get back to the kitchen where you belong, bitch?'

'How would one reply?' asked Janet, stunned by the letter.

'You can't, Janet. Repudiating that sort of mindless prejudice is beyond even your skilful hand. Let's be thankful that ninety-nine per cent of the letters are from fair-minded people who wish to express their views honestly. Though I confess if I knew his address I'd be tempted to reply for the first time in my life, "Up Yours".'

After a hectic week during which she seemed to be perpetually pursued by phone messages, Florentyna spent a quiet weekend with Richard. William was home from Harvard and was quick to show his mother a cartoon from the *Boston Globe* depicting her as a heroine with the head of an eagle, punching a bear on the nose. Annabel phoned from school to tell her mother that she wouldn't be home that weekend.

Florentyna played tennis with her son that Saturday and it took her only a few minutes to realise how fit he was and what a dreadful state she was in. She couldn't pretend walking around golf courses kept her in any real shape. With each shot it became more obvious that William wasn't trying very hard. She was relieved to be told that he couldn't play another set because he had a date that evening. She scribbled a note to Janet to order an exercycle from Hammacher Schlemmer.

Over dinner that night Richard told Florentyna that he wanted to build a Baron in Madrid and that he was thinking of sending Edward to check the building sites.

'Why Edward?'

'He's asked to go. He's working almost full-time for the group now and has even rented an apartment in New York.'

'What can have happened to his law practice?'

'He's become counsel to the firm and says that if you can change your whole career at forty, why shouldn't he? Since Daley's death he hasn't found it a full-time job proving you're worth a place in Congress. I must say he's like a schoolboy who's found himself locked up in a candy store. It's taken a great load off my shoulders. He's the only man I know who works as hard as you.'

'What a good friend he has turned out to be.'

'Yes, I agree. You do realise he's in love with you, don't you?'

'What?' said Florentyna.

'Oh, I don't mean he wants to leap into bed with you, not that I could blame him if he did. No, he simply adores you, but he would never admit it to anyone, although it wouldn't take a blind man to see that.'

'But I never –'

'No, of course you haven't, my darling. Do you think I would have been considering putting him on the board of Lester's if I thought I might lose my wife to him?'

'I wish he would find himself a wife.'

'He'll never marry anyone as long as you are around, Jessie. Just be thankful that you have two men who adore you.'

When Florentyna returned to Washington after the weekend she was greeted with another pile of the invitations that had been coming in with increasing frequency. She sought Edward's advice as to what she should do about them.

'Select about half a dozen of the major invitations to places where your views can be expected to reach the maximum number of people, and explain to the others that your work load does not permit you to accept at the moment. But remember to end each letter of refusal with a personal handwritten line. One day when you are seeking a bigger audience than the Ninth District of Illinois there will be people whose only contact with you will be that letter, and on that alone they will decide whether they are for or against you.'

'You're a wise old thing, Edward.'

'Ah, but you mustn't forget I'm a year older than you, my dear.'

Florentyna took Edward's advice and spent two hours every night dealing with the letters prompted by her speech on defence. At the end of five weeks she had answered every one, by which time her mail had almost returned to normal proportions. She accepted invitations to speak at Princeton and the University of California at Berkeley. She also addressed the cadets of West Point and the midshipmen at Annapolis and was to be the guest of Max Cleveland at a Washington lunch to honour Vietnam veterans. Everywhere she went Florentyna was introduced as one of America's leading authorities on defence. She became so involved and fascinated by the subject that it terrified her how little she really knew and only made her study the subject even more intensively. Somehow she kept up with her work in Chicago, but the more she became a public figure the more she had to assign tasks to her staff. She appointed two more assistants to her Washington office and another in Chicago at her own expense. She was now spending over one hundred thousand dollars a year out of her own pocket. Richard described it as reinvesting in America.

29

'ANYTHING THAT CAN'T WAIT?' asked Florentyna, glancing down at a desk full of correspondence that had arrived that morning. The 95th Congress was winding down and most members were once again more concerned about being re-elected than about sitting in Washington working on legislation. At this stage of the session assistants were spending almost all their time dealing with constituency problems rather than concentrating on national affairs. Florentyna disliked a system that made hypocrites of normally honest people as soon as another election loomed.

'There are three matters that I ought to draw to your attention,' said Janet in her habitually efficient manner. 'The first is that your voting record can hardly be described as exemplary. It has fallen from eighty-nine per cent during the last session to seventy-one per cent this session and your opponents are bound to jump on that fact, claiming that you are losing interest in your job and should be replaced.'

'But the reason I've been missing votes is that I've been visiting defence bases and accepting so many out-of-state engagements. I can't help it if half my colleagues want me to speak in their districts.'

'*I* am aware of that,' said Janet, 'but you can't expect the voters of Chicago to be pleased that you're in California and Princeton when they expect you to be in Washington. It might be wise for you to accept no more invitations from other members or well-wishers until the next session and if you make most of the votes during the last few weeks we may push you back above eighty per cent.'

'Keep reminding me, Janet. What's second?'

'Ralph Brooks has been elected State's Attorney of Chicago, so he should be out of your hair for a while.'

'I wonder,' said Florentyna, scribbling a note on her pad to remind herself to write and congratulate him. Janet placed a copy of the Chicago *Tribune* in front of her. Mr. and Mrs. Brooks stared up at her. The caption read: 'The new State's Attorney attends charity concert in aid of the Chicago Symphony Orchestra.'

'Doesn't miss a trick, does he?' commented Florentyna. 'I bet his voting record would always be over eighty per cent. And the third thing?'

'You have a meeting with Don Short at ten a.m.'

'Don Short?'

'He's a director of Aerospace Plan, Research and Development Inc. (A.P.R.D.),' said Janet. 'You agreed to see him because his company has a contract with the government to build radar stations for tracking enemy missiles. They are now bidding for the new navy contract to put their equipment into American warships.'

'Now I remember,' said Florentyna. 'Somebody produced an excellent paper on the subject. Dig it out for me, will you?'

Janet passed over a brown manila file. 'I think you'll find everything is in there.'

Florentyna smiled and flicked quickly through the papers. 'Ah, yes, it all comes back. I shall have one or two pointed questions for Mr. Short.'

For the next hour she dictated letters before reading through the briefing file. She found time to jot down several questions before Mr. Short arrived.

'Congresswoman, this is a great honour,' said Don Short, thrusting out his hand as Janet accompanied him into Florentyna's room as ten o'clock struck. 'We at Aerospace Plan look upon you as one of the last bastions of hope for the free world.'

It was very rare for Florentyna to dislike someone on sight, but it was clear that Don Short was going to fall firmly into that category. Around five foot seven and twenty pounds overweight, he was a man in his early fifties and nearly bald except for a few strands of black hair which had been carefully combed over the dome of his head. He wore a check suit and carried a brown leather Gucci briefcase. Before Florentyna had acquired her present hawkish reputation she had never been visited by the Don Shorts of this world, as no one thought it worthwhile to lobby her. However, since she had been on the Defence Sub-Committee Florentyna had received endless invitations to dinners, travel-free junkets, and had even been sent gifts ranging from bronze model F-15s to manganese nodules encased in lucite.

Florentyna only accepted those invitations that were relevant to the issues she was working on at the time, and with the exception of a model of Concorde she returned every gift she had been sent with a polite note. She kept the statue of Concorde on her desk to remind everyone that she believed in excellence whichever country was responsible. She had been told that Margaret Thatcher had a replica of Apollo 11 on her desk in the House of Commons and she assumed it was there for the same reason.

Janet left the two of them alone and Florentyna ushered Don Short into a comfortable chair. He crossed his legs, giving Florentyna a glimpse of hairless skin where his trousers failed to meet his sock.

'A nice office you have here. Are those your children?' he asked, jabbing a pudgy finger at the photos on Florentyna's desk.

'Yes,' said Florentyna.

'Such good-looking kids – take after their mother.' He laughed nervously.

'I think you wanted to talk to me about the XR-108, Mr. Short?'

'That's right; but do call me Don. We believe it's the one piece of equipment the U.S. Navy cannot afford to be without. The XR-108 can track and pinpoint an enemy missile at a distance of over ten thousand miles. Once the XR-108 is installed in every American carrier, the Russians will never dare attack America, because America will always be sailing the high seas, guarding her people while they sleep.' Mr. Short stopped almost as if he were expecting applause. 'What is more, my company's equipment can photograph every missile site in Russia,' he continued, 'and beam the picture straight on to a television screen in the White House Situation Room. The Russians can't even go to the john without us taking a photo of them.' Mr. Short laughed again.

'I have studied the capabilities of the XR-108 in depth, Mr. Short, and I wonder why Boeing claims it can produce essentially the same piece of equipment at only seventy-two per cent of your price.'

'Our equipment is far more sophisticated, Mrs. Kane, and we have a proven record in the field, having already supplied the U.S. Army.'

'Your company did not complete the tracking stations for the Army by the date specified in your contract, and handed the government a cost over-run of seventeen per cent on the original estimate – or, to be more precise – twenty-three million dollars.' Florentyna had not once looked at her notes.

Don Short started to lick his lips. 'Well, I'm afraid inflation has taken its toll on everyone, not least the aerospace industry. Perhaps if you could spare a little time to meet our board members, the problem would become clearer to you. We might even arrange a dinner.'

'I rarely attend dinners, Mr. Short. I have long believed that the only person who makes any profit over dinner is the maître d'.'

Don Short laughed again. 'No, no, I meant a testimonial dinner in your honour. We would invite, say, five hundred people at fifty dollars a head which you could add to your campaign fund, or to whatever you need the cash for,' he added, almost in a whisper.

Florentyna was about to throw the man out when her secretary arrived with some coffee. By the time Louise left, Florentyna had controlled her temper and made a decision.

'How does that work, Mr. Short?'

'Well, my company likes to give a helping hand to its friends. We understand some of your bills for re-election can be pretty steep, so we hold a dinner to raise a little cash and if all the guests don't turn up but still send their fifty dollars – well, who's to know?'

'As you say, Mr. Short, who's to know?'

'Shall I set that up then?'

'Why don't you, Mr. Short?'

'I knew we could work together.'

Florentyna just managed a tight-lipped smile as Don Short offered a moist hand before Janet showed him out.

'I'll be in touch, Florentyna,' he said, turning back.

'Thank you.'

As soon as the door closed the voting bells started to ring. Florentyna glanced up at the clock on which tiny white bulbs were flashing to show that she still had five minutes to reach the chamber. 'Well, there's one I can pick up,' she said, and left to run to the elevator reserved for members of Congress. When she reached the basement she jumped on the subway that went between Longworth and the Capitol and took a seat next to Bob Buchanan.

'How are you going to vote?' he asked.

'Good heavens,' said Florentyna, 'I don't even know what we are voting for or against yet.'

Her thoughts were still focused on Don Short and what she was going to do about his dinner.

'You're okay this time. It's lifting the retirement age cap from sixty-five to seventy, and on that one I am sure we can both vote the same way.'

'It's only a plot to keep old men like you in Congress, and see that I never get to chair any committees.'

'Wait until you're sixty-five, Florentyna. Then you might feel differently.'

The subway reached the basement of the Capitol and the two representatives took the elevator up to the chamber together. It pleased Florentyna that this diehard Republican now looked upon her as a fully fledged member of the club. When they reached the chamber they rested on the brass rail at the back, waiting for their names to be called.

'I never enjoy standing on your side of the chamber,' he said. 'After all these years, it still feels strange.'

'Some of us are quite human, you know, and I'll let you in on a secret: my husband voted for Jerry Ford.'

'Wise man, your husband,' chuckled Buchanan.

'Perhaps your wife voted for Jimmy Carter?'

The old man suddenly looked sad. 'She died last year,' he said.

'I *am* sorry,' said Florentyna. 'I had no idea.'

'No, no, my dear. I realised that, but rejoice in your family because they are not always with you, and the one thing I have discovered is that this place can only be a poor substitute for a real family, whatever you imagine you achieve. They've started calling the Bs so I will leave you to your thoughts . . . I shall find standing on this side of the aisle more pleasant in the future.'

Florentyna smiled and reflected how their mutual respect had been conceived in mutual mistrust. She was thankful that the party differences so crudely displayed on election platforms disappeared in the privacy of everyday work. A few moments later, they called the Ks and once she had punched her card into the voting pocket she went back to her office and phoned Bill Pearson, the Majority whip, to ask for an immediate interview.

'Must it be this minute?'

'This minute, Bill.'

'I suppose you want me to put you on the Foreign Affairs Committee.'

'No, it's far more serious than that.'

'Then you had better come around right away.'

Bill Pearson puffed away at his pipe as he listened to Florentyna recount what had happened in her office that morning. 'We know a lot of this sort of thing goes on, but we're rarely able to prove it. Your Mr. Short seems to have provided an ideal chance to catch someone with their radar scanner in the pie. You go through with the whole charade, Florentyna, and keep me briefed. The moment they hand over any money we'll jump on Aerospace Plan like a ton of bricks, and if in the end we can't prove anything, at least the exercise might make other members of Congress think twice before getting themselves involved in these sorts of shenanigans.'

Over the weekend Florentyna told Richard about Don Short, but he showed no surprise. 'The problem's a simple one. Some Congressmen have only their salaries to live on, so the temptation to pick up cash must sometimes be overwhelming, especially if they are fighting for a seat they could lose and have no assured job to fall back on.'

'If that's the case, why did Mr. Short bother with me?'

'That's also easy to explain. I receive half a dozen personal approaches a year at the bank. The sort of people who offer bribes imagine no one can resist the chance to make a quick buck without Uncle Sam finding out, because that's the way they would react themselves. You would be surprised how many millionaires would sell their mothers for ten thousand dollars in cash.'

Don Short phoned during the week and confirmed that a testimonial dinner had been arranged in Florentyna's honour at the Mayflower Hotel. He expected about five hundred people to be present. Florentyna thanked him, then buzzed

Louise on the intercom and asked her to write the date in the appointment book.

Because of the pressure Florentyna was under with Congressional business and out-of-state trips over the next few weeks, she nearly missed Don Short's testimonial dinner altogether. She was on the floor of the House supporting a colleague's amendment to a Small Businesses Bill, when Janet hurried into the chamber.

'Have you forgotten the Aerospace Plan dinner?'

'No, but it's not for another week,' said Florentyna.

'If you check your card, you'll find it's tonight and you're due there in twenty minutes,' said Janet. 'And don't forget there are five hundred people waiting for you.'

Florentyna apologised to her colleague and quickly left the chamber and ran to the Longworth garage. She drove out into the Washington night well above the speed limit. She turned off Connecticut Avenue at De Sales Street and left her car in a lot before walking through the side entrance of the Mayflower. She was a few minutes late, her thoughts far from collected, and arrived to find Don Short, dressed in a tight-fitting dinner jacket, standing in the lobby waiting to greet her. Florentyna suddenly realised that she had not had time to change and hoped that the dress she was wearing did not look too casual.

'We've taken a private room,' he said as he led her towards the lift.

'I didn't realise the Mayflower had a banquet room that could seat five hundred,' she said as the elevator doors closed.

Don Short laughed. 'That's a good one,' he said and led his guest into a room that – had it been packed – would have held twenty people. He introduced her to everyone present, which took a few moments; there were only fourteen guests.

Over dinner, Florentyna listened to Don Short's blue stories and tales of Aerospace Plan's triumphs. She wasn't sure that she could get through the whole evening without exploding. At the end of the dinner Don rose from his seat, tapped a spoon on his empty glass and made a fulsome speech about his close friend Florentyna Kane. The applause when he sat down was as loud as one could hope for from fourteen people. Florentyna made a short reply of thanks and managed to escape a few minutes after eleven, at least grateful that the Mayflower had provided an excellent meal.

Don Short escorted her back to the parking lot and as she climbed into her car, he handed her an envelope. 'I'm sorry so few people turned up, but at least all the absentees sent in their fifty dollars.' He grinned as he closed the car door.

After Florentyna had driven back to the Baron, she tore open the envelope and studied the contents: a cheque for twenty-four thousand three hundred dollars made out to cash.

She told Bill Pearson the whole story the following morning and handed over the envelope. 'This,' he said, waving the cheque, 'is going to open a whole can of worms.' He smiled and locked the twenty-four thousand three hundred dollars away in his desk.

Florentyna left for the weekend, feeling she had carried out her part of the exercise rather well. Even Richard congratulated her. 'Although we could have done with the cash ourselves,' he said.

'What do you mean?' asked Florentyna.

'I think the Baron's profits are going to take a big drop this year.'

'Good heavens, why?'

'A series of financial decisions implemented by President Carter which are harming the hotels while ironically helping the bank – we have inflation running at fifteen per cent while prime rate is sixteen. I fear the expense account business trip is the first cutback for most companies who have discovered the telephone is cheaper. So we are not filling all our rooms and we end up having to raise the prices – which only gives the business community even more reason to cut back on business travel. Into the bargain, food prices have rocketed while wages are trying to keep up with inflation.'

'Every other hotel group must be faced with the same problem.'

'Yes, but the decision to move the corporate offices out of the New York Baron last year turned out to be far more expensive than I budgeted for. 450 Park Avenue may be a good address but we could have built two hotels in the south in exchange for having that on our letterhead.'

'But that decision released three floors in the New York hotel which allowed us to operate the new banquet rooms.'

'And still the hotel only made a profit of two million while sitting on real estate worth forty million.'

'But there has to be a Baron in the centre of New York. You couldn't think of selling our most prestigious hotel.'

'Until it loses money.'

'But our reputation . . .'

'Your father was never sentimental about reputation when measured against profits.'

'So what are we doing about it?'

'I'm going to commission McKinsey and Company to carry out a detailed assessment of the whole group. They will give us an interim report in three months, and complete the study in twelve months. I've already spoken to a Mr. Michael Hogan at McKinsey – he's drawing up a proposal.'

'Surely moving in the top consultants in New York will cost us even more money?'

'Yes, it'll be expensive, but I wouldn't be surprised to discover that it will save us a considerable amount in the long run. We must remember that modern hotels all around the world are serving different customers from those your father built Barons for. I want to be sure we're not missing something that's staring us in the face.'

'But can't our senior executives give us that sort of advice?'

'When McKinsey moved into Bloomingdale's,' said Richard, 'they recommended that the store should change the location of seventeen of its counters from their traditional positions. Simple, you might say, but the profits were up twenty-one per cent in the following year when none of the executive staff had considered any changes were necessary. Perhaps we face the same problem without realising it.'

'Hell, I feel so out of touch.'

'Don't worry, Jessie darling, nothing is going to be acted on that doesn't meet with your full approval.'

'And how is the bank surviving?'

'Ironically, Lester's is making more money on loans and overdrafts than at any time since the Depression. My decision to move into gold when Carter won the election has paid off handsomely. If Carter is re-elected, I shall buy more gold. If Reagan captures the White House I shall sell the same day. But don't you worry. As long as you keep earning your fifty-seven thousand five hundred a year as a Congresswoman, I'll sleep easy knowing we have something to fall back on in bad times. By the way, have you told Edward about Don Short and the twenty-four thousand dollars?

'Twenty-four thousand three hundred. No, I haven't spoken to him in days, and when I do all he wants to talk about is how to run a hotel group.'

'I'm inviting him to join the Lester's board at the annual meetings. It will be the bank next.'

'He'll be running the whole show soon,' said Florentyna.

'That's exactly what I'm planning for when I become the First Gentleman.'

When Florentyna arrived back in Washington, she was surprised to find there was no message awaiting her from Bill Pearson. His secretary told her that he was in California campaigning, which reminded her how close the election was. Janet was quick to point out that the legislature was sleeping on its feet again, waiting for the new session, and that perhaps it might be wise for Florentyna to spend more time in Chicago.

On Thursday, Bill Pearson phoned from California to tell Florentyna that he had spoken with the ranking Republican and the chairman of the Defence Sub-Committee, and they both felt it would cause more trouble than it was worth to raise the issue before the election. He asked her not to declare the donation, because his investigation would be hampered.

Florentyna strongly disagreed with his advice and even considered raising the whole issue with the ranking committee members herself, but when she phoned Edward he counselled against such a move on the grounds that the whip's office undoubtedly possessed more information about bribery than she did, and it might look as if she were working behind their backs. Florentyna reluctantly agreed to wait until after the election.

Somehow Florentyna – with continual reminders from Janet – managed to push her voting record up to over eighty per cent by the end of the session, but only at the cost of turning down every invitation outside Washington that appeared in front of her, and she suspected there had been a whole lot more that Janet had prevented from landing on her desk. When Congress adjourned, Florentyna returned to Chicago to prepare for another election.

She was surprised to find, during the campaign, that she spent a considerable part of her time sitting in the Cook County Democratic headquarters on Randolph Street. Although Carter's first year had not lived up to the expectations of the American voters, it was well known that the local Republicans were finding it hard to convince anyone to run against Florentyna. To keep her occupied, her staff sent her off to speak on behalf of other Democratic candidates in the state as often as possible.

In the end, Stewart Lyle agreed to run again but only after he had made it clear to his committee that he was not going to stomp around the district night and day or waste any more of his money. The G.O.P. was not pleased with Lyle when he said in a private conversation – forgetting that nothing was private during an election campaign – 'There is only one difference between Kane and the late Mayor Daley – Kane is honest.'

The Ninth District of Illinois agreed with Stewart Lyle and sent Florentyna back to Congress with a slightly increased majority, but she noted the loss of fifteen of her colleagues from the House and three from the Senate. Among the casualties was Bill Pearson.

Florentyna called Bill at his home in California several times to commiserate, but he was always out. Each time she left a message on the answering machine, but he did not return her calls. She discussed the problem with Richard and Edward, who both advised her to see the Majority Leader immediately.

When Mark Chadwick heard the story he was horrified and said he would be in touch with Bill Pearson at once and speak to her later that day. Mark was as good as his word and phoned back to report something that chilled Florentyna: Bill Pearson had denied any knowledge of the twenty-four thousand three hundred dollars and was claiming that he had never discussed a bribe case with Florentyna. Pearson had reminded Chadwick that if Florentyna had received twenty-four thousand three hundred dollars from any source she was bound by law to report it either as a campaign contribution or as income. No mention of the money had been made on her campaign forms and, under House rules, she was not entitled to receive an honorarium of over seven hundred and fifty dollars from anyone. Florentyna explained to the Majority Leader that Bill Pearson had asked her not to declare the money. Mark assured Florentyna that he believed her but was not quite clear how she was going to prove that Pearson was lying. It was common knowledge, he added, that Pearson had been in financial trouble since his second divorce. 'Two alimonies when you're out of work would flatten most good men,' he pointed out.

Florentyna agreed to let Mark make a full investigation while she remained silent on the matter. Don Short rang during the week to congratulate her on her victory and to remind her that the contract with the Navy for the missile programme was up for discussion in the sub-committee that Thursday. Florentyna bit her lip after Don Short's next statement: 'I'm glad you cashed the cheque because I'm sure the money came in useful at election time.'

Florentyna immediately asked the Majority Leader to

postpone the vote on the missile programme until he had completed his enquiry on Bill Pearson. Mark Chadwick explained that he couldn't comply with her request because the allocated funds would go elsewhere if the decision were held up. Although Defence Secretary Brown didn't care which company was awarded the contract, he had warned them that all hell would break loose if a decision were postponed any longer. Finally, Chadwick reminded Florentyna of her own speech about members who held up defence contracts. She didn't waste any time arguing.

'Are you getting anywhere with your enquiries, Mark?'

'Yes. We know the cheque was cashed at the Riggs National Bank on Pennsylvania Avenue.'

'My bank, and my branch,' said Florentyna in disbelief.

'By a lady of about forty-five who wore dark glasses.'

'Is there any good news?' she asked.

'Yes,' replied Mark. 'The manager considered the sum large enough to make a note of the bill numbers in case some query arose later. How about that for irony?' She tried to smile. 'Florentyna, in my opinion, you have two choices. You can blast the entire thing open at Thursday's meeting or you can keep quiet until I have the whole messy business sorted out. One thing you can't do is talk publicly about Bill Pearson's involvement until I get to the bottom of it.'

'What do you want me to do?'

'The party would probably prefer you to keep quiet, but I know what I would do if the decision was left to me.'

'Thank you, Mark.'

'No one's going to love you for it. But that's never stopped you in the past.'

When Defence Sub-Committee chairman Thomas Lee gavelled the hearing to order, Florentyna had already been in her seat for several minutes making notes. The radar satellite contract was the sixth item on the agenda and she did not speak on the first five items. When she looked towards the press table and the seats occupied by the public she could not avoid the smiling Don Short.

'Item number six,' said the chairman, stifling a slight yawn at the length each subject on the agenda was taking. 'We must discuss today the three companies that have bid on the Navy's missile project. The Defence Department Office of Procurement will make the final decision, but they are still waiting our considered opinion. Who would like to open the discussion?'

Florentyna raised her hand.

'Congresswoman Kane.'

'I have no particular preference, Mr. Chairman, between Boeing and Grumman but under no circumstances could I support the Aerospace Plan bid.' Don Short's face turned ashen with disbelief.

'Can you tell the committee why you feel so strongly against Aerospace Plan, Mrs. Kane?'

'Certainly, Mr. Chairman. My reasons arise from a personal experience. Some weeks ago an employee of Aerospace Plan came to visit me in my offices in order to go over the reasons why his company should be awarded this contract. Later he attempted to bribe me with a cheque for twenty-four thousand three hundred dollars in exchange for my vote today. That man is now in this room and will no doubt have to answer to the courts for his actions later.'

When the chairman of the committee had finally brought the meeting back to order, Florentyna explained how the testimonial dinner had worked and she named Don Short as the man who had given her the money. She turned to look at him, but he had vanished. Florentyna continued her statement but avoided making any reference to Bill Pearson. She still considered that to be a party matter, but when she finished her story she couldn't help noticing that two other members of the committee were as white as Don Short had been.

'In view of this serious allegation made by my colleague, I intend to delay any decision on this item until a full enquiry has been carried out,' Chairman Lee announced.

Florentyna thanked him and left for her office immediately. She walked down the corridor, surrounded by reporters, but made no reply to any of their insistent questions.

She talked to Richard on the phone that night, and he warned her that the next few days were not going to be pleasant.

'Why, Richard? I've only told the truth.'

'I know. But now there are a group of people fighting for their lives on that committee and they only see you as the enemy, so you can forget the Marquis of Queensberry rules.'

When she read the papers the next morning, she found out exactly what Richard had meant.

'Congresswoman Kane Accuses Aerospace Plan of Bribery', ran one headline while another read, 'Company Lobbyist Claims Member of Congress Took Money as Campaign Contribution'. Once Florentyna had seen that most of the papers were running roughly the same story she jumped out of bed, dressed quickly, went without breakfast and drove straight to the Capitol. When she reached her office she studied all the papers in detail, and without exception they all wanted to know where the twenty-four thousand three hundred dollars had disappeared. 'And so do I,' said Florentyna out loud. The headline in the Chicago *Sun-Times* was the most unfortunate: 'Representative Kane Accuses Space Company of Bribery After Cheque Cashed'. True, but misleading.

Richard called to say that Edward was already on his way down from New York and not to talk to the press until she had spoken with him. She would not have been able to in any case because the FBI sent two senior agents to interview her at ten o'clock that morning.

In the presence of Edward and the Majority Leader, Florentyna made a complete statement. The FBI men asked her not to inform the press of Bill Pearson's involvement until they had completed their own investigation. Once again, she reluctantly agreed.

During the day some members of the House went out of their way to congratulate her. Others conspicuously avoided her.

In a lead story in the Chicago *Tribune* that afternoon the

paper wanted to know where the twenty-four thousand three hundred dollars had disappeared. They said it was their unfortunate duty to remind the public that Congresswoman Kane's father had been tried and found guilty of bribery of a public official in the Chicago courts in 1962. Florentyna could almost hear Ralph Brooks calling from the State Attorney's office to let them have all the salient details.

Edward helped Florentyna to keep her temper and Richard flew down from New York every night to be with her. Three days and three nights passed, while the papers kept the story running and Ralph Brooks made a statement from the State Attorney's office saying: 'Much as I admire Mrs. Kane and believe in her innocence I feel it might be wise in the circumstances for her to step down from Congress until the FBI investigation is completed.' It made Florentyna even more determined to stay put, especially when Mark Chadwick phoned to tell her not to give up. It could only be a matter of time before the guilty man was brought to justice.

On the fourth day, with no more news from the FBI, Florentyna was at her lowest point when a reporter from the *Washington Post* phoned.

'Mrs. Kane, may I ask how you feel about Congressman Buchanan's statement on Aerogate?'

'Has he turned against me as well?' she asked quietly.

'Hardly,' said the voice from the other end of the line. 'I'll read what he said. I quote: "I have known Representative Kane for nearly five years as a bitter adversary and she is many things that drive me to despair but, as we say in Tennessee, you'll have to swim to the end of the river to find anyone more honest. If Mrs. Kane is not to be trusted, then I do not know one honest person in either chamber of Congress."'

Florentyna phoned Bob Buchanan a few minutes later.

'Now don't you go thinking I'm getting soft in my old age,' he barked. 'You put a foot wrong in that chamber and I'll cut it off.' Florentyna laughed for the first time in days.

It was a cold December wind that whistled across the east front of the Capitol as Florentyna walked back alone to the

Longworth Building after the last vote that day. The newsboy on the corner was shouting out the evening headlines. She couldn't catch what he was saying – something, someone, arrested. She ran towards the boy, fumbling in her pocket for a coin, but all she could find was a twenty-dollar bill.

'I can't change that,' the boy said.

'Don't bother,' said Florentyna as she grabbed the paper and read the lead story first quickly and then slowly. 'Former Congressman Bill Pearson,' she read aloud as if she wanted to be sure the newsboy could hear, 'has been arrested by the FBI in Fresno, California, in connection with the Aerogate scandal. Over seventeen thousand dollars in cash was found hidden in the rear bumper of his new Ford. He was taken to the nearest police station, questioned and later charged with grand larceny and three other misdemeanours. The young woman who was with him at the time was also charged, as an accomplice.'

Florentyna leaped up and down in the snow as the newsboy quickly pocketed the twenty dollars and ran to sell his papers on another corner. He had always been warned about those Hill types.

'My congratulations on the news, Mrs. Kane.' The maître d'hôtel of the Jockey Club was the first of several to comment that evening. Richard had flown down from New York to take Florentyna to a celebration dinner. On her way into the oak-panelled room, other politicians and members of Washington society came over to say how pleased they were that the truth was at last out. Florentyna smiled at each one of them, a Washington smile that she had learned to develop after nearly five years in politics.

The next day the Chicago *Tribune* and the *Sun-Times* came out with glowing tributes to their representative's ability to stay calm in a crisis. Florentyna gave a wry smile, determined to back her own judgment in the future. Any comment from Ralph Brooks's office was conspicuously absent. Edward sent a large bunch of freesias, while William sent a telegram from Harvard: SEE YOU TONIGHT IF YOU'RE NOT THE WOMAN IN FRESNO STILL BEING HELD FOR FURTHER QUESTIONING. Annabel arrived home seemingly unaware of her mother's recent problems to announce she had been accepted at Radcliffe. Her headmistress at the Madeira School later confided to Florentyna that her daughter's acceptance had turned out to be a very close thing, although it couldn't have hurt that Mr. Kane had been at Harvard and that she herself had attended Radcliffe. Florentyna was surprised that her reputation was such that she could influence her daughter's future without lifting a finger and confessed to Richard later what a relief it was that Annabel's life was more settled.

Richard asked his daughter in what subject she planned to major.

'Psychology and social relations,' Annabel replied without hesitation.

'Psychology and social relations are not real subjects but merely an excuse to talk about yourself for three years,' Richard declared.

William, now a sophomore at Harvard, nodded in sage agreement with his father, and later asked the old man if he could up his allowance to five hundred dollars a term.

When an amendment to the Health Bill, prohibiting abortions after ten weeks, came up on the calendar, Florentyna spoke for the first time since the Aerogate scandal. As she rose from her place, she was greeted with friendly smiles and a ripple of applause from both sides of the aisle. Florentyna made a powerful plea for the life of the mother over that of the unborn child, reminding Congress that there were only eighteen other members who could even experience pregnancy. Bob Buchanan rose from his place and referred to the distinguished lady from Chicago as the worst sort of simpleton who would be claiming next that you could not discuss a future space programme unless one had circled the moon and he pointed out that there was only one member in either house who had managed that.

*

Within a few days Don Short and his twenty-four thousand three hundred dollars seemed to be a thing of the past as Florentyna returned to her normal hectic Congressional schedule. She had moved up two more notches on the Appropriations Committee, and when she looked around the table she began to feel like an old-timer.

30

WHEN FLORENTYNA RETURNED TO Chicago she found Democrats were voicing aloud their fears that having Jimmy Carter in the White House might not necessarily help their chances. Gone were the days when an incumbent could take it for granted that he would be returned to the Oval Office and take with him those of his party who were fighting marginal seats. Richard reminded Florentyna that Eisenhower was the last President to complete two terms.

The Republicans were also beginning to flex their muscles and after the announcement that Jerry Ford would not seek the Presidency, George Bush and Ronald Reagan appeared to be the front runners. In the corridors of Congress it was being openly suggested that Edward Kennedy should run against Carter.

Florentyna continued her daily work in the House and avoided being associated with either camp, although she received overtures from both campaign managers and more than her usual allocation of White House invitations. She remained non-committal, as she wasn't convinced that either candidate was right to lead the party in 1980.

While others spent their time campaigning, Florentyna put pressure on the President to take a stronger line when dealing with heads of state from the Warsaw Pact and pressed for a firmer commitment to NATO; but she appeared to make little headway. When Jimmy Carter told an astonished audience that he was surprised the Russians could go back on their word, Florentyna said despairingly to Janet that any Pole in Chicago could have told him that.

But her final split with the President came when the so-called students took over the American Embassy in Tehran on November 4, 1979, and held fifty-three Americans hostage. The President appeared to do little except make 'Born Again' speeches and say his hands were tied. Florentyna proceeded to bombard the White House by every means at her disposal, demanding that the President should stand up for America. When eventually he did attempt a rescue mission, it aborted, resulting in a sad loss of reputation for the United States in the eyes of the rest of the world.

During a defence debate on the floor of the House soon after this humiliating exercise, Florentyna departed from her notes to deliver an off-the-cuff remark. 'How can a nation that possesses the energy, genius and originality to put a man on the moon fail to land three helicopters safely in a desert?' She had momentarily forgotten that the proceedings of the House were now televised and all three networks showed that part of her speech on their evening news bulletins.

She didn't need to remind Richard of George Novak's wisdom in insisting on not renewing Lester's loan to the Shah and when the Russians marched over the Afghanistan border, Richard cancelled their holiday to watch the Olympics in Moscow.

The Republicans went to Detroit in July and chose Ronald Reagan with George Bush as his running mate. A few weeks later the Democrats came to New York and the Party confirmed Jimmy Carter with even less enthusiasm than they had showed for Adlai Stevenson. When the victorious Carter entered Madison Square Garden, even the balloons refused to come down from the ceiling.

Florentyna tried to continue her work in a Congress that was uncertain which would be the majority party in a few months' time. She pushed through amendments on the Defence Appropriations Bill and the Paperwork Reduction Act. As the election drew nearer, she began to fear that the fight for her own seat might be close when the Republicans replaced Stewart Lyle with an enthusiastic young advertising executive, Ted Simmons.

With Janet prodding her, she once again pushed her voting record up to around eighty per cent by only accepting invitations to speak in Washington or Illinois during the last six months prior to the election.

Carter and Reagan seemed to be living in Chicago, flying in and out of Illinois like two cuckoos in one clock. The polls were declaring it was too close to call, but Florentyna was not convinced after she had seen the candidates debate in Cleveland in front of a television audience estimated at one hundred million Americans. The next day Bob Buchanan told her that Reagan might not have won the debate, but he sure as hell hadn't lost it, and for someone trying to remove the White House incumbent that was all important.

As election day drew nearer, the issue of the hostages became more and more a focal point in the minds of the American people, who began to doubt that Carter could ever resolve the problem. On the streets of Chicago, supporters told Florentyna that they would return her to Congress, but they could not back Carter for a second term. Richard said he knew exactly how they felt and predicted that Reagan would win easily. Florentyna took his view seriously and spent the last few weeks of the campaign working as if she were an unknown candidate fighting her first election. Her efforts were not helped by a torrential rainstorm in Chicago that pounded the streets right up until election day.

When the last vote had been counted even she was surprised by the size of the Reagan victory, which took the Senate with him on his coat tails and only just failed to capture the House for the Republicans.

Florentyna was returned to Congress with her majority cut to twenty-five thousand. She flew into Washington, battered but not beaten a few hours before the hostages returned.

The new President lifted the spirit of the nation with his Inaugural Address. Richard, sitting in a morning coat, smiled all the way through the speech and applauded loudly at the section he quoted to Florentyna for several years after.

> We hear much of special interest groups, but our concern must be for a special interest group that has been too long neglected. It knows no sectional boundaries, crosses ethnic and racial divisions and political party lines. It is made up of men and women who raise our food, patrol our streets, man our mines and factories, teach our children, keep our homes and heal us when we're sick. Professionals, industrialists, shopkeepers, clerks, cabbies and truck drivers. They are, in short, we the people, this breed called Americans.

After the speech had been enthusiastically received the President gave a final wave to the crowd in front of the main stand and turned to leave the podium.

Two Secret Service men guided him through a human aisle created by the guard of honour.

Once the Presidential party had reached the bottom of the steps, Mr. Reagan and the First Lady climbed into the back of a large limousine obviously unwilling to follow the example of the Carters and walk down Constitution Avenue to their new home. As the car moved slowly off, one of the Secret Service men flicked a switch on his two-way radio. 'Rawhide returns to Crown' was all he said, and then, staring through a pair of binoculars, followed the limousine all the way to the White House gates.

When Florentyna returned to Congress in January 1981, it was a different Washington. Republicans no longer needed to beg support for every measure they espoused, because elected representatives knew the country was demanding change. Florentyna enjoyed the new challenge of studying the programme Reagan sent up to the Hill and was only too happy to support great sections of it.

She had become so preoccupied with amendments to the

Reagan budget and defence programme that Janet had to point out to her an item in the Chicago *Tribune* which might eventually remove her from the House.

> Senator Nichols of Illinois announced this morning that he would not be seeking re-election to the Senate in 1982.

Florentyna was sitting at her desk, taking in the significance of this statement when the editor of the Chicago *Sun-Times* called to ask her if she would be entering the race for the Senate in 1982. Florentyna realised that it was only natural for the press to speculate on her candidacy after three and a half terms as a representative.

'It doesn't seem that long ago,' she teased, 'that your distinguished journal was suggesting I should resign.'

'There was an English Prime Minister who once said that a week was a long time in politics! So where do you stand, Florentyna?'

'It's never crossed my mind,' she said, laughing.

'That's one statement no one is going to believe, and I am certainly not going to print. Try again.'

'Why are you pushing me so hard when I still have over a year to decide?'

'You haven't heard?'

'Heard what?' she asked.

'At a press conference held this morning at City Hall the State's Attorney announced that he's a candidate.'

'Ralph Brooks To Run For Senate,' ran the banner headline across the afternoon editions of the state's papers. Many reporters mentioned in their columns that Florentyna had not yet made a decision on whether she would challenge the State's Attorney. Once again pictures of Mr. and Mrs. Brooks stared up at Florentyna. The damn man seems to get better looking all the time, she grumbled. Edward called from New York to say he thought she should run but advised her to hold back until the Brooks publicity machine ran out of steam. 'You might even be able to orchestrate your announcement so that it looks as if you are bowing to public pressure.'

'Who are the party faithful backing?'

'My estimate is 60–40 in your favour, but since I'm no longer even a committeeman it's hard to predict. Don't forget it's over a year to the Primary so there's no need to rush in, especially now that Brooks has made his move. You can sit and wait until the time suits you.'

'Why do you think he announced so early?'

'To try and frighten you off, I suppose. Maybe he figures you might hold back until 1984.'

'Perhaps that's a good idea.'

'No, I don't agree. Never forget what happened to John Culver in Iowa. He decided to wait because he felt it would be easier later when weaker opposition was around so his personal assistant ran instead of him and won the seat.'

'I'll think about it and let you know.'

The truth was that Florentyna thought of little else during the next few weeks, because she knew that if she could beat Brooks this time, he would be finished once and for all. She was in no doubt that Ralph Brooks still had ambitions that stretched about sixteen blocks beyond the Senate. On Janet's advice, she now accepted every major invitation to speak in the state and turned down almost all other outside commitments. 'That will give you a chance to find out how the land lies,' said Janet.

'Keep nagging me, Janet.'

'Don't worry, I will. That's what you pay me for.'

Florentyna found herself flying to Chicago twice a week for nearly six months and her voting record in Congress was barely above sixty per cent. Ralph Brooks had the advantage of not living in Washington four days a week or having his record in court expressed in percentage terms. Added to that, Chicago's Mayor Jane Byrne was only halfway through her first term. There were those who said one woman in Illinois politics was quite enough. Nevertheless Florentyna felt confident after she had covered most of the state that Edward had been right, she did have a 60–40 chance of defeating

Ralph Brooks. In truth she believed that defeating Brooks might be harder than getting elected to the Senate, as the mid-term election traditionally ran against the White House incumbent.

One day Florentyna did leave clear in her diary was for the annual meeting of the Vietnam Veterans of America. They had chosen Chicago for the celebrations and invited Senator John Tower of Texas and Florentyna to be the key speakers. The Illinois press was quick to point out the respect with which outsiders treated their favourite daughter. The paper went on to say that the very fact that the vets could couple her with the chairman of the Senate's Armed Services Committee was high praise indeed.

Florentyna was carrying a full load in the House. She successfully sponsored the 'good Samaritan' amendment to the Superfund Act, making its implementation more flexible for companies that made genuine efforts to dispose of toxic wastes. Even Bob Buchanan supported her Good Samaritan amendment.

While she was leaning on the rail at the back of the chamber waiting for the vote on the final passage of her amendment, he told her that he hoped she would run for the Senate seat.

'You're only saying that because you want to see me out of this place.'

He chuckled. 'That would have been one compensation, I must admit, but I don't think you can stay here much longer if you're destined to live in the White House.'

Florentyna looked at him in astonishment. He didn't even glance towards her but continued to gaze into the packed chamber.

'I have no doubt you'll get there. I just thank God I won't be alive to witness your inauguration,' he continued before going off to vote for Florentyna's amendment.

Whenever Florentyna went to Chicago she avoided the question of her candidacy for the Senate, although it was obviously on everyone else's mind. Edward pointed out to her that if she did not run this time it might be her last chance for twenty years as Ralph Brooks was still only forty-four and it would be virtually impossible to defeat him once he was the incumbent.

'Especially when he has "the Brooks charisma",' mocked Florentyna in reply. 'In any case,' she continued, 'who would be willing to wait twenty years?'

'Harold Stassen,' Edward replied.

Florentyna laughed. 'And everyone knows how well he did. I'll have to make up my mind one way or the other before I speak to the Vietnam Vets.'

Florentyna and Richard spent the weekend at Cape Cod and were joined by Edward on the Saturday evening.

Late into the night they discussed every alternative facing Florentyna as well as the effect it would have on Edward's work at the Baron if he were to be in charge of the campaign. When they retired to bed in the early hours of Sunday morning they had come to one conclusion.

The International Room of the Conrad Hilton Hotel was packed with two thousand men and the only other women in sight were waitresses. Richard had accompanied Florentyna to Chicago and was seated next to Senator Tower. When Florentyna rose to address the gathering she was trembling. She began by assuring the vets of her commitment to a strong America and then went on to tell them of her pride in her father when he had been awarded the Bronze Star by President Truman, and of her greater pride in them for having served their country in America's first unpopular war. The veterans whistled and banged their tables in delight. She reminded them of her commitment to the M-X missile system and her determination that Americans would live in fear of no one, especially the Soviets.

'I want Moscow to know,' she said, 'that there may be some men in Congress who would be happy to compromise America's position but not this woman.' The vets cheered again. 'The present isolationist policy President Reagan seems determined to pursue will not help Poland in its present crisis or whichever nation the Russians decide to attack next. At some point we must stand firm, and we cannot afford to wait until the Soviets have camped along the Canadian border.' Even Senator Tower showed his approval of that sentiment.

Florentyna waited for complete silence before saying, 'I have chosen tonight, while I am assembled with a group of people whom everyone in America admires, to say that as long as there are men and women who are willing to serve their country as you have done, I hope to continue to serve in the public life of this great nation, and to that end I intend to submit my name as a candidate for the United States Senate.'

Few people in the room heard the word 'Senate' because pandemonium broke out. Everyone in the gathering who could stand, stood and those who couldn't banged their tables. Florentyna ended her address with the words, 'I pledge myself to an America that does not fear war from any aggressor. At the same time, I pray that you are the last group of veterans this country ever needs.'

When she sat down, the cheering lasted for several minutes and Senator Tower went on to praise Florentyna for one of the finest speeches he had ever heard.

Edward flew in from New York to mastermind the campaign while Janet kept in daily touch from Washington. Money flowed in from every quarter; the work that Florentyna had put in for her constituents was now beginning to pay off. With twelve weeks to go to the Primary, the polls consistently showed a 58–42 lead for candidate Kane across the state.

All through the campaign, Florentyna's assistants were willing to work late into the night, but even they could not arrange for her to be in two places at once. Ralph Brooks criticised her voting record along with the lack of real results she had achieved as a representative in Congress. Some of his attacks began to hit home while Brooks continued to show the energy of a ten year old. Despite this, he didn't seem to make much headway as the polls settled around 55–45 in her favour. Word reached Florentyna that Ralph Brooks's camp was feeling despondent and his campaign contributions were drying up.

Richard flew into Chicago every weekend and the two of them lived out of suitcases, often sleeping in the homes of downstate volunteers. One of Florentyna's younger campaign workers drove them tirelessly around the state in a small blue Chevette. Florentyna was shaking hands outside factory gates on the outskirts of cities before breakfast, attending grange meetings in the rural towns of Illinois before lunch, but somehow she still found time to fit in occasional banking associations and editorial boards in Chicago during the afternoon before the inevitable evening speech and a welcome night at the Baron. During the same period somehow she never missed the monthly meetings of the Remagen Trust.

When she did eat, it was endless Dutch-treat breakfasts and pot-luck dinners. At night before falling into bed she would jot down some more facts and figures – picked up in that day's travels – into a dog-eared black briefing book that was never far from her side. She fell asleep trying to remember names, countless names of people who would be insulted if she ever forgot the role they had played in her campaign. Richard would return to New York on Sunday night every bit as tired as Florentyna. Never once did he complain or bother his wife with any problems facing the bank or the Baron Group. She smiled up at him as they said goodbye at yet another cold February airport: she noticed he was wearing a pair of the blue leather gloves he had bought for his father in Bloomingdale's over twenty years before.

'I still have one more pair to go through Jessie, before I can start looking for another woman,' he said, and left her smiling.

Each morning Florentyna rose more determined. If she was sad about anything, it was how little she saw of William and Annabel. William, now sporting a Fidel Castro moustache, looked set for a summa cum laude while Annabel brought a different young man home each vacation.

From past experience, Florentyna had learned to expect a thunderbolt to land some time during an election campaign, but she had not imagined that a meteorite would accompany it. During the past year, Chicago had been shaken by a series of brutal local murders committed by a man the press had dubbed 'the Chicago Cut-throat'. After the killer had slashed the throat of each of his victims, he carved a heart on their foreheads to leave the police in no doubt who had struck again. More and more in public gatherings Florentyna and Ralph Brooks found that they were being tackled on the question of law and order. At night the streets of Chicago were almost deserted because of the reputation of the killer whom the police were unable to apprehend. To Florentyna's relief, the murderer was caught one night on the Northwestern University campus after he had been taken by surprise while in the act of attacking a college girl.

Florentyna made a statement the next morning in praise of the Chicago police force and wrote a personal note to the officer who made the arrest. She supposed that was the end of the matter until she read the morning paper. Ralph Brooks had announced that he was personally going to prosecute the case against the Chicago Cut-throat even if it resulted in his sacrificing the Senate seat. It was a brilliant stroke that even Florentyna had to admire. Papers all across the nation ran pictures of the handsome State's Attorney next to that of the vicious killer.

The trial began five weeks before the Primary and proceedings had obviously been speeded up because of the State's Attorney's influence. It meant Ralph Brooks was on the front page every day, demanding the death penalty so that the people of Chicago could once again walk the streets safely at night. Florentyna made press statement after press statement on the energy crisis, airport noise regulations, grain price supports, even Russia's troops movements on the Polish border after martial law was instituted and the Solidarity leaders were locked up, but she couldn't knock the

State's Attorney off the front page. At a meeting with the editorial board of the *Tribune*, Florentyna complained good-naturedly to the editor, who was apologetic but pointed out that Ralph Brooks was selling newspapers. Florentyna sat in her Washington office, impotently aware that she had no effective way of countering her opponent.

In the hope that the clash might give her a chance to shine for a change, she challenged Ralph Brooks to a public debate. But the State's Attorney informed the press that he could not consider any such confrontation while so grave a public responsibility rested on his shoulders. 'If I lose my chance to represent the good people of Illinois because of this decision, so be it,' he repeated again and again. Florentyna watched another percentage point slip away.

On the day that the Chicago Cut-throat was convicted, the polls showed that Florentyna's lead had fallen to 52–48. There were two weeks to go.

Florentyna was planning to spend those last fourteen days stumping through the state when the meteorite landed.

Richard phoned the Tuesday after the trial had ended to tell her that Annabel's roommate had called to say Annabel had not returned to Radcliffe on Sunday night, and she hadn't heard from her since. Florentyna flew to New York immediately. Richard informed the police and hired a private detective to find his daughter, and then sent Florentyna back to Chicago after the police had assured her that they would do whatever they could.

When Florentyna arrived back in Chicago she walked around in a daze, phoning Richard every hour, but he had no news for her. With a week to go, the polls showed Florentyna leading only 51–49 and Edward tried to make her concentrate on the campaign but the words of Bob Buchanan kept coming back to her. '*This place can only be a poor substitute for a real family.*' She began to wonder if only . . . After a bad weekend during which Florentyna felt she had lost more votes than she had gained, Richard called in excitement to say that Annabel had been found and that she had been in New York the whole time.

'Thank God,' said Florentyna, tears of relief welling up in her eyes. 'Is she all right?'

'She's okay, and resting in Mount Sinai hospital.'

'What happened?' asked Florentyna anxiously.

'She's had an abortion.'

Florentyna flew back to New York that morning to be with her daughter. On the return flight she thought she recognised a Party worker sitting a few rows back. There was something about his smile. Once she had arrived at the hospital she discovered that Annabel had not even realised she had been reported missing. Edward begged Florentyna to return to Chicago as the media were continually asking where she was. Although they had managed to keep Annabel's private life out of the newspapers, they were becoming highly suspicious of why Florentyna was in New York rather than Illinois. For the first time, she ignored Edward's advice.

Ralph Brooks was quick to leap in and suggest that she had returned to New York because there was a crisis at the Baron Group and that that had always been her first priority. With Edward pulling and Annabel pushing, Florentyna returned to Chicago on Monday night to find every paper in Illinois saying the election was too close to call.

On the Tuesday morning Florentyna read the headline that she most dreaded: 'Candidate's Daughter Has Abortion'. The article that followed revealed every detail, even down to the bed Annabel was in. 'Keep your head down and pray,' was all Edward said as he dragged her through a nerve-racking day.

Florentyna rose at six o'clock on election day and Edward drove her to as many polling places as she could reach in fourteen hours. At every stop, campaign workers waved blue and white 'Kane for Senate' placards and handed out leaflets on Florentyna's positions on the major issues. At one stop a voter asked Florentyna for her views on abortion. Florentyna looked at the woman indignantly and said, 'I can assure you that my views haven't changed,' before realising that the question was totally innocent.

Her workers were tireless in their efforts to get out every Kane supporter, and Florentyna didn't stop working until the polls closed. She prayed that she had held on in the way Carter had against Ford in 1976. Richard flew in that night with news that Annabel had returned to Radcliffe and was feeling fine.

When Florentyna returned to the Baron, husband and wife sat alone in their suite. Three televisions were tuned into the networks as the returns came in from all over the state deciding which one of them would be chosen to oppose the Republican candidate in November. At eleven o'clock, Florentyna had a two per cent lead. At twelve o'clock Brooks was one per cent ahead. At two o'clock, Florentyna had edged back into the lead by less than one per cent. At three o'clock she fell asleep in Richard's arms. He did not wake her when he knew the outcome because he wanted her to sleep.

A little later he nodded off himself and woke with a start to find her looking out of the window, her fist clenched. The television kept flashing up the result: Ralph Brooks selected as Democratic candidate for the Senate by seven thousand one hundred and eighteen votes, a margin of less than half a per cent. On the screen was a picture of Brooks waving and smiling to his supporters.

Florentyna turned around and stared at the screen once more. Her eyes did not rest on the triumphant State's Attorney but on a man standing directly behind him. Now she knew where she had seen that smile before.

Florentyna's political career had come to a halt. She was now out of Congress and would have to wait another two years before she could even hope to re-enter public life. After Annabel's problems, she wondered if the time had come to return to the Baron Group and a more private existence. Richard didn't agree.

'I would be sorry if you gave up politics after all the time you have put into it.'

'Perhaps that's the point. If I hadn't become so involved with my own life and taken a little more interest in Annabel, she might not be facing an identity crisis.'

'An identity crisis. That's the sort of garbage I'd expect to hear from one of her sociology professors, not from you. I haven't noticed William collapsing under the strain of an "identity crisis". Darling, Annabel has had an affair and was careless; it's as simple as that. If everyone who took a lover was considered abnormal, there would only be a few of us strange ones left. What she most needs at this moment is to be treated as a friend by you.'

Florentyna dropped everything and took Annabel to Barbados that summer. During long walks along the beach, she learned of the affair her daughter had had with someone at Vassar; Florentyna still couldn't get used to the idea of men going to women's colleges. Annabel wouldn't name the man and tried to explain that although she still liked him, she didn't want to spend the rest of her life with him. 'Did you marry the first man you went to bed with?' she asked. Florentyna didn't reply immediately, and then told her about Scott Forbes.

'What a creep,' said Annabel after she had heard the story. 'How lucky you were to find Dad in Bloomingdale's.'

'No, Annabel, as your father continually reminds me, he did the finding.'

Mother and daughter grew closer together in those few days than they had been for years. Richard and William joined them in the second week of the holiday, and they spent fourteen days together getting plump and brown.

Richard was delighted to find Annabel and Florentyna so relaxed in each other's company and touched when his daughter started referring to William as 'my big brother'. Richard and Annabel regularly beat William and Florentyna at golf in the afternoons before spending long evenings chatting over dinner.

When the holiday came to an end they were all sad to be returning home. Florentyna confessed that she did not feel like throwing herself back into the political fray, until Annabel insisted that the last thing she wanted was a mother who sat home and cooked.

It felt strange to Florentyna that she would not be fighting a campaign herself that year. During her battle with Brooks for the Senate, the Democrats had selected Noel Silverman, a capable young Chicago attorney, to run for her seat in Congress. Some members of the committee admitted that they would have held up the decision if they thought Brooks had had the slightest chance of winning the party's nomination for the Senate.

Many voters asked Florentyna to run as an independent candidate but she knew the party would not approve, especially as they would be looking for another Senatorial representative in two years' time: the other United States Senator, David Rodgers, had repeatedly made it clear that he would not be running for re-election in 1984.

Florentyna flew into Chicago to speak on behalf of Noel Silverman on several occasions and was delighted when he won the seat, even if only by three thousand two hundred and twenty-three votes.

Florentyna faced the fact that she would now have to spend two years in the political wilderness and it didn't ease the pain when she read the Chicago *Tribune*'s headline the day after the election:

BROOKS ROMPS HOME IN SENATE RACE

The Future

1982–1995

31

William first brought Joanna Cabot home at Christmas. Florentyna knew instinctively that they would be married, and not just because her father turned out to be a distant relation of Richard's. Joanna was dark-haired, slim and graceful – and shyly expressive of her obvious feelings for William. For his part William was attentive and conspicuously proud of the young woman who stood quietly by his side. 'I suppose I might have expected you to produce a son who has been educated in New York, lived in Washington and Chicago but ends up returning to Boston to choose his wife,' Florentyna teased.

'William is your son as well,' Richard reminded her. 'And what makes you think he'll marry Joanna, anyway?'

Florentyna just laughed. 'I predict Boston in the spring.' She turned out to be wrong: they had to wait until the summer.

William was in his final year as an undergraduate, and had taken his business boards and was waiting anxiously to be accepted at the Harvard Business School.

'In my day,' said Richard, 'you waited until you had finished school and had made a little money before you thought about marriage.'

'That just isn't true, Richard. You left Harvard early to marry me and for several weeks afterwards I kept you.'

'You never told me that, Dad,' said William.

'Your father has what in politics is called a selective memory.'

William left laughing.

'I still think . . .'

'They're in love, Richard. Have you grown so old you can't see what's staring you in the face?'

'No, but . . .'

'You're not yet fifty and you're already acting like an old fuddy-duddy. William is almost the same age as you when you married me. Well, haven't you anything to say?'

'No. You're just like all politicians: you keep interrupting.'

The Kanes went to stay with the Cabots early in the new year, and Richard immediately liked John Cabot, Joanna's father, and was surprised that, with so many friends in common, they had not met before. Joanna had two younger sisters, who spent the weekend running around Richard.

'I've changed my mind,' Richard said that Saturday night in bed. 'I think Joanna is just what William needs.'

Florentyna put on an extreme mid-European accent and asked: 'What if Joanna had been a little Polish immigrant who sold gloves in Bloomingdale's?'

Richard took Florentyna in his arms and said, 'I would have told him not to buy three pairs of gloves because it would work out cheaper just to marry the girl.'

Preparations for the forthcoming wedding seemed complicated and demanding to Florentyna, who remembered vividly how simply she and Richard had been married and how Bella and Claude had lugged the double bed up the stairs in San Francisco. Luckily Mrs. Cabot wanted to handle all the arrangements herself, and whenever something was expected of the Kanes, Annabel was only too happy to leap forward as the family representative.

In early January, Florentyna returned to Washington to clear out her office. Colleagues in Washington stopped and chatted with her as if she hadn't left the House. Janet was waiting for her with a pile of letters, most of them from people saying how sorry they were that Florentyna would not be returning to Congress but hoping that she would run for the Senate again in two years' time.

Florentyna answered every one of them but couldn't help wondering if something might go wrong in 1984 as well. If it did that would finish her political career completely.

Florentyna left the Capitol for New York only to find herself getting in everyone's way. The Baron Group and Lester's were being competently run by Richard and Edward. The group had changed considerably since Richard had implemented the many improvements suggested by McKinsey and Company. She was continually surprised by the new Baron of Beef restaurants that could now be found on every ground floor and thought she would never get used to the computer banks alongside the hairdresser's in the hotel lobby. When Florentyna went to see Gianni to check on the progress of the shops, he assumed she had only come in for a new dress.

During those first few months away from Washington, Florentyna became more restless than she could remember. She travelled to Poland twice and could only feel despair for her countrymen as she looked around at the devastation. She wondered where the Russians would strike next. Florentyna took advantage of these journeys to meet European leaders who continually referred to their fear that America was becoming more and more isolationist with each succeeding President.

When she returned to America once again the question of whether she should run for the Senate loomed in front of her. Janet, who had remained on Florentyna's staff, began to discuss tactics with Edward Winchester which included regular trips to Chicago for Florentyna who accepted any speaking engagements in Illinois that came her way. Florentyna felt relieved when Senator Rodgers called her over the Easter recess to say that he hoped she would run for his seat the following year and added that she could rely on his backing.

As Florentyna checked over the Chicago newspapers each week she could not help noticing that Ralph Brooks was already making a name for himself in the Senate. He had somehow managed to get on the prestigious Foreign Relations Committee as well as the Agriculture Committee – so important to Illinois farmers. He was also the only freshman Senator to be appointed to the Democratic Task Force on Regulatory Reform.

It made her more determined, not less.

William and Joanna's wedding turned out to be one of the happiest days of Florentyna's life. Her twenty-two-year-old son standing in tails next to his bride brought back to her memories of his father in San Francisco. The silver band hung loosely on his left wrist, and Florentyna smiled as she noticed the little scar on his right hand. Joanna, although she looked shy and demure, had already rid her future husband of some of his more eccentric habits, among them several gaudy ties and the Fidel Castro moustache William had been so proud of before he had met her. Grandmother Kane, as everyone now referred to Kate, was looking more and more like a pale-blue battleship in full steam as she ploughed through the guests, kissing some while allowing others – those few older than herself – to kiss her. At seventy-five she was still elegant without a suggestion of a failing faculty. She was also the one member of the family who could remonstrate with Annabel and get away with it.

After a memorable reception laid on by Joanna's parents at their Beacon Hill home – it included four hours of dancing to the ageless music of the Lester Lanin orchestra, William and his bride flew off to Europe for their honeymoon while Richard and Florentyna returned to New York. Florentyna knew that the time was fast approaching when she would have to make an announcement about the Senate seat, and she decided to phone the retiring Senator and seek his advice on how he would like her to word any statement.

She called David Rodgers at his office in the Dirksen Building. As she dialled the number, it struck her how odd it was that they now saw so little of each other when only a few months previously, they had spent half of their lives within a two hundred yard radius. The Senator wasn't in, so she left a message to say that she had called. He did not return her call for several days and finally his secretary rang to explain that his schedule had been impossibly tight. Florentyna reflected on the fact that this wasn't David Rodgers's style. She hoped that she was just imagining the rebuff until she discussed what was going on with Edward.

'There's a rumour going around that he wants his wife to take over the seat,' he told her.

'Betty Rodgers? But she's always claimed she couldn't abide public life. I can't believe she'd choose to continue his now that David's retiring.'

'Well, don't forget that since her children left home three years ago she's been on the Chicago City Council. Perhaps that's given her the taste for higher things.'

'How serious do you think she is?'

'I don't know, but a couple of phone calls and I can find out.'

Florentyna found out even before Edward because she had a call from one of her ex-assistants in Chicago, who said the Cook County party machine was talking about Mrs. Rodgers as if she were already the candidate.

Edward called back later the same day to say that he had discovered that the state committee was holding a caucus to consider putting Betty Rodgers's name up as the candidate, although the polls indicated that over eighty per cent of registered Democrats supported Florentyna as David Rodgers's successor. 'It doesn't help,' added Edward, 'that Senator Brooks is openly backing Betty Rodgers.'

'Surprise, surprise,' said Florentyna. 'What do you think my next move ought to be?'

'I don't think you can do anything at the moment. I know you have strong support on the committee and it's very much in the balance, so perhaps it might be wise not to become too closely involved. Just go on working in Chicago and appear to remain above it all.'

'But what if she is chosen?'

'Then you will have to run as an independent candidate and beat her.'

'It's almost impossible to overcome the party machine, as you reminded me a few months back, Edward.'

'Truman did.'

Florentyna heard a few minutes after the meeting was over that the committee had voted by a majority of 6–5 to place Betty Rodgers's name forward as the official Democratic candidate for the Senate at a full caucus meeting later in the month. David Rodgers and Ralph Brooks had both voted against Florentyna.

She couldn't believe that only six people could make such an important decision and during the following week she had two unpleasant phone conversations, one with Rodgers, the other with Brooks, who both pleaded with her to put party unity before personal ambition. 'The sort of hypocrisy you'd expect from a Democrat,' commented Richard.

Many of Florentyna's supporters begged her to fight but she was not convinced, especially when the state chairman called and asked her to announce formally, for the unity of the party, that she would not be a candidate on this occasion. After all, he pointed out, Betty will probably only do one six-year term.

Which will be long enough for Ralph Brooks, Florentyna thought.

She listened to much advice over the next few days, but on a trip to Washington it was Bob Buchanan who told her to read *Julius Caesar* more carefully.

'The whole play?' asked Florentyna.

'No, I should concentrate on Mark Antony if I were you, my dear.'

Florentyna called the Democratic Party chairman and told him she was willing to come to the caucus and state that she was not a candidate, but she was unwilling to endorse Betty Rodgers.

The chairman readily accepted the compromise.

The meeting was held ten days later at the Democratic State Central Commitee in the Bismarck Hotel on West Randolph Street, and when Florentyna arrived the hall was already packed. She could sense from the loud applause she received as she entered the room that the meeting might not go as smoothly as the committee had planned.

Florentyna took her assigned seat on the platform at the end of the second row. The chairman sat in the middle of the front row behind a long table with two Senators, Rodgers and Brooks, on his right and left. Betty Rodgers sat next to her husband and didn't once look at Florentyna. The secretary and treasurer completed the front row. The chairman gave Florentyna a polite nod when she appeared. The other committee members sat in the second row with Florentyna. One of them whispered, 'You were crazy not to put up a fight.'

At eight o'clock the chairman invited David Rodgers to address the meeting. The Senator had always been respected as a diligent worker for his constituents, but even his closest aides would not have described him as an orator. He started by thanking everyone for their support in the past and expressed the hope that they would now pass that loyalty on to his wife. He gave a rambling talk on his work during the last twenty-four years as a Senator and sat down to what might at best, have been described as polite applause.

The chairman spoke next, outlining his reasons for proposing Betty Rodgers as the next candidate. 'At least it will be easy for the voters to remember her name.' He laughed as did one or two people on the platform but surprisingly few in the body of the hall. He then went on to spend the next ten minutes expounding the virtues of Betty Rodgers and the work she had done as a city councillor. He spoke to a silent hall. And sat down to a smattering of applause. He waited a moment, then, in a perfunctory fashion, introduced Florentyna.

She had made no notes because she wanted what she had to say to sound off the cuff, even though she had been rehearsing every word for the past ten days. Richard had wanted to accompany her but she told him not to bother as everything had been virtually decided before the first word was spoken. The truth was that she did not want him there because his support might cast doubt on her apparent innocence.

When the chairman sat down, Florentyna came foward to the centre of the stage and stood right in front of Ralph Brooks.

'Mr. Chairman, I have come to Chicago today to announce that I am not a candidate for the United States Senate.'

She paused and there were cries of 'Why not?' and 'Who stopped you?'

She went on as though she had heard nothing. 'I have had the privilege of serving my district in Chicago for six years in the United States House of Representatives and I look forward to working for the best interests of the people in the future. I have always believed in party unity –'

'But not party fixing,' someone shouted.

Once again, Florentyna ignored the interruption. 'So I shall be happy to back the candidate you select to be on the Democratic ticket,' she said, trying to sound convincing.

An uproar started, amid which cries of 'Senator Kane, Senator Kane' were clearly audible.

David Rodgers looked pointedly at Florentyna as she continued. 'To my supporters, I say that there may come another time and another place, but it will not be tonight, so let us remember in this key state that it is the Republicans we have to defeat, not ourselves. If Betty Rodgers becomes the next Senator, I feel certain that she will serve the party with the same ability we have grown to expect from her husband. Should the Republicans capture the seat, you can be assured that I shall devote myself to seeing we win it back in six years' time. Whatever the outcome, the committee can depend on my support in this crucial state during election year.'

Florentyna quickly resumed her seat in the second row as her supporters cheered and cheered.

When the chairman had brought everybody to order, which he tried to do as quickly as possible, he called upon the next United States Senator from Illinois, Mrs. Betty Rodgers, to address the meeting. Until then, Florentyna had kept her head bowed but she could not resist glancing up at her adversary. Betty Rodgers clearly had not been prepared for any opposition and looked in an agitated state as she fidgeted with her notes. She read a prepared speech, sometimes almost in a whisper, and although it was well researched the delivery made her husband sound like Cicero. Florentyna felt sad and embarrassed for her and almost started to feel guilty about her own tactics but she still despised the committee for putting Betty Rodgers through such an ordeal. She began to wonder to what extremes Ralph Brooks would go to keep her out of the Senate. When Betty Rodgers sat down she was shaking like jelly, and Florentyna quietly left the platform and stepped out of a side door so that she would no longer embarrass them. She hailed a cab and asked the driver to take her to O'Hare airport.

'Sure thing, Mrs. Kane,' came back the reply. 'I do hope you're going to run for the Senate again. You'll win the seat easy this time.'

'No, I shall not be running,' Florentyna said flatly. 'The Democratic candidate will be Betty Rodgers.'

'Who's she?' asked the taxi driver.

'Senator Rodgers's wife.'

'What's she know about the job? Her husband wasn't that hot,' he said testily, and drove the rest of the way in silence. It gave Florentyna the opportunity to reflect that she would *have* to run as an independent candidate if she were ever going to have any chance of winning a seat in the Senate. Her biggest anxiety was splitting the vote with Betty Rodgers and letting a Republican take the seat. The party would never forgive her if that was the eventual outcome. It would spell the end of her political career. Brooks now looked as if he were going to win either way. She cursed herself for not beating him when she had the chance.

The cab came to a halt outside the terminal building. As she paid the driver he said, 'It still doesn't make sense to me. I'll tell you, lady, my wife thinks you're going to be President. I can't see it myself because I could never vote for a woman.'

Florentyna laughed.

'No offence meant, lady.'

'No offence taken,' she said, and doubled his tip.

She checked her watch and made her way to the boarding gate: another thirty minutes before take-off. She bought copies of *Time* and *Newsweek* from the news-stand. Bush on both covers: the first shots of the Presidential campaign were being fired. She looked up at the telemonitor to check the New York gate number: '12C'. It amused her to think of the extremes the officials at O'Hare would go to in order to avoid 'Gate 13'. She sat down in a red plastic swivel chair and began to read the profile on George Bush. She became so engrossed in the article that she did not hear the loudspeaker. The message was repeated. 'Mrs. Florentyna Kane, please go to the nearest white courtesy telephone.'

Florentyna continued reading about the Zapata Oil company executive who had gone through the House, the Republican National Committee, the CIA and the U.S. Mission in China to become Vice-President. A TWA passenger representative came over and touched her lightly on the shoulder. She looked up.

'Mrs. Kane, isn't that for you?' the young man said, pointing at a loudspeaker.

Florentyna listened. 'Yes, it is, thank you.' She walked across the lounge to the nearest phone. At times like this, she always imagined one of the children had been involved in an accident and even now she had to remind herself that Annabel was over twenty-one and William was married. She picked up the phone.

Senator Rodgers's voice came over loud and clear. 'Florentyna, is that you?'

'Yes it is,' she replied.

'Thank God I caught you. Betty has decided she doesn't want to run after all. She feels the campaign would be too great a strain on her. Can you come back before this place is torn apart?'

'What for?' asked Florentyna, her mind in a whirl.

'Can't you hear what's going on here?' said Rodgers.

Florentyna listened to cries of 'Kane, Kane, Kane', as clear as Rodgers's own voice.

'They want to endorse you as the official candidate and no one is going to leave until you return.'

Florentyna's fingers clenched into a fist. 'I am not interested, David.'

'But Florentyna, I thought . . .'

'Not unless I have the backing of the committee and you personally propose my name in nomination.'

'Florentyna, anything you say. Betty always thought you were the right person for the job. It was just that Ralph Brooks pushed her into it.'

'Ralph Brooks?'

'Yes, but Betty now realises that was nothing more than a self-serving exercise. So for God's sake come back.'

'I'm on my way.' Florentyna almost ran down the corridor to the taxi stand. A cab shot up to her side.

'Where to this time, Mrs. Kane?'

She smiled. 'Back to where we started.'

'I suppose you know where you're going, but I can't understand how an ordinary guy like me is meant to put any faith in politicians I just don't know.'

Florentyna prayed that the driver would be silent on the return journey so that she could compose her thoughts, but this time he treated her to a diatribe: on his wife, whom he ought to leave; his mother-in-law, who wouldn't leave him; his son, who was on drugs and didn't work, and his daughter, who was living in a California commune run by a religious cult. 'What a bloody country – beg your pardon, Mrs. Kane,' he said as they drew up beside the hall. God, how she'd wanted to tell him to shut up. She paid him for the second time that evening.

'Maybe I will vote for you after all when you run for President,' he said. She smiled. 'And I could work on the people who ride this cab – there must be at least three hundred each week.'

Florentyna shuddered – another lesson learned.

She tried to collect her thoughts as she entered the building. The audience had risen from their seats and were cheering wildly. Some clapped their hands above their heads while others stood on chairs. The first person to greet her on the platform was Senator Rodgers, and then his wife, who gave Florentyna a smile of relief. The chairman shook her hand heartily. Senator Brooks was nowhere to be seen: sometimes she really hated politics. She turned to face her supporters in the hall and they cheered even louder: sometimes she really loved politics.

Florentyna stood in the centre of the stage, but it was five minutes before the chairman could bring the meeting to order. When there was complete silence, she simply said: 'Thomas Jefferson once remarked: "I have returned sooner than I expected." I am happy to accept your nomination for the United States Senate.'

She was not allowed to deliver a further word that night as they thronged around her. A little after twelve thirty she crept into her room at the Chicago Baron. Immediately she picked up the phone and started dialling 212, forgetting that it was one thirty in New York.

'Who is it?' said a drowsy voice.

'Mark Antony.'

'Who?'

'I come to bury Betty, not to praise her.'

'Jessie, have you gone mad?'

'No, but I have been endorsed as the Democratic candidate for the United States Senate.' Florentyna explained how it had come about.

'George Orwell said a lot of terrible things were going to happen round about now, but he made no mention of you waking me up in the middle of the night just to announce you are going to be a Senator.'

'I just thought you would like to be the first to know.'

'Perhaps you'd better call Edward.'

'Do you think I ought to? You've already reminded me that it's one thirty in New York.'

'I know it is, but why should I be the only person you wake up in the middle of the night to misquote *Julius Caesar* to?'

*

Senator Rodgers kept his word and backed Florentyna throughout her whole campaign. For the first time in years she was free of pressures from Washington and could devote all her energies to an election. This time there were no thunderbolts or meteors that could not be contained, although Ralph Brooks's lukewarm support on one occasion and implied praise of her Republican opponent on another did not help her cause.

The main interest in the country that year was the Presidential campaign. The major surprise was the choice of the Democratic Presidential candidate, a man who had come from nowhere to beat Walter Mondale and Edward Kennedy in the Primaries with his programme dubbed the 'Fresh Approach'. The candidate visited Illinois on no less than six occasions during the campaign, appearing with Florentyna every time.

On the day of the election, the Chicago papers said once again that the Senate race was too close to call. The pollsters were wrong and the loquacious cab driver was right because at eight thirty Central time, the Republican candidate conceded an overwhelming victory for Florentyna. Later the pollsters tried to explain away their statistical errors by speculating that many men would not admit they were going to vote for a woman. Either way it didn't matter, because the new President-elect's telegram said it all:

WELCOME BACK TO WASHINGTON, SENATOR KANE.

32

NINETEEN EIGHTY-FIVE WAS to be a year for funerals, which made Florentyna feel every day of her fifty-one years.

She returned to Washington to find she had been allocated a suite in the Russell Building, a mere six hundred yards from her old Congressional office in the Longworth Building. For several days while she was settling in, she found herself still driving into the Longworth garage rather than the Russell courtyard. She also couldn't get used to being addressed as Senator, especially by Richard, who could mouth the title in such a way as to make it sound like a term of abuse. 'You may imagine your status has increased but they still haven't given you a raise in salary. I can't wait for you to be President,' he added. 'Then at least you will earn as much as one of the bank's Vice-Presidents.'

Florentyna's salary might not have risen, but her expenses had, as once again she surrounded herself with a team many Senators would envy. She would have been the first to acknowledge the advantage of a strong financial base outside the world of politics. Most of her old team returned and were supplemented by new assistants who were in no doubt about Florentyna's future. Her office in the Russell Building was in suite four hundred and forty. The other four rooms were now occupied by the fourteen assistants, led by the intrepid Janet Brown, whom Florentyna had decided long ago was married to her job. In addition, Florentyna now had four offices throughout Illinois with three assistants working in each of them.

Her new office overlooked the courtyard, with its fountain and cobble-stoned parking area. The green lawn would be a popular lunch place for Senate assistants during the warm weather, and for an army of squirrels in the winter.

Florentyna told Richard that she estimated she would be paying out of her own pocket over two hundred thousand dollars a year more than her Senatorial allowance, an amount which varies from Senator to Senator depending on the size of their state and its population, she explained to her husband. Richard smiled and made a mental note to donate exactly the same sum to the Republican Party.

No sooner had the Illinois State Seal been affixed to her office door than Florentyna received the telegram. It was simple and stark: WINIFRED TREDGOLD PASSED AWAY ON THURSDAY AT ELEVEN O'CLOCK.

It was the first time Florentyna was aware of Miss Tredgold's Christian name. She checked her watch, made two overseas calls and then buzzed for Janet to explain where she would be for the next forty-eight hours. By one o'clock that afternoon she was on board Concorde, and she arrived in London three hours and twenty-five minutes later at nine twenty-five. The chauffeur-driven car she had ordered was waiting for her as she emerged from Customs and drove her down the M4 motorway to Wiltshire. She checked into the Lansdowne Arms Hotel and read Saul Bellow's *The Dean's December* until three o'clock in the morning to counter the jet-lag. Before turning the light out she called Richard.

'Where are you?' were his first words.

'I'm booked into a small hotel at Calne in Wiltshire, England.'

'Why, pray? Is the Senate doing a fact-finding mission on English pubs?'

'No, my darling. Miss Tredgold has died, and I'm attending the funeral tomorrow.'

'I'm sorry,' said Richard. 'If you had let me know I would have come with you. We both have a lot to thank that lady for.' Florentyna smiled. 'When will you be coming home?'

'Tomorrow evening's Concorde.'

'Sleep well, Jessie. I'll be thinking of you – and Miss Tredgold.'

At nine thirty the next morning a maid brought in a breakfast tray of kippers, toast with Cooper's Oxford marmalade, coffee and a copy of the London *Times*. She sat in bed savouring every moment, an indulgence she would never have allowed herself in Washington. By ten thirty she had absorbed *The Times* and was not surprised to discover the British were having the same problems with inflation and unemployment as those that prevailed in America. Florentyna got up and dressed in a simple black knitted suit. The only jewelry she wore was the little watch that Miss Tredgold had given her on her thirteenth birthday.

The hotel porter told her that the church was about a mile away and as the morning was so clear and crisp she decided to walk. What the local had failed to point out to her was that the journey was uphill the whole way and his 'about' was a 'guesstimate'. As she strode along, she reflected on how little exercise she had taken lately, despite the pristine exercycle now lodged at Cape Cod. She had also allowed the jogging mania to pass her by.

The tiny Norman church, surrounded by oaks and elms, was perched on the side of the hill. On the noticeboard was an appeal for twenty-five thousand pounds to save the church roof; according to a little blob of red on a thermometer over one thousand pounds had already been collected. To Florentyna's surprise, she was met in the vestry by a waiting verger and led to a place in the front pew next to an imperious lady who could only have been the headmistress.

The church was far fuller than Florentyna had expected, and the school had supplied the choir. The service was simple and the address given by the parish priest left Florentyna in no doubt that Miss Tredgold had continued to teach others with the same dedication and common sense that had influenced the whole of Florentyna's life. She tried not to cry during the address as she knew Miss Tredgold would not have approved, but she nearly succumbed when they sang her governess's favourite hymn, 'Rock of Ages'.

When the service was over, Florentyna filed back with the rest of the congregation through the Norman porch and stood in the little churchyard to watch the mortal remains of Winifred Tredgold disappear into the ground. The headmistress, a carbon copy of Miss Tredgold – Florentyna found it hard to believe that such women still existed –said she would like to show Florentyna something of the school before she left. On their way back through the grounds, she learned that Miss Tredgold had never talked about Florentyna except to her two or three closest friends, but when the headmistress opened the door of a small bedroom in a cottage on the school estate, Florentyna could no longer hold back the tears. By the bed was a photograph of a vicar whom Florentyna recognised as Miss Tredgold's father and by its side, in a small silver Victorian frame, stood a picture of Florentyna graduating from Girls Latin next to an old Bible. In the bedside drawer, they discovered every one of Florentyna's letters written over the past thirty years; the last one remained unopened by her bed.

'Did she know I had been elected to the Senate?' Florentyna asked diffidently.

'Oh, yes, the whole school prayed for you that day. It was the last occasion on which Miss Tredgold read the lesson in chapel, and before she died she asked me to write to tell you that she felt her father had been right, and she had indeed taught a woman of destiny. My dear, you must not cry, her belief in God was so unshakeable that she died in total peace with this world. Miss Tredgold also asked me to give you her Bible and this envelope, which you must not open until you have returned home. It's something she bequeathed you in her will.'

As Florentyna left, she thanked the headmistress for all her kindness and added that she had been touched and surprised at being met by the verger when no one knew she was coming.

'Oh, you should not have been surprised, child,' said the

headmistress. 'I never doubted for a moment that you would come.'

Florentyna travelled back to London clutching the envelope. She longed to open it, like a child who has seen a package in the hall but knows it is for his birthday the following day. She caught Concorde at six thirty that evening, arriving back at Dulles by five thirty p.m. She was seated at her desk in the Russell Building by six thirty the same evening. She stared at the envelope marked 'Florentyna Kane' and then slowly tore it open. She pulled out the contents, four thousand Baron Group stock. Miss Tredgold had died presumably unaware that she was worth over a half a million dollars. Florentyna took out her pen and wrote out a cheque for twenty-five thousand pounds for a new church roof in memory of Miss Winifred Tredgold and sent the shares to Professor Ferpozzi to be placed at the disposal of the Remagen Trust. When Richard heard the story he told Florentyna that his father had once acted in the same way, but the sum required had been only five hundred pounds. 'It seems even God is affected by inflation,' he added.

Washington was preparing for another inauguration. On this occasion Senator Kane was placed in the VIP stand from which the new incumbent was to make his speech. She listened intently to the blueprint for American policy over the next four years, now referred to by everyone as the 'Fresh Approach'.

'You're getting nearer the podium every time,' Richard had told her at breakfast.

Florentyna glanced around among her colleagues and friends in a Washington where she now felt at ease. Senator Ralph Brooks, a row in front of her, was even nearer the President. His eyes never left the podium.

Florentyna found herself on the Defence Sub-Committee of the Appropriations Committee and on the Environment and Public Works Committee. She was also asked to chair the Committee on Small Business. Her days once again resembled a never-ending chase for more hours. Janet and her assistants would brief her in lifts, cars, planes, en route to vote on the floor, and even on the run between committee rooms. Florentyna was tireless in her efforts to complete her daily schedule and all fourteen staffers wondered how much they could pile on her before she cracked under the strain. In the Senate, Florentyna quickly enhanced the reputation she had made for herself in the House of Representatives by speaking only on matters on which she was well briefed, and then with compassion and common sense. She still remained silent on issues on which she did not consider herself well informed. She voted against her party on several defence matters and twice over the new energy policy provoked by the latest war in the Middle East.

As the only Democratic woman Senator, she received invitations to speak all over the nation and other Senators soon learned that Florentyna Kane was not the token Democratic woman in the Senate but someone whom they could never afford to underestimate.

Florentyna was pleased to find how often she was invited to the inner sanctum of the Majority Leader's office to discuss matters of policy as well as party problems.

During her first session as a Senator, Florentyna sponsored an amendment on the Small Business Bill, giving generous tax concessions to companies who exported over thirty-five per cent of their products. For a long time she had believed that companies who did not seek to sell their goods in an overseas market were suffering from the same delusions of grandeur as the English in the mid-century, and that if they were not careful, Americans would enter the twenty-first century with the same problems that the British had failed to come to terms with in the 1980s.

In her first three months she had answered five thousand four hundred and sixteen letters, voted seventy-nine times, spoken on eight occasions in the chamber, fourteen times outside and missed lunch on forty-three of the last ninety days.

'I don't need to diet,' she told Janet, 'I weigh less than

when I was twenty-four and opened my first shop in San Francisco.'

The second death was every bit as much of a shock because the whole family had spent the previous weekend together in Cape Cod.

The maid reported to the butler that Mrs. Kate Kane had not come down to breakfast as the grandfather clock chimed eight. 'Then she must be dead,' said the butler.

Kate Kane was seventy-nine when she failed to come down for breakfast and the family gathered for a Brahmin funeral. The service was held at Trinity Church, Copley Square and could not have been in greater contrast to the service for Miss Tredgold, for this time the bishop addressed a congregation who between them could have walked from Boston to San Francisco on their own land. All the Kanes and Cabots were present along with two other Senators and a Congressman. Almost everyone who had ever known Grandmother Kane, and a good many of those who had not, filled the pews behind Richard and Florentyna.

Florentyna glanced across at William and Joanna. Joanna looked as though she would be giving birth in about a month, and it made Florentyna feel sad that Kate had not lived long enough to become Great-Grandmother Kane.

After the funeral, they spent a sombre family weekend in the Red House on Beacon Hill. Florentyna would never forget Kate's tireless efforts to bring her husband and son together. Richard was now the sole head of the Kane family, which Florentyna realised would add further responsibility to his already impossible work load. She also knew that he would not complain and it made her feel guilty that she was unable to do much about making his life any easier.

Like a typical Kane, Kate's will was sensible and prudent; the bulk of the estate was left to Richard and his sisters, Lucy and Virginia, and large settlements were made on William and Annabel. William was to receive two million dollars on his thirtieth birthday. Annabel, on the other hand, was to live off the interest of a further two million until she was forty-five or had two legitimate children. Grandmother Kane hadn't missed much.

In Washington, the battle for the mid-term election had already begun and Florentyna was glad to have a six-year term before she faced the voters again, giving her a chance for the first time to do some real work without the biennial break for party squabbles. Nevertheless, so many of her colleagues invited her to speak in their states that she seemed to be working just as hard, and the only request she politely refused was in Tennessee: she explained she could not speak against Bob Buchanan, who was seeking re-election for the last time.

The little white card which Louise gave her each night was always filled with appointments from dawn to dusk indicating the routine for the following day:

'7.45: breakfast with a visiting foreign minister of defence. 9.00: staff meeting. 9.30: Defence Sub-Committee hearing. 11.30: interview with Chicago *Tribune*. 12.30: lunch with six Senate colleagues to discuss defence budget. 2.00: weekly radio broadcast. 2.30: photo on Capitol steps with Illinois 4-H'ers. 3.15: staff briefing on Small Business Bill. 5.30: drop by reception of Associated General Contractors. 7.00: cocktail party at French Embassy. 8.00: dinner with Donald Graham of the *Washington Post*. 11.00: phone Richard at the Denver Baron.'

As a Senator, Florentyna was able to reduce her trips to Illinois to every other weekend. On every other Friday, she would catch the U.S. Air flight to Providence, where she would be met by Richard on his way up from New York. They would then drive out on Route Six to the Cape, which gave them a chance to catch up with each other's week.

Richard and Florentyna spent their free weekends in Cape Cod, which had become their family home since Kate's death, Richard having given the Red House to William and Joanna.

On Saturday mornings, they would lounge around reading newspapers and magazines. Richard might play the cello while Florentyna would look over the paperwork she had brought with her from Washington. When weather permitted, they played golf in the afternoon and whatever the weather, backgammon in the evening. Florentyna always ended up owing Richard a couple of hundred dollars which he said he would donate to the Republican Party if she ever honoured her gambling debts. Florentyna always queried the value of giving to the Massachusetts Republican Party, but Richard pointed out that he also supported a Republican Governor and Senator in New York.

Patriotically, Joanna gave birth to a son on Washington's birthday, and they christened him Richard. Suddenly Florentyna was a grandmother.

People magazine stopped describing her as the most elegant lady in Washington and started calling her the best-looking grandmother in America. This caused a flurry of letters of protest including hundreds of photographs of other glamorous grannies for the editor to consider, which only made Florentyna even more popular.

The rumours that she would be a strong contender for the Vice-Presidency in 1988 started in July when the Small Business Association made her Illinoisan of the Year and a *Newsweek* poll voted her Woman of the Year. Whenever she was questioned on the subject, she reminded her enquirers that she had been in the Senate for less than a year and that her first priority was to represent her state in Congress, although she couldn't help noticing that she was being invited to the White House more and more often for sessions with the President. It was the first time that being the one woman in the majority party was turning out to be an advantage.

Florentyna learned of Bob Buchanan's death when she asked why the flag on the Russell Building was at half-mast. The funeral was on the Wednesday when she was due to offer an amendment to the Public Health Service Act in the Senate and address a seminar on defence at the Woodrow Wilson

International Centre for Scholars. She cancelled one, postponed the other and flew to Nashville, Tennessee.

Both of the state's Senators and its seven remaining Congressmen were present. Florentyna stood next to her House colleagues in silent tribute. As they waited to go into the Lutheran chapel, one of them told her that Bob had five sons and one daughter. Gerald, the youngest, had been killed in Vietnam. She thanked God that Richard had been too old and William too young to be sent to that pointless war.

Steven, the eldest boy, led the Buchanan family into the chapel. Tall and thin, with a warm open face, he could only have been the son of Bob and when Florentyna spoke to him after the service he revealed the same southern charm and straight approach that had endeared his father to her. Florentyna was delighted when she learned that Steven was going to run for his father's seat in the coming special election.

'It will give me someone new to quarrel with,' she said, smiling.

'He greatly admired you,' said Steven.

Florentyna was not prepared to see her photograph all over the major newspapers the next morning being described as a gallant lady. Janet placed a *New York Times* editorial on top of her press clippings for her to read:

> Representative Buchanan had not been well known to the citizens of New York, but it was a comment on his service in Congress that Senator Kane flew to Tennessee to attend his funeral. It is the sort of gesture that is rarely seen in politics today and is just another reason why Senator Kane is one of the most respected legislators in either House.

Florentyna was rapidly becoming the most sought-after politician in Washington. Even the President admitted that the demands on her time weren't running far short of his. But among the invitations that came that year there was one she accepted with considerable pride. Harvard invited her to run for election to the Board of Overseers in the spring and to address the Graduation Day ceremony that June. Even Richard put a note in his diary to keep the day free.

Florentyna looked up the list of those who had preceded her in this honour – from George Marshall outlining the plan to reconstruct post-war Europe to Alexander Solzhenitsyn describing the West as decadent and lacking in spiritual values.

Florentyna spent many hours preparing her Harvard address, aware that the media traditionally gave the speech considerable coverage. She practised paragraphs daily in front of a mirror, in the bath, even on the golf course with Richard. She wrote the complete text herself – in longhand, but accepted numerous amendments from Janet, Richard and Edward on its content.

The day before she was due to deliver the speech, Florentyna received a telephone call from Sotheby's. She listened to the head of the department and agreed to his suggestion. When they had settled on a maximum price, he said he would let her know the outcome immediately after the auction. Florentyna felt the timing could not have been better. She flew up to Boston that night, to be met at Logan airport by an enthusiastic young undergraduate who drove her into Cambridge and dropped her off at the Faculty Club. President Bok greeted her in the foyer and congratulated her on her election to the board, and then took her through to be introduced to the other overseers, who numbered among the thirty, two Nobel Prize winners, one for literature and one for science; two ex-cabinet secretaries, an Army general, a judge, an oil tycoon and two other university Presidents. Florentyna sat through the meeting amused by how courteous the overseers all were to one another and she could not help but contrast their approach with that of a House committee.

The guest room they put at her disposal brought back memories of Florentyna's student days and she even had to phone Richard from the corridor. He was in Albany dealing with some tax problems caused by Jack Kemp, the new Republican Governor of New York State.

'I'll be with you for the lunch,' he promised. 'By the way, I see tomorrow's speech was worthy of a mention by Dan Rather on C.B.S. 'News' tonight. It had better be good if you hope to keep me from watching the Yankees on channel eleven.'

'Just see you are in your place on time, Mr. Kane.'

'Just you make sure it's as good as your speech to the Vietnam Veterans of America, because I'm travelling a long way to hear you, Senator.'

'How could I have fallen in love with you, Mr. Kane?'

'It was, if I remember rightly, "Adopt an Immigrant Year", and we Bostonians were exhibiting our usual social conscience.'

'Why did it continue after the end of the year?'

'I decided it was my duty to spend the rest of my life with you.'

'Good decision, Mr. Kane.'

'I wish I were with you now, Jessie.'

'You wouldn't if you could see the room they've given me. I've only a single bed, so you would be spending the night on the floor. Be on time tomorrow, because I want you to hear this speech.'

'I will. But I must say it's taking you a long time to convert me to a Democrat.'

'I'll try again tomorrow. Good night, Mr. Kane.'

Richard was woken the next morning by the telephone at the Albany Baron. He assumed it would be Florentyna on the line with some Senatorial comment, but it turned out to be New York Air to say there would be no flights out of Albany that day because of a one-day action by maintenance workers that was affecting every airline.

'Christ,' said Richard, uncharacteristically, then jumped into a cold shower where he added some other new words to his vocabulary. Once he was dry, he tried to get dressed while dialling the front desk. He dropped the phone and had to start again.

'I want a rental car at the front entrance immediately,' he said, dropped the phone again and finished dressing. He then called Harvard, but they had no idea where Senator Kane was at that particular moment. He left a message explaining what had happened, ran downstairs, skipped breakfast and picked up the keys to a Ford Executive. Richard was held up in the rush-hour traffic and it took him another thirty minutes to find Route 90 East. He checked his watch: he would only have to do a steady sixty to be in Cambridge in time for the speech at two o'clock. He knew how much this one meant to Florentyna, and he was determined not to be late.

The last few days had been a nightmare, so much so he hadn't bothered Florentyna with the theft in Cleveland, the kitchen walk-out in San Francisco, the seizing of the hotel in Cape Town, tax problems over his mother's estate – all happening while the price of gold was collapsing because of the civil war in South Africa. Richard tried to put all these problems out of his mind. Florentyna could always tell when he was tired or over-anxious, and he did not want her to be worrying about situations he knew he could sort out eventually. Richard wound the car window down to let in some fresh air.

The rest of the weekend he was going to do nothing but sleep and play the cello; it would be the first break they had both had for over a month. No children, as William would be in Boston with his own family and Annabel in Mexico – leaving nothing more strenuous to consider than a round of golf for two whole days. He wished he didn't feel so tired. 'Damn,' he said out loud. He'd forgotten the roses – had planned to send them to Florentyna from the airport as usual.

Florentyna was given two messages just before lunch. The man from Sotheby's phoned to say that she had been successful in her bid, and a college porter delivered Richard's news. She was delighted by the first and disappointed by the second, although she smiled at the thought that Richard would be worrying about the roses. Thanks to Sotheby's, she now had something for him he had wanted all his life.

Florentyna had spent the morning in the formal graduation proceedings at the Tercentenary Theatre. The sight of all three networks setting up their cameras on the lawn for the afternoon ceremony made her feel even more nervous, and she hoped no one noticed that she had eaten almost nothing at lunch.

At one forty-five, the overseers left for the yard where alumni reunion classes had already gathered. She thought back to her own class . . . Bella . . . Wendy . . . Scott . . . Edward . . . and now she had returned, as Edward had predicted, as Senator Kane. She took her seat on the platform outside the Tercentenary Theatre next to President Horner of Radcliffe and looked down at the card on the other chair beside her. It read, 'Mr. Richard Kane – husband of Senator Kane'. She smiled at how much that would have annoyed him, and scribbled underneath, 'What took you so long?' She must remember to leave the card on the mantelpiece. Florentyna knew that if Richard arrived after the ceremony had begun he would have to find a seat on the lawn. The announcement of elections, conferring of honorary degrees, and reports of gifts received by the university, was followed by an address from President Bok. Florentyna sat and listened as he introduced her. She scanned the rows in front of her, as far as her eye could see, but was still unable to spot Richard.

'President Horner, distinguished visitors, ladies and gentlemen. It is a great honour for me today to present one of Radcliffe's most distinguished alumnae, a woman who has captured the imagination of the American people. Indeed, I know many of us believe that Radcliffe will one day have *two* Presidents.' Seventeen thousand guests burst into spontaneous applause. 'Ladies and gentlemen, Senator Florentyna Kane.'

Florentyna was shaking when she rose from her seat. She checked her notes as the great television lights were switched on, momentarily blinding her so that she could see nothing but a blur of faces. She prayed Richard's was among them.

'President Bok, President Horner. I stand before you more nervous now than I was when I first came to Radcliffe thirty-three years ago and I couldn't find the dining room for two days because I was too frightened to ask anyone.' The laughter eased Florentyna's tension. 'Now I see seated in front of me men and women, and if I recall correctly from my Radcliffe rule book, men may only enter the bedrooms "between the hours of three and five p.m." and "must at all times keep both feet on the ground". If the rule still exists today, I am bound to ask how the poor things ever get any sleep.'

The laughter continued for several seconds before Florentyna was able to start again. 'Over thirty years ago I was educated at this great university and it has set the standard for everything I have tried to achieve in my life. The pursuit of excellence has always been to Harvard of paramount importance and it is a relief to find in this changing world that the standards attained today by your graduates are even higher than they were in my generation. There is a tendency among the old to say that the youth of today do not compare with their forefathers. I am reminded of a carving on the side of one of the tombs of the Pharaohs which translated reads: "The young are lazy and preoccupied with themselves and will surely cause the downfall of the world as we know it."'

The graduates cheered while the parents laughed. 'Winston Churchill once said: "When I was sixteen, I thought my parents knew nothing. When I was twenty-one, I was shocked to discover how much they had picked up in the last five years."' The parents applauded and the students smiled. 'America is often looked upon as a great monolithic land mass, with a vast centralised economy. It is neither of these things. It is two hundred and twenty-five million people who make up something more diverse, more complicated, more exciting, than any other nation on earth and I envy all of you who wish to play a role in the future of our country and feel sorry for those who do not. Harvard University is famous for its tradition of service in medicine, teaching, the law, religion and the arts. It must be thought a modern tragedy that more young people do not consider politics an honourable and worthwhile profession. We must change the atmosphere in the corridors of power so that the very brightest of our youth does not dismiss, virtually without consideration, a career in public life.

'None of us has ever doubted for a moment the integrity of Washington, Adams, Jefferson or Lincoln. Why shouldn't we today produce another generation of statesmen who will bring back to our vocabulary the words duty, pride and honour without such a suggestion being greeted with sarcasm or scorn?

'This great university produced John Kennedy, who once said when receiving an honorary degree from Yale, "And now I have the best of both worlds, a Harvard education and a Yale degree."'

When the laughter had died down, Florentyna continued: 'I, Mr. President, have the best of every world, a Radcliffe education and a Radcliffe degree.'

Seventeen thousand people rose to their feet and it was a considerable time before Florentyna could continue. She smiled as she thought how proud Richard would be, because he had suggested that line to her when she was rehearsing in the bath, and she had not been sure that it would work.

'As young Americans, take pride in your country's past achievements, but strive to make them nothing more than history. Dcfy old myths, break new barriers, challenge the future, so that at the end of this century, people will say of us that our achievements rank alongside those of the Greeks, the Romans and the British in advancing freedom and a just society for all people on this planet. Let no barriers be unassailable and no aims too high and when the crazy whirligig of time is over, let it be possible for you to say as Franklin D. Roosevelt did, "There is a mysterious cycle in human events. To some generations much is given, of other generations much is expected, but this generation of Americans has a rendezvous with destiny."'

Once again, everyone on the lawn broke into spontaneous

applause. When it subsided, Florentyna lowered her voice almost to a whisper. 'My fellow alumni, I say to you, I am bored by cynics, I despise belittlers, I loathe those who think there is something sophisticated and erudite in running our nation down, because I am convinced that this generation of our youth, who will take the United States into the twenty-first century, has another rendezvous with destiny. I pray that many of them are present today.'

When Florentyna sat down she was the only person who remained seated. Journalists were to remark the next day that even the cameramen whistled. Florentyna looked down aware that she had made a favourable impression on the crowd, but she still needed Richard for final confirmation. Mark Twain's words came back to her: 'Sorrow can take care of itself, but to get the true benefit of joy, you must share it.' As Florentyna was led off the stage, the students cheered and waved, but her eyes searched only for Richard. Making her way out of the Tercentenary Yard, she was stopped by dozens of people, but her thoughts remained elsewhere.

Florentyna heard the words, 'Who will tell her?' while she was trying to listen to a student who was going to Zimbabwe to teach English. She swung around to stare at the troubled face of Matina Horner, the Radcliffe President.

'It's Richard, isn't it?' said Florentyna quickly.

'Yes, I'm afraid so. He has been involved in a car accident.'

'Where is he?'

'In Newton-Wellesley Hospital, about ten miles away. You must leave immediately.'

'How bad is it?'

'Not good, I'm afraid.'

A police escort rushed Florentyna down the Massachusetts Turnpike to the Route 16 exit as she prayed, Let him live. Let him live.

As soon as the police car arrived outside the main entrance of the hospital she ran up the steps. A doctor was waiting for her.

'Senator Kane, I'm Nicholas Eyre, chief of surgery. We need your permission to operate.'

'Why? Why do you need to operate?'

'Your husband has severe head injuries. And it's our only chance to save him.'

'Can I see him?'

'Yes, of course.' He led her quickly to the emergency room where Richard lay unconscious beneath a plastic sheet, a tube coming out of his mouth, his skull encased in stained white gauze. Florentyna collapsed on to the bedside chair and stared down at the floor, unable to bear the sight of her mutilated husband. Would the brain damage be permanent or could he recover?

'What happened?' she asked the surgeon.

'The police can't be certain, but a witness said your husband veered across the divider on the turnpike for no apparent reason and collided with a tractor-trailer. There seems to have been no mechanical fault with the car he was driving, so they can only conclude he fell asleep at the wheel.'

Florentyna steeled herself to raise her eyes and look again at the man she loved.

'Can we operate, Mrs. Kane?'

'Yes,' said a faint voice that only an hour before had brought thousands of people to their feet. She was led into a corridor and sat alone. A nurse came up. They needed a signature; she scribbled her name. How many times had she done that today?

She sat alone in the corridor, a strange hunched up figure in an elegant dress, on the little wooden chair. She remembered how she had met Richard in Bloomingdale's when she thought he had fallen for Maisie; how they made love only moments after their first row and how they had run away and with the help of Bella and Claude she had become Mrs. Kane; the births of William and Annabel; that twenty-dollar bill that fixed the meeting in San Francisco with Gianni; returning to New York as partners to run the Baron Group and Lester's; how he had then made Washington possible; how she had smiled when he played the cello for her; how he had laughed when she beat him at golf. She had always wanted to achieve so much for him, and he had always been selfless in his love for her. He must live so that she could devote herself to making him well again.

In times of helplessness one suddenly believes in God. Florentyna fell on her knees and begged for her husband's life.

Hours passed before Dr. Eyre returned to her side. Florentyna looked up hopefully.

'Your husband died a few minutes ago,' was all the surgeon said.

'Did he say anything to you before he died?' Florentyna asked.

The chief of surgery looked embarrassed.

'Whatever it was my husband said, I should like to know, Dr. Eyre.'

The surgeon hesitated. 'All he said, Mrs. Kane, was, "Tell Jessie I love her".'

Florentyna bowed her head.

The widow knelt alone and prayed.

It was the second funeral of a Kane in Trinity Church in as many months. William stood between two Mrs. Kanes dressed in black, as the bishop reminded them that in death there is life.

Florentyna sat alone in her room that night and cared no longer for this life. In the hall lay a package marked: 'Fragile, Sotheby Parke Bernet, contents one cello, Stradivarius.'

William accompanied his mother back to Washington on Monday; the news-stand at Logan airport was ablaze with headlines from her speech. Florentyna didn't even notice.

William remained at the Baron with his mother for three days until she sent him back to his wife. For hours Florentyna would sit alone in a room full of Richard's past. His cello, his photographs, even the last unfinished game of backgammon.

Florentyna began to arrive at the Senate by mid-morning.

Janet couldn't get her to answer her mail except for the hundreds of letters and telegrams expressing sorrow at Richard's death. She failed to show up at committee meetings and forgot appointments with people who had travelled great distances to see her. On one occasion, she even missed presiding over the Senate, a chore Senators took in turn when the Vice-President was absent – for a defence debate. Even her most ardent admirers doubted if she would ever fully regain her impetuous enthusiasm for politics.

As the weeks turned into months, Florentyna began to lose her best assistants who feared she no longer had the ambition for herself that they had once had for her. Complaints from her constituents, low key for the first six months after Richard's death, now turned to an angry rumble, but still Florentyna went aimlessly about her daily routine. Senator Brooks quite openly suggested an early retirement for the good of the party, and continued to voice this opinion in the smoke-filled rooms of Illinois's political headquarters. Florentyna's name began to disappear from the White House guest lists and she was no longer seen at the cocktail parties held by Mrs. John Sherman Cooper, Mrs. Lloyd Dreegar or Mrs. George Renchard.

Both William and Edward travelled regularly to Washington in an effort to try to stop her from thinking about Richard, and to bring her back to taking an interest in her work. Neither of them succeeded.

Florentyna spent a quiet Christmas at the Red House in Boston. William and Joanna found it difficult to adapt to the change that had taken place in so short a time. The once elegant and incisive lady had become listless and dull. It was an unhappy Christmas for everyone except the ten-month-old Richard who was learning to hoist himself up by pulling on anything he could get hold of. When Florentyna returned to Washington in the New Year, matters did not improve, and even Edward began to despair.

Janet Brown waited nearly a year before she told Florentyna that she had been offered the job of administrative assistant in Senator Hart's office.

'You must accept the offer, my dear. There is nothing left for you here. I shall serve out my term and then retire.'

Janet too pleaded with Florentyna but it had no effect.

Florentyna glanced through her mail, barely noticing a letter from Bella chiding her about not turning up for their daughter's wedding, and signed some more letters that she hadn't written or even bothered to read. When she checked her watch, it was six o'clock. An invitation from Senator Pryor to a small reception lay on the desk in front of her. Florentyna dropped the smartly embossed card into the waste-paper basket, picked up a copy of the *Washington Post* and decided to walk home alone. She had never once felt alone when Richard had been alive.

She came out of the Russell Building, crossed Delaware Avenue and cut over the grass of Union Station Plaza. Soon Washington would be a blaze of colours. The fountain splashed as she came to the paved walkway. She reached the steps leading down to New Jersey Avenue and decided to rest for a moment on the park bench. There was nothing to rush home for. She began to recall the look on Richard's face as Jake Thomas welcomed him as chairman of Lester's. He did look a fool standing there with a large red London bus under his arm. Reminiscing about such incidents in their life together brought her as near to happiness now as she ever expected to achieve.

'You're on my bench.'

Florentyna blinked and looked to her side. A man wearing dirty jeans and an open brown shirt with holes in the sleeves sat on the other end of the bench, staring at her suspiciously. He had not shaved for several days, which made it hard for Florentyna to determine his age.

'I'm sorry, I didn't realise it was your bench.'

'Been my bench, Danny's bench, these last thirteen years,' said the grimy face. 'Before that it was Ted's and when I go Matt gets it.'

'Matt?' repeated Florentyna uncomprehendingly.

'Yeah, Matt the Grain. He's asleep behind parking lot sixteen waiting for me to die.' The tramp chuckled. 'But I tell you the way he goes through that grain alcohol, Matt will never take over this bench. You not thinking of staying long, are you lady?'

'No, I hadn't planned to,' said Florentyna.

'Good,' said Danny.

'What do you do during the day?'

'Oh, this and that. Always know where we can get soup from church kitchens, and some of that stuff they throw out from the swanky restaurants can keep me going for days. I had the best part of a steak at the Monocle yesterday. I think I'll try the Baron tonight.'

Florentyna tried not to show her feelings. 'You don't work?'

'Who'd give Danny work? I haven't had a job in fifteen years – since I left the Army back in '70. Nobody wanted this old vet, should have died for my country in Nam – would have made things easier for everyone.'

'How many vets are there like you?'

'In Washington?'

'Yes, in Washington.'

'Hundreds.'

'Hundreds?' repeated Florentyna.

'Not as bad as some cities. New York they throw you in jail as quick as look at you. When are you thinking of going, lady?' he said eyeing her suspiciously.

'Soon. May I ask . . .?'

'You ask too many questions, so it's my turn. Okay if I have the paper when you leave?'

'The *Washington Post*?'

'Good quality, that,' said Danny.

'You read it?'

'No.' He laughed. 'I wrap myself up in it, keeps me warm as a hamburger if I stay very still.'

She passed him the paper. She stood up and smiled at Danny, noticing for the first time that he had only one leg.

'Wouldn't have a quarter to spare an old soldier?'

Florentyna rummaged through her bag. She had only a

ten-dollar bill and thirty-seven cents in change. She handed the money to Danny.

He stared at her offering in disbelief. 'There's enough here for both Matt and me to have some real food,' he exclaimed. The tramp paused and looked at her more closely. 'I know you, lady,' Danny said suspiciously. 'You're that Senator lady. Matt always says he's going to get an appointment with you and explain a thing or two about how you spend government money. But I told him what those little receptionists do when they see the likes of us walk in – they call the capital cops and grab the disinfectant. Don't even ask us to sign the guest book. I told Matt not to waste his valuable time.'

Florentyna watched Danny as he began to make himself comfortable on his bench by covering himself very professionally with the *Washington Post*. 'Any case, I told him you would be much too busy to bother with him, and so would the other ninety-nine.' He turned his back on the distinguished Senator from Illinois and lay very still. Florentyna said good night before walking down the steps to the street where she was met by a policeman outside the entrance to the underground parking lot.

'The man on that bench?'

'Yes, Senator,' said the officer. 'Danny, Danny One-Leg; he didn't cause you any trouble, I hope?'

'No, not at all,' said Florentyna. 'Does he sleep there every night?'

'Has for the past ten years, which is how long I've been on the force. Cold nights, he moves to a grate behind the Capitol. He's harmless enough, not like some of those at the back of lot sixteen.'

Florentyna lay awake the rest of the night only nodding off occasionally as she thought about Danny One-Leg and the hundreds suffering from the same plight as his. At seven thirty the next morning she was back in her office on Capitol Hill. The first person to arrive was Janet at eight thirty, and she was shocked to find Florentyna's head buried in *The Modern Welfare Society* by Arthur Quern. Florentyna looked up.

'Janet, I want all the current unemployment figures, broken down into states, and then into ethnic groups. I also need to know, with the same breakdowns, how many people are on social security and what percentage have not worked for over two years. Then I want you to find out how many of them have served in the armed forces. Compile a list of every leading authority. . . You're crying, Janet.'

'Yes, I am,' she said.

Florentyna came from behind her desk and put her arms round her. 'It's over, my dear, let's forget the past and get this show back on the road.'

33

IT TOOK EVERYONE IN Congress only a month to discover that Senator Kane was back with a vengeance. And when the President phoned her personally, she knew that her attacks on his Fresh Approach were coming home to the one house where things could be changed.

'Florentyna, I'm eighteen months away from election day and you are taking my Fresh Approach campaign apart. Do you want the Republicans to win the next election?'

'No, of course not, but with your Fresh Approach we only spent in one year on welfare what we spent on defence in six weeks. Do you realise how many people in this country don't even eat one square meal a day?'

'Yes, Florentyna, I do . . .'

'Do you also know what the figures are for people who sleep on the streets each night in America? Not India, not Africa, not Asia; I'm talking about America. And how many of those people haven't had a job in ten years; not ten weeks or ten months but ten years, Mr. President?'

'Florentyna, whenever you call me Mr. President I know I'm in trouble. What do you of all people expect me to do?

You have always been among those Democrats who advocate a strong defence programme.'

'And I still do, but there are millions of people across America who wouldn't give a damn if the Russians came marching down Pennsylvania Avenue right now, because they don't believe they could be any worse off.'

'I hear what you're saying, but you've become a hawk in dove's clothing, and those sort of statements may make wonderful headlines for you, but what do you expect me to do about it?'

'Set up a Presidential commission to look into how our welfare money is spent. I already have three of my staff working on the problem at the moment and I intend to present some of the facts they are unearthing about misuse of funds at the earliest date. I can promise you, Mr. President, the figures will make your hair curl.'

'Have you forgotten I'm nearly bald, Florentyna?' She laughed. 'I like the idea of a commission.' The President paused. 'I could even float the concept at my next press conference.'

'Why don't you do that, Mr. President? And tell them about the man who has been sleeping on a bench for thirteen years little more than a stone's throw away from the White House while you slumbered in the Lincoln bedroom. A man who lost a leg in Vietnam and doesn't even know he is entitled to sixty-three dollars a week compensation from the Veterans Administration. And if he did, he wouldn't know how to collect it, because his local V.A. office is in Texas, and if in an inspired moment they decided to send a cheque to him where would they address it? A park bench, near the Capitol?'

'Danny One-Leg,' said the President.

'So you know about Danny?'

'Who doesn't? He's had more good publicity in two weeks than I've had in two years. I'm even considering an amputation. I fought for my country in Korea, you know.'

'And you've managed to take care of yourself ever since.'

'Florentyna, if I set up a Presidential commission on welfare, will you give it your support?'

'I certainly will, Mr. President.'

'And will you stop attacking Texas?'

'That was unfortunate. A junior researcher of mine discovered Danny had come from Texas. But do you realise that in spite of the illegal immigrant problem, over twenty per cent of the people of Texas have an annual income of less than . . .?'

'I know, I know, Florentyna, but *you* seem to forget that my Vice-President comes from Houston and he hasn't had a day's rest since Danny One-Leg hit the front pages.'

'Poor old Pete,' said Florentyna. 'He will be the first Vice-President who has had something to worry about, other than where his next meal is coming from.'

'And you mustn't be hard on Pete, he plays his role.'

'You mean balances the ticket so that you can stay in the White House.'

'Florentyna, you're a wicked lady, and I warn you that I intend to open my press conference next Thursday by saying I have come up with a brilliant idea.'

'*You*'ve come up with the idea?'

'Yes,' said the President. 'There must be some compensation for taking the heat all the time. I repeat that I have come up with this brilliant idea of a Presidential commission on "Waste in Welfare" and . . .' the President hesitated for a minute '. . . that Senator Kane has agreed to be the chairman. Now will that keep you quiet for a few days?'

'Yes,' said Florentyna, 'and I'll try to report within one year so that you have time before the election to describe to the voters your bold new plans to sweep away the cobwebs of the past and usher in the Fresh Approach.'

'Florentyna.'

'I'm sorry, Mr. President. I couldn't resist that.'

Janet didn't know where Florentyna was going to find the time to chair such an important commission. Her appointment books already needed the assistant with the smallest handwriting to complete each page.

'I need three hours clear every day for the next six months,' said Florentyna.

'Sure thing,' said Janet. 'How do you feel about two o'clock to five o'clock every morning?'

'Suits me,' said Florentyna, 'but I'm not sure we could get anyone else to sit on a commission under those conditions.' Florentyna smiled. 'And we're going to need more assistants.'

Janet had already filled all the vacancies that had been created from resignations during the past few months. She had appointed a new press secretary, a new speech writer, and four more legislative researchers from some of the outstanding young college graduates who were now banging on Florentyna's door. 'Let's be thankful that the Baron Group can afford the extra cost,' Janet added.

Once the President had made his announcement, Florentyna set to work. Her commission consisted of twenty members, plus a professional support staff of eleven. She divided the commission itself, so that half were professional people who had never needed welfare in their lives nor given the subject much thought until asked to do so by Florentyna, while the other half were currently on welfare, or unemployed. A clean-shaven Danny, wearing his first suit, joined Florentyna's staff as a full-time adviser. The originality of the idea took Washington by surprise. Article after article was written on Senator Kane's 'Park Bench Commissioners'. Danny One-Leg told stories that made the other half of the committee realise how deep-seated the problem was and how many abuses still needed to be corrected, so that those in genuine need received fair recompense.

Among those who were questioned by the committee were Matt the Grain, who now slept on the bench Danny had vacated, and 'Charlie Wendon', an ingenious convict from Leavenworth who, for a parole deal arranged by Florentyna, told the committee how he had been able to milk a thousand dollars a week out of welfare before the police caught up with him. The man had so many aliases he was no longer sure of his own name; at one point he had supported seventeen wives, forty-one dependent children and nineteen dependent parents, all of whom were non-existent except on the national welfare computer. Florentyna thought he might be exaggerating until he showed the commission how to get the President of the United States on to the computer as unemployed, with two dependent children, living with his ageing mother at 1600 Pennsylvania Avenue, Washington, D.C. Wendon also went on to confirm something she had already feared, that he was small fry compared with the professional crime syndicates who thought nothing of raking in fifty thousand dollars a week through phony welfare recipients.

She later discovered that Danny One-Leg's real name was on the computer and that someone else had been collecting his money for the past thirteen years. It didn't take a lot longer to discover that Matt the Grain and several of his friends from parking lot sixteen were also on the computer although they had never received a penny themselves.

Florentyna went on to prove that there were over a million people entitled to aid who were not receiving it, while, at the same time, the money was disappearing elsewhere. She became convinced that there was no need to ask Congress for more money, just for safeguards designed to ensure that the annual pay-out of over ten billion dollars was reaching the right people. Many of those who needed help simply couldn't read or write, and so never returned to the government office once they had been presented with long forms to complete. Their names became an easy source of income for even a small-time crook. When Florentyna presented her report to the President ten months later, he sent a series of new safeguards to Congress for their immediate consideration. He also announced that he would be drawing up a new Welfare Reform Programme before the election. The press was fascinated by the way Florentyna had got the President's name and address on the unemployment computer; from MacNelly to Peters, the cartoonists had a field day, while the

FBI made a series of welfare fraud arrests right across the country.

The press praised the President for his initiative, and the *Washington Post* declared that Senator Kane had done more in one year for those in genuine need than the New Deal and the Great Society put together. This was indeed a 'fresh approach'; Florentyna had to smile. Rumours began to circulate that she would replace Pete Parkin as Vice-President when the election came round. On Monday she was on the cover of *Newsweek* for the first time and across the bottom ran the words: 'America's First Woman Vice-President?' Florentyna was far too shrewd a politician to be fooled by press speculation. She knew that when the time came, the President would stick with Parkin, balance the ticket and be sure of the south. Much as he admired Florentyna, the President wanted another four years in the White House.

Once again, Florentyna's biggest problem in life was in determining priorities among the many issues and people that competed for her attention. Among the requests from Senators to help them with their campaigns was one from Ralph Brooks. Brooks, who never lost the opportunity to describe himself as the state's senior Senator, had recently been appointed chairman of the Senate Energy Committee, which kept him in the public eye. He had received considerable praise for his handling of the oil tycoons and leaders of big business. Florentyna was aware that he never spoke well of her in private, but when proof of this came back to her she dismissed it as unimportant. She was surprised, however, when he asked her to share a TV commercial spot with him, saying how well they worked together and the importance of both Illinois Senators being Democratic. After she'd been urged to cooperate by the party chairman in Chicago, Florentyna agreed, although she had not spoken to her Senate colleague more than a couple of times a month during her entire term in Congress. She hoped her endorsement might patch up their differences. It didn't. Two years later when she came up for re-election, his support for her was rarely above a whisper.

As the Presidential election drew nearer, more and more Senators seeking re-election asked Florentyna to speak on their behalf. During the last six months of 1988 she rarely spent a weekend at home; even the President invited her to join him in several campaign appearances. He had been delighted by the public reaction to the Kane Commission report on welfare, and he agreed to the one request Florentyna made of him, although he knew Pete Parkin and Ralph Brooks would be furious when they heard.

Florentyna had had little or no social life since Richard's death, although she had managed to spend an occasional weekend with William, Joanna and her two-year-old grandson Richard at the Red House on Beacon Hill. Whenever she found a weekend free to be back at the Cape, Annabel would join her.

Edward, who was now chairman of the Baron Group and vice-chairman of Lester's Bank, reported to her at least once a week, producing results even Richard would have been proud of. On Cape Cod he would join her for golf, but unlike the results of her battles with Richard, Florentyna always won. Each time she did she would donate her winnings to the local Republican club in Richard's memory. The local G.O.P. man obligingly recorded the gifts as coming from an anonymous donor as Florentyna's constituents would have been hard put to understand her reasons for supporting both sides.

Edward left Florentyna in no doubt of his feelings for her and once hesitantly went so far as to propose. Florentyna kissed her closest friend gently on the cheek. 'I will never marry again,' she said, 'but if you ever beat me at a round of golf, I'll reconsider your offer.' Edward immediately started taking golf lessons, but Florentyna was always too good for him.

When the press got hold of the news that Senator Kane had been chosen to deliver the key speech at the Democratic convention in Detroit, they again started writing about her as a possible Presidential candidate in 1992. Edward became excited about these suggestions, but she reminded him that they had also considered forty-three other candidates in the last six months. As the President had predicted, Pete Parkin was livid when the suggestion was voiced that the Vice-Presidency would be handed to Florentyna but eventually calmed down when he realised that the President had no intention of dropping him from the ticket. It only convinced Florentyna that the Vice-President was going to be her biggest rival if she did decide to run in four years' time.

The President and Pete Parkin were re-nominated at a dull party convention, with only a handful of dissenters and favourite sons to keep the delegates awake. Florentyna wistfully recalled livelier conventions, such as the G.O.P.'s 1976 mêlée, during which Nelson Rockefeller had pulled a phone socket out of the floor in the Kansas City convention hall.

Florentyna's key speech was received by the delegates in decibels second only to those accorded to the President's speech of acceptance, and it caused posters and campaign buttons to appear on the final day with the words: 'Kane for '92'. Only in America could ten thousand campaign buttons appear overnight, thought Florentyna, and she took one home for young Richard. Her Presidential campaign was beginning without her even lifting a finger.

During the final weeks before the election, Florentyna travelled to almost as many marginal states as the President himself and the press suggested that her unstinting loyalty might well have been a factor in the Democrats' slim victory. Ralph Brooks was returned to the Senate with a slightly increased majority. It reminded Florentyna that her own re-election to the Senate was now only two years away.

When the first session of the 101st Congress opened, Florentyna found that many of her colleagues in both houses were openly letting her know of their support should she decide to put her name forward for the Presidency. She realised that some of them would be saying exactly the same thing to Pete Parkin, but she made a note of each one and always sent a handwritten letter of thanks the same day.

Her hardest task before facing re-election for the Senate was to steer the new Welfare Bill through both houses, and the job took up most of her time. She personally sponsored seven amendments to the bill which included the federal government being responsible for all costs, setting a nationwide minimum income, and a major overhaul of social security. She spent hours badgering, cajoling, coaxing and almost bribing her colleagues until the bill became law. She stood behind the President when he signed the new Act in the Rose Garden. Cameras rolled and shutters clicked from the ring of press photographers standing behind a cordoned-off area. It was the greatest single achievement of Florentyna's political career. The President delivered a self-serving statement and then rose to shake Florentyna's hand. 'This is the lady whom we can thank for "The Kane Act",' he said and whispered in her ear, 'Good thing the V.P.'s in South America or I would never hear the end of it.'

Press and public alike praised the skill and determination with which Senator Kane had guided the bill through Congress and the *New York Times* said that if she achieved nothing more in her political career, she would have placed on the books a piece of legislation that would stand the test of time. Under the new law, no one in genuine need would forfeit his rights, while at the other end of the scale, those who played the 'Welfare Charade' would now end up behind bars.

As soon as the fuss had blown over, Florentyna tried to return to the normal daily life of a Senator. Janet warned her that she must spend more time in the state now that the election was less than nine months away. Nearly all the senior members of the party offered their services to Florentyna when she came up for re-election, but it was the President who broke into a heavy schedule to support her and drew the biggest crowd when he spoke at the convention hall in Chicago. As they walked up the steps together to the strains of 'Happy Days Are Here Again' he whispered, 'Now, I am going to get my revenge for all the flak you've given me over the past five years.'

The President described Florentyna as the woman who had given him more problems than his wife and now he heard she wanted to sleep in his bed at the White House. When the laughter died down, he added, 'And if she does aspire to that great office, America could not be better served.'

The next day the press suggested that the statement was a direct snub to Pete Parkin and that Florentyna would have the backing of the President if she decided to run. The President denied this interpretation of what he had said, but from that moment on Florentyna was placed in the unfortunate position of being the front-runner for 1992. When the results of her Senate race came in even Florentyna was surprised by the size of her victory, as most Democratic Senators had lost ground in the usual mid-term election swing against the White House. Florentyna's overwhelming victory confirmed the party's view that it had found not only a standard-bearer but something far more important: a winner.

The week of the first session of the 102nd Congress opened with Florentyna's picture on the cover of *Time*. Full profiles of her life, giving the details of her playing St. Joan at Girls Latin and winning the Woolson Scholarship to Radcliffe, were meticulously chronicled. They even explained why her late husband had called her Jessie. She had become the best known woman in America. 'This charming fifty-six-year-old woman,' said *Time* in its summation, 'is both intelligent and witty. Only beware when you see her hand clench into a tight fist because it's then she becomes a heavyweight.'

During the new session, Florentyna tried to carry out the normal duties of a Senator but she was daily being asked by colleagues, friends and the press when she would be making a statement about her intentions to run or not for the White House. She tried to sidetrack them by taking more interest in the major issues of the day. At the time Quebec elected a left-wing government, she flew to Canada to participate in exploratory talks with British Columbia, Alberta, Saskatchewan and Manitoba about federation with America. The press followed her and after she returned to Washington, the media stopped describing her as a politician but America's first stateswoman.

Pete Parkin was already informing anyone and everyone who wanted to listen that he intended to run, and an official announcement was considered imminent. The Vice-President was five years older than Florentyna and she knew this would be his last opportunity to hear 'Hail to the Chief' played for him. Florentyna felt it might be her only chance. She remembered Margaret Thatcher telling her when she stood for Prime Minister, 'The only difference between the leader of a party being a man or a woman is, if a woman loses, the men won't give you a second chance.'

Florentyna had no doubt what Bob Buchanan would have advised had he still been alive. Read *Julius Caesar*, my dear, but this time Brutus and not Mark Antony.

She and Edward spent a quiet weekend together at Cape Cod, and while he lost yet another golf match they discussed the tide in the affairs of one woman, the flood and the possible fortune.

By the time that Edward returned to New York and Florentyna to Washington, the decision had finally been made.

34

'. . . AND TO THAT END I declare my candidacy for the office of President of the United States.'

Florentyna gazed into the Senate Caucus Room at the three hundred and fifty applauding members of the audience who occupied a space that the sergeant-at-arms insisted should only hold three hundred. Television camera crews and press photographers lobbed and dodged to prevent their frames from being filled with the backs of anonymous heads. Florentyna remained standing during the prolonged applause that followed her announcement. When the noise had finally ebbed Edward stepped up to face the battery of microphones at the podium.

'Ladies and gentlemen,' he said. 'I know the candidate will be delighted to answer your questions.'

Half the people in the room started to speak at once and Edward nodded to a man in the third row to indicate that he could ask the first question.

'Albert Hunt of the *Wall Street Journal*,' he said. 'Senator Kane, who do you think will be your toughest opponent?'

'The Republican candidate,' she said without hesitation. There was a ripple of laughter and some applause. Edward smiled and called for the next question.

'Senator Kane, is this really a bid to be Pete Parkin's running mate?'

'No, I am not interested in the office of Vice-President,' replied Florentyna. 'At best it's a period of stagnation while you wait around in the hope of doing the real job. At worst I am reminded of Nelson Rockefeller's words: "Don't take the number two spot unless you're up for a four-year advanced seminar in political science and a lot of state funerals." I'm not in the mood for either.'

'Do you feel America is ready for a woman President?'

'Yes, I do, otherwise I would not be willing to run for the office, but I will be in a better position to answer that question on November 3rd.'

'Do you think the Republicans might select a woman?'

'No, they don't have the courage for such a bold move. They will watch the Democrats make a success of the idea and copy it when the next election comes around.'

'Do you feel you have enough experience to hold this office?'

'I have been a wife, a mother, the chairman of a multimillion dollar corporation, a member of the House for eight years and a Senator for seven. In the public career I've chosen, the Presidency is the number one spot. So, yes, I believe I am now qualified for that job.'

'Do you expect the success of your Welfare Act to help you with the votes of the poor and black communities?'

'I hope the Act will bring me support from every sector. My main intent with that piece of legislation was to ensure that both those who contribute to welfare through taxation and those who benefit from the legislation will feel that the provisions made are both just and humane in a modern society.'

'After the Russian invasion of Yugoslavia, would your administration take a harder line with the Kremlin?'

'After Hungary, Czechoslovakia, Afghanistan, Poland and now Yugoslavia, the latest Soviet offensive on the Pakistan border reinforces my long-standing conviction that we must remain vigilant in the defence of our people. We must always remember that the fact that the two biggest oceans on earth have protected us in the past is no guarantee of our safety in the future.'

'The President has described you as a hawk in dove's clothing.'

'I'm not sure if that's a comment on my dress or my looks, but I suspect that the combination of those two birds looks not unlike the American eagle.'

'Do you feel we can keep a special relationship with Europe after the election results in France and Britain?'

'The decision of the French to return to a Gaullist government while the British voted for a new Labour Administration does not greatly concern me. Jacques Chirac and Roy Hattersley have both proved to be good friends of America in the past, and I see no reason why that should change in the future.'

'Do you expect Ralph Brooks's support for your campaign?'

It was the first question that had taken Florentyna by surprise. 'Perhaps you should ask him, but naturally I hope that Senator Brooks will feel pleased by my decision.' She could think of nothing else to add.

'Senator Kane, do you approve of the current Primary system?'

'No. Although I am not a supporter of a national Primary, the present system is by any standards archaic. America seems to have developed a process for the selection of a President that is more responsive to the demands of the network news programmes than it is to the needs of modern government. It also encourages dilettante candidates. To-day, you have a better chance of becoming President if you are temporarily out of work, having been left several million by your grandmother. You then have four years off to devote to running around the country collecting delegates, while the people best qualified for the job are probably doing a full day's work elsewhere. If I became President, I would seek to send a bill to the Congress which would not handicap anyone from running for the Presidency through lack of time or money. We must reinstate the age-old precept that anyone born in this country, with both the desire to serve and the ability to do the job, will not find themselves disqualified before the first voter goes to the polls.'

The questions continued to come at Florentyna from all parts of the room and she took the last one over an hour later.

'Senator Kane, if you become President, will you be like Washington and never tell a lie or like Nixon and have your own definition of the truth?'

'I cannot promise I will never lie. We all lie, sometimes to protect a friend or a member of our family, and if I was President perhaps to protect one's country. Sometimes we lie just because we don't want to be found out. The one thing I can assure you of is that I am the only woman in America who has never been able to lie about her age.' When the laughter died down Florentyna remained standing. 'I would like to end this press conference by saying that whatever the outcome of my decision today, I wish to express my thanks as an American for the fact that the daughter of an immigrant has found it possible to run for the highest office in the land. I do not believe such an ambition would be attainable in any other country in the world.'

Florentyna's life began to change the moment she left the room; four Secret Service agents formed a circle around the candidate, the lead one skilfully creating a passage for her through the mass of people.

Florentyna smiled when Brad Staimes introduced himself and explained that for the duration of her candidacy, there would always be four agents with her night and day, working in eight-hour shifts. Florentyna couldn't help noticing that two of the agents were women whose build and physical appearance closely resembled her own. She thanked Mr. Staimes but never quite became used to seeing one of the agents whenever she turned her head. The agents' tiny earphones distinguished them from well-wishers and Florentyna recalled the story about an elderly lady who attended a Nixon rally in 1972. She approached a Nixon aide at the end of the candidate's speech and said she would definitely vote for his re-election because he obviously sympathised with those who, like herself, were hard of hearing.

Following the press conference, Edward chaired a strategy meeting in Florentyna's office to work out a rough schedule for the coming campaign. The Vice-President had announced some time before that he was a candidate and several other contestants had thrown their hats into the ring, but the press had already decided that the real battle was going to be between Kane and Parkin.

Edward had lined up a formidable team of pollsters, finance chairmen and policy advisers who were well supplemented by Florentyna's seasoned staff in Washington led by Janet Brown.

First Edward outlined his day-by-day plan leading up to the first Primary in New Hampshire, and from there to California, all the way to the convention floor in Detroit. Florentyna had tried to arrange for the convention to be held in Chicago, but the Vice-President vetoed the idea; he wasn't challenging Florentyna on her home ground. He reminded the Democratic committee that the choice of Chicago and the riots that followed might have been the single reason that Humphrey lost to Nixon in 1968.

Florentyna had already faced the fact that it would be almost impossible for her to beat the Vice-President in the southern states so it was vital that she should get off to a strong start in New England and the Mid-West. She agreed that during the next three months she would devote seventy-five per cent of her energies to the campaign, and for several hours her team threw around ideas for the best use of that time. It was also agreed that she would make regular trips to the major cities that voted in the first three Primaries and, if she made a strong showing in New Hampshire, a traditionally conservative area, they would plan their forward strategy accordingly.

Florentyna dealt with as much of her Senate work as possible between making frequent trips to New Hampshire, Vermont and Massachusetts. Edward had chartered a six-seater Lear jet for her with two pilots available around the clock so that she could leave Washington at a moment's notice. All three Primary states had set up strong campaign headquarters, and everywhere Florentyna went she spotted as many 'Kane for President' posters and bumper stickers as she did for Pete Parkin.

With only seven weeks left until the first Primary Florentyna began to spend more and more of her time chasing the one hundred and forty-seven thousand registered Democrats in the state. Edward did not expect her to capture more than thirty per cent of the votes, but he felt that might well be enough to win the Primary and persuade doubters that she was an electoral asset. Florentyna needed every delegate she could secure before they arrived in the south, even if possible to pass the magic one thousand six hundred and sixty-six by the time she reached the convention hall in Detroit.

The early signs were good. Florentyna's private pollster, Kevin Palumbo, assured her that the race with the Vice-President was running neck and neck, and Gallup and Harris seemed to confirm that view. Only seven per cent of the voters said they would not under any circumstances vote for a woman, but Florentyna knew just how important seven per cent could be if the final outcome was close.

Florentyna's schedule included brief stops at over one hundred and fifty of New Hampshire's two hundred and fifty small towns. Despite the hectic nature of each day, she grew to love the classical New England milltowns, the crustiness of the Granite State's farmers and the stark beauty of its winter landscape.

She served as a starter for a dogsled race in Franconia and visited the most northerly settlement near the Canadian border. She learned to respect the penetrating insights of local newspaper editors, many of whom had retired from high-level jobs with national magazines and news services. She avoided discussions of one particular issue after discovering that New Hampshire residents stoutly defended their right to oppose a state income tax, thus attracting a host of high-income professionals from across the Massachusetts border.

More than once she had occasion to be thankful for the death of William Loeb, the newspaper publisher, whose outrageous misuse of the Manchester *Union Leader* had single-handedly destroyed the candidacies of Edmund Muskie and George Bush before her. It was no secret that Loeb had had no time for women in politics.

Edward was able to report that money was flowing into their headquarters in Chicago and 'Kane for President' offices were springing up in every state. Some of them had more volunteers than they could physically accommodate; the overspill turned dozens of living rooms and garages throughout America into makeshift campaign headquarters.

In the final seven days before the first Primary, Florentyna was interviewed by Barbara Walters, Dan Rather and Frank Reynolds, as well as appearing on all three morning news programmes. As Andy Miller, her press secretary, pointed out, fifty-two million people watched her interview with Barbara Walters and it would have taken over five hundred years to shake the hands of that number of voters in White

River Junction. Nevertheless her local managers still saw to it that she visited nearly every old people's home in the state.

Despite this, Florentyna had to pound the streets of New Hampshire towns, shaking hands with papermill workers in Berlin, as well as with the somewhat inebriated denizens of the VFW and American Legion posts, which seemed to exist in every town. She learned to work the ski-lift lines in the smaller hills rather than the famous resorts which were often peopled by a majority of non-voting visitors from New York or Massachusetts.

If she failed with this tiny electorate of the northern tip of America, Florentyna knew it would raise major doubts about her credibility as a candidate.

Whenever she arrived in a city, Edward was always there to meet her and he never let her stop until the moment she stepped back on to her plane.

Edward told her that they could thank heaven for the curiosity value of a woman candidate. His advance team never had to worry about filling any hall where Florentyna was to speak with potted plants rather than with Granite State voters.

Pete Parkin, who had a good luck streak with funeral duty, proved that the Vice-President had little else to do; he spent even more time in the state than Florentyna could. When the day of the Primary came, Edward was able to show that someone in the Kane team had contacted by phone, letter or personal visit one hundred and twenty-five thousand of the one hundred and forty-seven thousand registered Democrats but, he added, obviously so had Pete Parkin because many of them had remained non-committal and some even hostile.

On the final evening, Florentyna held a rally in Manchester which over three thousand people attended. When Janet told her that tomorrow she would be about one-fiftieth of the way through the campaign, Florentyna replied, 'Or already finished.' She went to her motel room a little after midnight followed by the camera crews of C.B.S., N.B.C., A.B.C., Cable News and four agents from the Secret Service, all of whom were convinced she was going to win.

The voters of New Hampshire woke up to drifting snow and icy winds. Florentyna spent the day driving from polling place to polling place thanking the party faithful until the last poll closed. At eleven minutes past nine, C.B.S. was the first to tell the national audience that the turnout was estimated at forty-seven per cent, which Dan Rather considered high in view of the weather conditions. The early voting pattern showed that the pollsters had proved right: Florentyna and Pete Parkin were running neck and neck, each taking over the lead during the night but never by more than a couple of percentage points. Florentyna sat in her motel room with Edward, Janet, her closest assistants and two Secret Service agents, watching the final results come in.

'The outcome couldn't have been closer if they had planned it,' said Jessica Savitch, who announced the result first for N.B.C. 'Senator Kane thirty-one per cent, Vice-President Parkin thirty, Senator Bill Bradley sixteen per cent and the rest of the voters scattered among five others who in my opinion,' added Savitch, 'needn't bother to book a hotel room for the next Primary.'

Florentyna recalled her father's words: *If the result of the New Hampshire Primary turns out to be satisfactory . . .*

She left for Massachusetts with six delegates committed to her; Pete Parkin had five. The national press declared no winner but five losers. Only three candidates were seen in Massachusetts, and Florentyna seemed to have buried the bogey that as a woman she couldn't be a serious contender.

In Massachusetts she had fourteen days to capture as many of the one hundred and eleven delegates as possible, and here her work pattern hardly varied. Each day she would carry out the schedule that Edward had organised for her, a programme that ensured that the candidate met as many voters as possible and found some way to get on the morning or evening news.

Florentyna posed with babies, union leaders and Italian restaurateurs; she ate scallops, linguine, Portuguese sweetbread and cranberries; she rode the MTA, the Nantucket ferry and the Alameda bus line the length of the Massachusetts Turnpike; she jogged on beaches, hiked in the Berkshires and shopped in Boston's Quincy Market, all in an effort to prove she had the stamina of any man. Nursing her aching body in a hot bath, she came to the conclusion that had her father remained in Russia, her route to the Presidency of the U.S.S.R. couldn't have been any harder.

In Massachusetts, Florentyna held off Pete Parkin for a second time, taking forty-seven delegates to the Vice-President's thirty-nine. The same day in Vermont, she captured eight of the state's twelve delegates. Because of the upsets already achieved by Florentyna, the political pollsters were saying that more people were answering 'Yes' when asked 'Could a woman win the Presidential election?' But even she was amused when she read that six per cent of the voters had not realised that Senator Kane was a woman. The press was quick to point out that her next big test would be in the south, where the Florida, Georgia and Alabama Primaries all fell on the same day. If she could hold on there she had a real chance, because the Democratic race had become a private battle between herself and the Vice-President. Bill Bradley, having secured only eleven per cent of the votes in Massachusetts, had dropped out because of lack of funds although his name remained on the ballot in several states and no one doubted he would be a serious candidate sometime in the future. Bradley had been Florentyna's first choice as running mate, and she already had the New Jersey Senator on her short list for consideration for Vice-President.

When the Florida ballots were counted, it came as no surprise that the Vice-President had taken sixty-two of the one hundred delegates and he repeated the trend in Georgia by winning 40–23, followed by Alabama where he captured twenty-eight of the forty-five voters, But Pete Parkin was not, as he had promised the press, 'trouncing the little lady when she puts her elegant toes in the south'. Parkin was increasingly trying to outdo Florentyna as a champion of the military, but his choice of legislation setting up the so-called 'Fort

Gringo Line' along the Mexican–American border was beginning to rebound on him in the south-west, where he had imagined he was unbeatable.

Edward and his team were now working several Primaries ahead as they criss-crossed back and forth across the country; Florentyna thanked heaven for her ample campaign funds as the Lear jet touched down in state after state. Her energy remained boundless and if anything it was the Vice-President who began to stammer and sound tired and hoarse at the end of each day. Both candidates had to fit in trips to San Juan, and when Puerto Rico held its Primary in mid-March, twenty-five of the forty-one delegates favoured Florentyna. Two days later, she arrived back in her home state for the Illinois Primary, trailing Parkin 164–194.

The Windy City came to a standstill as its inhabitants welcomed their favourite daughter, giving her every one of the one hundred and seventy-nine Illinois delegates so that she went back into the lead with three hundred and forty-three delegates. However, when they moved on to New York, Connecticut, Wisconsin and Pennsylvania, the Vice-President eroded the lead until he arrived in Texas trailing only five hundred and ninety-one to Florentyna's six hundred and fifty-five.

No one was surprised when Pete Parkin took one hundred per cent of the delegates in his home state; they hadn't had a President since Lyndon Baines Johnson and the male half of Texas believed that while J. R. Ewing might have had his faults, he had been right about a woman's place being in the home. The Vice-President left his ranch outside Houston with a lead of seven hundred and forty-three to Florentyna's six hundred and fifty-five.

Travelling round the country under such tremendous daily pressure, both candidates found an off-the-cuff remark or an unwary comment could easily turn out to be tomorrow's headline. Pete Parkin was the first to make a gaffe when he got Peru mixed up with Paraguay and the photographers went wild when he rode in a chauffeured Mercedes through Flint on one of his motorcades. Nor was Florentyna without her mishaps. In Alabama, when asked if she would consider a black running mate as Vice-President, she replied, 'Of course, I've already considered the idea.' It took repeated statements to persuade the press that she had not already invited one of America's black leaders to join her ticket.

Her biggest mistake, however, was in Virginia. She addressed the University of Virginia Law School on the parole system and the changes she would like to make if she became President. The speech had been written and researched for her by one of the assistants in Washington who had been with Florentyna since her days as a Congresswoman. She read the text through carefully the night before, making only a few minor changes, admiring the way the piece had been put together, and delivered the speech to a crowded hall of law students who received it enthusiastically. When she left for an evening meeting of the Charlottesville Rotary Club to talk on the problems facing cattle farmers, she dismissed all thought of the earlier speech until she read the local paper the next morning during breakfast at the Boar's Head Inn.

The Richmond *News-Leader* came out with a story that all the national papers picked up immediately. A local journalist covering the biggest scoop of his life suggested that Florentyna's speech was outstanding because it had been written by one of Senator Kane's most trusted staff members, Allen Clarence, who was an ex-convict himself, having been given a six-month jail sentence with a year's probation before going to work for Florentyna. Few of the papers pointed out that the offence had been drunken driving without a licence, and that Clarence had been released on appeal after three months. When questioned by the press on what she intended to do about Mr. Clarence, she said, 'Nothing'.

Edward told her that she must fire him immediately, however unfair it might seem, because those sections of the press who were against her – not to mention Pete Parkin – were having a field day repeating that one of her most trusted members of staff was an ex-con. 'Can you imagine who will be running the jails in this country if that woman is elected?' became Parkin's hourly off-the-cuff remark. Eventually Allen Clarence voluntarily resigned, but by then the damage had been done. By the time they reached California, Pete Parkin had increased his lead, with nine hundred and ninety-one delegates to Florentyna's eight hundred and eighty-three.

When Florentyna arrived in San Francisco, Bella was there to meet her at the airport. She might have put on thirty years, but she still hadn't lost any pounds. By her side stood Claude, one enormous son and one skinny daughter. Bella ran towards Florentyna the moment she saw her, only to be blocked by burly Secret Service agents. She was rescued by a hug from the candidate. 'I've never seen anything like her,' muttered one of the Secret Service men. 'She could kick start a Jumbo.' Hundreds of people stood at the perimeter of the tarmac chanting 'President Kane', and Florentyna, accompanied by Bella, walked straight over to them. Hands flew in Florentyna's direction, a reaction that never failed to lift her spirits. The placards read 'California for Kane' and for the first time the majority of the crowd was made up of men. When she turned to leave them and go into the terminal she saw scrawled all over the side of a wall in red, 'Do you want a Polack bitch for President?' and underneath in white, 'Yes'.

Bella, now the headmistress of one of the largest schools in California, had also, after Florentyna had won a seat in the Senate, become the city's Democratic committee chairwoman.

'I always knew you would run for President, so I thought I had better make certain of San Francisco.'

Bella did make certain, with her one thousand so-called volunteers banging on every door. California's split personality – conservative in the south, liberal in the north – made it hard to be the kind of centrist candidate Florentyna wanted to be. But her efficiency, compassion and intelligence converted even some of the most hardened Marin County left-wingers and Orange County Birchers. San Francisco's turnout was second only to Chicago's. Florentyna wished she had fifty-one Bellas because the vote in San Francisco was enough to give her sixty-nine per cent of the state. It had been Bella who had made it possible for Florentyna to arrive in Detroit for the convention with one hundred and twenty-eight more delegates than Parkin.

Over a celebration dinner, Bella warned Florentyna that the biggest problem she was facing was not 'I'll never vote for a woman' but that 'She has too much money'.

'Not that old chestnut. I can't do any more about that,' said Florentyna. 'I've already put my own Baron stock into the foundation.'

'That's the point – no one knows what the foundation does. I realise it helps children in some way, but how many children, and how much money is involved?'

'The trust last year spent over three million dollars on 3,112 immigrants from under-privileged backgrounds. Added to that, four hundred and two gifted children won Remagen Scholarships to American universities and one went on to be our first Rhodes Scholar to Oxford.'

'I wasn't aware of that,' said Bella, 'but I'm continually reminded that Pete Parkin built a feeble little library for the University of Texas at Austin. He's made sure that the building is as well known as the Widener Library at Harvard.'

'So what do you feel Florentyna should be doing?' asked Edward.

'Why don't you let Professor Ferpozzi hold his own press conference? He's a man the public will take notice of. After that everyone will know that Florentyna Kane cares about other people and spends her own money on them to prove it.'

The next day, Edward worked on placing articles in selected magazines and organised a press conference. They ended up with a small piece in most journals and newspapers, but *People* magazine did a cover picture of Florentyna with Albert Schmidt, the Remagen Rhodes Scholar. When it was discovered that Albert was a German immigrant whose grandparents had fled from Europe after escaping from a prisoner-of-war camp, David Hartman interviewed the young man the next day on 'Good Morning, America'. After that he seemed to be getting more publicity than Florentyna.

On her way back to Washington that weekend, Florentyna heard that the Governor of Colorado, whom she had never particularly considered a friend or political ally, had endorsed her without advance warning at a solar energy symposium in Boulder. Her approach to industry and conservation, he told the convention, offered the resource-rich western states their best hope for the future.

That day ended on an even higher note when Reuters tapped out the news right across America that the Welfare Department had delivered their first major report since the implementation of the Kane Act. For the first time since Florentyna's overhaul of the social service system, the number of welfare recipients leaving the register in a given year had surpassed the number of new applicants coming on.

Florentyna's financial backing was always a problem as even the most ardent supporters assumed she could foot her own campaign bills. Parkin, with the backing of the oil tycoons led by Marvin Snyder of Blade Oil, had never had to face the same problem. But during the next few days campaign contributions flowed in to Florentyna's office, along with telegrams of support and good wishes.

Influential journalists in London, Paris, Bonn and Tokyo began to tell their readers that if America wanted a President of international status and credibility there was no contest between Florentyna Kane and the cattle farmer from Texas.

Florentyna was delighted whenever she read these articles, but Edward reminded her that neither the readers nor the writers could pull any levers on any voting machines in America, although he felt for the first time they had Parkin on the run. He was also quick to point out that there were still more than four hundred of the three thousand three hundred and thirty-one delegates who after the Primaries and caucuses remained undecided. The political pundits estimated that two hundred of them were leaning towards the Vice-President while about a hundred would come out in favour of Florentyna. It looked as if it was going to be the closest convention roll call since Reagan ran against Ford.

*

After California, Florentyna returned to Washington with another suitcase full of dirty clothes. She knew she would have to cajole, coax and twist the arms of those four hundred delegates who still remained undecided. During the next four weeks, she spoke personally to three hundred and eighty-eight of them, some of them three or four times. It was always the women she found the least helpful, although it was obvious they were all enjoying the attention that was being showered on them, especially as in a month's time no one would ever phone them again.

Edward ordered a computer terminal for Florentyna's suite at the convention which had on-line access to the records at campaign headquarters. Information on all four hundred and twelve delegates who remained uncommitted, along with a short life history of each, right down to their hotel rooms in Detroit, was available. When he reached the convention city, he intended to be ready to put his final plan into operation.

For five days during the next week, Florentyna made certain she was never far from a television set. The Republicans were at the Cow Palace, San Francisco, haggling over whom they wanted to lead them, no one having excited the voters during the Primaries.

The choice of Russell Warner came as no surprise to Florentyna. He had been campaigning for the Presidency ever since he had become Governor of Ohio. The press's description of Warner as a good Governor in a bad year reminded Florentyna that her main task would be to defeat Parkin. Once again, Florentyna felt it was going to be easier to defeat the Republican standard-bearer than the opposition within her own party.

The weekend before the convention, Florentyna and Edward joined the family on Cape Cod. Exhausted, Florentyna still managed to beat Edward in a round of golf, and she thought he looked even more tired than she felt. She was thankful that the Baron was run so well by its new, young directors, who now included William.

Florentyna and Edward were both due to fly into Detroit on Monday morning where they had taken over yet another Baron. The hotel would be filled with Florentyna's staff, supporters, the press and one hundred and twenty-four of those uncommitted delegates.

As she said good night to Edward and then to the Secret Service men and women – whom she was beginning to treat as her adopted family – on Sunday night, Florentyna knew the next four days were going to be the most important in her political career.

35

WHEN JACK GERMOND OF the *Baltimore Sun* asked Florentyna on the plane when she had started working on her acceptance speech, she replied, 'Since my eleventh birthday.'

On the flight from New York to Detroit Metro Airport, Florentyna had read through her acceptance speech, already drafted in case she was nominated on the first ballot. Edward had predicted that she would not secure victory on the first roll call, but Florentyna felt she had to be prepared for any eventuality.

Her advisers considered the result was much more likely to be known after the second or even the third ballot by which time Senator Bradley would have released his one hundred and eighty-nine delegates.

During the previous week, she had drawn up a short list of four people whom she thought worthy of consideration to join her on the ticket as Vice-President. Bill Bradley still led the field and Florentyna felt he was her natural successor to the White House, but she was also considering Sam Nunn, Gary Hart and David Pryor.

Florentyna's thoughts were interrupted when the plane landed and she looked out of the windows to see a large, excited crowd awaiting her. She couldn't help wondering how many of them would also be there tomorrow when Pete Parkin arrived. She checked her hair in her compact mirror; a few white strands were showing in the dark hair but she made no attempt to disguise them, and she smiled at the thought that Pete Parkin's hair had remained the same implausible colour for the past thirty years. Florentyna wore a simple linen suit and her only piece of jewelry was a diamond-studded donkey.

Florentyna unbuckled her seat belt, rose and ducked her head under the overhead compartment. She stepped into the aisle and as she turned to leave, everyone in the plane began applauding. She suddenly realised that if she lost the nomination, this would be the last time that she would see them all together. Florentyna shook hands with all the members of the press corps, some of whom had been on the trail with her for five months. A crew member opened the cabin door and Florentyna stepped out on to the staircase, squinting into the July sun. The crowd let up a yell of 'There she is', and Florentyna walked down the steps and straight towards the waving banners because she always found that direct contact with the voters recharged her. As she touched the tarmac, she was once again surrounded by the Secret Service who dreaded crowds they could never control. She might sometimes think of being assassinated when she was alone, but never when she was in a crowd. Florentyna clasped outstretched hands and greeted as many people as possible before Edward guided her away to the waiting motorcade.

A line of ten small new Fords reminded her that Detroit had finally come to terms with the energy crisis. If Pete Parkin were to make the mistake of being driven in a Mercedes in this city, she would be the Democratic choice before Alabama cast its first vote. Secret Service men filled the first two cars while Florentyna was in the third, with Edward in front by the driver. Florentyna's personal doctor rode in the fourth and her staff filled the remaining six 'mighty midgets', as the new small Ford had been dubbed. A press corps bus followed at the rear with police outriders dotted up and down the motorcade.

The front car moved off at a snail's pace so that Florentyna could wave to the crowds, but as soon as they reached Interstate 94, the cars travelled into Detroit at a steady fifty miles an hour.

For twenty minutes Florentyna relaxed in the back seat during the drive into the mid-town New Centre area, where the motorcade exited at Woodward Avenue, turned south towards the river, and slowed down to about five miles an hour as the crowds filled the street to catch a glimpse of Senator Kane. Florentyna's organising committee in Detroit had distributed one hundred thousand handbills showing the exact route she would take when she arrived in the city, and her supporters cheered her all the way to the Baron Hotel east of the Renaissance Centre on the Detroit River. The Secret Service begged her to change the route but she wouldn't hear of it.

Dozens of photographers and television crews were poised awaiting her arrival as Florentyna stepped out of her car and climbed the steps of the Detroit Baron; the whole area was lit up by flashbulbs and arc lights. Once she was inside the hotel lobby, the Secret Service men whisked her away to the twenty-fourth floor, which had been reserved for her personal use. She quickly checked over the George Novak Suite to see that everything she required was there because she knew that this was going to be her prison for the next four days. The only reason she would leave that room would be either to accept the nomination as the Democratic Party candidate or to declare her support for Pete Parkin.

A bank of telephones had been installed so that Florentyna could keep in touch with the four hundred and twelve wavering delegates. She spoke to thirty-eight of them before dinner that night and then sat up until two o'clock the next morning, going over the names and backgrounds of those whom her team genuinely felt had not made up their minds.

Next morning, the Detroit *Free Press* was filled with pictures of her arrival in Detroit, though in truth she knew Pete Parkin would receive the same enthusiastic coverage tomorrow. At least she was relieved that the President had decided to remain on the sidelines when it came to supporting either candidate. The press had already treated that as a moral victory for Florentyna.

She put the newspaper down and began to watch the closed circuit television to see what was going on in the convention hall during the first morning. She also kept an eye on all three channels at lunchtime in case any one network came up with some exclusive piece of news that the other two had missed and on which the press would demand her instant reaction.

During the day, thirty-one of the wavering delegates were brought to meet her on the twenty-fourth floor. As the hour progressed, they were served coffee, iced tea, hot tea and cocktails. Florentyna stuck to iced tea or she would have been drunk by eleven o'clock.

She watched in silence as Pete Parkin arrived in *Air Force II* at the Detroit airport. One assistant told her that his crowd was smaller than the one that had turned out for her yesterday, while another said it was larger. She made a mental note of the assistant who said that Parkin's crowd was larger today and decided to listen to his opinions more carefully in the future.

Pete Parkin made a short speech at a specially set-up podium on the tarmac, his Vice-Presidential seal of office glistening in the sun. He said how delighted he was to be in the city that could rightly describe itself as the car capital of the world. 'I should know,' he added, 'I've owned Fords all my life.' Florentyna smiled.

By the end of two days under 'house arrest', Florentyna had complained so much about being cooped up all day that on Tuesday morning the Secret Service took her down in a freight lift so that she could stroll along the river front and enjoy the fresh air and the low skyline of Windsor, Canada, on the opposite bank. She had gone only a few paces before she was surrounded by well-wishers who wanted to shake her hand.

When she returned, Edward had some good news: five uncommitted delegates had decided to vote for her on the first ballot. He estimated that they only needed another seventy-three to be over the magic one thousand six hundred and sixty-six. On the monitor she followed the programme on the floor of the convention hall. A black school superintendent from Delaware expounded Florentyna's virtues and when she mentioned her name the blue placards filled the hall with 'Kane for President'. During the speech that followed red placards demanding 'Parkin for President' were in equal abundance. She paced around the suite until one thirty by which time she had seen forty-three more delegates and spoken on the phone to another fifty-eight.

The second day of the convention was devoted to the major platform speeches on policy, finance, welfare, defence and the key speech by Senator Pryor. Time and time again, delegates would declare that whichever of the two great candidates was selected, they would go on to beat the Republicans in November; but most of the delegates on the floor kept up a steady hum of conversation, all but oblivious to the men and women on the platform who might well make up a Democratic cabinet.

Florentyna broke away from the welfare debate to have a drink with two delegates from Nevada who were still undecided. She realised their next stop would probably be Parkin, who would also promise them their new highway, hospital, university or whatever excuse they came up with to visit both candidates. At least tomorrow night they would have to come down finally in someone's favour. She told Edward she wanted a fence put up in the middle of the room.

'Why?' asked Edward.

'So that wavering delegates have somewhere to sit when they come to meet me.'

Reports flowed in during the day about what Pete Parkin was up to, which seemed to be much the same as Florentyna except that he was booked into the Westin Hotel at the

Renaissance Centre. As neither of them could go into the convention arena, their daily routines continued: delegates, phone calls, press statements, meetings with party officials, and finally bed without much sleep.

On Wednesday, Florentyna was dressed by six o'clock in the morning and was driven quickly to the convention hall. Once they had arrived at the Joe Louis Arena, she was shown the passage she would walk down to deliver her acceptance speech if she were the chosen candidate. She walked out on to the platform and stood in front of the banked microphones, staring out at the twenty-one thousand empty seats. The tall, thin placards that rose from the floor high into the air proudly proclaimed the name of every state from Alabama to Wyoming. She made a special note of where the Illinois delegation would be seated so that she could wave to them the moment she entered the hall.

An enterprising photographer who had slept under a seat in the convention hall all night began taking photographs of her before he was smartly ushered out of the hall by the Secret Service. Florentyna smiled as she looked toward the ceiling where two hundred thousand red, white and blue balloons waited to cascade down on the victor. She had read somewhere that it would have taken fifty college students, using bicycle pumps, one week to fill them with air.

'Okay for testing, Senator Kane?' said an impersonal voice from she could not tell where.

'My fellow Americans, this is the greatest moment in my life, and I intend to . . .'

'That's fine, Senator. Loud and clear,' said the chief electrician as he walked up through the empty seats. Pete Parkin was scheduled to go through the same routine at seven o'clock.

Florentyna was driven back to her hotel where she had breakfast with her closest staff, who were all nervous and laughed at each other's jokes, however feeble, but fell silent whenever she spoke. They watched Pete Parkin doing his usual morning jog for the television crews; it made them all hysterical when someone in an N.B.C. windcheater holding a mini-camera accelerated past a breathless Vice-President three times to get a better picture.

The roll call vote was due to start at nine that evening. Edward had set up fifty phone lines direct to every state chairman on the convention floor so that he could be in constant touch if something unexpected happened. Florentyna was seated behind a desk with only two phones, but at the single touch of a button she had access to any of the fifty lines. While the hall was beginning to fill they tested each line and Edward pronounced that they were ready for anything, and now all they could do was use every minute left to contact more delegates. By five-thirty that evening, Florentyna had spoken to three hundred and ninety-two of them in three days.

By seven o'clock the Joe Louis Arena was almost packed, although there was still a full hour to go until the names were placed in nomination. No one who had travelled to Detroit wanted to miss one minute of the unfolding drama.

At seven-thirty, Florentyna watched the party officials begin to take their seats on the stage and she remembered her days as a page at the Chicago Convention when she had first met John Kennedy. She knew then that they had all been told to arrive at certain times; the later you were asked the more senior you were. Forty years on, and she was hoping to be asked last.

The biggest cheer of the evening was reserved for Senator Bill Bradley, who had already announced he would address the convention if there was a deadlock after the first ballot. At seven forty-five, the Speaker of the House of Representatives, Marty Lynch, rose and tried to bring the convention to order but he could scarcely make himself heard above the klaxons, whistles, drums, bugles and cries of 'Kane' and 'Parkin' from supporters trying to outscream each other. Florentyna sat watching the scene but showed no sign of emotion. When finally there was a semblance of order, the chairman introduced Mrs. Bess Gardner, who had been chosen to record the votes, although everyone in the hall knew that the results would flash up on to the vast video screen above her head before she even had a chance to confirm them.

At eight o'clock the chairman brought his gavel down; some saw the little wooden hammer hit the base but no one heard it. For another twenty minutes the noise continued as the chairman still made no impression on the delegates. Eventually at eight twenty-three Marty Lynch could be heard asking Rich Daley, the mayor of Chicago, to place the name of Senator Kane in nomination; ten more minutes of noise before the mayor was able to deliver his nominating speech. Florentyna and her staff sat in silence through a speech that described her public record in the most glowing terms. She also listened attentively when Senator Ralph Brooks nominated Pete Parkin. The reception of both proposals by the delegates would have made a full symphony orchestra sound like a tin whistle. Nominations for Bill Bradley and the usual handful of predictable favourite sons followed in quick succession.

At nine o'clock, the chairman looked down into the body of the hall and called upon Alabama to cast its vote. Florentyna sat staring at the screen like a prisoner about to face trial by jury – wanting to know the verdit even before she had heard the evidence. The perspiring chairman of the Alabama delegation picked up his microphone and shouted, 'The great state of Alabama, the heart of the south, casts twenty-eight votes for Vice-President Parkin and seventeen votes for Senator Kane.' Although everyone had known how Alabama was going to vote since March 11th, over four months before, this didn't stop Parkin posters from being waved frantically, and it was another twelve minutes before the chairman was able to call on Alaska.

'Alaska, the forty-ninth state to join the Union, casts seven of its votes for Senator Kane, the forty-second President of the United States, three for Pete Parkin and one for Senator Bradley.' It was the turn of Florentyna's followers to unleash a prolonged uproar in support of their candidate, but Parkin led the field for the first half hour until California declared two hundred and fourteen for Senator Kane, ninety-two for Parkin.

'God bless Bella,' said Florentyna, but had to watch the Vice-President go back into the lead with the help of Florida, Georgia and Idaho. When they reached the state of Illinois the convention nearly came to a halt. Mrs. Kalamich, who had welcomed Florentyna the first night in Chicago nearly twenty years before, had been chosen as vice-chairman of the Illinois Democratic Party in convention year to deliver the verdict of her delegates.

'Mr. Chairman, this is the greatest moment of my life' – Florentyna smiled as Mrs. Kalamich continued – 'to say to you that the great state of Illinois is proud to cast every one of its one hundred and seventy-nine votes for its favourite daughter and the first woman President of the United States, Senator Florentyna Kane.' The Kane supporters went berserk as she took the lead for the second time, but Florentyna knew her rival would create the same effect when the moment came for Texas to declare their allegiance, and in fact Parkin went ahead for a second time with one thousand four hundred and forty delegates to Florentyna's one thousand three hundred and seventy-one after his home state had given their verdict. Bill Bradley had picked up ninety-seven delegates along the way and now looked certain to end up with enough votes to prevent there being an outright winner on the first round.

As the chairman pressed forward with each state – Utah, Vermont, Virginia – the network computers were already flashing up on the screen that there would be no winner on the first ballot, but it was ten forty-seven before Tom Brokaw announced the first round verdict: one thousand five hundred and twenty-two for Senator Kane, one thousand four hundred and eighty for Vice-President Parkin, one hundred and eighty-nine for Senator Bradley and one hundred and forty for favourite sons.

The chairman told the delegates that Senator Bradley would now address them. Another eleven minutes passed before he could speak. Florentyna had talked to him on the phone every day of the convention and steadfastly avoided asking him to join her ticket as Vice-President, because she felt such an offer would smack of bribery rather than of choosing him because she felt he was the right man to succeed her. Although Ralph Brooks was the favourite for the post in the Parkin camp, Florentyna couldn't help wondering if Pete Parkin had already offered Bradley the chance to join him.

At last the senior Senator from New Jersey was able to address the convention. 'My fellow members of the Democratic Party,' he began. 'I thank you for the support you have given me during this election year, but the time has come for me to withdraw from this Presidential race and release my delegates to vote the way their conscience guides them.' The hall fell almost silent. Bradley spoke for several minutes about the sort of person he wanted to see in the White House but did not openly support either candidate. He closed with the words: 'I pray you will select the right person to lead our country,' and was cheered for several minutes after he had returned to his seat.

By this time, most people in suite 2400 of the Baron had no nails left; only Florentyna remained outwardly calm, although Edward noticed that her fist was clenched. He quickly returned to work on the green section of his master printout, which showed only the Bradley delegates, but there wasn't much he could do while they were all on the floor except phone the chairman of each state committee and keep them working. The phones came ringing back; it seemed that the Bradley delegates were also split down the middle. Some of them would even continue to vote for Bradley in the second round in case the convention became deadlocked and had to turn to him in the end.

The second roll call vote started at eleven twenty-one with Alabama, Alaska and Arizona showing no changes. The balloting dragged on from state to state until they recorded the Wyoming decision at twelve twenty-three. At the end of the second round, the convention was still undecided, with the only important change being that Pete Parkin had taken a slight lead – 1,629–1,604 – while ninety-eight delegates had remained uncommitted or faithful to Senator Bradley.

At twelve thirty-seven the chairman said, 'Enough is enough, we'll start the roll call again tomorrow evening at seven o'clock.'

'Why not first thing tomorrow morning?' asked one of Florentyna's sleepless, young aides as he was leaving the arena.

'As the boss pointed out,' said Janet, 'elections are run for the benefit of the networks, and ten o'clock tomorrow morning just isn't prime time.'

'Are the networks going to be responsible for which candidate we choose?' he asked.

They both laughed. The sleepless aide repeated the same comment twenty-four hours later – when neither of them laughed.

The exhausted delegates slumped off to their rooms, aware that on a third ballot most states freed their delegates from their original pledges, which meant that they could now vote any way they pleased. Edward and his team didn't know where to start, but they picked up the printout and went through each delegate from Alabama to Wyoming for a third time that night, hoping they would have a plan for every state by eight o'clock the next morning.

Florentyna hardly slept that night and at ten past six she walked back into the living room of her suite in a dressing gown to find Edward still poring over the lists.

'I'll need you at eight,' he said, not looking up at her.

'Good morning,' she said, and kissed him on the forehead.

'Good morning.'

Florentyna stretched and yawned. 'What happens at eight?'

'We speak to thirty Bradley and undeclared delegates an hour all through the day. I want you to have spoken to at least two hundred and fifty by five this afternoon. We'll have all six phones manned every minute of that time so that there will never be less than two people waiting to speak to you.'

'Won't eight be a little early?' asked Florentyna.

'No,' said Edward. 'But I won't bother the west coast delegates until after lunch.'

Florentyna returned to her room realising yet again how much thought Edward had put into her whole campaign, and she remembered Richard saying how lucky she was to have two men who adored her.

At eight o'clock, she started work with a large glass of orange juice by her side. As the morning proceeded, the team became more convinced that the first roll call that evening would give the majority to their candidate. The feeling in that room was turning to one of victory.

At ten forty Bill Bradley rang to say that if his delegates caused another deadlock he was going to recommend they vote for Florentyna. Florentyna thanked him.

At eleven thirty-seven Edward passed Florentyna the phone. This time it wasn't a well-wisher.

'It's Pete Parkin here. I think we ought to get together. Can I come and see you immediately?'

Florentyna wanted to say 'I'm far too busy' but only said 'Yes'.

'I'll be right over.'

'Whatever can he want?' said Edward as Florentyna handed him back the phone.

'I have no idea, but we don't have long to wait before we find out.'

Pete Parkin arrived via the freight lift with two Secret Service agents and his campaign manager.

After unnatural pleasantries had been exchanged – the two candidates hadn't spoken to each other for the past six months – and coffee poured, the contenders were left alone. They sat in comfortable chairs facing each other. They might as well have been discussing the weather, not which one of them should rule the Western world. The Texan got straight down to business.

'I am prepared to make a deal with you, Florentyna.'

'I'm listening.'

'If you withdraw I'll offer you the Vice-Presidency.'

'You must be –'

'Hear me out, Florentyna,' said Parkin, putting up his massive hand like a traffic cop. 'If you accept my offer, I will only serve one term if elected, and then I'll support you for the job in 1996 with full White House backing. You're five years younger than I am and there is no reason why you shouldn't complete two full terms.'

Over the previous thirty minutes Florentyna had thought of many reasons why her rival might want to see her, but she had not been prepared for this.

'If you don't accept my offer and I win tonight, I'll be giving the number two spot to Ralph Brooks, who has already confirmed that he is willing to run.'

'I'll call you by two this afternoon,' was all that Florentyna said.

Once Pete Parkin had left with his aides, Florentyna discussed the offer with Edward and Janet, who both felt that they had come too far to give in now. 'Who knows what the situation might be in four years' time?' Edward pointed out. 'You might be like Humphrey trying to recover from Johnson. In any case, we only need a deadlock this time and Bradley's delegates will push us comfortably over the top on the fourth ballot.'

'And I bet Parkin knows that,' added Janet.

Florentyna sat motionless listening to her different advisers and then asked to be left alone.

Florentyna phoned Pete Parkin at one forty-three and politely declined his offer, explaining she was confident that she was going to win on the first ballot that night. He made no reply.

By two o'clock the press had got hold of the news of the secret meeting and the phones in suite 2400 never stopped as they tried to find out what had happened. Edward kept Florentyna concentrating on the delegates and with each call she was becoming more and more assured that Pete Parkin's move had been made more out of desperation than confidence. 'He's played his final card,' said Janet, smirking.

At six o'clock everyone in suite 2400 was back in front of the television: there were no longer any delegates left to speak to; they were all on the convention floor. Edward still had his phone bank linked up to all the state chairmen and the early reports back from them indicated that the feeling they had picked up votes all through the day was accurate.

Exactly at the point when Florentyna relaxed and felt confident for the first time, the bombshell fell. Edward had just handed her yet another iced tea when C.B.S. flashed up on the screen 'Newsbreak' and a camera went over to Dan Rather, who told a stunned audience only fifteen minutes before the roll call was due to start that he was about to interview Vice-President Parkin on the reason for his secret meeting with Senator Kane. The C.B.S. camera panned down on the florid face of the big Texan and to Florentyna's horror, the whole thing was going out live on the vast screen in the convention hall. She remembered that the Rules Committee had decided to allow anything to go up on the screen that might affect the delegates; this was meant to stop rumours spreading around the convention hall about what was really going on outside, to be sure that what had happened between Ford and Reagan in the 1980 convention over the picking of a running mate could never happen again. It was the first time that the delegates in the hall had been unanimously silent for four days.

The camera switched back to the C.B.S. interviewer.

'Mr. Vice-President, we know you had a meeting with Senator Kane today. Can you tell me the reason you asked to see her?'

'Certainly, Dan. It was first and foremost because I am interested in the unity of my party and above all, Dan, in beating the Republicans.'

Florentyna and her staff were mesmerised. She could see the delegates on the floor hanging on every word and she was helpless to do anything but listen.

'Can I ask what took place at that meeting?'

'I asked Senator Kane if she would be willing to serve as

my Vice-President and make up a Democratic team that would be unbeatable.'

'How did she reply to your suggestion?'

'She said she wanted to think the offer over. You see, Dan, I believe together we can lick the Republicans.'

'Ask him what my final answer was,' said Florentyna, but it was no use; the cameras were already switching to a half-crazed convention hall ready for the first vote. Edward phoned C.B.S. and demanded equal time for Florentyna. Dan Rather agreed to interview Senator Kane immediately, but Florentyna knew that they were already too late. Once the voting had started the committee had agreed that nothing would go on that screen except the ballot tally. No doubt they would have to revise the rule by the next convention, but all Florentyna could think of was Miss Tredgold's views on television: '*Too many instant decisions will be made that will later be regretted.*'

The chairman banged his gavel and called upon Alabama to begin the roll call and the Camellia State showed a two-vote switch to Parkin. When Florentyna lost one delegate from Alaska and two from Arizona she knew her only hope was another deadlock so that she could put her version of the meeting with Parkin on television before the next vote. She sat and watched herself lose one vote here and a couple there but when Illinois held firm she hoped the tide might turn. Edward and the team had been working the phones non stop.

Then the next blow came.

Edward received a call from one of his campaign managers on the floor to say that Parkin assistants had started a rumour in the hall that Florentyna had accepted his offer. A rumour he knew Florentyna would never be able to trace back directly to Parkin or have time to rebut. Although as each state's turn came to vote, Edward fought to stem the tide. When they reached West Virginia, Parkin only needed twenty-five more delegates to go over the top. They gave him twenty-one, so he needed four from the penultimate state, Wisconsin. Florentyna was confident that all three delegates from Wyoming, the final state to vote, would remain loyal to her.

'The great state of Wisconsin, mindful of its responsibility tonight' – once again the hall was totally silent – 'and believing in the unity of the party above all personal considerations gives all its eleven votes to the next President of the United States, Pete Parkin.'

The delegates went berserk. In suite 2400 the result was met with stunned silence.

Florentyna had been beaten by a cheap but brilliant trick. And its true genius was that if she denied everything and gave her version of Parkin's behaviour, the Democrats might well lose the White House to the Republicans and she would be made the scapegoat.

Thirty minutes later, Pete Parkin arrived at the Joe Louis Arena amid cheers and the strains of 'Happy Days Are Here Again'. He spent another twelve minutes waving to the delegates and when at last he managed to bring the hall to silence he said: 'I hope to stand on this platform tomorrow night with the greatest lady in America and place before the nation a team that will whip the Republicans so that those elephants will never forget it.'

Once again the delegates roared their approval. During the next hour Florentyna's staff crept back to their rooms until Edward was left alone with her.

'Do I accept?'

'You have no choice. If you don't, and the Democrats lose, the blame will be placed at your door.'

'And if I tell the truth?'

'It will be misunderstood; they will say you're a bad loser after your opponent had held out the olive branch of reconciliation. And don't forget President Ford predicted ten years ago that the first woman President would have to have been Vice-President before the American people would find the idea acceptable.'

'That might be true, but if Richard Nixon were alive today,' said Florentyna bitterly, 'he would be on the phone to Pete Parkin congratulating him on a trick far superior to any he pulled off against Muskie or Humphrey.' Florentyna yawned. 'I'm going to bed, Edward, I will have made a decision by the morning.'

At eight thirty Pete Parkin sent an emissary to ask if Florentyna had made up her mind. She replied that she wanted to see him again in private.

This time, Parkin arrived with three television companies in tow and as many reporters who could get hold of red press passes. When they were alone, Florentyna found it hard to control her temper even though she had decided not to remonstrate with Parkin but simply asked if he would confirm that he intended to serve one term.

'Yes,' he said, looking Florentyna straight in the eye.

'And at the next election you'll give me your full backing?'

'You have my word on that,' he said.

'On those terms I'm willing to serve as Vice-President.'

When he had left the room, Edward listened to what had taken place and said, 'We know exactly what his word is worth.'

As she entered the convention hall later that night, Florentyna was greeted by a cascade of noise. Pete Parkin held her hand up high, and the delegates once more roared their approval. Only Ralph Brooks looked sour.

Florentyna felt her acceptance speech as Vice-Presidential candidate was below her best, but they cheered her just the same. However, the biggest cheer of the evening was raised for Pete Parkin when he addressed the delegates; after all, he had been introduced as their new hero, the man who had brought honest unity to the party.

Florentyna flew to Boston and retreated to Cape Cod the next morning after a nauseating press conference with the Democratic candidate, who kept referring to her as 'that great little lady from Illinois'.

When they parted, in full view of the press, he kissed her on the cheek. She felt like a prostitute who had accepted his money and found it was too late to change her mind about going to bed.

36

Taking advantage of the fact that the campaign did not start until after Labour Day, Florentyna returned to Washington to catch up on her neglected Senatorial duties. She even found time to visit Chicago.

She spoke to Pete Parkin on the phone every day and certainly he could not have been more friendly and cooperative about fitting in with her arrangements. They agreed to meet at his White House office to discuss the final plan for the campaign. Florentyna tried to fulfil all her other commitments before the meeting so she could devote herself entirely to electioneering during the last nine weeks.

On September 2nd, accompanied by Edward and Janet, Florentyna arrived at the west wing of the White House to be greeted by Ralph Brooks, who clearly remained a trusted lieutenant of the candidate. She was determined not to be the cause of any friction between herself and Brooks so near the election, especially as she knew that Brooks had expected to be the Vice-Presidential candidate himself. Senator Brooks took them from the reception area through to Pete Parkin's office. It was the first time Florentyna had seen the room she might occupy in a few weeks, and she was surprised by the warmth, with its yellow walls and ivory moulding. Fresh flowers sat on Parkin's mahogany desk, and the walls were hung with Remington oil paintings. Parkin's love of the west, Florentyna thought. The late summer sun flooded in through the south-facing windows.

Pete Parkin jumped up from behind his desk and came

over to greet her, just a little too effusively. Then they all sat around a table in the centre of the room.

'I think you all know Ralph,' said Pete Parkin with a slightly uncomfortable laugh. 'He's worked out a campaign strategy which I am sure you'll find most impressive.'

Ralph Brooks unfolded a large map of the United States on the table in front of them. 'I feel the main consideration to keep uppermost in our minds is that to capture the White House we must have two hundred and seventy electoral college votes. Although it is obviously important and satisfying to win the popular vote, as we all know it's still the electoral college which selects the next President. For this reason, I have coloured the states black that I feel we have least chance of winning, and white those that are traditionally safe in the Democrat column. That leaves the key marginal states which I've marked in red, which between them make up one hundred and seventy-one electoral college votes.

'I believe both Pete and Florentyna should visit all the red states at least once, but Pete should concentrate his energies in the south while Florentyna spends most of her time in the north. Only California, with its massive forty-five electoral votes, will have to be visited by both of you regularly. During the sixty-two days left before the election, we must use every spare minute on states where we have a genuine chance and make only token visits to those fringe areas we captured in the 1964 landslide. As for our own white states, we must be prepared to visit them all once so that we cannot be accused of taking them for granted. I consider Ohio a no-hoper as it's Russell Warner's home state, but we mustn't let the Republicans assume Florida is theirs just because Warner's running mate was once the state's senior Senator. Now I've also worked out a daily routine for you both, starting next Monday,' he continued, handing the candidate and Florentyna separate sheaves of paper, 'and I think you should be in contact with each other at least twice a day, at eight o'clock in the morning and eleven o'clock at night, always Central Time.'

Florentyna found herself impressed by the work Ralph Brooks had put in before the briefing and could appreciate why Parkin had become so reliant on him. For the next hour Brooks answered queries that arose from his plan, and agreement was reached on their basic strategy for the campaign. At twelve thirty, the Vice-President and Florentyna walked on to the north portico of the White House to speak to the press. Ralph Brooks seemed to have statistics for everything: The press, he warned them, were divided like everyone else. One hundred and fifty papers with twenty-two million readers were already supporting the Democrats, while one hundred and forty-two with twenty-one point seven million readers were backing the Republicans. If they needed to know, he added, he could supply the relevant facts for any paper in the country.

Florentyna looked out across the lawn at Lafayette Square, dotted with lunchtime strollers and picnickers. If elected, she would rarely again be able to visit Washington's parks and memorials. Not unaccompanied, anyway. Parkin escorted her back to the Vice-President's office when the press had asked all the usual questions and received the usual answers. When they returned to the office they found that Parkin's Filipino stewards had set up lunch on the conference table. Florentyna came away from the meeting feeling a lot better about how matters were working out, especially since the Vice-President had twice in Brooks's hearing referred to their earlier agreement concerning 1996. Still Florentyna considered that it would be a long time before she could totally trust Parkin.

On September 7th she flew into Chicago to start her part of the election campaign but found that even though the press was still hard put to keep up with the daily routine she put herself through, she lacked the drive that had been a trademark of her earlier campaigning.

The Brooks plan ran smoothly for the first few days as Florentyna travelled through Illinois, Massachusetts and New Hampshire. She met with no surprises until she arrived in New York where the press was waiting in large numbers at the Albany airport. They wanted to know her views about Pete Parkin's treatment of Mexican Chicanos. Florentyna confessed that she didn't know what they were talking about, so they told her that the candidate had said that he had never had any trouble with Chicanos on his ranch; they were like his own children. Civil rights leaders were up in arms all over the country and all Florentyna could think of to say was, 'I am sure he has been misunderstood or else his words have been taken out of context.'

Russell Warner, the Republican candidate, said there could be no misunderstanding. Pete Parkin was simply a racist. Florentyna kept repudiating these statements although she suspected they were rooted in truth. Both Florentyna and Pete Parkin had to break off from their scheduled plans to fly to Alabama and attend the funeral of Ralph Abernathy. Ralph Brooks described the death of an aide as timely. When Florentyna heard what he had said she nearly swore at him in front of the press.

Florentyna continued her travels through Pennsylvania, West Virginia and Virginia, before going on to California, where she was joined by Edward. Bella and Claude took them out to a restaurant in Chinatown. The manager gave them a corner alcove where no one could see them, or more important, hear them, but the relaxed break only lasted for a few hours before Florentyna had to fly on to Los Angeles.

The press was becoming bored with the petty squabbles between Parkin and Warner over everything except real issues, and when the two candidates appeared together on a television debate in Pittsburgh, the universal opinion was that they had both lost, and that the only person of Presidential stature in the whole campaign was turning out to be Senator Kane. Many journalists expressed the view that it was a tragedy that Senator Kane had ever let it be known she was willing to be Pete Parkin's running mate.

'I'll write what really happened in my memoirs,' she told Edward. 'Only by then who will care?'

'In truth, no one,' replied Edward. 'How many Americans could tell you the name of Harry Truman's Vice-President?'

The next day, Pete Parkin flew into Los Angeles to join Florentyna for one of their few joint appearances. She met him at the airport. He walked off *Air Force II* holding up Missouri's *Unterrified Democrat*, the only paper which had run as its headline 'Parkin Wins Debate'. Florentyna had to admire the way he could make a rhinoceros look thin-skinned. California was to be the last stop before returning to their own states, and they held a final rally in the Rose Bowl. Parkin and Florentyna were surrounded by stars, half of whom were on stage for the free publicity they were guaranteed whichever candidate was in town. Along with Dustin Hoffman, Al Pacino and Jane Fonda, Florentyna spent most of her time signing autographs. She didn't know what to say to the girl who, puzzled by her signature, asked: 'Which was your last movie?'

The following morning, Florentyna flew back to Chicago while Pete Parkin left for Texas. As soon as Florentyna's 707 touched down in the Windy City, she was greeted by a crowd of over thirty thousand people, the biggest any candidate had had on the campaign trail.

On the morning of the election she voted at the elementary school in the Ninth District, in the presence of the usual group of reporters from the networks and the press. She smiled for them, knowing she would be forgotten news within a week if the Democrats lost. She spent the day going from committee room to polling places to television studio, and ended up back at her suite in the Chicago Baron a few minutes after the polls had closed.

Florentyna indulged herself with her first really long hot bath in over five months and a change of clothes that was not affected by whom she was spending the evening with. Then she was joined by William, Joanna, Annabel and Richard who, at the age of six, was being allowed to watch his first election. Edward arrived just after ten thirty and for the first time in his life saw Florentyna with her shoes off and her feet propped up on a table.

'Miss Tredgold wouldn't have approved.'

'Miss Tredgold never had to do seven months of campaigning without a break,' she replied.

In a room full of food, drink, family and friends, Florentyna watched the results come in from the east coast. It was obvious from the moment that New Hampshire went to the Democrats and Massachusetts to the Republicans that they were all in for a long night. Florentyna was delighted that the weather had been dry right across the nation that day. She had never forgotten Theodore H. White telling her that America always voted Republican until five on election day. From that time on, working men and women on their way home decide whether to stop at the polls; if they do and *only* if they do, the country will go Democratic. It looked as though a lot of them had stopped by, but she wondered if it would turn out to be enough. By midnight, the Democrats had taken Illinois and Texas but lost Ohio and Pennsylvania and when the voting machines closed down in California, three hours after New York, America still hadn't elected a President. The private polls conducted outside the voting stations proved only that the nation's largest state wasn't wild about either candidate.

At the George Novak Suite in the Chicago Baron, some ate, some drank, some slept. But Florentyna remained wide awake throughout the whole proceedings and at two thirty-three, C.B.S. announced the result she had been waiting for: California had been won by the Democrats, the returns showing 50.2 to 49.8, a margin of a mere three hundred and thirty-two thousand votes, giving the election to Parkin. Florentyna picked up the phone by her side.

'Are you calling the President-elect to congratulate him?' asked Edward.

'No,' said Florentyna. 'I'm calling Bella to thank her for putting him there.'

37

Florentyna spent the next few days in Cape Cod having a total rest, only to find she kept waking at six each morning with nothing to do except wait for the morning papers. She was delighted when Edward joined her on Wednesday, but couldn't get used to him affectionately addressing her as 'V.P.'

Pete Parkin had already called a press conference at his Texas ranch to say he would not be naming his cabinet until the New Year. Florentyna returned to Washington on November 14th, for the lame-duck session of Congress, and prepared for her move from the Russell Building to the White House. Although her time was fully occupied in the Senate and Illinois, it came as a surprise to her that she spoke to the President-elect only two or three times a week and then on the phone. Congress adjourned two weeks after Thanksgiving, and Florentyna returned to Cape Cod for a family Christmas with a grandson who kept calling her Grannie President.

'Not yet,' she replied.

On January 9th the President arrived in Washington and held a press conference to announce his cabinet. Although Florentyna had not been consulted on his new appointments no one was expecting any real surprises: Charles Selover was made Secretary of Defence and would have been everyone's choice. Paul Rowe retained his position as Director of the CIA, Pierre Levale became Attorney-General and Michael

Brewer, National Security Adviser. Florentyna didn't raise an eyebrow until he came to his choice for Secretary of State. She sat in disbelief when the President declared: 'Chicago can rightly be proud of having produced the Vice-President as well as the Secretary of State.'

By Inauguration Day, Florentyna's personal belongings in the Baron had been packed up and were all ready for delivery to the Vice-President's official residence on Observatory Circle. The huge Victorian house seemed grotesquely large for a family of one. For this Inauguration, Florentyna's whole family sat in seats one row behind Pete Parkin's wife and daughters, while Florentyna sat on one side of the President, Ralph Brooks sat immediately behind him. When she stepped forward to take the oath of office, her only thought was to wish that Richard were there by her side to remind her she was getting closer and closer. Glancing sideways at Pete Parkin, she concluded that Richard would still have voted Republican.

The Chief Justice, William Rehnquist, gave her a warm smile as she repeated after him the oath of office for the Vice-President.

'"I do solemnly swear that I will support and defend the Constitution of the United States against all enemies, foreign and domestic. . . ."'

'"I do solemnly swear that I will support and defend the Constitution of the United States against all enemies, foreign and domestic. . . ."'

Florentyna's words sounded clear and confident, perhaps because she had learned the oath by heart. Annabel winked at her as she returned to her seat amid deafening applause.

After the Chief Justice administered the Presidential oath to Parkin, Florentyna listened intently as America's new chief executive delivered his Inaugural Address about which she had not been consulted and hadn't even seen in final draft until the night before. Once again he referred to her as the greatest little lady in the land.

After the Inauguration ceremony was over, Parkin, Brooks and Florentyna joined Congressional leaders for lunch in the Capitol. Her Senate colleagues gave Florentyna a warm welcome when she took her place on the dais. After lunch they climbed into limousines for the drive down Pennsylvania Avenue that would lead the Inaugural parade. Sitting in the enclosed viewing stand in front of the White House. Florentyna watched the floats, marching bands and assorted governors roll by representing every one of the fifty states. She stood and applauded when the farmers of Illinois saluted her, and then after making a token visit to every one of the Inaugural balls she spent her first night in the Vice-President's house and realised the closer she got to the top, the more alone she became.

The next morning, the President held his first cabinet meeting. This time Ralph Brooks sat on his right-hand side. The group, visibly tired from the seven Inaugural balls the night before, assembled in the Cabinet Room. Florentyna sat at the far end of the long oval table, surrounded by men with whose views she had rarely been in accord in the past, aware that she was going to have to spend four years battling against them before she could hope to form her own cabinet. She wondered how many of them knew about her deal with Parkin.

As soon as Florentyna had settled into her wing of the White House, she appointed Janet as head of her personal office. Many of the positions left vacant by Parkin's staff she also filled with her old team from the campaign and Senate days.

Of the remaining staff she inherited, she quickly learned how valuable their skills and special qualifications would have been had they not disappeared one by one as the President offered them executive branch jobs. Within three months, Parkin had denuded her office of all the most competent staff, even reaching into her inner circle of advisers.

Florentyna tried not to show her anger when the President

offered Janet the position of Under Secretary of the Department of Health and Human Service.

Janet didn't hesitate over the new opportunity: and in a handwritten letter to the President she accepted the great compliment he had paid her but explained in detail why she felt unable to consider any government position other than to serve the Vice-President.

'If you can wait four years, so can I,' she explained.

Florentyna had often read that the life of the Vice-President was, to quote John Nance Garner, 'not worth a bucketful of warm spit', but even she was surprised to find how little real work she had to do compared with her days in Congress. She had received more letters when she had been a Senator. Everyone seemed to write to the President or their Congressman. Even the people had worked out that the Vice-President had no power. Florentyna enjoyed presiding over the Senate for important debates, because it kept her in contact with colleagues who would be helping her again in four years' time. They made sure she was aware of what was being said covertly in the halls of Congress, as well as on the House and Senate floor. Many Senators used her to get messages through to the President, but as time went by she began to wonder whom she should use for the same purpose, as the days turned into weeks in which Pete Parkin did not bother to consult her on any major issue.

During her first year as Vice-President, Florentyna made goodwill tours to Brazil and Japan, attended the funerals of Willy Brandt in Berlin and Edward Heath in London, carried out on-site inspections of three natural disasters and chaired so many special task forces that she felt qualified to publish her own guide to how the government works.

The first year went slowly, the second even slower. The only highlight was being sent to represent the government at the crowning of King Charles III in Westminster Abbey after Queen Elizabeth II's abdication in 1994. Florentyna stayed with Ambassador John Sawyer at Winfield House, conscious of how similar their respective roles were in the matter of form over substance. She seemed to spend hours chatting about how the world was run and what the President was doing on subjects such as the building up of Russian troops on the Pakistan border. She gained most of her information from the *Washington Post* and envied Ralph Brooks's real involvement as Secretary of State. Although she kept herself well informed as to what was going on in the world at large, for only the second time in her life she was bored. She longed for 1996, fearing her years as Vice-President would yield very few positive results.

Once *Air Force II* had landed back at Andrews, Florentyna returned to her work and spent the rest of the week checking through the State and CIA traffic that had piled up in her absence abroad. She rested over the weekend despite C.B.S. informing the public that the dollar had suffered as a result of the international crisis. The Russians were massing more forces on the Pakistan border, a fact which the President had dismissed in his weekly press conference as 'not of great importance'. The Russians, he assured the assembled journalists, were not interested in crossing any borders into countries that had treaties with the United States.

During the following week the panic seemed to subside and the dollar recovered. 'It's a cosmetic recovery' – Florentyna pointed out to Janet – 'caused by the Russians. The international brokers are reporting that the Bank of Moscow is selling gold which is exactly what they did before invading Afghanistan. I do wish bankers would not treat history on a week-to-week basis.'

Although several politicians and journalists contacted Florentyna to stress their fears, she could only placate them as she watched proceedings from the wings. She even considered making an appointment to see the President but by Friday evening most Americans were on their way home for a peaceful weekend convinced the immediate danger had passed. Florentyna remained in her office in the West Wing that Friday evening and read through the cables from ambassadors and agents on the Indian sub-continent. The more she read the more she felt unable to share the President's relaxed stance. As there was very little she could do about it, she neatly stacked up the papers, put them into a special red folder and prepared to go home. She checked her watch. Six thirty-two. Edward had flown down from New York, and she was due to join him for dinner at seven thirty. She was laughing about the thought of filing her own papers when Janet rushed into the office.

'There's an intelligence report that the Russians are mobilising,' she said.

'Where's the President?' was Florentyna's immediate reaction.

'I've no idea. I saw him leaving the White House by helicopter about three hours ago.'

Florentyna reopened her file and stared back down at the cables while Janet remained standing in front of her desk.

'Well, who *will* know where he is?'

'You can be sure Ralph Brooks does,' said Janet.

'Get me the Secretary of State on the line.'

Janet left for her own office while Florentyna checked through the reports again. She quickly went over the salient points raised by the American ambassador in Islamabad before rereading the assessments of General Pierce Dixon, the chairman of the joint chiefs of staff.

The Russians, it was reliably documented, now had ten divisions of troops on the Afghanistan-Pakistan border and their forces had been multiplying over the past few days. It was known that half their Pacific fleet was sailing towards Karachi, while two battlegroups were carrying out 'exercises' in the Indian Ocean. General Dixon directed an increased intelligence watch when it was confirmed that fifty MIG 25s and SU 7s had landed at Kabul military airport at six that evening. Florentyna checked her watch: nine minutes past seven.

'Where is the bloody man?' she said out loud. Her phone buzzed.

'The Secretary of State on the line for you,' said Janet. Florentyna waited for several seconds.

'What can I do for you?' asked Ralph Brooks, sounding as if Florentyna had interrupted him.

'Where is the President?' she asked for a third time.

'At this moment he's on *Air Force I*,' said Brooks quickly.

'Stop lying, Ralph. It's transparent, even on the phone. Now tell me where the President is.'

'Halfway to California.'

'If we have the Soviets on the move and an increased intelligence watch, why hasn't he been advised to return?'

'We have advised him, but he has to land to refuel.'

'As you well know, *Air Force I* doesn't need to refuel for that length of journey.'

'He isn't on *Air Force I*.'

'Why the hell not?'

No reply came.

'I suggest you level with me, Ralph, even if it's only to save your own skin.'

There was a further pause.

'He was on his way to see a friend in California when the crisis broke.'

'I don't believe it,' said Florentyna. 'Who does he think he is? The President of France?'

'I have everything under control,' said Brooks, ignoring her comment. 'His plane will touch down at Colorado airport in a few minutes' time. The President will immediately transfer to an Air Force F15 and be back in Washington within two hours.

'What type of aircraft is he on at the moment?' asked Florentyna.

'A private 737 owned by Marvin Snyder of Blade Oil.'

'Can the President enter the secure National Command System network from the plane?' asked Florentyna. No reply was forthcoming. 'Did you hear what I said?' she rapped out.

'Yes,' said Ralph. 'The truth is that the plane doesn't have complete security.'

'Are you telling me that over the next two hours any ham radio enthusiast could tune into a conversation between the President and the chairman of the joint chiefs of staff?'

'Yes,' admitted Ralph.

'I'll see you in the Situation Room,' said Florentyna, and slammed down the phone.

She came out of her office almost on the run. Two surprised Secret Service officers quickly followed her as she headed down the narrow staircase past small portraits of former Presidents. Washington faced her on the bottom of the stairs before she turned into the wide corridor that led to the Situation Room. The security guard already had the door open that led into the secretarial section. She passed through a room of buzzing telexes and noisy typewriters while yet another security man opened the oak-panelled door of the Situation Room for her. Her Secret Service men remained outside as she marched in.

Ralph Brooks was seated in the President's chair giving orders to a bevy of military personnel. Four of the remaining nine seats were already occupied – around a table that almost took up the whole room. Immediately to the right of Brooks sat the Secretary of Defence, Charles Selover, and on his right the Director of the CIA, Paul Rowe. Opposite them sat the chairman of the joint chiefs of staff, General Dixon, and the National Security Adviser, Michael Brewer. The door at the end of the room that led into the Communications area was wide open.

Brooks swung around to face her. Florentyna had never seen him with his coat off and a shirt button undone.

'No panic,' he said. 'I'm on top of everything. I'm confident the Russians won't make any move before the President returns.'

'I don't expect that's what the Russians have in mind,' said Florentyna. 'While the President is unexplainably absent, we must be prepared for them to make any move that suits them.'

'Well, it's not your problem, Florentyna. The President has left me in control.'

'On the contrary, it *is* my problem,' said Florentyna firmly refusing to take a seat. 'In the absence of the President the responsibility for all military matters passes to me.'

'Now listen, Florentyna, I'm running the shop, and I don't want you interfering.' The gentle buzz of conversation between personnel around the room came to an abrupt halt as Brooks stared angrily at Florentyna. She picked up the nearest phone. 'Put the Attorney-General on the screen.'

'Yes, ma'am,' said the operator.

A few seconds later Pierre Levale's face appeared on one of the six televisions encased in the oak panelling along the side of the wall.

'Good evening, Pierre, it's Florentyna Kane. We have an increased intelligence watch on our hands and for reasons I am not willing to discuss the President is indisposed. Will you make it clear to the Secretary of State who holds executive responsibility in such a situation?'

Everyone in the room stood still and stared up at the worried face on the screen. The lines on Pierre Levale's face had never been more pronounced. They all knew he had been a Parkin appointment, but he had shown on past occasions that he thought more highly of the rule of law than of the President.

'The Constitution is not always clear on these matters,' he began, 'especially after the Bush-Haig showdown, following the attempt on Ronald Reagan's life. But, in my judgment, in the President's absence all power is vested in the Vice-President, and that is how I would advise the Senate.'

'Thank you, Pierre,' said Florentyna still looking at the screen. 'Please put that in writing and see that a copy is on the President's desk immediately on completion.' The Attorney-General disappeared from the screen.

'Now that that's settled, Ralph, brief me quickly.'

Brooks reluctantly vacated the President's chair, while a staff officer opened a small panel below the light switch by the door. He pressed a button and the beige curtain that stretched along the wall behind the President's chair opened. A large screen came down from the ceiling with a map of the world on it.

Charles Selover, the Secretary of Defence, rose from his chair as different coloured lights shone all over the map. 'The lights indicate the position of all known hostile forces,' he said as Florentyna swung around to face the map. 'The red ones are submarines, the green ones aircraft, and the blue ones full army divisions.'

'A West Point plebe looking at that map could tell you exactly what the Russians have in mind,' said Florentyna, as she stared at the mass of red lights in the Indian Ocean, green lights at Kabul airport and blue lights stretched along Afghanistan's border with Pakistan.

Paul Rowe then confirmed that the Russians had been massing armies on the Pakistan border for several days and within the last hour a coded message from a CIA agent behind the lines suggested that the Soviets intended to cross the border of Pakistan at ten o'clock Eastern Standard Time. He handed her a set of decoded cables and answered each of her questions as they arose

'The President told me,' said Brooks pointedly when Florentyna had read the final message, 'that he feels Pakistan is not another Poland and that the Russians wouldn't dare to go beyond the Afghanistan border.'

'I think we are about to find out if his judgment is sound,' she said.

'The President,' he added, 'has been in touch with Moscow during the week, as well as the Prime Minister of England, the President of France and the West German Chancellor. They all seem to agree with his assessment.'

'Since then the situation has changed radically,' said Florentyna sharply. 'It's obvious that I shall have to speak to the Soviet President myself.'

Once again Brooks hesitated. 'Immediately,' Florentyna added. Brooks picked up the phone. Everyone in the room waited while the circuit was linked. Florentyna had never spoken to President Romanov before and she could feel her heart beating. She knew her phone would be monitored to pick up the slightest reaction she unwittingly displayed, as it would be for the Soviet leader. It was always said that it was this device that had enabled the Russians to run roughshod over Jimmy Carter.

A few minutes later Gorbachev came on the line. 'Good evening, Mrs. Kane,' he said, not acknowledging her title, his voice as clear as if he were in the next room. After four years at the Court of St. James the Russian President's accent was minimal and his command of the language impressive. 'May I ask where President Parkin is?'

Florentyna could feel her mouth go dry. The Soviet President continued before she could reply.

'In California with his mistress, no doubt.' It didn't surprise Florentyna that the Russian President knew more about Parkin's movements than she did. It was now obvious why the Russians had chosen ten o'clock to cross the Pakistan border.

'You're right,' said Florentyna. 'And as he will be indisposed for at least another two hours you will have to deal with me. I therefore wish you to be left in no doubt that I am taking full Presidential responsibility in his absence.' She could feel small beads of sweat but didn't dare to touch her forehead.

'I see,' said the former head of the KGB. 'Then may I ask what is the purpose of this call?'

'Don't be naïve, Mr. President. I want you to understand that if you put one member of your armed forces over the border with Pakistan, America will retaliate immediately.'

'That would be very brave of you, Mrs. Kane,' he said.

'You obviously don't understand the American political system, Mr. President. It requires no 'bravery' at all. As Vice-President I am the one person in America who has nothing to lose and everything to gain.' This time the silence was not of her making. Florentyna felt her confidence growing. He had given her the chance to continue before he could reply. 'If you do not turn your battle fleet south, withdraw all ten army divisions from the border with Pakistan and fly your MIG 25s and SU 7s back to Moscow, I shall not hesitate to attack you on land, sea and air. Do you understand?'

The phone went dead.

Florentyna swivelled around.

By now the room was a buzz again with professionals who

had previously only played 'games' in this situation and now waited like Florentyna to see if all their training, experience and knowledge was about to be tested.

Ralph Brooks held a hand over the mouthpiece of his phone and reported that the President had landed in Colorado and wanted to speak to Florentyna. She picked up the red security phone by her side.

'Florentyna? Is that you?' came down the phone in a broad Texas accent.

'Yes, Mr. President.'

'Now hear me, lady. Ralph has briefed me and I am on my way back immediately. I'll be with you in under two hours. So don't do anything rash – and be sure the press don't get to hear of my absence.'

'Yes, Mr. President.' The phone went dead.

'General Dixon?' she said, not bothering to look at Brooks.

'Yes, ma'am,' said the four-star general who had not spoken until then.

'How quickly can we mobilise a retaliatory force into the battle area?' she asked the chief of staff.

'Within the hour, I could have ten squadrons of F 111's in the air from our bases in Europe, directed towards targets in the U.S.S.R. The Mediterranean Fleet is in almost constant contact with the Russians, but perhaps we should move it closer to the Indian Ocean.'

'How long would it take to reach the Indian Ocean?'

'Two to four days, ma'am.'

'Then issue the order, General. And, if possible, make it two.'

Florentyna didn't have to wait long for the next report to come up on the screen. It was the one she feared most. The Russian fleet still ploughed on relentlessly towards Karachi while more and more Soviet divisions were massing at Salabad and Asadabadon on the Afghanistan border.

'Get me the President of Pakistan,' said Florentyna.

He was on the line in moments.

'Where is President Parkin?' was his first question.

'Not you as well?' Florentyna wanted to say, but in fact replied, 'On his way back from Camp David. He will be with us shortly.' She briefed him on the actions she had taken to date and made it clear how far she was willing to go.

'Thank God for one brave man,' said Murbaze Bhutto.

'Just stay on the open line and we will keep you briefed if anything changes,' said Florentyna, ignoring the compliment.

'Shall I get the Russian President back?' asked Ralph Brooks.

'No,' said Florentyna. 'Get me the Prime Minister of Britain, the President of France and the Chancellor of West Germany.'

'She checked her watch: seven thirty-five. Within twenty minutes Florentyna had spoken to all three leaders. The British agreed to her plan, the French were sceptical but would cooperate, while the Germans were unhelpful.

The next piece of information Florentyna received was that Russian MIG 25s at Kabul Military Airport were being prepared for take-off.

Immediately she ordered General Dixon to place all forces on standby. Brooks leaned forward to protest but by then everyone present had placed their careers in the hands of one woman. Many of them watched her closely and noted she showed no emotion.

General Dixon came back into the Situation Room. 'Ma'am, the F111's are now ready for take-off, the Sixth Fleet is steaming full speed towards the Indian Ocean and a brigade of paratroopers can be dropped at Landi Kotal on to the borders of Pakistan within six hours.'

'Good,' said Florentyna quietly. The telex continued to rap out the message that the Russians were still advancing on every front.

'Don't you think we should renew contact with Gorbachev before it's too late?' asked Brooks. Florentyna noticed his hands were shaking.

'Why should we contact him? I have nothing to add. If we turn back now it will always be too late,' said Florentyna quietly.

'But we must try to negotiate a compromise, or by this time

tomorrow the President will look like a jackass,' said Brooks standing over her.

'Why?' asked Florentyna.

'Because in the end you will have to give in.'

Florentyna made no reply but swivelled back in her chair to face General Dixon who was standing by her side.

'In one hour, ma'am, we will be over Soviet airspace.'

'Understood,' said Florentyna.

Ralph Brooks picked up the ringing phone by his side. General Dixon returned to the Operations Room.

'The President is preparing to land at Andrews Air Force Base. He'll be with us in twenty minutes,' Brooks told Florentyna. 'Talk to the Russians and tell them to back off until he returns.'

'No,' said Florentyna. 'If the Russians don't turn back now you can be certain they will let the whole world know exactly where the President was at the moment they crossed the Afghanistan border. In any case I am still convinced they will turn back.'

'You've gone mad, Florentyna,' he shouted, rising from his chair.

'I don't think I have ever been saner,' she replied.

'Do you imagine the American people will thank you for involving them in a war over Pakistan?' asked Brooks.

'It's not Pakistan we're discussing,' said Florentyna. 'India will be next, followed by West Germany, France, Britain and finally Canada. And you, Ralph, would still be looking for excuses to avoid any confrontation even when the Soviets were marching down Constitution Avenue.'

'If that's your attitude I wash my hands of the whole affair,' said Brooks.

'And no doubt you will receive the same footnote in history as the last person who carried out that ignominious act.'

'Then I shall tell the President you overruled me and countermanded my orders,' said Brooks, his voice rising with every word.

Florentyna looked up at the handsome man who was now red in the face. 'Ralph, if you're going to wet your pants, can you please go and do it in the little boys' room and not the Situation Room?'

Brooks stormed out.

'Twenty-seven minutes to go, and still no sign of the Russians turning back,' whispered Dixon in her ear. A message came through on the telex that the fifty MIG 25s and SU 7s were taking off and would be over Pakistan air space within thirty-four minutes.

General Dixon was back by her side. 'Twenty-three minutes, ma'am.'

'How do you feel, General?' Florentyna tried to sound relaxed.

'Better than the day I marched into Berlin as a lieutenant, ma'am.'

Florentyna asked a staff major to check all three networks. She began to realise what Kennedy had been through over Cuba. The major pressed some buttons in front of him. C.B.S. was showing a Popeye cartoon, N.B.C. a basketball game and A.B.C. an old Ronald Reagan movie. She checked through everything on the little TV screen once again but there was no change. Now she could only pray she would be given enough time to be proved right. She sipped at a cup of coffee that had been left at her elbow. It tasted bitter. She pushed it to one side as President Parkin stormed into the room, followed by Brooks. The President was wearing an open-necked shirt, a sports jacket and check trousers.

'What the hell is going on?' were his first words. Florentyna had stepped out of the President's chair, when General Dixon came forward.

'Twenty minutes to go ma'am.'

'Now brief me quickly, Florentyna,' demanded Parkin, taking his place in the President's chair. She sat down on the President's right and told him what she had done right up to the moment he walked in.

'You fool,' he shouted when she had finished. 'Why didn't you listen to Ralph? He would never have got us into this trouble.'

'I am aware of exactly what the Secretary of State would have done presented with the same set of circumstances,' said Florentyna coldly.

'General Dixon,' said the President, turning his back on Florentyna. 'What is the exact position of your forces?' The general briefed President Parkin. Maps continually flashing up on the screen behind him showed the latest Russian position.

'In sixteen minutes' time the F 111 bombers will be over enemy territory.'

'Get me the President of Pakistan,' said Parkin, banging the table in front of him.

'He's holding on an open line,' said Florentyna quietly.

The President grabbed the phone, hunched his shoulders over the table and started speaking in a confidential tone.

'I'm sorry it's worked out this way, but I have no choice but to reverse the Vice-President's decision. She didn't understand the full implication of her actions. Now I don't want you to feel that we are deserting you. Be assured we will negotiate a peaceful withdrawal from your territory at the first possible opportunity,' said Parkin.

'For God's sake you can't desert us now,' said Bhutto.

'I must do what is best for all of us,' replied Parkin.

'Like you did in Afghanistan.'

Parkin ignored the comment and slammed down the phone.

'General?'

'Yes, sir,' said Dixon stepping forward.

'How much time have I got?'

He looked up at the small digital clock, suspended from the ceiling in front of him. 'Eleven minutes and eighteen seconds,' he said.

'Now listen and listen carefully. The Vice-President took on too much responsibility in my absence and I must now find a way out of this mess without egg landing on all our faces. I'm sure you agree, General.'

'Anything you say, Mr. President, but in the circumstances I'd stick with it.'

'There are wider considerations that go beyond the military. So I want you to –'

A yell went up from the far side of the room from a hitherto unknown colonel. For a moment he stopped even the President speaking.

'What is it?' shouted Parkin.

The colonel now stood to attention. 'The Russian fleet has turned back and is now heading south,' he said, reading a cable.

The President was speechless. The colonel continued, 'The MIG 25s and SU 7s are flying north-west to Moscow.' A cheer went up drowning the rest of the colonel's pronouncement. Telexes buzzed out confirmation all over the room.

'General,' said Parkin, turning to the chairman of the joint chiefs, 'we've won. It's a triumphant day for you and America.' He hesitated for a moment before adding, 'And I want to know that I'm proud to have led my country through this hour of peril.'

No one in the Situation Room laughed, and Brooks quickly added, 'Congratulations, Mr. President.' Everyone started cheering again, while several personnel walked over to congratulate Florentyna.

'General, bring your boys home. They've carried out a fantastic operation. Congratulations, you too did a great job.'

'Thank you, Mr. President,' said General Dixon. 'But I feel the praise should go to –'

The President turned to Ralph Brooks and said, 'This calls for a celebration, Ralph. All of you will remember this day for the rest of your lives. The day we showed the world America couldn't be pushed around.'

Florentyna was now standing in the corner as if she had had nothing to do with what had happened in that room. She left a few minutes later as the President continually ignored her. She returned to her office on the first floor and put away the red file, slamming the cabinet closed, before returning home. No wonder Richard had never voted Democrat.

*

'A gentleman's been waiting for you since seven thirty,' were the first words the butler said when she returned to her home on Observatory Circle.

'Good God,' said Florentyna out loud and rushed through to the drawing room where she found Edward, eyes closed, slumped on the sofa in front of the fire. She kissed him on the forehead and he woke immediately.

'Ah, my dear, been rescuing the world from a fate worse than death, no doubt?'

'Something like that,' said Florentyna, pacing up and down as she told Edward everything that had happened at the White House that evening. Edward had never seen her so angry.

'Well, I'll say one thing for Pete Parkin,' Edward said, when she had reached the end of her story, 'he's consistent.'

'He won't be after tomorrow.'

'What do you mean?'

'Precisely that. Because I'm going to hold a press conference in the morning to let everybody know exactly what happened. I'm sick and tired of his devious and irresponsible behaviour, and I know that most people who were in the Situation Room tonight will confirm everything I've told you.'

'That would be both rash and irresponsible,' said Edward, staring into the fire in front of him.

'Why?' asked Florentyna, surprised.

'Because America would be left with a lame-duck President. You might be the hero of the hour, but within days you would be despised.'

'But –' began Florentyna.

'No buts. On this occasion you will have to swallow your pride and be satisfied with using what happened tonight as a weapon to remind Parkin of his agreement over the one-term presidency.'

'And let him get away with it?'

'And let *America* get away with it,' said Edward, firmly.

Florentyna continued pacing and didn't speak for several

minutes. 'You're right,' she said finally. 'I was being short-sighted. Thank you.'

'So might I have been if I had experienced what you went through at first hand.'

Florentyna laughed. 'Come on,' she said and stopped pacing for the first time. 'Let's have something to eat. You must be starving.'

'No, no,' said Edward, looking at his watch. 'Although I must confess, V.P., that you're the first girl who's kept me waiting three and a half hours for a dinner date.'

Early the next morning the President phoned her.

'That was a great job you did yesterday, Florentyna, and I appreciate the way you carried out the earlier part of the operation.'

'You hardly showed it at the time, Mr. President,' she said, barely controlling her anger.

'I intend to address the nation today,' said Parkin, ignoring Florentyna's comment, 'and although this isn't the time to tell them I shall not be seeking re-election, when the time does come I shall remember your loyalty.'

'Thank you, Mr. President,' was all Florentyna could manage to say.

The President addressed the nation at eight o'clock that night on all three networks. Other than a passing mention of Florentyna he left the distinct impression that he had been in complete control of operations when the Russians turned back.

One or two national newspapers suggested that the Vice-President had been involved in the negotiations with the Russian leader, but as Florentyna was not available to confirm this Parkin's version went almost unchallenged.

Two days later Florentyna was sent to Paris for the funeral of Giscard d'Estaing. By the time she returned to Washington the public was worked up about the final game of the World Series and Parkin was a national hero.

*

With the first Primary little more than eight months away, she told Edward that the time had come to start planning for the 1996 Presidential campaign. To that end, Florentyna accepted invitations to speak all over America, and during the year she addressed voters in thirty-three states. She was delighted to find that wherever she went the public took it for granted she was going to be the next President. Her relationship with Pete Parkin remained cordial, but she had had to remind the President that the time was drawing near for him to make the announcement about his intentions to serve only one term in office, so that she could officially launch her campaign.

One Monday in July, when she had returned to Washington from a speaking engagement in Nebraska, she found a note from the President saying that he would be making those intentions clear in a statement to the nation that Thursday. Edward had already started work on a strategic outline for a '96 campaign so that, as soon as the President had announced that he would not be running again, the Kane effort would be ready to move into top gear.

'His timing is perfect, V.P.,' he said. 'We have fourteen months before the election campaign, and you needn't even declare you're the candidate before October.'

Florentyna sat alone in the Vice-President's office that Thursday evening waiting for the President to deliver his statement. The three networks were carrying his speech and all of them had talked of the rumour that, at sixty-five, Parkin was not considering a second term. Florentyna waited impatiently as a camera panned down from the façade of the White House and into the Oval Office, where President Parkin sat behind his desk.

'My fellow Americans,' he began, 'I have always believed in keeping you informed of my plans as I do not want any speculation about my personal future, as to whether I shall be running again for this onerous office in fourteen months' time' – Florentyna smiled – 'I therefore wish to take this opportunity to make my intentions clear so that I can complete this session without involving myself in party politics.' Florentyna nearly leaped out of her seat in delight as Parkin now leaned forward in what the press referred to as 'his sincere stance' before continuing. 'The President's job is here in the Oval Office serving the people and to that end I announce that although I shall be a candidate for President at the next election, I will leave the electioneering to my Republican opponents while I continue to work for your best interests in the White House. I hope you will allow me the privilege of serving you for another four years. God bless you all.'

Florentyna was speechless for some moments. Finally she picked up the phone by her side and dialled the Oval Office. A woman's voice answered.

'I'm on my way to see the President immediately.' Florentyna slammed down the phone and walked out of her room towards the Oval Office.

The President's private secretary met her at the door. 'The President is in conference right now, but I expect him to be free at any moment.'

Florentyna paced up and down the corridor for thirty-seven minutes before she was finally shown in.

Her first words were, 'Pete Parkin. You're a liar and a cheat,' spitting out the words even before the door had closed.

'Now just a minute, Florentyna, I feel for the good of the nation . . .'

'For the good of Pete Parkin, who can't keep his end of any bargain, God help this country. Well, I can tell you one thing, I am not willing to run as your Vice-President for a second term.'

'I'm sorry to hear that,' said the President, sitting down in his chair and making a note on the pad in front of him, 'but I naturally accept your decision with regret. Not that it would have made a lot of difference.'

'What do you mean?' said Florentyna.

'I wasn't intending to ask you to join me on the ticket for a second time, but you have made the whole problem a lot easier for me by refusing to be considered. The party will now understand why I had to look to someone else for the coming election.'

'You would lose the election if I ran against you.'

'No, Florentyna, we would both lose and the Republicans might even win the Senate and the House. That wouldn't make you the most popular little lady in town.'

'You won't get my backing in Chicago. No President has ever won the election without Illinois and they will never forgive you.'

'They might if I replaced one Senator from the state with another.'

Florentyna turned cold. 'You wouldn't dare,' she said.

'If I pick Ralph Brooks, I think you will find he's a popular enough choice. So will the people of Illinois when I say that I see him as my natural successor in five years' time.'

Florentyna left without another word. She must have been the only person who had ever slammed the Oval Office door.

38

WHEN FLORENTYNA WENT OVER the details of the Parkin meeting for Edward the following Saturday on the golf course at Cape Cod, he confessed that the news came as no great surprise.

'He may not be much of a President, but he knows more about Machiavellian politics than Nixon and Johnson put together.'

'I should have listened to you in Detroit when you warned me this would happen.'

'What did your father always say about Henry Osborne? Once a skunk, always a skunk.'

There was a slight breeze and Florentyna threw a few blades of grass into the air to determine its direction. Satisfied, she took a ball from her golf bag, set it up and hit a long drive. To her surprise the wind took the ball slightly to the right and into some brush.

'Didn't properly anticipate the wind, V.P., did you?' volunteered Edward. 'I can only believe this must be my day to beat you, Florentyna.' He hit his ball right down the centre of the fairway, but twenty yards shorter than Florentyna's.

'Things are bad, Edward, but not yet that bad,' she said, smiling, and proceeded to take the first hole with a chip out of the rough and a long putt.

'Early days,' said Edward, as they were about to tee off on the second hole. He asked Florentyna about her future plans.

'Parkin is right: I can't make a fuss as such an outburst would only play into the hands of the Republicans; so I have decided to be realistic about my future.'

'And what does that mean?'

'I'll see this fourteen months out as Vice-President and then I'd like to return to New York as chairman of the Baron Group. I've had an almost unique view of the company since my continual travelling around the globe, and I think I shall be able to institute some new ideas that could put us far ahead of any of our competitors.'

'Then it sounds as though we have an interesting time ahead of us,' Edward said, smiling as he joined her to walk to the second green. He tried to concentrate on his game while Florentyna went on talking.

'I would also like to join the board of Lester's. Richard always wanted me to find out how a bank worked from the inside. He never stopped telling me he paid his directors a higher salary than the President of the United States.'

'You'll have to consult William on that, not me.'

'Why?' asked Florentyna.

'Because he's taking over as chairman on January 1st next year. He knows more about banking than I ever will. He's inherited all Richard's natural instincts for high finance. I'll stay on as a director for a few more years, but I'm confident that the bank couldn't be in better hands.'

'Is he old enough for such a responsibility?'

'Same age as you were when you first became chairman of

the Baron Group,' said Edward.

'Well, at least we'll have one President in the family,' Florentyna said as she missed a two-foot putt.

'One hole each, V.P.' Edward marked his card and studied the two hundred and ten yard dog-leg that lay in front of him. 'Now I know how you intend to occupy half of your time. So do you have anything planned for the other half?'

'Yes,' said Florentyna. 'The Remagen Trust has lacked direction since the death of Professor Ferpozzi. I have decided to head it up myself. Do you know how much the trust has on deposit nowadays?'

'No, but it would only take one phone call to find out,' said Edward, trying to concentrate on his swing.

'I'll save you a quarter,' said Florentyna. 'Twenty-nine million dollars, bringing in an annual income of nearly four million dollars. Edward, the time has come to build the first Remagen University with major scholarships for the children of first-generation immigrants.'

'And remember, V.P., gifted children, whatever their background,' said Edward, teeing up.

'You're sounding more and more like Richard every day,' she laughed.

Edward swung. 'I wish my golf was as good as his,' he added as he watched his little white ball head high and far before hitting a tree.

Florentyna didn't seem to notice. And after she had hit her ball firmly down the middle of the fairway, they both walked off in different directions. They could not continue their conversation until they had reached the green where Florentyna went on talking about where the new university would be built, how many students it should admit in its first year, who should be the first President. She ended up losing the third and fourth holes. Florentyna began to concentrate on her game but still had to scramble to square the match by the ninth.

'I shall be particularly pleased to give your hundred dollars to the Republican party today,' Florentyna said.

'Nothing would give me more pleasure than seeing Parkin and Brooks bite the dust.'

Florentyna sighed as she hit a bad short iron from the tee towards the tenth green.

'I'm far from beaten yet,' said Edward.

Florentyna ignored him. 'What a waste my years in government have been,' she said.

'No, I can't agree with that,' said Edward, still practising his swings. 'Six years in Congress, a further eight in the Senate and ending up the first woman Vice-President. And I suspect history will ultimately record your role over the invasion of Pakistan far more accurately than Parkin has felt necessary. Even if you have achieved less than you'd hoped, you've made the task a lot easier for the next woman who wants to go the whole way. Ironically I believe if you were the Democratic candidate at the next election, you would win easily.'

'The public opinion polls certainly agree with you.' Florentyna tried to concentrate, but sliced her tee shot. 'Damn,' she said as her ball disappeared into the woods.

'You're not at the top of your game today, V.P.,' said Edward. He proceeded to win the tenth and eleventh holes but then threw away the twelfth and thirteenth with over-anxious putts.

'I think we should build a Baron in Moscow,' said Florentyna when they had reached the fourteenth green. 'That was always my father's ultimate ambition. Did I ever tell you that the Minister for Tourism, Mikhail Zokovlov, has long tried to interest me in the idea? I have to go on that frightful culture trip to Moscow next month which will be a wonderful opportunity to discuss the idea with him in greater detail. Thank God for the Bolshoi Ballet, borsch and caviar. At least they've never tried to get me in bed with some handsome young man.'

'Not while they know about our golf deal,' chuckled Edward.

They split the fourteenth and fifteenth and Edward won the sixteenth hole. 'We are about to discover what you are like under pressure,' said Florentyna.

Edward proceeded to lose the seventeenth by missing a putt of only three feet so that the match rested on the last hole. Florentyna drove well, but Edward, thanks to a lucky bounce off the edge of a small rise, came within a few feet of her. He put his second shot only twenty yards from the green and found it hard to suppress a smile as they walked down the centre of the fairway together.

'You have a long way to go yet, Edward,' said Florentyna, as she sent her ball flying into a sand trap.

Edward laughed.

'I would remind you how good I am with a sand wedge and putter,' said Florentyna, and proved her point by pitching the ball only four feet from the hole.

Edward chipped up from twenty yards to within six feet.

'This may be the last chance you'll ever have,' she said.

Edward held his putter firmly and jabbed at the ball and watched it teeter on the edge of the hole before disappearing into the cup. He threw his club high into the air and cheered.

'You haven't won yet,' said Florentyna, 'but no doubt it will be the nearest you'll ever get.' She steadied herself as she checked the line between ball and hole. If she sank her putt, the match was halved and she was off the hook.

'Don't let the helicopters distract you,' Edward said.

'The only thing that is distracting me, Edward, is you. Be warned, you will not succeed. Since the rest of my life depends on this shot, you can be assured that I shall not make a mistake. In fact,' she said, taking a step back, 'I shall wait until the helicopters have passed over.'

Florentyna stared up into the sky and waited for the four helicopters to fly past. Their chopping noise grew louder and louder.

'Did you have to go to quite such lengths to win, Edward?' she asked as one of the helicopters began to descend.

'What the hell is going on?' said Edward anxiously.

'I have no idea,' said Florentyna. 'But I suspect we are about to find out.'

Her skirt whipped around her legs as the first helicopter landed a few yards off the green of the eighteenth hole. Even as the blades continued to rotate an army colonel leaped out and rushed over to Florentyna. A second officer jumped out and stood by the helicopter, carrying a small black briefcase. Florentyna and Edward stared at the colonel as he stood to attention and saluted.

'Madam President,' he said. 'The President is dead.'

Florentyna clenched her hand into a tight fist as the eighteenth hole was surrounded by agents from the Secret Service. She glanced again at the black nuclear command briefcase which was now her sole responsibility, the trigger she hoped she would never have to pull. It was only the second time in her life she felt what real responsibility meant.

'How did it happen?' she asked calmly.

The colonel continued in clipped tones. 'The President returned from his morning jog and retired to his room to shower and change for breakfast. It was over twenty minutes before any of us felt that something might be wrong so I was sent to check, but it was already too late. The doctor said he must have had a massive coronary. He has had two minor heart attacks during the last year, but on both occasions we managed to keep them out of the press.'

'How many people know of his death?'

'Three members of his personal staff, his doctor, Mrs. Parkin and the Attorney-General, whom I informed immediately. On his instructions, I was detailed to find you and see that the oath of office is administered as quickly as is convenient. I am then to accompany you to the White House where the Attorney-General is waiting to announce the details of the President's death. The Attorney-General hopes that these arrangements meet with your approval.'

'Thank you, Colonel. We had better return to my home immediately.'

Florentyna, accompanied by Edward, the colonel, the officer with the black box and four Secret Service agents, climbed aboard the Army aircraft. As the chopper whirled up into the air, Florentyna gazed down at the eighteenth green where her ball, a diminishing white speck, remained four feet from the hole. A few minutes later, the helicopter landed on the grass in front of Florentyna's Cape Cod house while the other three remained hovering overhead.

Florentyna led them all into the living room, where young Richard was playing with his father and Bishop O'Reilly, who had flown in for a quiet weekend.

'Why are there helicopters flying over the house, Grandma?' Richard asked.

Florentyna explained to her grandson what had happened. William and Joanna rose from their chairs, not sure what to say.

'What do we do next, Colonel?' asked Florentyna.

'We'll need a Bible,' said the colonel, 'and the oath of office.'

Florentyna went to her study table in the corner of the room and from the top drawer took out Miss Tredgold's Bible. A copy of the Presidential oath was not as easy to find. Edward thought it might be in Theodore White's *The Making of the President: 1972*, which he remembered was in the library. He was right.

The colonel phoned the Attorney-General, and checked that the wording was correct. Pierre Levale then spoke to Bishop O'Reilly and explained how he should administer the oath.

In the living room of her Cape Cod home, Florentyna Kane stood beside her family, with Colonel Max Perkins and Edward Winchester acting as witnesses. She took the Bible in her right hand and repeated the words after Bishop O'Reilly.

'I, Florentyna Kane, do solemnly swear that I will faithfully execute the office of President of the United States and will to the best of my ability, preserve, protect and defend the Constitution of the United States, so help me God.'

Thus Florentyna Kane became the forty-third President of the United States.

William was the first to congratulate his mother and then they all tried to join in at once.

'I think we should leave for Washington, Madam President,' the colonel suggested a few minutes later.

'Of course.' Florentyna turned to the old family priest. 'Thank you, Monsignor,' she said. But the bishop did not reply; for the first time in his life, the little Irishman was lost for words. 'I shall need you to perform another ceremony for me in the near future.'

'And what might that be, my dear?'

'As soon as we have a free weekend Edward and I are going to be married.' Edward looked even more surprised and delighted than the moment he heard Florentyna had become President. 'I remembered a little too late,' she continued, 'that if you fail to complete a hole in match-play competition, it is automatically awarded to your opponent.'

Edward took her in his arms as Florentyna said, 'My darling, I will need your wisdom and your strength, but most of all your love.'

'You've had them for nearly forty years already, V.P. I mean . . .'

Everyone laughed.

'I think we should leave now, Madam President,' the colonel prompted. Florentyna nodded in agreement as the phone rang. Edward walked over to the desk and picked it up. 'It's Ralph Brooks. Says he needs to speak to you urgently.'

'Would you apologise to the Secretary of State, Edward, and explain I am not available at the moment.' Edward was about to convey the message when she added, 'And ask him if he would be kind enough to join me at the White House.'

Edward smiled as the forty-third President of the United States walked towards the door. The colonel accompanying her pressed a switch on his two-way radio and spoke softly into it: 'Baroness returning to Crown. The contract has been signed.'

The End

Kane and Abel

JEFFREY ARCHER

William Lowell Kane and Abel Rosnovski, one the son of a Boston millionaire, the other a penniless Polish immigrant – two men born on the same day on opposite sides of the world, their paths destined to cross in the ruthless struggle to build a fortune.

The marvellous story, spanning sixty years, of two powerful men linked by an all-consuming hatred, brought together by fate to save . . . and destroy . . . each other.

'Archer has a gift for a plot that can only be described as genius' *Daily Telegraph*

'A storyteller in the class of Alexandre Dumas' *Washington Post*

'A master entertainer' *Time*

'Probably the greatest storyteller of our age' *Mail on Sunday*

HarperCollins*Publishers*

Shall We Tell the President?

JEFFREY ARCHER

At 7.30 one evening the FBI learn of a plot to kill the first woman President of the United States – the 1572nd such threat of that year. At 8.30 five people know all the details. By 9.30 four of them are dead.

FBI agent Mark Andrews alone knows when. He also knows that a senator is involved. He has six days to learn where – and how. Six days to prevent the certain death of the President.

'The only difference between this book and *The Day of the Jackal* is Archer is a better writer' *Chicago Tribune*

'Here is terror, outrageous and top-notch' *Vogue*

'Probably the greatest storyteller of our age'
Mail on Sunday

HarperCollins*Publishers*

Not a Penny More, Not a Penny Less

JEFFREY ARCHER

One million dollars – that's what Harvey Metcalfe, lifelong king of shady deals, has pulled off with empty promises of an oil bonanza and instant riches. Overnight, four men – the heir to an earldom, a Harley Street doctor, a Bond Street art dealer and an Oxford don – find themselves penniless. But this time Harvey has swindled the wrong men. They band together and shadow him from the casinos of Monte Carlo to the high-stakes windows at Ascot and the hallowed lawns of Oxford.

Their plan is simple: to sting the crook for exactly what they lost. To the penny.

'A most exhilarating debut' *Observer*

'Marvellously plotted, with just the right amounts of romance, wit and *savoir-faire*' *Publishers Weekly*

'A master entertainer' *Time*

'Probably the greatest storyteller of our age' *Mail on Sunday*

HarperCollins*Publishers*

A Quiver Full of Arrows

JEFFREY ARCHER

Two friends fall under the spell of a New York beauty – with quite unexpected results.

An offhand remark is taken seriously by a Chinese sculptor, and a British diplomat becomes the owner of a priceless work of art.

An insurance claims advisor has a most surprising encounter on the train home to Sevenoaks.

The openings to three of this marvellous collection of stories that ends with a hauntingly-written, atmospheric account of two undergraduates at Oxford in the thirties, a tale of bitter rivalry that ends in a memorable love story.

'Stylish, witty and constantly entertaining . . . Jeffrey Archer has a natural aptitude for short stories'
The Times

'Somerset Maugham never penned anything so swift or so urbanely satiric as this' *Publishers Weekly*

'Probably the greatest storyteller of our age'
Mail on Sunday

HarperCollins*Publishers*

First Among Equals

JEFFREY ARCHER

In the 1960s four ambitious new MPs take their seats at Westminster. Over three decades they share the turbulent passions of the race for power with their wives and families, men and women caught up in a dramatic game for the highest stakes of all. But only one man can gain the ultimate goal – the office of Prime Minister . . .

'We haven't had a better novel about Parliament since Anthony Trollope' *Scotsman*

'Another example of the author's mastery of the pure art of storytelling' *Daily Telegraph*

'Probably the greatest storyteller of our age' *Mail on Sunday*

HarperCollins*Publishers*

A Matter of Honour

JEFFREY ARCHER

Adam Scott listens to the reading of his father's will, aware that the financial benefit can only be pitiful. The Colonel, after all, had nothing to leave – except a letter he had never opened himself, a letter Adam fears can only bring further disgrace to the family name.

Against his mother's wishes, Adam opens the letter, and immediately realises his life can never be the same again. The contents leave him with no choice but to follow a course his father would have described as *a matter of honour.*

'It's possible that you will be able to tear yourself away from *A Matter of Honour* – your house could burn down, the bomb could drop. Otherwise you will be glued to every page' *Cosmopolitan*

'This is Jeffrey Archer's best book yet . . . he keeps the pages turning like a stiff wind' *Sunday Times*

'Probably the greatest storyteller of our age' *Mail on Sunday*

HarperCollins*Publishers*